Praise for *USA TODAY* bestselling author Michele Hauf

"With action-packed excitement from start to finish, Hauf offers an original storyline full of quirky, fun characters and wonderful descriptions. And the sexual tension between CJ and Vika sparkles. Readers won't want to put this one down."
—*RT Book Reviews* on *This Wicked Magic*; Top Pick

"This quirky story has a fair amount of humor and a lot of heart as well."
—*HarlequinJunkie.com* on *The Vampire Hunter*

"*Kiss Me Deadly* is an addictive read, one that won't be put down until the final page is completed."
—*Examiner.com*

Praise for Karen Whiddon

"A nice backstory and exciting plot make this a must-read."
—*RT Book Reviews* on *The Wolf Siren*

"Original and exciting, the constant tension—both dangerous and sexual—will keep readers on the edge of their seats."
—*RT Book Reviews* on *The Wolf Prince*

"*The Lost Wolf's Destiny* is action-packed with a lot of twists and turns that lead the reader on an amazing ride."
—*Fresh Fiction*

THE BILLIONAIRE WEREWOLF'S PRINCESS

&

FINDING THE TEXAS WOLF

USA TODAY BESTSELLING AUTHOR
MICHELE HAUF
AND
KAREN WHIDDON

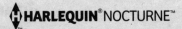

HARLEQUIN® NOCTURNE™

Recycling programs
for this product may
not exist in your area.

ISBN-13: 978-1-335-83216-0

The Billionaire Werewolf's Princess & Finding the Texas Wolf

Copyright © 2018 by Harlequin Books S.A.

The publisher acknowledges the copyright holders
of the individual works as follows:

The Billionaire Werewolf's Princess
Copyright © 2018 by Michele Hauf

Finding the Texas Wolf
Copyright © 2018 by Karen Whiddon

Printed in U.S.A.

CONTENTS

THE BILLIONAIRE WEREWOLF'S PRINCESS   7
Michele Hauf

FINDING THE TEXAS WOLF   307
Karen Whiddon

Michele Hauf is a *USA TODAY* bestselling author who has been writing romance, action-adventure and fantasy stories for more than twenty years. France, musketeers, vampires and faeries usually populate her stories. And if Michele followed the adage "write what you know," all her stories would have snow in them. Fortunately, she steps beyond her comfort zone and writes about countries and creatures she has never seen. Find her on Facebook, Twitter and at michelehauf.com.

Books by Michele Hauf

Harlequin Nocturne

Her Werewolf Hero
A Venetian Vampire
Taming the Hunter
The Witch's Quest
The Witch and the Werewolf
An American Witch in Paris

The Saint-Pierre Series

The Dark's Mistress
Ghost Wolf
Moonlight and Diamonds
The Vampire's Fall
Enchanted by the Wolf

In the Company of Vampires

Beautiful Danger
The Vampire Hunter
Beyond the Moon

Visit the Author Profile page
at Harlequin.com for more titles.

THE BILLIONAIRE
WEREWOLF'S PRINCESS

Michele Hauf

To Marcy V.
I'm so glad you persisted after that initial email to me.

Chapter 1

Paris

Indigo DuCharme's chin wobbled as she held up her head and bravely looked over the busy ballroom. She stood at the top of a stairway that curled down to the marble dance floor. Her heart pounded so loudly she couldn't focus on the waltz played by the orchestra. Her eyes threatened to tear up, but she blamed this on the brilliant glints from half a dozen chandeliers suspended above the dancers.

Clutching her pink tulle skirt with both hands, she toyed with the embroidered red poppies she'd added days ago. She'd also sewn a pocket in the skirt to keep her cell phone. She forced herself not to check her text messages again. For the sixth time. Or maybe the thirteenth time. Because...

He had jilted her.

The last text she'd read from him, ten minutes earlier, had the audacity to state: Sorry, hooked up with Melanie this evening. You and me? Sex was great. But never connected beyond the sheets, yeah?

Fingers curling into her palms, Indi winced as her perfectly manicured fingernails dug into her skin. Never connected? Beyond the sheets? She'd been dating Todd for over a month. They'd seen each other practically every day. She'd cooked for him. Shopped for him. Had sex with him and made sure he was a happy camper, meaning that she didn't always orgasm but he did. All week she'd been planning her dress and hair for tonight's date. The Summer Soiree charity ball was one of her favorites. And she looked...

...so pretty.

Indi had felt like a star when she arrived by limo two hours earlier. Todd always met her for dates; his work as a stock trader kept him at the office at all hours. Indi had glided out of the limo, her long, lush, poppy-red-and-pink tulle skirts floating about her legs. The beaded bodice hugged her like a dream and she had dusted her décolletage with fine glitter. Her blond hair was pulled up in a messy bun with tendrils framing her face. She wore a pink, cat-ears tiara, which she sold through her online business, Goddess Goodies. Her makeup was dramatic and sexy. Todd loved the smoky eye shadow and her dark matte red lipstick. Or so he'd said.

Had it all been a lie? Had she merely been a prolonged hookup? Who the hell was Melanie? And just how long could Indi hold off tears before she risked mascara running down her cheeks?

A waiter, wielding a tray of goblets shimmering with bubbles, appeared before her. "Champagne?"

Indi shook her head and forced a smile. She felt no mirth whatsoever. Reaching up to adjust the cat ears, she remembered how putting them on tonight had reminded her of the joy she'd felt as a kid. She'd worn cat ears for fun as a child, and then, after a few bad romances in high school, as a sort of confidence boost.

The cat ears had been the first of many luxury accessories she now offered at her online store. Goddess Goodies bought out-of-season and damaged designer gowns—sometimes they were donated directly from the designers. Indi refurbished them, and then rented them for the price of shipping and cleaning. As well, she sold some gowns outright for a pretty penny. Indi's business was designed to boost confidence and empower women, and to give the opportunity to those who might not be able to afford a pretty dress for prom or an important event. Goddess Goodies was treading toward its first million-dollar year. And that should make her feel on top of the world.

It was difficult to celebrate her feminine power when her goddess had just been trampled on by an asshole. Would her love life ever catch up to the success she was experiencing in her business life?

"Doubt it," she whispered, and sniffed back a tear.

Screw it. She grabbed a champagne goblet from another passing waiter's tray and tilted it back. It was number five, or six, that she'd consumed since realizing Todd had dumped her.

"One more," she muttered, and veered toward another waiter, her footsteps a bit unsure. "And then I'm going to blow this Popsicle stand."

"Indigo!"

Dread climbed Indi's neck at the sound of a familiar and falsely friendly voice. Sabrina Moreau, who hosted this ball, had never met a strand of pearls she didn't like, or, for that matter, an older married man.

She tended to wear both as if battle prizes strung about her neck.

"Bree," Indi said, while sweeping another goblet of champagne off a passing tray. Her world wobbled, but she ignored the easy drunk that was riding her spine and up the back of her neck.

"That is the most gorgeous dress I've seen," Bree cooed. "One of your creations?"

"Of course. It's Gucci restyled. Mint green certainly is your color."

Bree blushed, which only emphasized how terrible the pale green did look on her artificially tanned skin. "Jean-Paul likes me in green. Where's your date? For as lovely as you look this evening, it can't be solo. You always have a handsome stunner on your arm."

"Todd is…" An asshole. And her heart split to even think that she'd thought she could love the guy. Had she thought that? No, not love. Certainly not so fast. But she'd invested a lot of time in him over the past month. "We broke up. And you know me, I'd never miss a ball, especially when I've got the dress."

"Oh, sweetie. That's so sad."

Tell her about it. Tightening her lips seemed to keep the tears at bay. Why had she stopped to talk to Bree? She needed to be out of here. Away from the too-happy glow of crystal chandeliers and laughing couples. Now. Someplace dark and quiet so she could lick her wounds.

"How old are you, Indi?"

Indi quirked an eyebrow at that delving question.

"Well, you know what I mean. We're not getting any younger, are we? Time to wrangle one and get him to put a ring on it. Am I right?" Bree rubbed Indi's forearm and patted her on the shoulder. "Do you want me to fix you up?"

"No." Because she was no longer in the market for

rich assholes who liked to spend weekends on their yachts while working all hours and making business calls between kisses and—oh, yeah—between orgasms that never quite pleased her. "I'm good, Bree. Really."

Not really.

Where the hell was the exit?

"Well, if you need—"

Indi's tolerance level dropped out the bottom of her Swarovski crystal strappy heels. She turned and fled from Bree's prying questions, suspecting she might look like Cinderella fleeing the ball. It was near midnight. But she couldn't wear the false smile anymore.

And tears had started to spill without volition.

Aiming down the hallway toward the front doors, she suddenly stopped and spun, thinking an escape out the back would be much easier. The paparazzi always lurked out front. And while she was no A-list celebrity, she didn't want to risk photobombing any shots with her distraught tear-streaked mug. She could walk down the street and hail a cab.

Weaving through the coat-check area and then down a darkened hallway, she passed a few waiters who informed her she wasn't authorized to be in this area of the building. Flipping them off, Indi mumbled something about not feeling well and needing to be away from the crowd. Finally, escape loomed ahead.

Pushing the back doors open, she wandered through what must be the loading area. Filing around a parked truck that smelled of diesel fuel, she clutched her skirt so it wouldn't skim the ground. She'd spent last Saturday afternoon adding the red chiffon poppies to this dress to give color and interest to what had been a crop of beaded green leaves growing up from the hem.

Finally making the cobblestone street, she looked both ways. La rue Joséphine was to the left; that's where all the cabs would be parked. Yet the promise of bright streetlights and neon revealing her tears to all made her turn to the right.

She'd walk a bit. Even if her heels were much too high for a comfortable stroll and the uneven cobblestones made walking with some decorum a joke. She inhaled deeply, as she thought it would help, but instead, the sudden influx of stale air only increased her tears. And she started to sob. The champagne made her head swim.

Who was she kidding? She was drunk. Which was probably why she hadn't toppled over yet. The drunkeness was counterbalancing the wobbly-heels-to-ground ratio. Ha!

She wandered by a homeless man sitting on a piece of cardboard. He cast her a wide-eyed look.

"What?" she said testily. "This is Paris. Haven't you ever seen a woman in a ball gown wandering the streets in the middle of the night?"

She just needed to find a quiet place to break down and bawl. Loud and long. To let the goddess who had been standing at the top of the steps feeling so pretty and special exude the pain of such a sharp and cruel rejection. And then she'd find her way home to curl in on herself.

At the very least, Todd could have texted her *before* she'd left for the soiree tonight. The bastard!

"Melanie," she muttered, and wandered forward. The woman sounded high-maintenance. And like she'd go down on a man on the first date.

What was wrong with her? She was a nice person. Reasonably pretty. Not too big and not too thin. She had always agreed to whatever Todd wanted to do. She ate at the restaurants he'd chosen, and she even wore the tight red dress that pushed up her tits to her throat when he'd asked her to. What had she done wrong?

"Wasn't I good enough for him?"

Tears spilled down her cheeks. Indi pushed forward, wandering mindlessly, then turned down another, narrower street. She knew this neighborhood from girls' nights out with her BFF. Maybe?

Pausing, she thrust out her arms to balance as her heel wobbled in a crack between cobblestones. Where in Paris was she?

"Who cares?"

Unable to fight the call to release her hurt, Indi released her tears, loudly.

Ryland James stood in the center of a dark, quiet street in FaeryTown. The sword he held in his right hand curved like a scimitar, and was bespelled to kill faeries. He'd found it in a tree years ago, guarded by a dryad, and had claimed it as his own. Of late, Sidhe Slayer was the whispered title he'd been hearing about himself.

He didn't need a label. Someone had to stop the collectors who snuck in at midnight from Faery through this, a thin place insinuating FaeryTown. It was smack-dab in the middle of the eighteenth arrondissement of Paris. The collectors arrived in pairs and, if they could get past him, would seek the first human they could find and assume control of that person's body, then steal a human baby and take it back to Faery.

Not on his guard.

Checking his watch, he noted four minutes until midnight. FaeryTown was normally bustling this late at night, but when Ry walked onto the scene the residents scattered, shuffling behind doors and peering out windows to witness the slaughter.

Lifting his chin, he sniffed the air. His werewolf

senses were attuned and he picked up the usual odors of faery presence and very little from humans. Faery-Town overlay this part of Paris. Humans could walk through and would never know faeries occupied the same space only on a different dimension. Humans hadn't the ability to see faeries, such as he did.

The sudden sound of a human voice—crying—alerted Ry. He swung about to spy a woman in a fancy pink gown wandering along the brick wall that fronted a human-owned bakery, yet the faeries, in their altered dimension, used it as a dust den that lured in vampires addicted to their ichor. Hair pulled up and looking like a princess, the woman choked out tears and sobs. He noted the sparkly ears on her head. And the streaks of mascara running down her cheeks.

Why was he seeing her now? When he focused on the FaeryTown layer of this area, he saw only the sidhe and their ilk. Any humans present slipped away into the background. She was so vivid. Almost as if she treaded FaeryTown herself. But she wasn't faery. Even though her gorgeous breasts sparkled above the pink fabric. That wasn't faery dust, just glitter that women loved to dust all over themselves. No, she smelled human—coppery and tinged with the earthy presence of skin and bone and yet also a delicious overlayer of perfume and soft woman.

Ry shook his head. He shouted at her. "Hey! Get out of here! You can't be here right now."

She dismissed his worry with a swinging gesture of her hand and plopped down to sit on the curb. Her skirts fluffed around her, the hem edged with dirt, and…she was missing a shoe.

She should not be able to see him.

She sniffed loudly, then muttered, "Can you call me

a cab? I seem to have gotten lost. My phone is here—" she patted her fluffy skirt "—somewhere…"

"I don't have time for that." Two minutes until midnight. Gripping the enchanted sword firmly, Ry swung it behind him, pointing toward the main street that edged the border of FaeryTown. "Get out of this area. It's not safe. I'll call you a cab later."

"He dumped me!" she announced.

Ry winced at the woman's utter lack of recognition for the imminent danger. There was no way she could be in FaeryTown unless she also had the sight or had somehow gained admittance. Humans couldn't simply enter FaeryTown unless they could see it. And it appeared that she was merely wandering the streets…

Why was this gorgeous princess wandering about alone?

"Listen, Princess Pussycat," he hissed. "Bad things are going to happen. Right now. So run!"

As he spoke the final word, the fabric between Faery and the mortal realm glimmered. The gray night sky above a two-story building tore and shimmered along the edges of that tear.

Ry swore. The woman on the curb still sobbed, her head caught against her open palms. He felt a moment of compassion for her. What asshole would be so cruel to such a pretty woman?

But really? Things were about to get rough.

Swinging his sword arm, Ry prepared as the first of the collectors entered this realm. The creature's body was long and wispy, barely holding the form of a human. It was black, so black it was like peering into a void in the shape of the creature. And yet it sparkled with so much faery dust it was as though that void formed a black hole speckled with stardust.

Not about to become enchanted by the sight, Ry

swung toward the approaching collector. It floated nearer, and when it spied him, it stretched its maw wide to reveal a piranha row of vicious teeth.

"What the hell is that?" the woman called.

"I don't know how you can see this, but you need to listen to me and run!"

"I lost my shoe."

"Mademoiselle! I'm serious!" He swung the sword but missed the collector.

It soared high, the wispy tail of its form spilling black, oily fog over Ry's head. He swept the substance aside to keep an eye on the creature. Out the corner of his eye he again saw the fabric between realms glimmer. Always, they arrived in pairs.

"This is crazy," the woman said. She stood and wobbled. Drunk? Had to be. "I need a cab. I can't find my pocket. My skirts are tangled… Hey, that thing is swooping toward you!"

Ry averted his attention from the crazy lush sight of the most gorgeous woman he'd ever seen to the sparkling black void that aimed for his throat. Its curved, sharp talons wrapped about his throat. Gagging, Ry stumbled backward. Slipping his sword arm back and thrusting the tip up, he managed to stab the thing, but not in the substantial main body, instead only in the wispy tail. It released him and, with a twist of its misty shape, soared toward its approaching partner.

"That way!" Ry pointed down the street. "Go!"

"What are those things? And why are you so angry with me? Can a girl get a break?" She now stood in the street not ten feet from him. "I have only ever tried to please people. And what do I get? Dumped at the ball. Todd is such an asshole."

"Fuck Todd!" Ry said hastily.

"Right?"

One of the collectors took note of the woman. She wouldn't have time to get to the street and out of Faery-Town.

Ry raced for her, grabbed her by the arm and shoved her between the dust den and another brick wall. She screamed and landed on her hands and knees, which he regretted, but only so long as it took for him to turn and dodge the lunging collector.

Now he was angry. And the twinge of a shift crawled across his scalp. His werewolf did not like these nasty things from Faery. Ry's upper body, of its own volition, shifted. T-shirt tearing at the seams, his shoulders grew wider and his head assumed wolf shape.

Growling, Ry marched toward the collector and led it back to the center of the street. He swung his sword repeatedly. When it shot upward into the sky, hovering above him, Ry positioned himself below, waiting. In his peripheral vision he could see the other collector approaching the alley where he'd shoved the woman.

The creature above him dropped like a rock. He thrust up the sword, and it pierced the collector's heart. Ichor spilled over Ry's fur and wolf-shaped head and down his arms and paws. Without a death scream, the thing dissipated into black faery dust.

But the next sound sent a chill up his spine. The scream was not that of annoyance, drunkenness or a jilted woman. It was of fear—and pain.

The collector slashed a razor talon across the woman's décolletage. She fainted. And the thing turned to gnash its teeth at Ry as he approached. Sword thrusting as he ran, Ry caught the creature as it lunged toward him. More black dust and the eerie, quiet dissipation of the collector in the air before him.

On the ground was a scatter of pink fabric. A sparkly

rhinestone shoe peeked out from the fluff. The woman's chest bled where the collector had scratched her.

Shaking off his werewolf with a seamless shift back to human shape, Ry bent over her. "Damn it, how did you manage this?" He touched two fingers to the side of her neck. The collectors' bite was deadly to humans, but he wasn't sure about their talons. The things were literally bags of floating poison.

He felt a heartbeat, but it pulsed and then slowed. Quickly.

Instinctually, he knew. "She's going to die."

And that did not sit well with him. This was his beat. He was responsible for any and all who got in the way of his efforts to keep the collectors off the streets. And she was an innocent. Just like those he was trying to protect.

Lifting her into his arms, Ry rushed down the street, deeper into FaeryTown. He knew no more collectors would arrive tonight. There were never more than two nightly.

"Sorry to make your night worse, Princess," he said as he turned, heading toward the faery healer he had once or twice used for his own injuries. "We're going to have to talk about how you were able to breach FaeryTown."

She moaned in his arms and muttered something about Todd not deserving her.

"Todd's a jerk," he said. "Any man should be proud and honored to have your company."

Unless she was a pill. Hell, even the pretty ones could be tough to deal with. But damn, she smelled great. Sweet and soft, like something he wanted to taste.

Giving his head a shake to chase away that random thought, Ry kicked the door to the faery healer's home. This was not a situation he wanted to be in right now.

Standing on Hestia's doorstep? She wasn't going to be happy.

"To the devil with you!" a voice hollered from behind the door.

To be expected. They had a history.

But the woman in his arms would soon be history if he didn't hurry. Ry kicked the door again, and the chains on the other side broke, the door slamming inside against the wall. He rushed across the threshold and down the tight, narrow hallway to the healing room where Hestia helped so many of her afflicted species. He laid the woman on the bed of leaves and vines that immediately coiled and twisted to embrace her arms and one exposed shoeless foot.

Ry turned to the fuming faery behind him. Her skin tone was a shade of cotton-candy pink, which she accented with a green slip of a dress. She was tiny, compared to his hulking height, and yet her annoyance hit him like a punch to the gut. If violet eyes could ever burn with the flames of hatred, hers did.

"I know, I don't deserve your help after the last time," he began. "Please, Hestia, she's an innocent. Got caught between me and a collector. See that scratch on her collarbone?"

The healer bent to inspect the woman. She then licked the wound with a snake-long tongue. Shaking her head, she announced, "She will die."

"No. You can heal her. I know you can. Do this, and I promise I'll never ask for another healing from you again."

Hestia looked him up and down. Lately, with his battles against the collectors, he took on a lot of injuries that challenged his innate ability to quickly heal. And she knew it. And the last time they'd spoken? She had nearly died to save him from a fatal wound. And she might have thought he cared for her more than he really had. It had been a fling. Apparently, though, she had thought differently.

"You willing to pay for this?" she asked. "Lots of mortal realm euros?"

Money meant nothing to him. And he had far too much of it. She could ask for untold riches and it would be like handing over a few bills to her.

"One million," she said.

He nodded eagerly. "I'll send a courier with the cash as soon as the banks open tomorrow."

She eyed him cautiously. For as much as she hated him—and had every right to—she had to know he was good on his word. But she tilted her head and asked, "What does this one mean to you?"

"Her? I hadn't met her until five minutes ago. I don't want an innocent to die because she got in my way."

The healer nodded, then pointed over his shoulder. "Very well. Go stand out in the hallway. It will take some time."

Chapter 2

The beautiful man with impossible muscles—he wore an oddly tattered shirt that revealed oh, so many tight, bulging muscles—held a sword and fought weird black creatures that flew in the air about him. In the middle of Paris.

And as Indi was lying there on the ground, watching with her mouth hanging open, she thought, for a moment, the tall, handsome man...changed. When he looked at her, his head was shaped like a wolf's.

The eerie image made Indi scream, and she pushed herself up abruptly. And hit her head on something above her. Dropping her cheek back onto the hardwood floor, she groaned.

That had been a weirdly detailed dream. Very real. Almost as if she could smell the strange black creatures' ozone scent and hear the man's sexy voice as he had bent over her. Prodding her. Asking if she was okay.

Eyelids flashing open, Indi darted her gaze about the room. She was lying on the floor? Not a familiar floor, either. She didn't have hardwood in her home. And…what had she hit her head on?

Rolling to her side, she realized she still wore the ball gown. The beaded leaves on the bodice crunched as her body turned on the wood floor. Above her stretched a flat piece of wood, supported by a table leg…

"Why am I lying under a table? Oh…"

It hurt her brain to talk. Had someone taken it out, rolled it across the ground like a *pétanque* ball, then shoved it back in through her ear? Mercy, what a bender. Champagne hangovers were the worst!

But this didn't look like her friend Janet's floor. And Janet had moved to New York two months ago.

Where was she? And how had she gotten here?

"When I got up this morning I couldn't figure why you were under the table," a male voice suddenly said.

A pair of bare feet, with a slouch of blue jeans hanging over them, stopped but a foot from her face. Indi placed both palms on the floor before her and craned her head up as far as she could manage, but her neck ached, so her line of sight only stretched as far as his crotch. Not a terrible sight to wake up to. Just…unexpected.

She dropped and rolled to her back.

"You insisted on crawling under there after I deposited you on the couch last night," he said. He bent to display two mugs. "Coffee?"

Heartbeat suddenly racing, Indi inhaled deeply a few times to calm her panic. But really, she *should* be panicking. "Where am I? Who are you? I, uh…"

"My name's Ryland James. I don't know your name. You were buttered when I found you last night."

Buttered? Hell yes, she'd been so drunk.

"When you found me? What the hell? What did you…?" She winced. No, she was still dressed. Which didn't mean much. If the man had had his way with her while she was inebriated…

"You stumbled onto a strange scene," he said, sitting on the black leather sofa and setting one coffee cup on the floor near her shoulder. "I wanted to bring you home, make sure you were safe, but I didn't know where you lived. And…after a bunch of wild-and-craziness you passed out. For the night."

She closed her eyes and slapped a palm to her chest. Wild and crazy? Seriously? She'd let that bastard Todd get to her that much? And now she was lying on the floor in a strange man's home.

The coffee smelled deceptively good. But from experience, she knew if she drank any she'd get sick. Hangovers were never kind to her.

She spoke her fears. "I need to get out of here."

"I can drive you home if you'll give me your address."

"I don't think I should do that. I can hail a cab."

"Suit yourself. I'm not going to hurt you. I just wanted to make sure you were okay after…"

Indi skimmed her fingers over her chest and throat. Something hurt. She winced at the slight pain and felt the rough line of skin along her collarbone. Had she been cut?

"It should heal more quickly than you expect," the man, Ryland, said. "I tried to get you out of there, but you were, well…"

Buttered.

"Sorry. Some guy broke up with you?"

She'd told him that? What had happened last night?

"He dumped me at the ball. And I was feeling so pretty." She sniffed, feeling all the emotions well in her gut again. Oh, she couldn't do the ugly cry in front of this handsome stranger!

Turning and crawling out from under the table, she managed to bump the coffee cup and topple it. It soaked into her skirt.

"I'm so sorry."

"Don't worry about it."

A strong hand helped her to stand by grabbing her upper arm. And when she swayed near his chest, Indi smelled fresh, outdoorsy aftershave on him. Or maybe it was his innate scent. Like wild captured yet never tamed. The man was handsome. Long dark hair, trimmed mustache and a beard that was short and hinted at the dark hairs that might grow on his chest. And so many muscles in the biceps she clung to.

Indi had never been one to let opportunity pass, but…

She also wasn't stupid.

"Thank you for, uh…" She wandered to the door, tugging up her wet skirt and realizing a long piece of it dragged behind. The outer tulle layer had torn, and the hem was blackened with dirt. One of the chiffon poppies dangled from a thread.

"Oh, God, you must think I'm the worst case. I was…upset. And yes, he broke my heart. I have this tendency to get attached, too—" What was she doing? She didn't need to detail her pitiful emotional failings to a stranger. "I needed a good cry and…"

She turned, thinking Ryland looked like the man she'd seen in her dreams. He had been. She'd never forget such a handsome face. And those brown eyes pierced her with intensity. "Last night." Peering intently at him, she asked, "Did you change?"

"Did I, uh, what?" He set the mug on the table and approached her.

Indi backed up until her shoulders hit the door. She slumped. Her head was spinning and she predicted the hangover would play revenge on her soon. And she did not want the guy to witness that.

"Change," she muttered, though she wasn't sure why she'd asked him that. How could a person change? Yet she had seen something odd last night. Maybe? "Were there flying creatures?"

He bent before her, and long brown hair spilled over his chest and the T-shirt that he wore inside out to expose the seams. Earth-brown eyes studied her for a pitiful moment. "I think you might still be a little drunk, Princess Pussycat."

"Princess…" She reached for the top of her head and felt the cat ears sitting up there, but at a tilt. "I'm not drunk. Not anymore. And my name is…"

She should leave. Right now. Before things got weird.

Indi turned and grabbed the doorknob, hoping the door wasn't locked and that he didn't have plans to toss her in a dirt pit in his basement. It opened. She exhaled and dashed across the threshold.

"I hope you feel better!" he called after her. "And I hope the guy who did that to you gets his just. No woman deserves to be treated so poorly."

Indi paused at the top of a stairway that led down to the building's entry. She lifted her skirts and imagined she must look a nightmare to him. A kind man who had only wanted to ensure that she was safe last night.

"My name's Indigo," she said, then took the stairs, hands firmly clutching both railings for support.

By some strange luck that she was not accustomed to, a cab was parked curbside. Indi climbed into the back seat, gave the driver her address in the eighth arrondissement, then flopped down, hugging the seat as if it were a life raft. Shoving her hand in her skirt pocket, she was relieved her phone was still in there. She checked her texts. There were none.

Had she expected to hear from Todd after his night with Melanie?

Oh, that she could even think of him again. Stupid, stupid, stupid!

She needed to talk to Janet. To spill all the details of her horrible, terrible, no-good very humiliating night. She'd call her when she got home.

Ten minutes later, the cabbie offered to help her to the front door, but Indi said she'd manage. She paid him with a scan of the credit card app on her phone and then meandered up to the house.

Her head wasn't quite so spinny now, but her limbs felt heavy. As if she'd run a marathon. Exhaustion hit her hard as she opened the front door and wandered inside. She could only think to lie down. Right. Now.

She eyed the alpaca rug before the white velvet couch and stepped down into the sunken living room. Dropping the phone on the couch, and then falling to her knees, Indi collapsed onto her stomach on the soft, inviting rug. She curled her fingers into the fur and closed her eyes.

And then she fell asleep.

For a very long time.

Ry strolled into the small office he kept in the fourth arrondissement. His secretary, Kristine, blew him the usual good-morning kiss and handed him a full and steaming mug of coffee.

"How'd hunting go last night?" she asked while focusing on a spreadsheet she had opened on the laptop before her. Her long purple nails clattered on the keys.

"It was..." Ry sipped the coffee and winced. He

could never get her to add even a smidge of cream to the wicked black concoction she brewed. "Different."

That got her attention. Turning on the swivel chair and crossing her legs, she dangled a very large pink vinyl high heel and eyed him through a flutter of thick false lashes. She didn't need to speak. He could hear her thoughts plainly.

"A human woman stepped onto the scene while I was slashing through collectors."

"Oh, *mon cher*. That is not acceptable. How did that happen? I thought FaeryTown wasn't something we humans could even access."

"Exactly. Not unless you're wearing an ointment to see the sidhe. I'm not sure how she saw me or the collectors, but she did, and…" He sipped again. He probably shouldn't tell Kristine everything. But then, she was a confidante, and he trusted her with the information about his nature. "She was scratched by one of them. Would have died had I not rushed her to a healer. By the way, I need to send Hestia a million-euro check."

Kristine sighed. "Really? The old girlfriend? I'll take care of that."

"She was not a girlfriend. More a—"

Kristine put up a palm. "Nope. Don't want you to mansplain that one to me. So, what happened after that big adventure?"

"I took her home with me, and she spent the night on the floor under the coffee table."

"Ryland Alastair James."

He winced at the admonishing tone. "I put her on the couch, but she wouldn't stay there. She was drunk and…the healer drugged her with some wacky faery stuff. I'm surprised she could even stand to run away from me this morning."

"You let her run away? Without making sure she got home safe? Who are you?"

He sighed heavily. Kristine knew him well. Normally he would never allow a woman to run off like that without seeing to her safety. But she had been freaked by him. And he'd not been given an opportunity to explain the cut on her chest, which might have been a good thing, all things considered.

"She'll be fine," he said. "And both collectors are dead. No babies stolen last night."

Kristine crossed her arms, and her dangling foot increased in bobbing speed.

"I don't know her last name, so it's not like I can look her up and check in on her. She was dressed fancy and I think she's probably well-off."

"Doesn't mean she made it home safely."

"I accept your admonishment, and confess I'm worried about her, too. But there's nothing I can do now."

"Can't you track her down with your sniffer? Didn't you once tell me you werewolves can smell a peppermint candy five miles away?"

"She wasn't wearing peppermint. She smelled like champagne and roses." And not just any kind of rose perfume. She'd smelled like fresh-from-the-garden roses.

"Was she pretty?"

"Does that matter?"

"No, but she's going to stay in your brain until you know what became of her after she fled your place. Fled! Seriously, Ry, what did you do to her?"

"I offered her coffee."

Kristine chuckled and turned back to her work. "Only you can manage to simultaneously slay weird faery marauders and hook up with a pretty young thang."

"We didn't hook up. I set her on the couch and…in the morning I found her under my coffee table."

Kristine raised an eyebrow in judgment.

"And that's the end of this conversation. Did you compile research on the Severo Foundation?"

"I did. And I've a report for you. I'll print it up and bring it into your office in two twitches. This is a good one, *cher*. You'll want to donate to them."

"Thanks, Kristine. Give me ten minutes before you come in. I need to—"

"Think about the poor sweet thang that fled your place this morning?" She winked at him. "You have some weird problems."

Ry entered his office and closed the door behind him, thinking Kristine was right on. But oddly, the human interference last night had been the weirdest. Not the faeries.

Only a desk, a chair and a couch decorated his tiny office space. The far wall opposite the door was completely window, and no cabinets blocked the view of the nearby Seine River. He didn't do the fancy. Much as his multibillion-dollar philanthropic foundation could afford it. He wasn't into the bling or showing off his riches. It wasn't him. And while he could put on a suit and blend in with the wealthy at the snap of a finger, he preferred the casual look and lifestyle.

Yet he did do the expensive watch. He liked to know the time to the exact second. And right now it was eleven fifteen, on the nose.

He sat on the leather sofa and stretched his arms along the back of it. Clouds were rolling in, and rain was in the forecast, yet the color of the sky was wildly vivid.

"Indigo," he muttered.

Interesting name for a woman. She'd been more of

a soft pink last night, mixed with a few streaks of jet-black mascara. Poor thing.

Kristine was right. He should have followed her out of his building this morning. But he'd watched from his loft and seen the waiting cab. She'd beelined into it and it had pulled away. She'd made it home safe.

What hell of a hangover would she have? If not from the alcohol, but from the mysterious concoction of herbs and who-knew-what Hestia had given her?

"Should have gotten her last name," he said with a regretful twinge that he felt in his heart. "She was pretty."

And she had seen too much. That wasn't good. He needed to keep his secret, and the secret of FaeryTown, from the human public. And if she had seen him in those few moments when his rage caused him to partially shift, then he needed to make sure she thought it was just an effect of the alcohol. Not the truth.

Because his truth always managed to fuck things up.

Indi lifted her head from the alpaca rug. It was dark. Really dark. She was lying on the floor in her living room for reasons that escaped her...

"Ah, really?"

She dropped her head and realized she must have slept the entire day. Twenty-four hours had passed since Todd dumped her last night. And what had happened after that had been even more remarkable. She'd watched a handsome man with P90X abs and biceps kill weird sparkly creatures with a sword. And then she'd woken up under his coffee table.

"This is definitely one for the diary," she muttered as she sat up. "Oh, my aching bones, have I become an old lady?"

She pressed a hand to her back and winced as she

stretched. Either she was growing old quickly or sleeping on the floor was no longer something she could do and recover from with ease. Her college days had often found her sleeping on the floor, or a table, or even in a big box once.

"Shouldn't have sucked down all that champagne."

With some groans and grunts, she managed to stand. Inspecting her tattered and dirty gown made her moan. "It was so pretty. *I* was pretty. Asshole."

Grabbing her phone from the couch, she intended to call Janet, but...

"It's ten at night?"

Now she stomped toward the curving marble staircase and her second-floor bedroom. She didn't bother to turn on the lights. Passing through the bedroom, she clutched the cat ears still clinging to her head and tossed them onto the king-size bed. Tripping a few more times on her torn hem, she made it into the bathroom and flicked on the lights as she stopped before the wide vanity mirror specially lighted for putting on makeup.

Indi chirped out an abbreviated scream. Then she slapped both palms over her mouth. Staring back at her from the mirror was a bedraggled bit of tattered lace and smeared makeup. Her mascara had streaked down her cheeks, but—perhaps when she'd been passed out on the floor—most of it had rubbed off. Had that happened before or after she was at the handsome stranger's place?

"He saw me looking like this? Oh, Indi, you really know how to impress a guy, don't you?"

Her hair was half out of the messy bun. One jut of hair managed to stick straight out on the left side. "What hurricane did I walk through?" She pulled out a leaf from her hair. "Where did this— Oh, I want to die! I just…"

She slammed her hands to the vanity and shook her head. But instead of tears, laughter burst out. Lung-tugging, gut-clenching laughter. Dropping and settling onto the soft pom-pom rug in front of the tub, Indi laughed until her ribs ached.

"Lowest point in my life? Last night," she muttered. "Lesson learned? Lay off the champagne. Never date a guy whose most important accessories are his cell phone and day-planner app. And…" She sighed and wiggled her toes through the tear in the pink tulle. "Always thank the handsome stranger who rescues you from the idiocy of yourself." And from a strange creature she thought might have been trying to eat her. "Did I thank him? I don't think I did. Ryland James? And he never did answer my question."

She had seen things while shivering in the alley last night. More than a few weird things. And he had most definitely changed into…something different. It hadn't been the alcohol. Couldn't have been.

"Who are you kidding, Indi? Of course it was the champagne. People don't change shapes."

She touched her chest where she had rubbed over a cut earlier this morning at her rescuer's place. Her skin felt smooth now.

Indi stood and studied her collarbone in the mirror. The skin did not show a cut or mark of any kind. And if she had been hurt, shouldn't there be, at the very least, a faint or red mark?

Was it possible she'd imagined it all?

"Anything is possible," she said to the tawdry prin-cess in the mirror.

He'd called her Princess Pussycat. And his eyes had smiled before his mouth had.

Indi smiled. A weak, pitiful and bedraggled smile, but it was the best she could manage. It would be a crime not to see that man again. And she really did need to thank him. At least some man had been concerned about her last night.

More important, she wanted to ask him questions. To make sure she wasn't going crazy and hadn't started to imagine strange creatures walking the streets of Paris.

"Tomorrow," she said to the disaster in the mirror. "Now a shower, and a bath, and maybe another shower after that."

Chapter 3

The next day

"The proposal is very well done." Ry laid the file folder on Kristine's desk. He'd been in the office all day making phone calls and was ready to kick back with a beer and some sports TV.

"The Severo Foundation is amazing." Kristine brought up the website on her laptop. "Started by Stephan Severo decades ago to buy up forested land in Minnesota to protect the natural wolf population."

"And I do appreciate that it's also helping the Save the Wolf Foundation. His son wants to take the project international."

"Yes. Pilot Severo continued to support the project after his father died," Kristine said. "I dug a little deeper with my research. Most isn't in the proposal. Pilot is not werewolf. His mother, Belladonna Severo, is a vampire and his father was werewolf. Pilot was born straight human. I kind of relate to him." Kristine tapped her highly lacquered red lips in thought. "He was born into a body that was so different from what others must have expected of him. And can you imagine the parents' disappointment when their son was not a werewolf or vampire, but rather merely human?"

"I can," Ry said.

His thoughts flickered back to that day he'd first discovered he was different. Not quite the werewolf he'd always believed he was. And then his mother had confirmed it, and his entire world had been tipped off its axis. The time had been seventeen minutes and twenty-one seconds past three in the afternoon. Not a good time. Not something a seventeen-year-old man should have to experience.

"Get me a phone meeting set up with Pilot Severo," he said. "I want to send him funds and would also like to be a part of the international project, if possible."

"Perfect." Kristine typed as they conversed. Multitasking, as usual. Something Ry appreciated but could never manage himself. "It's morning in the States. I'll give them a ring in another hour."

"You don't have to stay late, Kristine."

"You know I don't mind. And I want to finalize the donations for the upcoming charity ball. You know the full moon is this weekend? You heading out to your castle?"

"I, uh…" Ry winced as he considered that this full moon would be different from the previous one. He had a new commitment that wouldn't allow him to leave the city. To escape from the possibility of being seen in his shifted form. "I don't think I can."

"You can't stay in the city. Not unless you hook up with that new girl fast. And by *fast* I mean in the three days before the weekend. Don't you need to have sex before the full moon to keep the werewolf at bay? You up for that challenge?"

"Always." He cast her a charming smirk. "But I don't think I'll see her again. She ran out on me so quickly. I do have some solutions available."

"Uh-huh. But even if you do find a woman to have sex with the day before and after the full moon, there's still the night of the full one, *mon cher*. Don't you need to wolf out no matter what?"

"That I do."

"Maybe FaeryTown can go one night without you."

"If I miss one night of patrol, then a baby could be stolen from his or her crib, never to be seen again. Do you think that's fair for me to put my needs before one so innocent?"

"But you'll wolf out during the full moon. *In Paris.*"

"That's something I'm going to have to deal with. I don't see any other option, Kristine. Text me the appointment after you've talked with Severo. I'll see you tomorrow afternoon."

He left the office in the wake of an unenthusiastic "sure" from his secretary. He knew she was right. She knew she was right. A werewolf shouldn't risk staying in a populated city on the night he was called by the moon to shift to his half-man/half-wolf shape. And while he wasn't a wild and crazy beast intent on destroying or maiming humans in that shape, he didn't need to be seen loping about the Parisian streets with tail wagging and tongue lolling. That was inviting trouble for him and every other werewolf who needed to remain a myth to all humans.

Yet if he went to his private property in the countryside, as he did every night of the full moon, then FaeryTown would be left unguarded for the collectors to come through.

As he strode down the sidewalk and angled for his parked Alfa Romeo, Ry wished the choice was easier. But then, nothing good ever came easily.

Indi slept until three o'clock the next afternoon. She decided to mark it off as the worst night of her life. Getting dumped, being chased by a creature and then being sort-of kidnapped by a man she didn't know.

But it was the memory of that mystery man that compelled her this afternoon. Pouring herself a cup of coffee, then dousing it with creamer, she curled up on the couch, wrapped a light summer blanket about her bare shoulders and pulled the laptop up to browse online.

"Ryland James," she said as she typed in his name.

Not expecting to find anything more than a Facebook page, she was surprised when the first page of Google spilled down a whole list of hits. And the image bar featured some paparazzi shots of the man wearing either a tux or a well-tailored business suit, and in all of them he was either facing away from the camera or had his hand up to block his face.

She clicked on the first entry posted by a dishy entertainment channel. A photo showing Ryland James leaving what looked like a nightclub with a hand blocking his face was captioned Parisian Billionaire Camera-Shy.

"Billionaire?" she whispered. "What have you stumbled onto, Indi?"

She scanned the article and it mentioned that Ryland James was a philanthropist who gave away billions but was noted as media-shy, and while he was occasionally seen with a date, no woman could ever be pinned to him as a long-term relationship. He was always the talk of the party when he arrived, and socialites listed him as their BILF—*B* standing for *billionaire*—on their social media pages.

"I was rescued by a billionaire?" She couldn't help the incredulous tone. But at the same time… "Why have I never heard of him before?"

She was a socialite. She participated in all social media and liked to know who was who and what they were doing with whom and for how long. Of course, she'd never followed the philanthropy hashtag before. As a trust-fund baby, she'd grown up, admittedly, with a silver spoon in her mouth. But now that she was on her own, she was perfectly happy to create her own riches. And was doing a great job at it.

And yet.

"Why would a billionaire be out in the middle of the night wielding a sword and chasing weird monsters?"

Because that was what she'd witnessed. Much as she didn't want anyone to hear her say it out loud, she had seen exactly that. Monsters. Big, black, sparkly monsters that had sort of faded out in a long wispy tail of darkness. And a tall, muscled, handsome man who had swung a sword like a Viking marauder.

"And I woke up under his coffee table. If only I had known he was rich, I would have stayed for breakfast. Ha!"

No, she wasn't the gold-digging type. Generally, a man's checkbook did not influence his attractiveness. And hadn't she given up on rich, self-involved men because of the extremely humiliating dumpage from Todd?

"For sure. No more rich businessmen."

Scanning through a few articles on him, she didn't learn much more, other than that he had been wooed by major modeling agencies and had refused contracts from all of them. Was known for driving a black Alfa

Romeo down the Champs-élysées at top speed. And could be rude to reporters when they pushed him for information. A rumor that he'd once dated Lady Gaga could not be confirmed. However, according to a tabloid, they had been in the same New York concert hall on the same night and both had left in the same limo.

Teasing her tongue along her upper lip, Indi double-clicked on the one photo that showed his face. The man was so freaking gorgeous. He wore his long dark brown hair loose, yet in other pictures it was pulled back behind his head. Always, the shirts he wore strained across strapping biceps and pecs. And the mustache and trimmed beard framed some seriously kissable lips.

"Billionaire or not, I most certainly need to thank him. And ask him the burning questions. Today. I do remember where he lives."

Now to figure out what to wear when thanking a man for saving her life, while also wanting to enhance her assets without looking desperate. But she had just been dumped. She really should go into mourning for a bit.

"He's not worth it," she muttered, dismissing Todd with the breezy apathy she should have had the other night. But if she hadn't been so distraught she would never have had a few too many drinks and wandered the streets, *and* she would never have run into Monsieur Sexy Billionaire.

"Not chasing after another rich man," she said, confirming her drunken decision to forgo them. "But I do need some answers."

Grabbing her half-empty coffee mug and heading down the hall to her bedroom, Indi tore off her robe and entered her closet to stand naked, perusing the possibilities. She owned a lot of clothes, and she wouldn't apologize for the extravagance. Shopping was in her blood.

Her closet had always been bigger than her bedroom since she could remember, even from when she was a toddler. Dressing up made her happy, just as wearing cat ears gave her confidence. Besides, her job required she seek out vintage, and off-season, designer clothing. If she happened on the perfect item of clothing for herself, she would never deny that want.

She touched the red dress. "Too aggressive." And it was the one Todd had always asked her to wear. "Never going to wear that dress again." It was Betsey Johnson. She'd gotten it off the rack during a discards sale. "I'll make a few adjustments to it, then sell it on the site." She pulled out the pink lace number. "Too summer-wedding." A white pantsuit with navy pinstripes was what she called her power suit. "Too businessy."

The blue sundress with a fitted bodice and full skirt would look great with some rhinestone heels.

"Or some stop-him-dead-in-his-tracks gladiator sandals."

Decided, Indi went about getting on her A-game.

An hour later, she stood before the door to Ryland James's apartment. At least, she hoped it was his place. When she'd fled the other morning, she was pretty sure she'd walked down four flights of stairs. This was the only apartment on the fourth floor.

She knocked and someone called out from the other side of the door to "hold on."

Primping, she quickly pushed up the girls. A lather of her pistachio-almond moisturizer over her décolletage, and some soft heather eye shadow along with pale lips, had given her a summery look. She liked to wear her hair pulled up, and today she'd gone with a bouncy ponytail high at the back of her head, with long strands teased out to frame her face.

Why she was nervous was beyond her. It wasn't as

though she intended to throw herself at the man. She was getting over a breakup. And she didn't do rebound guys. That was crazy waiting to happen. But she did have good reason to return to his place today. And that reason was what made her anxious.

The door opened to reveal a man a good foot taller than her, wearing loose jeans that hung low on his hips to reveal gorgeous cut muscles that veed toward his crotch. He wore no shirt, so she followed those ridges upward, over abs of steel and pecs that might have been formed from stone. Indi finally met the man's piercing brown gaze. His smile beamed.

And she lost all means of rational communication.

The prettiest pair of blue eyes gazed up at him. Blue? Maybe more like blue violet. They emulated jewels, for sure. For a few seconds Ry forgot his name. Not that he needed to know his name. A guy should remember a thing like that. But…ah, hell, what was going on in his brain?

"Princess," he said. "Minus the pussycat ears. I didn't expect to see you again."

"Oh." She looked aside.

He immediately picked up on her sullen expression. "But I'm happy to. I just wasn't sure you'd remember, uh…things."

She shrugged and offered him a straight smile. "I remember more than I probably want to. And I remembered where you live. I hope you don't mind that I stopped by. I wanted to talk to you, and I didn't have a phone number, so…"

"I'm glad you stopped by. Come in. I was warming up some nachos in the oven. You hungry?"

"I, uh…maybe? If I'm interrupting your meal—"

"Not at all. I left work early today and felt like bumming around home, catching up on some reading for business projects. Come in." He grabbed his T-shirt from the back of a chair and pulled it on. "Have a seat on the sofa. Uh, unless you prefer under the coffee table?"

She gaped at him, then shook her head and nodded a grinning acknowledgment to the dig.

Ry took in her gorgeous pale skin, which was exposed from shoulder to neck to cleavage, and then her pretty knees and down to those very sexy sandals that wrapped thin leather straps up to her knees. Up along the soft blue dress. Her breasts rose from the low-cut top in a sensual yet not-too-blatant invitation. And he couldn't stop looking at her mouth, pursed and the palest pink. And were those lashes for real? So thick and black and...

She paused and looked over the coffee table. Offering him a smirking grin, she sat on the sofa. "I can't believe I slept under your table."

"Me, either. Couldn't have been too comfy. You look like you're feeling one hundred percent better," he said as he wandered into the kitchen to peek into the oven. Another ten minutes and the cheese would be melted. "How are you feeling?"

She turned and looked over the back of the sofa. "Good. Not quite a hundred percent. Still a bit tired. I guess I went on a crazy bender. Slept on my floor when I got home, too. Apparently, when drunk, I'm a floor sleeper."

"Does that happen often?"

"The drunk?" Her laugh was soft but she waved off the levity with a gesture. "Not usually. But champagne goes straight to my head. I shouldn't have had that fifth goblet."

Ry whistled and wandered over to sit on the arm of

the couch. "Believe it or not, wine is my bête noire. I can't handle the vino."

"Really? A big guy like you? It must take quite a few bottles to get you wasted."

"Try one glass. I'm not sure what it is, but it lays me flat. And I can drink vodka and whiskey like it's juice. Weird."

He didn't normally reveal himself so boldly like that, but he'd sensed her need for reassurance. The woman had lain under his coffee table all night.

"You must have thought I was a case," she said. "And when I got a look at what I looked like when I got home? I can't believe you didn't think I was a homeless person."

"Wearing a designer gown and diamonds? The homeless are never so stylish."

She laughed. "Yeah, I guess. But they weren't diamonds. I never go for the splash when rhinestones will do." She leaned an elbow on the back of the sofa and pulled up a knee, catching it with a palm. "I needed to come see you because I don't think I ever thanked you. You were so kind to make sure I didn't lie abandoned in some dark alleyway. I can't imagine what would have happened to me if you'd walked away. So, thank you."

"You're welcome. I'm not much for leaving a helpless woman in a dangerous situation. I hope you weren't too freaked to wake here in the morning."

"I was, but that's to be expected. And speaking of dangerous situations, I do have questions."

This was the part Ry should have foreseen, but still it had snuck up on him. Questions. Always questions. And they were never easy to answer. "Like what?"

The oven timer went off and, thankful for a moment of respite, he rushed over to pull out the nachos. He'd made a whole pan of chips with jalapeños, tomatoes, onions, shredded chicken, black beans and heaps of cheese. His favorite comfort food. A guy could never find good nachos in Paris.

"You have to share these with me," he called over his shoulder, and was surprised when she answered from close by.

Indigo leaned over the pan of steaming nachos and inhaled. "That smells heavenly. Last time I had something like this was when I visited a girlfriend in the States. You can't find good nachos in Paris."

"Exactly. I use pickled jalapeños on them. That's the secret recipe."

She rubbed her palms together. "Dish me up!"

Could he get so lucky that she'd forget she'd come here with questions? With hope, maybe she would.

Chapter 4

It had been a while since Ry enjoyed the company of a woman so much. And since he'd felt so comfortable with one. Usually his dates were high-maintenance, slipping into the bathroom every half hour to check their makeup, texting or doing God knew what on their ever-present cell phones. He had yet to see Indigo glance at her phone.

They both sat on the sofa, facing the slanted windows that lined the east side of his flat from the floor, where they rose vertically about six feet up the wall, then angled at forty-five degrees to the top of the high ceiling.

Indi's hand rested on her stomach and she'd slouched down and declared, "You've ruined me for any other kind of nachos. I am your servant for life. Pay me with melty cheese and those fabulous pickled jalapeños."

"I have never seen such a pretty, petite woman put

down the cheese and chips with such gusto. I promise to call you next time I have a nacho craving."

She met his fist with her own. And Ry tilted his head against the back of the sofa and slouched down as well. He'd had a couple of beers in the fridge, and the now empty bottles sat on the coffee table. An evening sharing brews and junk food with a pretty woman? This was a hell of a lot easier than doing the fancy-restaurant thing and then trying to figure out if he should suggest a museum or a boring concert. And how to read a woman regarding whether she was on board for sex or if she was the sort who had a three-date minimum or even longer.

But he reminded himself this wasn't a date. The woman had been dumped by her boyfriend. And Ry did not do the rebound-guy thing. No way. He didn't need that kind of baggage to sort through.

He wasn't sure what was going on besides that he was warming to Indi fast and hoped they could get to know each other better. As more than friends, if that appealed to her. It did to him. When she decided to start dating again, he wanted to be tops on her list of potential dates.

Indi suddenly sat upright, turned to face him and asked, "Now about what I really came here for."

Ah, hell. The fun couldn't have lasted forever. Ry sat up and set the empty plate on the table, then prepared to face the tough questions.

"This is going to sound strange," she began, "but… why do I feel as if I was drugged the other night?"

Because she had been. "You did say champagne goes straight to your head."

"True, but I've been on a champagne bender once before. This was different. The aftereffects have been exhausting. I've slept like Sleeping Beauty minus the beauty part. I didn't even get up until three today. It's like I'm fighting to come back from an illness, or something. And I still don't feel right. Tired and achy. Usually after a bender I puke, pass out, then wake with a headache. But a few hours later, I'm good to go. You didn't... I mean, I don't think you would. You seem like a nice man. But... I have to ask."

He picked up on where she was headed. "I did not roofie you, Indi."

"Oh. Right. I mean, it's never happened to me before, so I wouldn't know what to expect. I'm sorry, but I had to ask."

"Understandable. Let me see if I can help you to sort out things."

Ry shoved a hand over his hair, then pulled it back and held his hand at the back of his head. How to explain this to her without going into so much detail she'd develop even more questions... Could he trust her with the details? She already knew some things, so he'd only get caught if he tried to twist them into something they had not been.

"And while you're at it, what were those black things?" she asked. "I saw them. They were...creatures. Totally black and creepy and yet weirdly sparkly."

Ry blew out his breath and dropped his hair. No way around this one. And lying never felt right to his soul. He'd have to give her the truth. Some of it. She seemed smart and capable of handling such information. And if not, she could run away from him again, and he wouldn't go after her. She'd just think she'd met a totally whacked guy with a weird way of looking at the world.

"You were drugged," he said. "Or rather, you were treated with a complex healing process that involved herbs and some..." He couldn't say *faery magic*. No human was that open-minded. "And I'm sure that was what has you feeling so blown now."

"Herbs? What the hell?" She pressed her palm over the base of her throat. Today there were no signs she'd even been injured by the collector. "I remember something about getting cut. Maybe from the creature's claws? Then you picked me up and carried me... And then I draw a blank. Ryland, please. I know this is crazy, but I need to fill in the blanks so I don't think I'm going nuts."

"You're not nuts. At least, as far as I know. I don't know you well." He winked, but she didn't return the playful vibe.

Right. She was worried, and he had no right to keep her in the dark.

"There was a creature," he confessed. "Two of them. I was there to slay them. Which I did. Because if I had not stopped them they would have entered the mortal realm fully and done some terrible things."

Indigo thrust up a palm between them. But she didn't speak.

Ry felt compelled to clasp her hand and give it a reassuring squeeze, then he set it on her leg. "This is going to be tough to hear, but you have to keep an open mind. Okay?"

She nodded. Winced. Closed her eyes tightly. Then opened one eye and nodded again.

"First," Ry said, "I need to know if you've been in that area of the eighteenth before. At night?"

"A lot of times. I used to party there with friends a few years ago. Janet and I did the Club Rouge for her going-away party this spring. Why?"

"No reason. Well, yes, there is a reason. That particular section of Paris is a strange place. Actually, it's called a thin place. Two worlds overlap."

She didn't react, but her attention grew fierce. He was jumping deep, but something about the woman made him feel as if she wouldn't be satisfied with anything but that dive, so Ry continued. "Do you know about faeries?"

"You mean like the little twinkly ones I see in my garden?"

He bent to level their gazes. "You see faeries?"

She shrugged. "Not all the time, but I have. And just that you're asking about it means that I don't have to say to you 'don't think I'm weird.'"

"I don't think you're weird. You've seen actual faeries before?"

"I guess so. Out of the corner of my eye. I believe in faeries. Just like I'm sure all the other mythical creatures exist in the world. Not that I've seen anything but a few faeries. I've have never run in to a vampire, but until something is disproven, I keep an open mind."

Ry's exhale released a lot of tension. "Good. Because those black sparkly creatures were from Faery."

"Really?" Her response was so enthusiastic Ry leaned away from her. Would it have been easier if she'd laughed at his fantastical suggestion and walked out on him? Much less to explain that way. "But those creatures were big. The same size as you. Can faeries be all sizes and shapes?"

He nodded. "Basically. They are a species, and within the species are hundreds, probably thousands of breeds."

"Cool."

So far, so good. Time to hold his breath and do the free dive to the deepest depths.

"That part of Paris you were in last night is called FaeryTown," Ry said. "It's where the realm of Faery overlaps the mortal realm. It's always been there. Humans aren't aware of it. They walk through never knowing that faeries are all around them, living, existing, doing drugs."

"Drugs?"

"Rather, the faeries sell their dust to—" Er, she probably didn't need to know about vampires and their addiction to faery dust right now. "Anyway, I saw you sitting on the curb, and you could *see* me."

"I did see you." Her eyebrows narrowed. She was starting to think too much.

Ry jumped in for the save. "At that moment, I realized I shouldn't have been able to see you, so I figured that you had somehow breached the fabric between the two realms and were actually in FaeryTown. And since you say you've seen faeries in your garden, then maybe you have the sight."

"Is that an ability to see faeries?"

"Yes. I have it. And that's what allows me to enter FaeryTown and to interact with its inhabitants."

"Which is why you were there with a big sword and hell gleaming in your eyes?"

"You did see those black things flying above me."

"I did. Not nice?"

"The nastiest of the not nice. I can't allow them to enter the mortal realm, so I go there every night to slay them."

"Every night?"

"At midnight. One or two collectors come through from Faery."

"Collectors? That's what you call the black sparkly things?"

"Yes. And while you don't need to know everything, just know that it would be a very bad situation if one got through to this realm. Meaning, they pierced the borders of FaeryTown and completely entered the human realm."

"Uh-huh." She rapped her fingers on her leg a few times, then tilted her head at him. Her big blue eyes were so deeply colored they were almost violet. Faeries had violet eyes. But she wasn't faery. He'd sense her faery nature if she was. And she had bled the other night. Red blood. Faery blood was clear and sparkly.

"So you're like Batman, then?"

"Batman?" Ry crimped his eyebrows. "I just fell off this conversational thread."

"Well, I, uh—" she tapped a finger against her lip and squinted one eye shut "—kind of sort of…googled you."

"To be expected."

"I know you're a famous billionaire philanthropist. That's totally Bruce Wayne. And then you fight the bad guys at night?" She shrugged. "Batman."

"I, uh, would never call myself that, but whatever works for you." Probably more like wolfman, but he was trying to avoid that branch of conversation right now.

"So…" Indigo placed her hand over her throat again. "One of those things, a collector, scratched me. I think?"

"Yes. And they are deadly to humans. By the time I got to your side, your breathing was shallow. You were going to die."

She gaped at him.

"I carried you to a faery healer and she saved your life. She owed me one. Well, not exactly, but I wasn't going to take a no from her because of our history."

"Your history?"

"It's not important. Hestia agreed to heal you. I didn't watch, but it took about twenty minutes. And whatever she gave you—the herbs or faery magic she worked on you—must be what's making you so tired and feeling as if you've been hit by a truck."

"That was how I felt yesterday. Only a small car this evening. So a real live faery healed me? Kept me from dying?"

He nodded.

"And then you carried me here to take care of me?"

"I wouldn't call letting you crawl under a table taking care of you."

"I was probably delirious."

"Close."

"Okay, so faeries exist and they are doing some bad things in Paris, and you go out nightly with your sword to make sure it doesn't happen."

"I try my best."

"What are these collectors doing? Killing people?"

"No, uh…" He winced.

"Ryland." She touched his leg and it sent such a shock of intense desire through him that he sucked in a breath. But now was no time to kiss her. Even if the compulsion was screaming for just that right now. "You seem like a smart man. Doing good for others by giving away your money. Avoiding the celebrity because that's not you. I did creep on you online. Don't hold that against me. Anyway, you don't seem like a man prone to flights of fancy."

"I never take to fanciful flight."

Her smile was so cute, curling the corners of her lips like a heart. "I think I can believe everything you've told me. I want to, anyway. It's the best explanation for my worst night ever. But you have to tell me everything. Please?"

"I don't know what else there is to say. As for what

I've told you, I would normally never tell things like this to anyone. Well, I tell Kristine."

"A girlfriend?"

"No, my secretary. She knows me inside and out. And she knows that this realm is populated by more than merely humans."

"You keep saying *human* like it's something you're not." She dipped her head to meet his gaze. "Are you a faery?"

"I thought you wanted to hear about the collectors."

"I do, but… Okay. Tell me."

He hadn't dodged that one and knew the bullet would ricochet around to hit its target soon enough. Stalling for time had never been his thing. He always liked to come right out with it. Unless it related to revealing his true nature.

"Collectors have only recently been infiltrating this realm," he said. "I know because I got curious after a news reports about stolen infants."

"I remember that a few weeks ago. Such an awful thing. Something like three newborn babies taken from their cribs."

"Right. Do you know about how faeries take human infants from their beds and replace them with change-lings?"

"I've only read about such a thing in faery tales. That's something that really happens?"

"It does. Or it did. It's been almost thirty years since any major baby thefts have occurred and changelings were left behind. Related to Faery, that is. But it's started again. Only this time, the faeries have decided not to leave a changeling in the human baby's place. They just take the baby and run."

"What do they want the babies for?" She pressed fingers to her lips. "Oh, my god, do they eat them?"

"No. Faeries have a thing for half-breeds. Unless its half demon. That's a long story. But suffice, they raise the humans in Faery and when they are grown, breed them with their own. It's not like a breeding farm. Some are treated as family. But it's how things have always been done."

"That's fucked."

"Gotta agree with that assessment."

"It sounds like human trafficking."

"When you put it that way, it is similar."

"You're protecting innocent babies. That's so honorable."

"I try. I've gone out every night for the past two weeks. Each night I slay one or two collectors. They often come in pairs, sometimes just the one."

Ry stood and paced to the windows that looked out over the city. Twilight was creeping up and the streetlights below fought with the remaining daylight. The sky was a hazy azure-and-gray violet. Behind him, he heard Indigo shift on the sofa.

"You don't have to buy everything I've told you," he said over his shoulder. "But it's the truth. And…" He turned to face her. "You can't tell anyone about this."

"Who would believe me? I've got enough problems without adding crazy faery lady to the list. And I do believe you. Can I just say it's kind of cool to know you? I mean, you really are Batman."

"Call me what you want. But I'm not a superhero. All I want is to stop innocent families from having their precious children stolen."

"I wish there was a way I could help you. I'm glad you trusted me to tell me."

She walked up beside him, and when he sensed she was looking up at him Ryland met her gaze. The outside light gleamed in her eyes and gave her skin a soft matte texture that looked finer than the most expensive silk. He wanted to kiss her. He should kiss her.

"One last question," she said. "And this one is the most important."

"Shoot."

"When I was hiding out in the alley, watching you battle the collectors with your sword, I saw something."

"Like what?"

"I saw you change. Briefly. Your whole body bulked up and your face… Ry, what are you?"

Chapter 5

"I should have kissed you when I was thinking about it," Ry said.

Indi's jaw dropped open. The man had been... "You were thinking about kissing me?"

He nodded. Smirked. A sexy move that crinkled the corner of one eye. "Just now."

Indi forgot her question. Had she asked him something? The man wanted to kiss her? "Then why are you standing there staring at me?"

His smirk curled to an outright grin. And as he leaned forward, kiss forthcoming, the delicious aura of him surrounded Indi with a fresh, outdoorsy gush of man and might. Overwhelmed by his stature and the sudden glee that invaded her core, she could but remember to close her mouth as his lips touched hers and one of his hands slid across her back to firmly take her in hand.

This was a slow and focused seduction of her senses

that lifted Indi onto her tiptoes to taste his lips, his teeth, his tongue. He clutched her tighter and deepened the kiss. The move made her feel safe and owned, yet also alive and sensual. The man knew how to hold a woman.

Gliding her hand up his chest, she slipped her fingers through the ends of his long hair and clutched at it, inadvertently pulling him closer to her, into her, if possible.

She sighed against his mouth as he tilted his head to change their angle. And when his other hand slid down her hip and over her ass, Indi couldn't resist lifting a leg to hook at his hip. And then the other leg. He held her there, wrapped about him, sinking into his taste, his smell, the hardness of his body and the gentle control of holding her.

Something perfect about this moment. But she wasn't going to analyze right now. Now was for pressing her breasts against his chest. Her nipples hardened and the man who held her groaned into their kiss. It sent an erotic hum through Indi's system. She rocked her hips forward, wanting the sensations to travel deep, and knew she was growing wet. Just from a kiss. A stunning, all-consuming kiss.

All of a sudden, Ry broke their connection and said, "Whew!"

Indi realized she'd actually jumped into his arms and decided that had been a bit forward, so she disengaged from him. With reluctance. Tugging at her ponytail and stretching her gaze along the floor, she couldn't prevent a giddy grin.

"I think I forgot my name," she confessed. And then when she looked up into his eyes, and he delivered her a waggle of eyebrows, she lost it and broke into a giggle. "Seriously, that was some kind of powerful kiss."

"I could give you another one. Unless that one was too much to handle?"

"Oh, I can handle a lot. Bring it."

Ry's smile collided with hers. And with a giggle, Indi again jumped up to fit her legs about his waist. He reached around and cupped her derriere, all while diving deep into her.

Had she come here to make out with the man? It hadn't been her intent. She'd had questions. That had been answered. Most of them. Yet the flexing of his pecs and abs against her torso enticed her to abandon her previous worries and simply fall into the moment.

Hot and firm, his mouth. And he knew exactly how to kiss her. She clung to his wide biceps as he opened her mouth in a deep, lush takeover. He wanted to be inside her? Yes, yes, and oh, baby, yes, please.

"You are some kind of delicious, Princess Pussycat."

"I like when you call me that. But it reminds me of my tattered dress that will never get clean. How could you have thought me a princess when I must have looked like—"

The next kiss was immediate and urgent. And it felt like the admonishment it had been meant to be. She'd been going down the route of complaining and putting herself down, and Ry stopped her. Bless him.

Clutching at his hair behind his neck, she curled it around her fingers and felt her toes curl within the strappy gladiator sandals. Had a kiss ever been so sensual? Targeted to her very core? Every part of her reacted to every part of him. And if she could get any closer to him she would, but she was already clinging to him for all the sweet, hot contact he would give her.

When they finally parted, she lingered in his arms this time, enjoying the feel of his warm chest against her torso and she hugged him. She wrapped her fingers about each of his biceps. So strong. Then she re-membered how he'd wielded the sword as if a Viking warrior.

And those creatures. *Collectors*. From Faery.

Indi slid down from the embrace and tugged at her skirt. "You're very sneaky," she said.

One of Ry's eyebrows lifted in question.

"That was a well-timed kiss. And the follow-up kisses distracted me from the question I asked you. But I can't forget. What I saw that night is seared into my brain."

She gave one of his biceps a squeeze, feeling the strength in his pulsing reaction. She felt sure many men who worked out were as solid and pumped as him. But did they wander about a place where faeries and hu-mans overlapped carrying big swords? And did they... change?

"What are you, Ryland?"

He stepped back from her, swooping a hand over his hair, a devastatingly sexy move that spilled the brown locks over an ear and forward against his neck and under his jaw. Indi's fingers wiggled, anticipating an-other glide through that delicious darkness.

And yet he looked down at her with an expression she couldn't figure. Challenge? Or an intense anxiety that he tried to bolster with silence?

"Are you a faery, too?" she prompted, unwilling to ignore her curiosity. "Because, you know, I am on board with all the faery stuff. Apparently."

He was the last example of what she'd expect a faery should look like. But then, those black sparkly things had never been in her mental catalog of what should and shouldn't be a faery. The few she'd thought to see in the backyard garden had been no higher than her index finger and had looked human and had sported glittery wings.

He exhaled heavily, one of those disapproving sighs that could go either way. Resignation or acceptance.

Indi dared to meet his gaze again, and this time he nodded and shoved his hands in his front pockets. Walking to the windows, he stood there for a while. The streetlights beamed and, while the sky was yet light, the moon was nearly full. It hung above the distant spire of the Eiffel Tower. A pretty picture. Made even more intriguing by the silhouette of the handsome yet seemingly troubled man standing before her.

"Ryland?"

"Just Ry, okay?" he said softly. "That's what all my friends call me."

She was relieved he had added her to his friends list. But after that kiss, and the following one, and then the next one, she had been hoping for something a little more than merely being friends.

"The things I told you," he said, still facing the window, "about FaeryTown and what I've been doing, have to be kept in strictest confidence."

"Of course. Like I've said, no one would believe me anyway."

"I'm not sure why I told you. Well, I had to. You were there. And for some reason beyond my ken you could see Faery. And, of course, if you believe in faeries, then you should understand there's a whole lot of other sorts out there that are best believed as only myth."

"Like vampires and witches?"

He nodded and turned to her. "Does that freak you out?"

Indi gestured calmly with splayed hands. "Do I look freaked?"

Now he narrowed his gaze at her, and there was that growing smirk again. "You don't. But maybe you'll go home and have a real good think about everything we've discussed and then the freak will pounce on you."

She shrugged. "Possible. But I'd like to fall on the side of me being a smart woman who can rationalize and decide for herself what is real and what is not. Show me a faery? I believe. Tell me vampires exist? Next time some guy flashes fangs at me, I'm going to guess it would be wise to run. Not sure what to do if I ever meet a witch, though."

"You wouldn't know it if you had met a witch. Or a vampire, for that matter. Unless he flashes his fangs at you. And then? How would you know if he's real or one of those poseurs that dances in the clubs and has a weird fetish?"

"Exactly. The world is filled with oddities. But what about mermaids?" she asked suddenly as her thoughts drifted. "Do they exist? Oh, please, tell me they do, because I so want to see one of those someday."

"They do, but you'd never want to meet one. They're vicious."

"Seriously? Have you met one? How do you know about all these creatures, Ry? If you're not a faery…?"

"I'm part faery," he said suddenly. And before Indi could ask for clarification, he added, "But mostly werewolf."

Chapter 6

He should not have stopped kissing her. Because then *the* question had been asked.

Ry had a thing about the first kiss. A man could tell a lot about a woman from that kiss. Awkward and graceless? There was always room for improvement. Sloppy and aggressive? Nerves could be the culprit, or just an overzealousness with which he didn't want to deal. Firm and accepting, yet also the woman jumped into his arms and wraps herself about him like she was made to fit his body?

Mercy.

His heart was still thumping from that incredible contact. And he wished his erection would chill. Because there were more important matters. Like his confession about being part faery, part werewolf to a perfectly human woman. He never did that. And on the one occasion he had told all? He'd known her for months, and her name was Kristine, and he trusted her implicitly with his secret because she knew all too well that secrets could be painful.

He'd known Indigo for less than forty-eight hours. Didn't know her last name. Wasn't even sure she believed in faeries or if she was playing along with him until she could laugh at his stories later. Who was this incredibly compelling woman who had loosened his lips so much that he'd laid it all out there like that?

That was it, wasn't it? That kiss of hers had loosened him up.

And now?

He wanted more from this woman. And for some reason, his better judgment had abandoned ship and decided he needed to tell all.

"Werewolf?" she said. Her voice was soft and awe-filled. Or was that fear? She stared up at him, hands clasped together below her chin. It looked like wonder in her gaze, but he could be wrong. Could be disgust. "And faery?"

With a heavy sigh, Ry knew he wouldn't be able to push her out the door and send her on her merry way now. The deep dive had occurred. Now to surface without sustaining too much damage.

"Sit down," he said.

She sat immediately. Eagerness lifted her chin, and yes, that was weird awe in her beaming gaze. "That's what I saw," she said. "I thought you changed to something like a wolf. Your head and shoulders and chest… they were—"

"I didn't realize it happened. In the moment, my anger and the fury at trying to destroy the collector overwhelmed and I briefly shifted. You shouldn't have had to see that."

"Why? It didn't scare me. I mean, from what I recall. Still kinda fuzzy from that whole adventure. And sore." She pressed a hand to her back and arched it forward. "I wonder if I could talk to that faery healer. Ask her what she did to me, and how long it's going to take to feel better?"

"Give it a few more days. You went through a lot the other night. And I'm sure I shoved you less than gently to get you out of the way."

"You were trying to protect me."

"A lot of good that did. You almost died, Indigo."

"There is that. I have no memory of a near-death experience, though. But let's talk about you. Come sit by me. Tell me about being a werewolf. And a faery! Please?"

In for the dive, Ry sat next to Indi and pressed his palms together before him as he summoned the strength and downright calm to put himself out there. He didn't have to tell her all. He would never do that. Because he didn't know her. But she knew too much. Enough that leaving her hanging would only push her away from him, and could likely result in her telling others his secret.

For once, Ry wished he had a vampire's skill of persuasion. They could change a human's mind, convince them they'd never been bitten. Or that they had never seen a werewolf shift halfway while battling vicious critters from Faery.

"Okay, here goes," he said.

She wiggled expectantly and leaned forward.

"I was born werewolf. My mother was a werewolf, and my father..." This part he didn't need to go into detail. "It's a twisty thing. My father was a faery, but my mother was married to the pack leader. She had an affair. Leave it at that. So I'm half-and-half, but I have more werewolf tendencies than faery. I don't have wings," he said quickly as she opened her mouth to speak.

"Oh." Her shoulders dropped. "I was going to ask about that. Do you have a tail?"

Her fascination disturbed him on a level he couldn't quite measure. Such a question made him angry, and a little humiliated. But why he felt that way went back to being ousted from the pack because he was part faery. Too many bad memories.

"I don't have a tail. In my *were* shape. *Were* means man. Werewolf means half man, half wolf. Like you saw the other night. Though I didn't shift completely. If so, my clothes would have split and fallen off and…you would have known for certain you'd seen a werewolf."

"Your clothes fall off? Is it like an Incredible Hulk thing?"

"Incredible…?" Ry couldn't help a chuckle. "What's with you and the superheroes?"

She shrugged. "I like comic-book heroes. Anything wrong with that?"

"Nothing at all. Not like the Hulk. When I shift to werewolf my body grows a little taller, more muscular and hairy, and my head takes on wolf shape, as do my legs and feet and hands. I'm mostly man but a lot of wolf."

"And you're naked?"

"Uh, yes?"

"Sorry, I like to have all the details. Helps me to picture it better. And then you run around naked in the city?"

"I never shift to werewolf in the city. Not completely, anyway. It would be foolish and asking for trouble. We of the paranormal ilk know the only way we can survive in the mortal realm is to keep our truths hidden."

"Wow, I suppose so. That's got to be tough. Trying

to survive in a world that doesn't believe in you. And if they did, they'd think you're a monster. You're not a monster, are you?"

"Do I look like a monster?"

"Not now you don't." But she wasn't completely on board with believing otherwise, he suspected.

"I'm not a monster, Indi." He clasped her hand and rubbed the back of it along his cheek. She smelled so good. And he didn't scent fear in her. Interesting. "I am a man first and foremost, who happens to have a proclivity for nature and running about as a wolf, especially on the night of the full moon. I also shift to wolf shape, which is exactly the creature you know as a wolf."

"Four legs and a howl?"

He nodded.

"That's so interesting. Do you have wolf friends?"

Despite the odd and uncomfortable questions, at the very least, Ry could be thankful she was open and not screaming right now. "Wolf friends? You mean who I run about with in the forest?"

She nodded.

"Yes. And no. Most werewolves live in packs. I haven't been in one for a while." Not by choice, either. "When I shift I do it alone. I own some property a couple hours out of Paris that is wooded and has a lot of acreage. If I encounter another of my species while shifted, we might have a tussle or just avoid each other. We're protective of our property."

"Alpha?"

"Yes, but I'm considered a lone wolf after leaving my pack."

"Why did you leave?"

"That's not something I want to get in to right now."

He pulled up her hand again and this time kissed the knuckles. "Any more questions?"

"Well, tons! I mean, how does the whole faery thing work in? If you don't have wings? You can't fly?"

"Can't fly. Don't have the desire to fly. I have a faery sigil on my hip that allows me some weak faery magic and the sight that I've already explained to you. And I do dust when I come."

"You what?"

Ry smirked. That was always an interesting one to explain. And it only happened with a forceful orgasm. Something he tried to avoid when with women. Otherwise, how to explain the sudden glitter explosion? The jacking off when he got home thing was getting stale, though.

"When faeries have sex," he explained, "they put out dust when they orgasm. I, uh, do that."

Indi's jaw dropped open, so he pushed it closed and then she caught his hand with hers, thumbing the side of his hand as she stared at it.

"A werewolf," she said in that awe-filled voice. "Who would have thought? You're not even Batman, you're Wolfman."

"I don't like that term. Just call me Ry."

"Ry. Ryland James. The billionaire werewolf who fights crime. What compelled you, a werewolf, to fight the bad faeries?"

"As I've explained, they are stealing human children. Isn't that reason enough to want to stand up and make it stop?"

"You're amazing. So selfless. And your philanthropy. You're quite the package, Ry."

And his own package was starting to harden again. She hadn't dropped his hand, and each time she stroked her thumb over his skin he grew a little harder. He'd love to kiss her until she begged him to strip her bare and have sex with her on the sofa. But she might like that. And he was in a weird place. A little freaked that he'd spilled all to her.

Could he trust his instincts right now?

"You probably need to give what I've told you a good think," he mused.

Pulling out of her grasp, he tapped her lips and pondered another kiss. That was the easy way out. Now was no time to press the easy button.

"I need to repeat how important it is to keep this information about me quiet," he said. "If the paparazzi and tabloids ever got wind of this—"

"Oh, never. I promise." She made an *X*-ing motion over her chest. "I swear to you. I won't tell."

He could almost believe her. "The photographers for those trashy rags have their ways. They find out I have a new friend? They'll go after you."

"Why?"

"Those bastards are always trying to dig up something on me. Can't accept that I don't do interviews and that there is nothing to tell. Except that there is a lot to tell. Which is why I avoid the press like the plague."

"And that only makes them go after you all the more?"

"Exactly. I'd rather battle hundreds of collectors than face down one hungry tabloid reporter. They're ruthless."

"I've seen that. I myself am a socialite." She beamed, but it wasn't one of those entitled poses, but was rather sweet actually. "I attend a lot of balls and social events. I've never been in the spotlight like a celebrity, but I do understand. You can trust me, Ry. We don't know each other that well, but we've been through something together. And... I want to know you better."

"I'd like to get to know you better. Can we go out on a date? Something official? I mean, if you can handle dating someone who isn't human."

"I'd love that. And you seem very human to me. How about this weekend?"

He winced. "Can't. Full moon."

"Oh." Her shoulders slumped, but then she perked up. "Oh? So you and the full moon…?"

"I have to shift on the night of the full moon. Which is going to be an issue this month. I've only been slaying the collectors for a couple weeks. This weekend will present a challenge. I normally leave for my cabin on the night before the full moon. There I have the freedom to shift without worry of being caught out. But I can't leave Paris this weekend. I have to be in Faery-Town at midnight to stop the collectors."

"But if you shift to werewolf in FaeryTown, will humans see you? You said they couldn't see FaeryTown, so…" She offered a hopeful shrug.

Ry hadn't considered that. *Could* he shift in Faery-Town? Of course, he wouldn't be seen by humans. But he risked the chance of his werewolf leaving Faery-Town for regular Paris. And would that wild part of him be satisfied with a romp about the city? No trees or fields? No long stretches of human-free acreage to let loose and howl in?

He'd have to figure this out within the next few days.

"It's something to consider. Can we make the date for next week? Sunday maybe? Because the day before and after it's full I also…have needs."

"Like what?"

The days before and after the full moon? He also wanted to shift, but that compulsion could be squelched with sex. A lot of it. How to work that out this weekend? "Another one of those things you don't need to know about."

"You certainly are a man of mystery. But I'm glad you felt comfortable enough to share some of those secrets with me. You can trust me, Ry. Sunday?"

"Later in the day, after I've returned to Paris."

"Maybe we could do a late-afternoon picnic?"

"Sounds like a plan." He grabbed his cell phone from the coffee table and handed it to her. "Enter your info for me so I can call you. I don't even know your last name."

"I'm Indigo DuCharme."

"Of course. A princess wouldn't have any other but a romantic name. We'll figure things out Sunday morning when I give you a call."

"I can't wait. In the meantime, I'm going home to—"

"Google werewolves?"

She bowed her head, because he'd hit it right on the nose. "Maybe." Indi typed in her name and phone number, then also put in her address.

"What you read online will only be fiction," Ry explained, feeling the need to do so. "Although some writers do get a few things right. Just take it all with a huge chunk of salt, okay?"

"Deal. I imagine it may be weird for you to have someone asking you questions about yourself, but I'm going to warn you that I may have many more questions on Sunday."

"It is weird, but I'm not feeling so nervous about this as I was when you initially asked me. Maybe we both need a few days to let this sink in. If by Sunday you're not on board with me, then I'll understand." He took the phone from her.

"Sounds like a plan."

Indi stood. He'd just given her an opportunity to

leave. And while he wanted her to stay for a few more kisses, Ry guessed her brain was humming with so much new, strange and curious information that she would need to be away from him for awhile, take it in and give it a good think.

She thrust out her hand for him to shake. Really? They'd gone beyond that silly gesture.

Ry pulled her in and bent to kiss her. The woman's body melded to his as if fitting into a mold. And as his hard-on gave him away, Ry delved deeper into the kiss to grasp her sweetness just in case he might never see her again. Parting from her happened with a sigh from them both.

"Sunday is so far away," she said, walking to the door. "It's going to be a long week. Thanks, Ry, for being honest."

"Thank you for not freaking out. But if you freak later, you can call me and we'll cancel plans."

"No canceling. And besides, my BFF is always on call for my freak-outs."

"No telling the BFF about me."

"Right. I can tell her I met a handsome man, though. She'd never forgive me if I kept that one to myself."

Another kiss sent her on her way. And Ry waited in the doorway, listening as her footsteps sounded down the stairs.

What had he just done? Revealing himself to a woman he barely knew? Something was wrong with him.

"Or maybe it's finally right."

Chapter 7

Days later

After slaying the two collectors in FaeryTown, Ry hopped in the Alfa Romeo and headed out of Paris. For reasons that were innate, the full moon always seemed to pull hardest at him around midnight. The witching hour? More like the wolfing hour. Even though, rationally, he knew the moon would hit its peak fullness around 2:00 a.m. this month. Other months it could be fullest during the day, but no matter, his werewolf waited until midnight to clamor for release.

But he could hold it back with the knowledge that soon he'd let out his werewolf and it would be free to run. The drive to the cabin was one of the prettiest trips when he managed it during the day. His night vision was excellent, and as he neared his property, he spied groups of deer in the ditches and the paralleling forest.

Ry pulled up the long curving gravel drive to his

place and left the car out front. He'd considered having a garage built to protect the Alfa, but he wasn't so hung up on material possessions, and while he kept it maintained, he wasn't owned by the upkeep of it.

He unlocked the front door and tossed his duffel bag to the floor. It was cool and quiet inside. He didn't bother to close the door because he immediately began to strip and toss aside his clothes.

Nothing felt better than a four-legged lope through the forest. And it was rare he got farther than the front doorway when he came here for two or three days of quiet and relaxation.

Shifting was immediate. His limbs loosened and shortened and coalesced to that of a gray wolf, which, when standing next to a natural wolf, would be perhaps six or eight inches taller and longer, but not much bigger.

Strutting out into the night, the wolf loped around the fieldstone walls and then raced toward the grassy field spotted with wildflowers. When he reached the forest, he let out a long and rangy howl that was answered by another natural wolf many miles off. He would ignore the howl. It was merely a property marker, not an invitation.

Charging through the forest, the night crisp against his fur, the wolf reached the small clearing that was lit like a stage with cool white moonlight.

And as the beast soared into the wild grasses and, briefly, all four limbs were off the ground, again the shift overtook Ry and his body lengthened. His legs grew and tight, furred muscles wrapped about his burly chest. He landed on legs similar to a man's, yet his feet were powerful paws with claws that could dig into the ground for propulsion, or kick and kill with a slice of those sharp weapons.

Head growing and yet remaining in wolf shape, Ry stood tall. He thrust back his shoulders and arms, and lifted his chest. His lungs deflated as he let out a howl that mastered the night and laid claim to his territory.

And with a sniff of the air and a tilt of its ear, the werewolf tracked a nearby fox. He took off toward the small creature, the invigorating rush of adrenaline, and the release after a month in human form, quickening his strides.

The website had been updated. The bills were paid. And the new product samples had been delivered an hour earlier. Indi looked over the many assorted boxes that she'd received from companies vying to be featured by Goddess Goodies' new self-care line. While she'd thus far stuck with adding a few hair accessories and one pretty moonstone necklace to the website, Janet had suggested she branch out to a few more female-centric items. Books on self-care. Healthy teas. Crystals. And…why not a vibrator? Self-pleasure was a big part of being a happy, gorgeous goddess. So Indi had agreed to at least consider the vibrators.

And the research could prove interesting, if not also satisfying.

Chuckling at what her job description required, Indi stood up from the boxes she'd unpacked and stretched. She'd been working all morning. Her office was the front living area at the side of the house. It was walled on the curved side with windows and sat up two short steps from the main sunken living room. A dressmaker's dummy, currently wearing vintage Alexander McQueen, was her main project. While she employed a staff in a small warehouse, and they managed the bulk of the sewing and online orders, she did choose a few gowns to revamp because she loved the process of redesigning what had been a gorgeous piece to begin with, and she was an excellent seamstress. Home economics had been a favorite course in high school, and she'd taken fashion, textiles and business in college.

It was Saturday and the sun was high in the sky. She tried to keep her weekends free and not work too much. And she did have fresh peaches in the fridge…

Stripping away her clothes, Indi walked away from work and into the weekend.

Later, she floated on an inflatable lounge chair in the pool behind her home, eyes closed and one hand clasped about a peach sangria. No swimsuit. Nudity was her thing. Her shrubs were tall enough that she didn't worry about nosy neighbors.

Indi wondered what Ry was up to. She'd told him she had intended to give the news about his nature a good think. But she'd been so busy the past few days she hadn't taken a moment to look up *werewolf* online.

The man was a werewolf.

Half werewolf. And half faery.

And why was she not überfreaked about that? Shouldn't she be worried that he was mentally disturbed and that to date him could put her in a dangerous situation with a psychopath? It was a stretch to go there with a man who had only been kind to her, but she had to consider the psychopath possibility. The world had gotten less kind and more strange. And that was just the humans.

Yet at the same time, she had seen those black sparkly faeries. Collectors, he'd called them. And she had witnessed Ry partially shift. His entire head had changed to a wolf's head. Despite being drunk that night, she would never doubt her instincts, which confirmed everything he'd told her was true.

Now to decide where she stood with all this information. Could she date a werewolf? Because he'd intimated he'd wanted to get to know her better. What was different about him than any other man?

"Besides that he can change into a wolf," she muttered. The sun beamed across her skin, glistening in the water droplets. "I wonder if he has sex with other wolves. As a wolf? Would he have sex with me as a wolf?"

Because those were the squicky questions that needed answers.

But she was rushing far ahead of herself. First things first. Ryland James was an amazingly sexy man that she wanted to date. And their first date was already on the calendar. He was also, seemingly, very kind, philanthropic and concerned for others. The man was keeping babies safe from abduction. It didn't get any more honorable than that. He really was a superhero.

And didn't all the superheroes have a dark and secret affliction that made them different from the rest? Something that would challenge anyone to love them and welcome them into their life?

Like being a man who was also a wolf?

He hadn't said anything about his dating history. He didn't look like a man who had trouble finding dates. Certainly, he could not be desperate. Indi reasoned he probably didn't need to reveal what he was to a girlfriend. If he left Paris to shift only during the full moon? Would be easy enough to keep his secret safe.

And yet he'd shared that secret with her. She wanted to honor that trust. And she would.

A weird twinge at her back folded Indi in the water. Toppling off the inflatable chair, she clutched at her back, unable to reach up as high as where the pain was while trying to keep the sangria up in the air. Spitting

out water, she kicked her way to the edge of the pool
and propped an elbow on the edge.

What was up with the sudden shot of pain up and
down her spine? It had zapped her and yet faded as
quickly as it had come upon her.

"I really need to talk to that healer."

The exhaustion was gone, but now that she thought
about it, she'd winced at a stretch of pain in her back
this morning when she reached for a dress in her closet.
She'd never had the flu, so she didn't know what a body
ache should feel like. But this was not normal. She was
an active young woman, not a creaky geriatric.

"Something weird happened that night in Faery-
Town. And I need to know what that was."

Ry had called the healer Hestia. Indi had no recall
about being in her presence or witnessing what she had
done to her. And Ry had acted defensive about her when
Indi prodded for more information. Did the man have
something going on with the healer?

With a wince at the snapping tug in her spine, she
pulled herself up and sat at the pool's edge. Her phone
rang and she leaned over to grab it. "It's him." Had he
changed his mind about their date?

Had she?

She pressed a hand to her chest to still her frantic
heartbeats. No, it was all good. So far, anyway. She
could go on a date with a werewolf. Talk about an adventure.

"Ry, good to hear from you. You still at your cabin?"

"Yes. It's not really a cabin, it's more a… Just
thought I'd give you a call, see what you were up to. I
hope that's okay."

That was encouraging. The man had been thinking of her.

"As a means to honor my no-working-on-weekends rule, I'm floating in the pool, getting some sun."

"You have a pool?"

"Yes, I do live in the eighth."

"Fancy neighborhood. Then you're doing well with your goddess thing, eh?"

"Not too shabby. It's a lot of work, but I love it. And I have a small but awesome bunch of employees. Later I get to do some field testing for a new product I may introduce with the next site update."

"Puppy ears?"

She laughed. "No. It's not an accessory."

"What is it?"

Should she tell him? She had felt as if they'd crossed the more-than-friends barrier with those fabulous kisses.

"Indi?"

"It's vibrators," she said as casually as she could manage. A trace of her finger across the water's surface tracked the glint of sun. "A lot of them. A dozen different companies want me to consider their product to sell on our site."

"Seriously? And you have to— I suppose product testing is important. Wow. I'm glad I called you. This is the most interesting conversation I've had in a while."

"Seriously? Because I think our conversation at your place the other night took the cake."

"For you, yes. For me? Vibrators are extremely interesting."

She laughed. "Chick toys interest you? I'm liking you more and more, Monsieur James. Are you returning to Paris soon?"

"Probably tonight. I drove out to the cabin last night after I slayed the collectors. I'll see how I feel about shifting after that. What I really need to do is stop slaying and figure out the source. Who is sending them in the first place."

"Otherwise you could end up slaying them forever with no end in sight. Makes sense. How could you find out something like that?"

"I'll have to talk to my brother."

"Brother?"

"Half brother. I have…hundreds of half siblings."

"Seriously?"

"My faery dad is a manslut. That's about the only way to put it. But I only know a few. Never, one of my half brothers, makes his home in Paris. I'm stopping by his place on the way in tonight. You mentioned you wanted to do a picnic tomorrow? What should I bring?"

"Nothing. Let me make all the food. Maybe you could bring wine. No, wait. You and wine don't mix. Bring beer."

"I can do that. Can I pick the place?"

"Yes, surprise me."

"What time should I pick you up?"

"How about a midday siesta? Around four?"

"I've got your address. I'll see you tomorrow afternoon."

"In the meantime, I have a lot of research to do."

"And now I'm going to have some sweet dreams thinking about you and your research. Thank you, Indi."

The phone clicked off and she smiled to herself. The man would dream about her jilling off? She could dig it.

It was a Saturday night. The Moulin Rouge and the Pigalle area featured assorted strip clubs, and the sex shops weren't far away, either. People were out partying, drinking, making general merriment…and even not-so-general merriment.

Wishing he was holding a drink instead of flexing his fingers in readying them to wield an enchanted weapon, Ry stood in FaeryLand, sword sheathed at his back and shaking out his hands at his sides. He shook because it was the night following the full moon and his werewolf was jonesing for release like a drug addict hungered for the needle. And the only way to subdue that jittery need was to shift. Or to have sex until he was sated.

But he wasn't having sex with a pretty blond woman who liked to wear cat ears and could eat as many nachos as he could at one sitting. No, he was waiting for some creepy, sparkly creature to come charging for him, talons flashing in the moonlight, intent on taking out the werewolf who stood between it and human babies.

Something wrong with that scenario.

Beside him stood Never, the half faery and half vampire who had been sired by the same faery Ry had. Never stood as tall as Ry but was lanky and dark. He did not spare the guy-liner. Ry was sure the man had to blow-dry his hair to get it to stand up all spiky on the top like that. Add in the black shredded jeans, boots and chains and spikes all over his clothing? Ry thought he looked like a goth reject from *The Rocky Horror Picture Show*.

"Doesn't it hurt to sit?" Ry had noticed the spikes that formed a spade on his brother's ass pocket.

"Depends on who I'm sitting on," Never said drily.

He wasn't a big talker. At least, he and Ry hadn't quite found their groove yet. They didn't go out of their way to spend time with each other. And that was only because Ry sensed the man liked to be alone.

He'd met him years ago, here in FaeryTown, when Never strolled up to him and insisted Ry smelled familiar. And then he'd mentioned their father's name and they'd had a drink and hadn't actually hugged and promised to call each other every weekend, but they had become as amiable as two weirdos could be.

"I seriously have not noticed anything out of the ordinary over the past few weeks," Never said. "'Course, my current chick lives across the river in the fifth." Moonlight gleamed in his violet eyes. Eyes that sported red pupils. "I've never seen what you call a collector. And I do spend a lot of time in FaeryTown."

Ry checked his wristwatch. "In three minutes you'll be a believer. Pay attention. I need to know where they're coming from and, most important, who is sending them. I can't keep up this slaying for much longer."

"What's wrong if a few human babies go missing?"

"Really?" He cast Never a look of disdain.

His brother shrugged. "They're so noisy and smelly."

"Remind yourself to always use condoms, all right, bro?"

"What's a condom?" Never chuckled and nodded. "You think I want to take after our dad? By-blows spread all over the world *and* in two realms? For all we know we've got siblings in Daemonia, too. Make that three realms!"

"I do know one of The Wicked is related to us. So it is possible." The Wicked were half demon and half faery. Faeries hated demons, and the half-breeds were ostracized to a strange and distant part of Faery. Most escaped to the mortal realm for freedom from such oppression. "Think she married a werewolf, actually."

"Right, that's Beatrice," Never said. "I've met her. She rocks. You want me to introduce you to her?"

Ry hadn't any burning desire to gain siblings, but he wouldn't push them away, either. "Too busy at the moment. Check with me in a few months. Here one comes."

They watched as the fabric between Faery and the mortal realm undulated, sparkled and spit out a collector.

"Wow," Never said. "Now, that's working the glam Goth look."

Chapter 8

Indi loved the Luxembourg Garden. It had once been Marie de' Medici's private garden on the south side of the royal palace, which still stood. Now the lush emerald grounds were neatly manicured and populated with statues, trees, groomed hedges and flowers. The metal chairs around the octagonal pond were occupied by parents watching their children play with the rentable model boats. Photographers wandered with their attention on their cameras, and lovers held hands and giggled and embraced.

Ry had led her away from the crowd, down an aisle of horse chestnut trees and to a secluded spot. The grass was off-limits for sitting, so Ry spread out the blanket she'd packed on the bench and helped her set out the food. Egg-salad sandwiches with spicy pickle relish, cut veggies and the requisite soft cheese with a long chewy baguette. And a growler of craft beer that Ry said was his favorite. Except he'd forgotten to bring along glasses, so they took turns drinking from the awkward growler. But it was all good.

The sun was high. The birds chirped. And not too many tourists wandered by their spot under the shade of the tree canopy.

Having consumed six of the eight sandwich halves Indi had brought along, Ry now laid back, head resting on Indi's lap. He closed his eyes. His long body stretched the length of the bench, and his biker boots, which were loosely laced at the tops, propped against the iron armrest. His T-shirt had ridden up to reveal a notch of chiseled abs. And his hair, pulled into a neat queue, splayed to one side across a shoulder.

Finishing off the last carrot stick, Indi toed the picnic basket closer and rested her sandaled feet on the wicker edge. Ry reached up to stroke his fingers over her hair, which she'd combed back into a ponytail again today, sans cat ears. The tickle of his touch behind her ear felt great and she quickly went from fun and chatty to hot and horny.

But she wasn't one for public displays of affection. Not the intense kind she imagined happening with this hot specimen of man. It involved kisses melting into tongue lashing over skin and body parts. And, oh, so many gasping moans.

"How did it go at your cabin?" she asked him to divert her lusty thoughts.

"As usual. But with the added driving back and forth. Saw my brother Never last night. He's going to look into things for me. He hasn't a clue who might be sending the collectors into this realm, but he spends a lot of time in FaeryTown. If anyone there knows anything, he'll be able to root it out."

"You live such a fascinating life."

"I'm not Batman, Indi."

"I know. But it must be interesting, probably difficult, straddling two worlds at once. Not to mention the added fact that you are a minor celebrity who is always being hounded by the paparazzi."

"Only during special events. Which I'm attempting to do less of lately. No time what with the midnight watches."

"I love a good event." She stroked her fingers down his cheek and teased them through his trimmed beard. "The ball gowns and diamonds. The glitter and the high heels."

"Sounds like it doesn't matter what the event is, so long as you get to dress up."

"I have been attending balls since I was five or six. My parents were always going to one or another. I begged my mom to take me along. I could live in a ball gown."

"Is that so? Then today's ensemble is definitely dressing down for you."

She wore another sundress, fitted green seersucker with thin straps and deep cleavage. As deep as size 34-Bs could manage.

"Not as far dressed down as I would like," she said. "It's either a ball gown or nothing at all for me."

His gaze found hers in an upside-down smirk. "Are you a nudist?"

"That I am. Give me skin or give me ruffles and rhinestones. I do enjoy being a girl."

"I also enjoy that you're a girl." He rolled to his side, facing her stomach, and slid his wide palm up her torso, not quite reaching her breast. "I had a dream about you last night."

"Did it involve vibrators?"

He laughed unexpectedly. "Maybe?"

"I hope it was more satisfying for you than my night

was. I spent it going over some SKU numbers the factory screwed up."

"Then definitely more satisfying. We guys do tend to think about sex." He winked at her. "A lot."

"Sex is never terrible to think about." And that they were talking about it wasn't bad, either. It was a bit daring, considering how short a time they had known each other. So…why not push it? Once again, Indi's curiosity raced to the fore. "I know this may be forward, but tell me about werewolves and sex?"

"That is rushing things."

"You're not interested in me?"

"I'm very interested in you, Indi. But as a man and a woman."

"That's good to know. But still, I couldn't find any information on Google…"

"All right, all right, I'll give you the basics. Werewolf sex. It's like two humans going at it when I'm in were shape."

"Were shape is your man form, like you are now."

"Yes. I'm all male right now."

"You most certainly are," she said in breathy agreement.

The man chuckled.

"But it can be different?" Indi prompted.

"If I was dating a female werewolf, we might go at it in our shifted forms."

"Do you know a female werewolf?"

"Not well enough to have sex with her. I have a friend from my former pack. But she's engaged. And I've only ever thought of her as a buddy. Besides, it's been years since we've talked."

"Do you want to have sex that way?"

He shrugged. "When I'm in werewolf shape I think as a man and as a wolf, so things are different to experience. And I don't always recall, when I'm back in this form, the things I did when in another shape. So, yes, it's something I would do because it comes naturally to me. It is what I am. But I spend most of my time as a man, so I do most things as a man and that is great, too."

"Have you ever had sex with a human woman while in werewolf shape?"

"I haven't. But I could."

"Would you want to?"

He quirked an eyebrow. "Not sure. The opportunity hasn't presented itself. And the question would be more would *she* want to? Does that freak you out?"

"The opportunity hasn't presented itself, so I guess not."

"Do you always ask your dates about how they prefer sex *before* you've had sex with them?"

"Sometimes. I am a curious chick. But now that you ask, it does seem like a good thing to communicate beforehand. I mean, most people tend to stumble through the act. Why not go into it informed and educated?"

"Like learning that the woman you are dating likes to research vibrators?"

"Exactly." And he'd just said they were dating. Score! "Maybe I'll let you help with the research sometime."

He sat up abruptly and scooted over to sit close to her. "I'm in."

And together they laughed and collected their things and repacked the basket.

Ry checked his watch. "It's six fifty-seven."

"It's early. Want to head to my place for a swim?" Indi offered as they strolled down the tree-lined alley toward the main pond in the park.

"I don't have swim trunks," Ry said.

"Somehow I don't think I'll mind that missing item one bit."

"Fine, but if I'm going in the buff, then you have to as well."

"I did confess to being a nudist." She winked at him. "Skinny-dipping it is!"

Out behind Indi's home the fieldstone patio stretched around a kidney-shaped pool. She dropped a couple of fluffy white towels she'd retrieved from the bathroom on the double lounge chair with the canopy over it, then joined Ry as he stared off toward the maple copse that marked the back of the lot.

"You have a lot of land for midtown Paris," he said.

"It's one of the larger lots in the city. It's been in my family for generations. We can trace ownership of this land back to the seventeenth century and some royal vicomte from King Louis XIV's court."

"Impressive."

"You didn't happen to know him, did you? Louis XIV?"

He cast her a strange look.

"I thought werewolves were immortal. Like vampires?"

"We can live three, four, sometimes five hundred years. But I'm only twenty-nine. Sorry to disappoint."

"I'm not disappointed. What about faeries?"

"Life span? A long freaking time." He wandered to the pool's edge and tugged off his T-shirt. At the sight of his wide, muscled back Indi caught her lower lip with her teeth. He turned a look over his shoulder at her. "We going to do this?"

The waggle of his eyebrows was all the invite Indi needed. She unzipped the back of her dress and stepped up beside him. "I'll have you know," she said, "if I see you in the buff I will probably want to have my way with you."

"Challenge accepted."

He unzipped his jeans and dropped trou so quickly, Indi paused with her dress halfway down and managed to step back in time as the tremendous splash from his cannonball into the pool soaked her feet and calves.

Tossing her dress aside, she dove into the pool and surfaced ten feet away from the man who treaded water with a shit-eating grin on his face. She lunged forward into a front crawl and swam toward the deepest end. When she reached the edge she turned to find him floating on his back, spitting up water like a fountain.

"This is heated!" he called.

"Of course it is. Otherwise my skin would goose-pimple and my tits would turn to rocks."

"Sounds painful." He lifted a hand from his floating position and made a rubbing motion with his thumb and forefinger. "Why don't you swim over here and let me make sure that doesn't happen?"

The sexy tease had begun, and Indi was all for it. She swam over to Ry and dove to swim under him and come up on the other side. When she surfaced, he pulled her to him to kiss.

They floated, but if she stretched she could just touch the bottom of the pool with her big toe. She didn't need the support, as Ry's arms held her against him. And with that security, she bent her legs and wrapped them about his hips. It was a position she seemed to naturally go into when kissing him. Seeking haven and finding it with ease.

He shifted to float on his back, which broke the kiss, but he didn't let her go. Lying on top of him, she laid her head against his neck and closed her eyes to take in every hard and slick bit of him that supported every wanting, wet bit of her.

His hand slid down her ass and cupped it. His erection nudged her thigh. It was a sizable asset that put her product research to shame.

"Let's move to the shallow end," he said. With a swish of his hands, Ry directed them around and he sailed them both across the pool. "Your tits against me are making things so hard."

"I noticed. Can you swim when you are a wolf?"

"Very well, but not in deep waters. Wolves weren't designed for that kind of movement. But I'm doing pretty well right now, aren't I?"

His shoulders hit the lowest step of four and he sat up and pulled her onto his lap. Indi straddled him. The water sloshed at their shoulders and made her breasts buoyant, lifting the tops of them above water.

Ry bowed and kissed each one. Then he gently cupped them both and kissed her beneath the water, sucking in a nipple. She rose onto her knees, lifting her breasts out of the water, and the man spread one arm across her back, holding her to him as he devoured her.

The hot, sucking tease shimmied through her system and coiled in her core and lower to her groin. Indi arched her back, showing him how much she liked what he was doing. She clutched at his wet hair and tilted back her head.

"Indi, your breasts are perfect."

"A little small," she said before she could catch herself. Goddesses did not put themselves down.

"Nope. I like this size. Made for my mouth. Mmm…" He nipped her gently, and one of his wide hands squeezed her derriere. "They're so hard. You're not cold out of the water?"

"Against you? I feel like I'm pressed against an inferno. And it is so good." She bowed and kissed him deeply, clasping his jaw with both hands as she swung out her legs to float behind her. "Let's do this," she said. "I want you, Ry."

"I've wanted you since the moment you looked up at me from under my coffee table."

"Really? Not before that, when I was drunk and apparently dying?"

"I was too worried about you then. Now? You're fine. And I do mean fine."

Swimming her out a little ways, so she could still feel the bottom, Ry held her securely and kissed her deeply. His free hand slipped between her legs. With a sensual hiss, Indi reacted to him finding her clit. She squeezed his arm, digging in her nails.

"That okay?"

"Oh, yes. You don't have any trouble without a map, do you? Oh… That. Right. There."

He performed a slow circling rhythm. It moved in a tight counterclockwise motion that was first firm and then a little gentler, and then back to the firm command. Her body shuddered at the instant-orgasm move.

Indi leaned in and kissed Ry's shoulder as his motions brought her to an edge she didn't want to grip, and couldn't, for she was surrounded by water and man. And when he tilted his head to breathe against her neck, moving his lips to kiss up under her jaw, and his finger hit the right spot, she came in a shout of release and joy.

Wrapping herself about him and shivering with the incredible muscle-clenching excitement of the orgasm, Indi kissed his forehead because that was where her mouth landed. His fingers nudged at her breast. A tweak of her nipple stirred the orgasm to a second wave, and that made her clutch him all the tighter. And then she released her muscles, letting him go and slipping into the water.

It was only when he caught her across the back and pulled her to him that she remembered it was probably a good idea not to drown.

"You come like the proud, sexy woman you are."

"That was…a surprise. Especially for, you know, a new lover. You focused right in on the task." She shivered and sighed, sliding her hand down his abs. Her fingers landed on his cock. Mercy, she could feel its power in her grasp. "My turn to get you off."

He hissed as she pistoned her hand about his length. "You've got a nice firm grip. Oh, Indi…"

He floated backward to notch his shoulders and head against the pool edge. She kissed him, long and deep, teasing him to dance with her tongue, while jacking him faster and faster.

"I probably shouldn't come in your pool," he said through a tight jaw.

"That's what the chemicals are for. Come on, lover. Let go." She lashed her tongue under his chin and felt his shiver. "For me?"

The man closed his eyes and let out a moan as his hips bucked and she held his erection firmly. He swore and bucked harder. And she noticed the surface of the water before him glittered in the setting sunlight. He'd said something about faery dust when he came. Wow. He really was part faery.

Ry pulled himself up to sit at the edge and then with one arm swung up Indi to sit beside him. She caught her balance against his thigh, then noticed the purple mark on his hip.

"What's that?"

"That's the faery in me," he said, and stood, offering her his hand to help her stand.

Once upright, she bent to study the marking, which looked like a violet design drawn by a tattoo artist before the actual ink was administered. "It's sort of like a mandala."

"It's supposed be the source of my faery magic, but…eh, it's just a mark. I've never experienced any real magic with it. It might be what makes my blood sparkle, and well…" He glanced over the water. "I did mention faeries put out dust when they come."

"My pool has never looked prettier. I love glitter, you know that. I want more. We need to do it again." She grabbed his hand and tugged him over to the chaise longue. "Hurry, before we dry off!"

She dove onto the chaise and Ry crawled on top of her, dripping hair splattering her chest and throat. "Water's not the best lube."

"No, but it makes your skin slick and I want to lick you." She pushed him to the side and, with another nudge, he surrendered to lie on his back. "Where should I start?" She looked him up and down.

The man's cock was already hard again, and she couldn't not look at it, again, and again, and…

"Right here." She bowed and licked the bold red head of his erection. The heavy shaft bobbed, so she held it firmly and squeezed at the base.

Ry's groan was a mixture of surprise and satisfaction. He gripped her by the wet hair and eased his hand along her neck as she took him in her mouth and brought him to another, trembling, shouting orgasm. This time the sparkle misted into the air in the wake of his ejaculation. Faint, but it glittered on his skin and her fingers.

"Cool."

Ry kissed her nose and grabbed his watch. "You girls and your love for glitter. I've gotta say, this is much easier than trying to come up with an excuse like maybe the glitter came from the woman's makeup. Or else having sex in the dark."

"I can't imagine."

"It's an issue, that's for sure." He checked his watch. "Ah, hell. I have to get going. It's almost eleven thirty. Mind if I use your bathroom before I leave?"

"It's upstairs and through my bedroom. You'll see it. Will you grab an extra towel and bring it down? I want to wrap up my hair."

"Be right back." He kissed her, then wandered inside the house.

Indi stood and stretched her luxuriously aching muscles. This had been a perfect date. Could a girl get a hallelujah?

"Oh."

Too soon to celebrate. She caught her hand at her back, wincing at the stinging pain that focused in her spine, but high up, too high to reach. Not like the usual aches and pains she would expect if she'd lifted something wrong or had maybe gyrated too much while in the pool having sex with a hunky werewolf.

Ry returned and placed a towel over her head. He bent to look into her eyes. "You still feeling some pain? Is that from the other night?"

She nodded. "I don't know what it is, but it sneaks up on me, and it seems to be getting stronger. I wonder if I sprained something when I stumbled in the alleyway."

"Possible. I'll look for the healer tonight and ask her what's up. Maybe she can enlighten me to what she used on you and if it has any side effects." He bent and pulled up his jeans. "By the way, that is a hell of a lot of vibrators you have in your bedroom."

Indi giggled and fluffed the towel over her hair. "That it is."

"If I wasn't in such a hurry I'd help you with your research."

"There's always tomorrow."

"Sign me up?"

"Consider yourself recruited. Do you work tomorrow?"

"Yes, I go in to the office every weekday. Kristine has a new list of potential recipients that I want to go through and call for interviews."

"Who are your recipients?"

"Mostly paranormal-related causes. Though the one I'm excited about buys land to protect natural wolves. They want to start an international office."

"Sounds right up your alley. I'll be out and about tomorrow running errands. Is it all right if I stop by your office with lunch?"

"That'd be thoughtful of you. Would you mind bringing along something for Kristine, as well? I'll foot the bill."

"I can do that. My phone is inside on the kitchen counter. Leave your office address in the contacts and I'll see you then."

He pulled on his shirt, then flipped his wet hair over a shoulder. Kissing her, the man growled. "It's tough walking away from you."

"That'll give you more incentive to walk back to me."

"I like the sound of that. Thanks for today. I like spending time with you. And having sex with you."

"Ditto. See you tomorrow, lover boy. Can I call you lover wolf? It sounds sexy."

He waggled his hand before him. "Whatever makes you happy?"

"I'll think about it. Good luck stopping the big bad

sparklies tonight. Be careful!" she called as he wandered into her house.

Wrapping the towel around her body and tucking it in front, Indi collected the wet towels and dropped them in the hamper that connected to the laundry room.

She wasn't sure she had the energy or desire to do any research tonight. She was a woman sated. Who was dating a werewolf. How strange was that? Was she prepared for this? Could she do this?

Up until a few days ago, her life had been exquisitely normal. Ball gowns and tiaras? Check. Wolf fur and big, deadly swords?

"Check," she whispered, and then smiled. "Bring on the not normal. I'm in for the ride."

Chapter 9

Indi gave her name to the doorman at the business building overlooking the Seine. He said she was "on the list," so he let her walk through to the elevator bay. It wasn't a swanky building, was rather run-down, but it might have been glorious in its 1920s heyday, judging by the aging azure-and-maroon art deco tilework on the walls.

Once in the elevator, she thought that this getting dumped thing was not so bad after all. Look at the rebound man she'd scored!

"Not a rebound guy," she whispered. "Please don't let him be a rebound. That never ends well. He's the new guy. The new wolf," she muttered as the doors opened and she walked out onto the third floor.

There were four office doors to choose from, and three of them had brass plaques that detailed more than a few last names or a product name. She chose the door without the plaque and walked in.

A woman behind the desk looked up from the laptop. She was certainly…oh. Indi was briefly taken aback by her stature and broad shoulders as she stood and offered a wide hand to shake.

"You must be Indigo DuCharme. The cat ears are gorgeous, and don't get me started on your shoes. *Très magnifique!*" she cooed in a deep voice. "Ry said you might stop in today. I'm Kristine."

"Nice to meet you, Kristine. Ry mentions you often."

"He'd better. I do keep his life on course, and you'll never find a faster typist than me, sweetie. Even with these luscious nails." She fluttered her, indeed, glossy and lushly violet nails for Indi to see.

"Is Ry in?"

"He's in his office. You bring him lunch?"

"Yes." Indi held up the take-out bag. "And for you, too. Do you like crepes? I picked up some with everything on them and salads for sides."

"That was so sweet of you, Indigo. Thank you."

She set out the boxed lunch for Kristine on her desk, then gestured she was going in to see Ry.

Ry met her at the door to his office, opened it and invited her in. "Smells like cheese and ham."

"And mushrooms and basil and lots of other stuff. I told the chef to toss everything in them."

"I'm hungry." He closed the door and then tugged her by her free hand to stand in his embrace. The kiss was masterful, and delving, and she was glad she'd not snuck any of the spinach before coming here. "You taste better than lunch."

"Well, if you're not hungry anymore, I can eat them both."

"Not so fast." He grabbed the lunch bag and gestured for her to sit on the couch. "So you met Kristine."

"I did."

Ry sat next to her and Indi leaned in close and whispered, "You do know your secretary is a man, right?"

He chuckled and handed her a box and a plastic fork. "Kristine is a woman. She just hasn't transitioned yet. Won't take my money to pay for the surgery. Stubborn. And I love her like a sister. Not even like a half-blood sister, either. She and I are tight."

Endeared by his acceptance and love for the woman, Indi felt awful she'd called her a man. She had difficulty knowing how to label some people, but knew the label wasn't so important as simply accepting them as human beings. But when it came to humans…

"Don't tell her I said that," she said, opening the box. "I feel terrible."

"You shouldn't. It's natural to not understand people who aren't like you."

"You mean like understanding you?"

"I think we get along pretty well, even for our differences."

They clicked forks and both dug in to the steaming crepes. "We do indeed. But tell me this. Is Kristine… paranormal?"

"Nope, as human as you are. Paranormals live in the city, but we're not everywhere. At least, not we wolves. Most of us tend toward the country."

"Then why do you live in the city?"

"It's the furthest thing from what I had, and…" He frowned.

Indi suspected some bad memories were struggling in his brain.

"It works for me right now."

"It's good to be close to all the action, I guess. How did it go last night?"

"Only one collector came through. Stabbed it right through the heart. Er, if they have hearts. Not sure about that one. But the thing disappeared in a silent scream and a cloud of sparkling dust."

"Can they speak? Maybe you could capture one and question it?"

"I've considered that. But I don't think they can speak or make vocal utterances. They do have a mouth. I've seen the rows of teeth and felt them on my skin, but still haven't heard a peep from them."

"Curious. But your half brother is looking into finding who controls them? That must be the person who wants the babies. It's so strange."

"Strange is normal in Faery. So are malevolence, violence and tricksters. Faery is not a place for the weak. My faery father has asked me to go there and—"

Indi paused with a forkload of crepe before her mouth, waiting for him to elaborate, but Ry instead set down his fork and opened the door. "Kristine, would you mind bringing in something for us to drink?"

"Sure, boss, be right in."

Indi waited silently for the transaction to occur. Kristine winked at her when she handed Ry two bottles of water, then closed the door behind her.

He sat down again and handed her a bottle, then resumed eating.

"Uh…" She twisted off the bottle cap. "And?"

"And?" he asked, looking to her with question.

"You were saying something about your father wanting you to go to Faery."

Ry sighed. She was learning that he did that a lot, usually when he didn't want to tell her something. What more could the man possibly have to tell that could shock her?

"That slipped out. I don't talk about my father much. I don't like to."

"Fair enough. But Faery is out for you?"

"Definitely. It's not my home." He tilted back half the bottle of water. "It was nice of you to bring lunch. And I'm sorry because I looked for the healer last night, to ask her about how you've been feeling, and wasn't able to find her. Tonight, I promise I will camp out on her doorstep until she talks to me. You feel any better today?"

"In general, I feel fine. No longer exhausted. But I keep experiencing weird twinges of pain right between my shoulder blades and lower. It has to be a pulled muscle."

"Probably. But I'll ask. If she'll talk to me."

"What does that mean?"

"Hestia and I had some issues a few years back. She doesn't like me very much."

"But she was nice enough to save a dying human woman when you asked. Unless." Indi looked to him. "Were you two dating?"

"What? No. Maybe. No. It was just…" He dropped his fork onto the foam box and then wobbled his hand before him. "A few nights. She was in love with the idea of making it something more. I was not."

"And I take it she never got over it?"

Ry shrugged. "Apparently not. You women are a tough bunch to figure out most of the time."

"It is in our nature to be contrary. But if she doesn't like you, maybe she did something to me?"

"I can't imagine she would be so vindictive. She has no reason to harm you. And like you said, it's probably pulled muscles. How often do you do something so physical as dodging collectors?"

"Never. But I am a swimmer. I'm not out of shape."

"You don't have to tell me that. I've seen your shape. It's sexy."

He kissed her cheek, and warmth flushed Indi's

cheeks. "You can take a gander at my shape any time you like. As for the aches and pains, they'll go away." She stood and looked for a wastebasket to toss her box in.

"You can leave the garbage and Kristine will take care of it," he offered. "You going to eat that salad?"

"No, you can have it." She sat on the comfy office chair behind his desk. The far wall was all windows, and boasted a view of the Seine, and just down the river loomed the Notre Dame Cathedral. "This is a small office. You certainly don't go in for bold and flashy, do you?"

"Why spend the money I hate on stupid things?"

"You hate your money?"

He tilted his head back against the wall and set the salad aside. "More delving questions from the sexy swimmer in the cat ears."

"I am sexy." She tapped the black velvet ears she wore today; they went with the black velvet trim on her pink sundress. "And the ears are my thing."

"They are. I like them."

"So, the money," she prompted, knowing she was pushing it with her nosy questions.

Ry leaned forward to prop his elbows on his knees and clasped his hands between them. "My faery father wants me to move to Faery. I refuse. I like the mortal realm. It's all I've ever known. He tried to bribe me right after I left the pack. I didn't know at the time, when he plucked a couple leaves off a maple tree and handed them to me, that would change my life forever."

"Leaves?"

"Faeries can enchant things. They've a talent manipulating human objects. Those leaves turned to thousand-dollar bills in my hand. My first compulsion was to toss them, but I'm not stupid. And I wasn't bringing

in much cash at the time, being on my own and trying
to make a living. So I invested the cash. Within months
it grew to millions. Billions within a few years."

"How is that possible?"

"It's the enchantment. The damn investment keeps
multiplying. And I can't give it away fast enough."

"Wow. I wish I had your problems."

"It's not money I want. It came from a person from
whom I don't care to take charity. So I give it all away
as fast as I can."

"Doesn't it ever change back to leaves?"

"It would if my father died. Then all his magic would
die with him. And he's been around for more than many
centuries. Not sure about faery years. He's old, but I
don't expect him to start pushing daisies anytime soon,
despite his suggestions otherwise. If you ask him, he's
on his last leg. I doubt that very much. He's a pompous
bit of wing and sparkle."

"You and your father don't get along. Can I ask
why?"

"Not today."

She sighed and caught her chin in her hand. "Fine.
I can deal. I'm thinking learning about the paranormal should be taken in small chunks and not tossed at
me all at once."

"I imagine it would be like an alien learning about
earth. There's so much to learn, Indi. Don't worry about
it. I'm just glad you can accept."

"Like I said. Show me proof." She leaned her elbows
onto the desk, but before her a stack of papers lured
her eye. It was the gold engraving and soft violet paper
that caught her attention. She tilted her head to read
it. "You're going to the Hermès ball in two nights?"

"No. I hate those things."

"I thought you said you go to them to schmooze."

"I do, but the photographers…and with the midnight slaying calls. I try to avoid them as much as possible."

"I get that, but this one's for raising awareness for endangered species. Like wolves?" She winked at him, feeling the giddy stir that always accompanied the planning and anticipation for a fancy event. "There's got to be some of your people at an event like that. Why don't you go? The charity seems like something that would be right up your alley."

"It is. And I should learn more…" With a sigh, he offered, "I don't have a date."

She cast him a gaping stinky-eye look.

Ry laughed. "But it's in two nights."

"You think I can't put together a ball gown and makeup in forty-eight hours? Ry, my natural habitat is a ballroom. I breathe tulle and eat rhinestones like candy. Oh, please, take me with you. I know we've only started this thing between the two of us, but—"

"But what?" His eyes glinted with a tease that reminded her of their dip in the pool. And then afterward, sprawled on the chaise longue. Had it not meant as much to him as it had to her?

"Well," she began cautiously, "if you took me along, you wouldn't have to introduce me as your girlfriend."

"What would you be? My female friend? The chick who begged to come along?"

She nodded eagerly, knowing she seemed desperate, but also sensing he was stringing her along. They *were* dating.

Ry flipped his hair over a shoulder and winked at her. "Your natural habitat, eh?"

"I've been gliding across a ballroom floor since I was a little girl."

"That's right. It's either the big fancy or nothing at

all for you. And I've seen you in both scenarios. Know which one I like best?"

"You can have both options because I love nothing better than, after the big fancy, to strip it all away."

"You don't need to tempt me with such promises. You had me at those big pleading blue eyes. All right, then. It's a date."

"Yes!" She clapped her hands in glee.

Ry narrowed his gaze on her. "Why do I suspect you're less excited about going with me and more excited about the fancy dress-up?"

"Because it's true! I love to dress up and be a princess." She spun around the side of the desk and approached him.

"A Princess Pussycat. Promise you'll wear the kitty ears?"

Bending over him, Indi leaned in and whispered in his ear, "If you promise to make me purr after we've danced all night."

"Oh, that I can do." Tapping his forefinger on her lips, he added, "But we'll have to pull a Cinderella."

"What do you mean?"

"Me and my midnight FaeryTown date."

"Oh, right. But after Batman fights the bad guys he goes home to someone, right?"

"I believe that's Alfred."

"Then I'll be your Alfred tomorrow after the ball."

"I'd much prefer Catwoman purring in my bed, waiting for my return."

"Meow."

Indi straddled his legs and kissed him, running her fingers through his loose hair and snuggling her breasts against his chest. He hugged her closer and deepened the kiss until all she knew was the taste and fire of him coiling within her.

Had she in mind to give up on rich, self-possessed men? She had. And she had done so. Ry was the furthest thing from self-possessed. And she felt his wide and giving heart every time she was near him.

"Yay! It's a black-and-white ball. I have the perfect dress. And the shoes. Oh, wait. I think that pair is broken. I have to go home and figure this out."

"You do that. I've a lot of phone calls to make this afternoon. It might be a long day that stretches into tomorrow."

"I'm good. Much as I'd love to spend more time with you, I have a ball gown to create."

"Can we meet up on the night of the event? What time does the ball start?"

"Seven. But one must never arrive exactly at the starting time. Fashionably late is de rigueur."

"Then I'll pick you up at seven."

The next night

"Three down…" Ry checked his watch. "In four minutes, seventeen seconds. A new time."

He sheathed his sword behind his back and jumped over the pile of dissipated collectors. The ash had fallen like soot and sparkled. He had the stuff in his hair and on his shoulders and arms.

Shaking briskly, he got rid of most of what had fallen on him.

He eyed the direction in which the healer lived. Hestia would talk to him. If he approached her with his heart in his hands. Women. That one, in particular, knew how to hold a grudge. He'd not told Indi all the sordid details. That he and Never had been on a binge one evening right here in FaeryTown and Ry had tried a drink called Devil's Spit. He'd never been so wasted in his life. Or horny.

He'd laid eyes on Hestia and sweet-talked her right into her bed. For three days straight. That was how long it had taken for the loopy space-out effects of that bizarre drink to wear off. He'd woken on the fourth morning, Hestia gazing at him adoringly and calling him her one true love.

And Ry had run from that bed as quickly as possible. He'd not been in a place for a true love, or even a girlfriend. But that hadn't kept him from returning to her for healing a time or two. He'd not noticed her adoring looks or possessive hand clasps until that third time, when he crawled to her doorstep after a violent fight with another lone wolf who had been attempting to claim FaeryTown as his own—it belonged to no wolf—and had left him with a blade stuck through his lung. Hestia had given him her vita that night, and had nearly died in the process. She'd saved him.

But that still hadn't made him want to call her his girlfriend. She had seen it another way, and had raged at him, calling him a tease and saying that he had been stringing her along.

"Women," he muttered.

Now as he reluctantly walked toward Hestia's place, Never called out to him from the open door of a faery club that vibrated with weird harp and electronic tones. Ry nodded acknowledgment but kept on walking. Never would follow.

And he did. He might be funny-looking, but the guy was predictable.

"How's tricks?" Ry asked as he slowed his strides and they wandered side by side. A blue-skinned faery fluttered past them wearing a sandwich board that advertised "Bliss'shrooms direct from Faery." The contraband mushrooms were probably fake, but the Sidhe Cortege made a pretty penny extorting the weak. "You do any sleuthing?"

"I did," Never said. "Riske wants to talk to you."

"Is that so?" He'd just been thinking of the Sidhe Cortege. Riske was the ringleader of the Mafia-like organization that worked the mortal realm. "Tell him to come talk to me. My office is in the fourth."

"You know he's le Grande Sidhe, right? Big man on campus. The grand poohbah."

"I thought he was the leader of the Sidhe Cortege."

"Exactly. I've worked a few jobs for him. Thug stuff."

Ry cast a gaze down his half brother's lean form. Faeries were strong as fuck. He certainly wouldn't stand against Never's strength. Not for long. As well, he was an excellent marksman with any weapon he could get his hands on.

"He's fair, but brutal," Never continued. "Me asking him questions for you? That put up his hackles."

"Does he know who is behind sending the collectors to this realm?"

"He wouldn't say. Wants to discuss it with you face-to-face."

"Then I guess I'll have a talk with the big faery on campus. I got a gig tomorrow night, though. When does he want to do it?"

"Tomorrow night."

Ry's smirked. Wasn't that always the way it went? "I'll be in FaeryTown at midnight again," he said. "I can talk with him after that."

"I'll let him know. And, uh, no bringing along any humans."

"Wouldn't dream of it. You see Hestia anywhere?"

"I think she's down at the jazz club. You don't want to go in there tonight."

"And why is that?"

"Her girlfriend is hanging all over her. She's a witch."

An involuntary shiver skittered down Ry's spine. "Witches creep me out."

"That they do. You want to head to that new night-club down the street? I'll match you in dust shots."

His brother had a hunger for faery ichor, as opposed to blood, and he drank it like water. Indi had texted him a "good night" earlier as she'd made it an early evening after a long day of work.

"Sounds like a plan." Ry would order the dust-free vodka shots.

Chapter 10

Indi answered her ringing phone. Her heart dropped when she saw it was a call from Ry. It was six thirty and she was dressed up and ready for the ball—

She wouldn't think the worst. That way lay madness. "Hey, Ry. What's up?"

"I'm going to have to meet you at the ball. Kristine has an emergency and she needs me to pick her up. I'm headed toward the eleventh right now."

The ball was at the Grand Palais in the eighth. If he had to pick up his secretary, he'd never make it to her place by seven.

"I see." Indi clutched the back of the chair. Tears bubbled at the corners of her eyes. This could not happen a second time in such close proximity to the previous disastrous jilting. It. Could. Not.

"Indi, you there?"

She nodded.

"Listen, I'm not ditching you tonight. Promise. I

would never do that. And I feel terrible that I can't pick you up, so I've sent a limo for you. It's on the way right now. If I could change things, I would, but Kristine…"

"Of course. She's like your sister. You sure things will work out? If you don't think you can make it…"

"I'll be there. I've got the tux on and I intend to dance with you all night under that amazing glass ceiling at the palace. Now, don't let those tears fall."

She quickly swiped at a tear that loosened from the corner of her eye.

"I know this is freaky news for you," he said. "I'm not that insensitive. I'm shooting for getting to the palace around seven-thirty. Will you wait for me on the *escalier d'honneur* leading into the ballroom?"

She nodded again.

"You're going to have to verbalize, Indi."

"Sorry. I… Sure." Her hand shook as she smoothed it down the gown's sleek black taffeta bodice. "I'll be there."

"And so will I. Promise. Now go check for the limo. It's probably already arrived."

She glanced out the front window. Sure enough, a black limo rolled up to the curb.

Again, Indi nodded. Why was she finding it so hard to speak? It wasn't as if Ry was going to pull a Todd on her.

Maybe. How well did she really know the guy?

"Ah, hell, maybe I can find someone else to drive Kristine."

"No!" Indi blurted, finding her courage. "It's fine, Ry. And if something happens that keeps you from attending the ball—"

"Nothing will. Swear to it. See you in a bit. Okay?"

"Yes. See you there."

She clicked off and almost dropped the phone her

hands shook so much. Pressing a palm to her heart, she leaned over and breathed deeply.

It couldn't happen to her again. It simply must not.

Ry glanced over at Kristine, who sat on the passenger seat. Head bowed and mascara streaked, she gazed out the window.

A couple of assholes had decided to tease the chick who wasn't their idea of what a woman should be. They'd pushed her around on the Métro and she'd rushed out of the subway car but had caught her elbow in the automatic doors. A bruise had darkened her skin.

This had happened once before, and she'd told him about it after the fact. He'd made her promise, if it ever happened again, to call him immediately. It had only taken him fifteen minutes to get to the subway stop. Good thing he'd been ready to go, all dressed up.

He turned the car down Kristine's street in the fifth arrondissement. She lived in a cozy top-floor flat owned by an elderly couple who were always inviting her to join them for breakfast. Ry was glad she lived in a good, safe neighborhood. But assholes would never go away. And she was, to most, different. He could relate to her in a vague way. Both of them appeared to be something they were not. But he'd never try to compare himself to her, and her troubles.

He pulled the Alfa to a stop and leaned across the shift to stroke a finger along her cheek. She offered him a weak smile. "They were idiots. You know that, right?"

"I do know that. I feel more terrible that you were on your way to pick up your girl. I forgot all about the ball. I never would have called—"

"I'm glad you called. I'm always here for you, Kristine. Always."

"You're my guy, Ry. The big brother I never had."

"You know it."

"You'd better get going."

He grabbed her by the wrist to stop her quick escape. "Not until I know you're not going to head up there and wolf down that hidden supply of vanilla mochi I know you keep in the freezer."

She laughed at that one. "You know me too well. And I am so lucky to have a friend like you, Ryland James. I hope this new girl realizes that, too."

"We're not serious. Just having some fun."

"You'd better adjust your fun meter. I saw the way she looked at you. That woman is head over heels for the wolf in the billionaire's clothing."

"I don't think she's attracted to my money. She's a trust-fund baby. Has her own fortune."

"Good to know. And that does explain her excellent taste in footwear. Those togs she had on the other day were not cheap. Let me go. I don't want you to stand her up."

"I'll get there in time. I've got a good fifteen minutes yet. Nothing will keep me from showing up to dance with the Princess Pussycat."

"You know that sounds like a drag-queen name."

"It does?"

Kristine shook her head. "Just teasing." She leaned in and kissed his cheek. "Love you, *cher*."

"Love you back. No mochi!"

"Just one?"

He tilted a concerned look at her.

"Oh, you're right. A girl can't eat just one. I'll watch reruns of *Braquo* instead. You know I love to moon over Jean-Hugues Anglade."

"That I do. See you at the office, Kristine."

Ry waited until she was inside the building foyer before pulling away. The ball was on the right bank just off the Champs-élysées. He could get there in twenty minutes if the traffic cooperated.

He turned the corner. Behind him, a work truck screeched its brakes as it turned and pulled up close enough to touch bumpers. Ahead, flashing red lights alerted him there had been an accident. Three cars before him were all stopped. He scanned for a way out, but he was in the middle of a block.

"Shit."

Laying on the horn wasn't going to help the situation, but he did it anyway. The woman in the car ahead of him flipped him off. And behind him the trucker's horn blasted the neighborhood.

Pulling out and making a sharp turn—he only had to back up and forward once with the sleek sports car—Ry drove in the opposite lane about four car lengths before the police vehicle pulled out from the right and flashed its lights at him.

Shaking his head, Ry shifted into Park and decided he'd deserved that one. The police officer approached and took down his name and information from his license, then scanned inside the car.

"Monsieur, I'll ask you to please step out of the vehicle."

About to protest, and unsure why such a request had been issued, Ry figured it best to comply. If only to move things along. He got out, hands held up before him. The officer then scanned inside his car again.

"Is there a problem, Officer?"

"Yes, Monsieur James, there is. Can you tell me the reason for the weapon you have hanging on the back interior wall of your vehicle?"

Ah, hell. He'd forgotten the three-foot-long battle sword he used to slay collectors from Faery come to steal human babies. He'd put hooks on the back wall to keep it close and for easy access. Once again, he wished he had the powers of persuasion that vampires possessed. They could whisper or touch humans and make them forget their names, let alone seeing a deadly weapon in the back seat of an Alfa Romeo.

And in his next thought, he wondered what Batman would do in a situation like this one.

Chapter 11

"Do not hyperventilate," Indi whispered as she stood at the top of the stairs looking down over the bustling ballroom. Hundreds of couples dressed in black and white and dazzling with diamonds, silver, gold and colored gemstones socialized and took selfies and danced to the orchestra's invitation. It was eight thirty. Ry had not shown.

"He promised he'd be here. He will be here."

Or maybe not, the scared, traumatized part of her whispered back.

Maybe it was time she took a break from men altogether. Focused on her business. Ball gowns and tiaras? Only on purchase orders and invoices from now on.

She was wearing the black blingy cat ears tonight. They matched her gown. Janet had requested a selfie STAT in her text a few minutes ago, but Indi had been too disheartened to reply. She wouldn't get to swish around on the dance floor in this gorgeous gown because…

Clutching her skirts, she closed her eyes as a familiar waltz began. She loved to waltz. Her daddy had taught her when she was able to stand on his toes and he'd swirl her about the dance floor like a Beauty to his kind and loving Beast.

"The beast isn't going to arrive tonight," she whispered.

Catching a sigh at the back of her throat, Indi forced a smile to a passing couple, who nodded acknowledgment to her.

Below the three massive crystal chandeliers suspended from the steel beams that arched and created the glass ceiling, the party attendees spun and swirled and laughed and chattered. Unaware that Indi's heart was breaking anew.

She considered looking for the champagne, but nixed that idea. Tonight would not be another replay of the previous Humiliating Experience. If Ry didn't show, she'd lift her head and walk out with shoulders thrust back. Her entire business was based on a woman's confidence and knowing herself. She was a goddess. And goddesses could handle shit, like men who had no idea how important it was to stand by their word.

"Exactly," she muttered.

Whatever trouble Kristine had been in? She hoped it was worth it.

In her next thought, Indi chastised herself for thinking such a thing. Ry would never have jilted her without good reason. As little as she yet knew him, the things she had learned about him proved he was an honorable man. Tonight had simply been Kristine's turn to receive his honor.

Glancing up through the glass ceiling high above,

she wished it was darker. Easier to make a quick exit that way, and not be seen by too many.

Maybe it was time to design a sort of breakup survival kit for her website? No. That would defeat the purpose of her brand—imparting strength and confidence to her customers.

Lifting her shoulders and drawing in a breath through her nose, Indi nodded. She was fine. She would not let this tiny moment in her life affect her any more than it should. She'd turn and walk out, go home and strip off her fabulous dress, then shed a few tears. But ultimately, she'd get over it. As quickly as she'd gotten over Todd.

Men could be so thoughtless and self-involved. Why had she allowed herself to pick up with another man so soon after the last? It was her fault she was standing alone right now.

But she didn't want to berate herself. It wasn't her fault. She could date whom she wished, and whenever she wished. And she could have fun with a man for a fling, or longer. She'd find "the one" someday. Probably a werewolf wasn't her best match anyway.

It sounded good when she thought it in her head, but Indi's heart was squeezing. She really liked Ry. And...

Just and.

Indi spun to leave and she walked right into Ry's arms. He hugged her, enveloping her in a sudden and delicious warmth. He smelled like wild and nature and a hint of peppermint. The hard pillar of his body overwhelmed and then offered solace.

Nuzzling his nose aside her ear, he said, "I'm sorry. I had an unavoidable delay."

She hugged him tightly, squeezing her eyelids and knowing a tear ran down her cheek. Tonight she'd used the waterproof mascara. Live and learn.

"Can you forgive me?" he asked, and pulled away to search her face.

She quickly swiped at the tear. "Of course. Nothing's wrong. It's all good."

"No, it's not. I know exactly what you were thinking, standing here all alone. It happened again. Another man treated you like crap."

She shrugged and wasn't able to look him in the eye. He'd guessed it right on the mark.

"It kills me that you had to go there." He stroked his fingers down the curl hugging the side of her head, then tapped her cat ears. "All I can do is try to make the rest of the night as good as it can be."

"It's already improved one hundred percent." And her heart jumped with glee. She'd judged him harshly. He was a man of his word. "You really work the tuxedo. Damn, you are so fine."

"Yeah?" He swept his loose hair over a shoulder. "Well, look at you, Princess Pussycat. You just happen to have that gown hanging in your closet?"

She smoothed her palms over the black taffeta skirt. "Believe it or not, yes. I've not worn it until now. And see." She lifted the skirt a little to reveal the white underskirt she added.

"That's like the stuff you wore the night I saw you in FaeryTown."

"Tulle. It's princess fabric all the way."

"I do know the fashion was most important to you tonight. But…" He eyed her sweetly, a grin curling his mouth.

"But what?" Indi touched the cat ears. "Is my tiara on crooked?"

"Nope. You're missing something." He reached into his inner suit pocket and pulled out a folded piece of blue tissue paper. "It's nothing fancy. But when I passed it in a store window yesterday, it screamed Indigo DuCharme."

"You got me a gift? I love presents." Her heartbeat jittered for a new and wondrous reason. She took the paper and carefully unfolded it. Inside coiled a delicate silver chain, and the pendant was the tiniest silver paw print. "Oh, my God, this is perfect."

"A little kitty paw," Ry said.

"Oh? Sure. But I was thinking it was a wolf paw. I want it to be a wolf paw, okay?"

"I think a wolf's paw would be bigger—" She met his gaze and his mouth softened. "A wolf's paw it is. Let me help you with it. I practiced because those things are so delicate, but the screw clasp is easier for me."

He took the necklace and when his hand brushed her neck, Indi shivered. A good, so-happy-he-made-it shiver. She should never have doubted him. But she hadn't known him long, and... Enough of that. The man was here. And he'd been thinking of her so much that he'd brought her a gift. The night could not get any better.

But she was open to letting it become the best. It was time to get her dance on.

Ry traced the silver chain around to the front and base of her neck, where the paw rested. "My princess," he said.

He bowed to kiss her, and even though partiers wandered near them, Indi suddenly felt as if they were the only two in the room. The vast airy ballroom suddenly quieted so she could hear her heartbeats mingle with Ry's. And the warm, masculine scent of him permeated her pores, inviting her to tug him closer and deepen the kiss.

Every part of her sparkled with a giddy thrill. She stood up on her Jimmy Choo tiptoes, clasping his lapels. He smelled like earth and fresh grass, with a hint of wild that wrapped about her senses.

"You like to dance?" he asked.

"I do. The waltz is my favorite."

"Mine, too. Shall we?"

He offered her his hooked arm and Indi threaded her arm through it. She had attended many an event and ball, and often on the arm of her date or a handsome friend, but this was the first time one had ever been so gentlemanly. Or had given her a gift.

They descended the half-curved stairs to the main floor. The nervous anticipation over wondering if she had been dumped fled. She walked to the dance floor alongside the sexiest guy in the room. Ry bowed grandly to her, and offered his hand, then whisked her into the music. They danced three waltzes in a row.

Ry was a remarkable dancer, and she was more than impressed that his talents matched hers. And she claimed a good mastery of the dance. His hand held out hers as he led her around the floor, while his other hand hugged her bare back. The back of her dress was cut low to her waist. It offered a connection of skin against skin that curled a giddy warmth over her entire body and tightened her nipples. The two of them so close amongst so many. It felt surreal. Truly, like a Disney scene of the prince and princess dancing. But neither was royalty, and that suited Indi fine. Ry was hers and she was most definitely his.

Six dances later, the orchestra segued into a quickstep. Ry suggested they find refreshment because he never could grasp the syncopations required for the dance. That worked for Indi. Her skirts impeded any frantic steps and she needed a break from the crowded dance floor.

They avoided the wine and champagne and instead

tried the craft beer offered by a local brewery. But only a few sips. Because the next dance was a tango, and while Indi was only a little familiar with the steps, it didn't matter. Standing in Ry's arms, following his moves, she felt like the luckiest woman alive. And she noticed the stares from the other women. Or rather, eyeballs focused like lasers on Ry. The man did work the tuxedo. But it might also have been that he was sex on a stick, penguin suit or not.

And she had seen him sans clothes. Pity, all the other women would never have that opportunity. Not while Indi had him in her arms.

At the end of the tango, they lingered in each other's embrace at the edge of the dance floor under subdued lighting.

Ry kissed her and stroked a strand of loose hair over her ear. "You sparkle."

"It's glitter dust. A standard. One must never pass up the chance to sparkle, be it man-made or—" she let her gaze fall to his crotch "—faery-made."

"Oh, I've got some sparkle for you, Princess." He tugged her away from the lights and into a private area against the wall.

"Do you have to leave soon?" she asked.

He checked his watch. "It's only ten thirty. Still got a while before duty calls. Fortunately, the police officer let me keep my sword."

"The police officer?"

"I did say I had good reason for being late." He kissed her again. "But enough about me. I want this whole night to be Indi, Indi and even more Indi. You smell so good. What is that scent? It's almost like candy."

"It's my skin cream, scented with almonds and pistachios."

"Delicious. Food does tend to appeal to we men." He nuzzled his nose into her hair. "I'd like to eat you right here and now."

Now that was a suggestion that she could get behind. Or under. Or however he would like her positioned.

"Remember what I said about getting naked after the ball?" she said.

"Haven't forgotten. As pretty as this dress is, I want to slide it off you and drop it to the floor. Then…" He kissed her earlobe. "I'm going to taste every inch of your delicious skin. Slowly. Deeply."

Indi moaned wantonly. "You are making it difficult to want to head back to the dance floor."

"We can leave early? Stop by your house before I need to take up the sword?"

As much as that suggestion appealed… "No, I love to dance, and you're the first man since my father who actually knows how to dance with me."

She winced at the sudden pain in her back. She'd forgotten about that annoying pain because it hadn't reared up since early this morning when she took a quick dip in the pool.

"Still not feeling one hundred percent?" he asked.

She gave him the standard nod/shrug because she didn't want to complain tonight. "Let's extend this break," she said. "Give me ten minutes and then I'll be ready for another waltz, or maybe even a fox-trot."

"I love the fox-trot. It's fast. Think you can keep up?"

"Just watch me."

"Ryland!"

Ry turned to seek out the man who called to him and nodded. To her, he said, "One of my clients. I fund his charity for rehousing The Wicked, who come here from Faery. He's one himself."

"I'm going to need all the details on that interesting paranormal stuff later. Why don't you say hello to him?" she said. "I'm going to slip out back and wander through the herb gardens. Breathe in some fresh air. Meet me out there?"

"The guy can talk up a storm."

"That's okay. I'm not going anywhere. Come find me when you can."

"Thank you. I'll make it quick." He kissed her cheek and then turned to shake hands with the man.

The Wicked? She couldn't wait to learn about that, or them, or whatever it meant.

Indi followed the hallway out to the gardens. Not many were out in the subtly lit formal gardens. The back courtyard was narrow but long, and a thick line of hedges butted up against the very end and blocked the view of the Seine. The sounds of music from inside segued into the background as Indi inhaled the lush scents and wandered from flower to flower. As she strolled the crushed shell walk, she let her fingers glide across the glossy green leaves of a thigh-high boxwood shrubbery. Everything smelled green and open. And here, the mint and thyme bloomed. The heady scents lured her as if Chanel perfume.

Leaning over, she inhaled the lush sweetness. What had begun as a harrowing will-he-show-or-won't-he-show? was turning out to be the best night of her life. The man could dance! And he had been so apologetic. Easy to forgive him when he was so handsome. And sexy. And smelled like a dream she wanted to linger with between the sheets. Bring on the sparkle! And, well—what *was* wrong with him?

"Not a thing," she whispered, and a smile curled her lips.

The police officer had let him keep his sword? She would need to learn more about that later, as well. But whatever had delayed Ry from getting here on time didn't matter now. He had kept his promise. And she was looking forward to later, when the man intended to taste every inch of her skin. She wished he didn't have to leave her to go slay a couple bad faeries. She wanted him with her all night. But if her superhero had a calling, far be it from her to keep him from that. She would have him later. In his bed. All night long.

"Oh!" The pain at her back stabbed mercilessly.

Indi looked about to see if anyone had remarked her sudden cry. Stumbling forward, she approached the back of the garden, where the lighting was subdued and segued into shadows.

Another sharp pain caused her to misstep on her five-inch heels. Arm thrust out to seek an anchor, Indi sought a bench to sit down. The pain grew fierce. Unrelenting.

"What the hell is wrong with me?"

Ry told Nestor Arch about the international wolf project. Nestor possessed an interest in all paranormal charities—as did Ry. He texted a note to Kristine to arrange to have him speak with Pilot Severo. With more financial backers the project would have an excellent chance at getting off the ground. Checking his watch, he realized he'd been chatting for fifteen minutes. Informing Nestor he had a date he didn't want to leave alone for too long, Ry turned to search for Indi.

His phone rang, and just when he thought to ignore it, some intuition made him tug it out and check the screen. "Princess, what's up?"

"Ry…" She gasped and moaned. "Oh, Ry, hurry. Something's happened."

"Indi, where are you?" He scanned the ballroom

floor. All the women were dressed in black and white. It was difficult to home in on her.

"I'm out in the garden. Oh! I don't know what it is. It's... Oh, please come out here. I'm at the back near the hedges, where it's dark. Hurry!"

Dashing toward the hallway that led outdoors, Ry suddenly checked his pace. He didn't want to draw attention. He filed down the hallway and into the garden. His shoes crushed the shell walk and he scanned the low-lit area. Half a dozen couples chatted and sipped champagne.

He lifted his head and sniffed the air. Beyond an intoxicating layer of flowers, he could scent almonds and pistachios. Indi must have stood right here. Following the lingering scent trail, he walked to the back of the garden. A stone bench was placed before a high shrub, and beside that a lonely marble angel bowed her head.

"Indi?" he whispered.

"Back here!"

Back here was... Was she on the other side of the shrubbery?

He noticed a narrow part in the shrubs and slipped through. The street paralleling the Seine flashed with passing headlights, but didn't illuminate this part of the garden. Indi's dark dress camouflaged her body, but the glint from the rhinestones in the cat ears helped him to find her. She was bent over, hand pressed to a tree trunk.

He rushed over and touched her shoulder, leaned down to study her face.

"Something's wrong," she said. "It hurt so bad."

"Your back?" He was about to smooth a palm down her back; the dress was cut low and had allowed him to caress her bare skin as they'd danced, but she stood abruptly. "What is it? Indi?"

"I don't know. I think…something came out of my back."

"What?"

"Will you take a look? It hurt like someone slashed a knife down my spine and then I could feel something… move. Oh, Ry. This is freaking me out."

"Turn around." He glanced over his shoulder, confirming they were alone and no curious bystanders were in the vicinity. Any passing cars would not make them out against the dark shrubs.

Indi turned and the glint from a passing headlight beamed through the tree canopy and caught on the things on her back. Things that had not been there earlier. What the hell? Really? Ry gaped as he looked over her skin and took it all in.

"Ry, what is it? Maybe I scratched myself when I was pushing through the shrubbery. The pain came on so suddenly I wanted to hide in case— I don't know. It's not painful anymore. Ry?"

He pressed a palm to her back but didn't touch the appendages that were so small yet that was probably because they were new and… He didn't have words. How could something like this have occurred?

"Ry, you're freaking me out. What's wrong? What do I have on my back?"

"Wings," he muttered simply. "You've sprouted wings, Indi."

Chapter 12

She couldn't have heard him correctly.

"What are you talking about?" Indi shoved at Ry when he attempted to pull her into his arms. She stumbled backward, but he caught her by the wrist so she wouldn't topple into the shrubs.

Laughter echoed out from the garden on the other side of the hedgerow, but she was feeling no mirth now. "Is that some kind of joke?"

"Princess, you've sprouted wings. I'm telling you the truth." And when she began to protest, he shoved a hand in his suit pocket and pulled out his phone. "I'll show you."

Ry swung around behind her and snapped a shot of her back. "There's poor lighting out here, but with the flash…you can plainly see."

He handed her the phone and she almost dropped it when she realized what she was looking at. It was a dark shot, but the flash lit up the center of her back.

And there, looking like crisply unfolded insect append-ages, were two small iridescent wings. Each about the size of her hand.

She shoved the phone at him. Grasping frantically for her back, she couldn't reach up high enough to feel them. "What is going on?"

"I don't know. This is…"

"It was that stupid healer you took me to. She did something to me!"

He scratched his jaw. "Maybe…"

"Ry! Really? Your frustrated ex-lover put some kind of weird curse on me?"

"She's not my— I'm sorry, Indi. I don't know what Hestia did to you, but I doubt she could do something like this. I am at a loss. I've never seen anything like this before."

"But you know faeries and all that stuff. Does it look like faery wings to you?"

"They come in all sizes, colors and shapes. But I don't know what else it could be. Can I… I want to touch them. Make sure they're—"

"Real? Oh, Ry, this is crazy!"

"Please, Indi, I'll be careful. Can I do that?"

Releasing a heavy sigh, her shoulders dropping, Indi nodded. Would she ever again attend a ball and *not* have it end disastrously? Who grew wings? This was beyond crazy. Yet she'd been feeling pains in her back since the night she was scratched by the collector creature.

"What if I turn into one of those black sparkly things?" She pressed a palm over her thundering heart-beats. "Oh, my god, this is so not a good night. And I was thinking it was the best night ever."

"The best night? It is, Indi. I mean…" Ry winced. "I got to spend all this time dancing with you and holding you in my arms. It's been so awesome."

"It has been. Truly, the best night. But, Ry…" She sniffed back a burgeoning tear. "Oh, touch them, then. Tell me they're not real."

He kissed her on the crown of the head, then walked around behind her again. "I'm just going to touch them gently…"

Indi shivered as she suddenly felt a warmth at the junction where the wings clung to her back. It was an intensely visceral touch that seemed to vibrate throughout her system.

"Does that hurt?" Ry asked.

She shook her head. "No. I feel your touch. Intensely. Like you might have touched my hand. That means… Oh, my God, they're real?"

"They seem to be growing out from your back. I haven't studied faery wings up close before…"

He swung around in front of her and pulled her against his chest. The warmth of him was ridiculous. His overwhelming strength and masculinity gave her some solace. She felt safe in his arms. But safe from what?

"Am I turning into a faery?" she whispered.

"I'm sorry, Indi, I don't have answers. But we'll get some. It's…" He checked his watch. "Eleven thirty."

"You've got to get to FaeryTown. And I want to go home and cry."

"I won't have time to bring you home. And I don't want to put you in a cab. I'm bringing you along with me. After the collectors have been dealt with we'll find the healer and ask her about this. Is that all right with you?"

She nodded against his chest. "I do want you to stay with me. I don't want to be alone."

When he stepped away and shrugged off his suit coat, she couldn't prevent a few teardrops. Ry wrapped his coat about her shoulders, to hide the wings, most likely. She tugged it close over her chest and couldn't manage to lift her head to look at him.

"You go ahead and cry," he said. "It's weird. And strange. But I'm here for you. Do you understand that?"

She nodded again and sniffed back the tears. The last thing she wanted was for anyone inside to see her with mascara running down her cheeks. Been there, done that. Had wings been the result of that crazy night after the last charity ball?

"We can get to the valet stand from the garden," Ry said. "We don't have to go back inside. Come on, Princess Pussycat."

Ry parked the Alfa in his usual spot half a block away from where FaeryTown began, and reached behind the seats for the battle sword. The cop had believed his story about donating it to a charity action. Good going with the fast thinking.

But he didn't grasp it, because instead his hand went to Indi's bowed head. A soft tendril of her hair spilled over his wrist. She sat sideways on the passenger seat, facing him, her knees pulled up and an arm wrapped across her legs. Volumes of black taffeta spilled to the floor in a lush puddle. She still wore his suit coat. She'd tugged off the cat ears and there was a tear streak through her blush on the one cheek.

"You going to be okay?"

She shrugged.

"Stupid question. I'll make this fast, then come back for you and we'll go look for the healer. Okay?"

She nodded.

"Stay in the car. I don't want you to get—"

"I got it," she snapped. "If you think I'm eager to go anywhere near that wacky faery stuff, you're mistaken. I'll be here. Trying to figure this out. Go kill some nasty monsters, then hurry back to me. Please?"

"This will be the fastest the Sidhe Slayer has ever laid his victims to ash. Promise." He kissed the crown of her head, then grabbed the sword and marched down the street.

He hated leaving Indi alone and vulnerable. Not because he expected anyone to wander by and give her trouble. She had been shaking, for heaven's sake. The woman had no idea what was going on with her. Nor did he. Wings? How crazy was that? But he'd touched them. Had seen the skin on her back seamlessly fused into the cartilage and sheer fabric of the tiny wings. They were real.

"If that bitch did something to her," he muttered as he turned into FaeryTown, "she will feel the cut of my blade."

Yet even as he thought it, he didn't believe Hestia would be so vindictive. Not unless it directly affected him. To harm some random human he hadn't even known that night? No, it was impossible to fathom.

He didn't have time to check his watch. The fabric between realms glimmered and spit forth two collectors at once. Ry charged them both. With a swing and a thrust to the left, he took out the first one before it got a chance to see what was coming for it. Turning, he growled...and felt the angry shift to werewolf overtake him. He thrust up his blade into the other collector.

Easy. Quick. He looked at the paw holding the sword hilt—he never had to marvel how easy it was to shift without volition. Outrage and anger always did it for him.

With a shake of his arm, he shifted back to were form and lowered the sword. He couldn't sheathe it because he didn't wear one over his dress shirt and trousers.

"You're getting very efficient at that," Never said as he walked up behind Ry. "Didn't even tear your coat."

Ry swung, lifting his sword to slash.

"Whoa! It's me. Your bro."

He lowered the sword and pushed the hair from his face. "Sorry. Didn't your daddy ever teach you not to walk up behind a guy holding a dangerous weapon?"

"You know my daddy. And there's your answer."

Exactly. Ry could only be thankful he had been raised by his own kind—well, the pack, whom he'd once thought were his own kind.

"You're looking a bit too spiffy for a round of slaying," Never commented. "What's up with the penguin suit?"

"I had a commitment. I'm forced to walk two paths lately with these vicious collectors."

"You're obviously managing." Never nodded down the street toward the section that was always busy with nightclubs and ichor dens. "You remember your meeting with Riske this evening?"

Ah, hell, he had forgotten. If he was going to get anywhere in solving this problem, and stop slaying collectors, he did need to speak to the man. Faery. But more important, he needed to get back to Indi. He'd only been away from the car ten minutes. He didn't want her sitting alone, wondering what had become of him. The poor woman had been through enough rejection, and near rejections, that he didn't need to add to that humiliation. She was so vulnerable right now.

"I'll take you to him." Never started walking down the street.

"I can't meet the man tonight. Indi is waiting. She can't be alone."

The dark faery swung around, shaking his head and splaying out his hands. "You are going to stand up le Grande Sidhe? I know you're not stupid, Ryland."

Ry winced. "I don't want to. And the last thing I want is to piss off the leader of a faery Mafia. But something's happened. I need to find Hestia. Indi is…"

"Talk to Riske first. Then you can talk to the healer. Yes?"

Ry glanced down the street. The Alfa was parked just around the corner. When he inhaled, he could smell Indi's sweet scent. Wings?

"Will you do me a favor?" he asked Never.

"Depends." The faery gestured for him to follow as he started to walk again. And when Ry didn't, he stomped a foot. "You shouldn't keep Riske waiting."

Ry said, "I need you to go sit with Indi until I return."

"Babysit your girlfriend? What's going on with her? Why are you so nervous? Because I can feel it coming off you in waves, man. You are not in a good place. This isn't like you."

"I just exterminated two collectors. It's the adrenaline."

"No, it's something more." Never stopped before a building elaborately decorated in violet arabesques resembling something from Chinatown. "What's going on with your woman?"

"She's not my—" Actually, she was his woman. And he would do anything to protect her. "Will you go sit with her, Never? She's had a shock tonight. Don't let her go wandering. Got that?"

Never nodded. "Whatever it takes to get your ass to this meeting." He opened the door and gestured for Ry to walk through. "You should probably leave the sword out here. That's not going to go over well."

With a huff of resignation, Ry set the sword against the outer wall and cast a glance around. Faeries strolled by, but when he met their gazes they quickly looked away. The sword was enchanted with magic from the mortal realm, designed to slay the sidhe. None of them would risk touching it.

He crossed the threshold and Never pointed down a long dark hallway. "End of the hall. Knock twice. Don't speak until you're spoken to."

"Thanks, Never. Now go to the car and sit with Indi."

The dark faery saluted him and strode off.

And Ry hoped this detour would be worth the emotional trauma his absence might create in one very scared and vulnerable human woman.

When the car door opened, Indi lifted her head. Her heartbeats speeded with anticipation. In slid Ry, er... not Ry, but some lanky, dark-haired man with enough spikes on his clothing to cause serious damage, and more mascara under his eyes than she had ever worn.

"Hey, Indigo, right? I'm Never," he said quickly.

"Ry's half brother? Where is he? Did something happen?"

"Everything is cool. Ry wanted me to come sit with you so you're not alone. He'll be back soon enough. Man, this is a nice car. Real leather." He whistled in appreciation.

"Where is he? Did something go wrong with the collectors?"

"Nope. He slayed both in less than ten seconds. That man is incredible with the sword. But he forgot he had a meeting with a very high-ranked sidhe leader that he wouldn't want to disappoint. He might have info for him on the whole stolen-baby thing."

"Oh." She let her leg slide down from the seat, and

her foot landed on the car floor, where her dress had puddled. She was tired and wanted to go home and sleep, and hope to wake from this weird nightmare. She wriggled her shoulders but couldn't feel the wings at her back. Had they disappeared?

"So, what's up with you? Ry said you are not doing well."

"He didn't tell you?"

Never adjusted the seat so he could lean back and stretch out his long legs. "He told me you were in the way the other night when he was slaying and got hurt."

"Did he tell you he took me to a healer who fucked me up?"

Now the man turned, curiosity glittering in his violet eyes. "How so?"

Indi narrowed her gaze on his eyes. They weren't exactly violet, maybe a bit of red mixed into the pupils. Such a strange color, but oddly pretty. Also disconcerting.

"Hey." The man snapped his fingers in front of her face.

Indi shook out of the impolite stare. "Right. It happened at the ball tonight. I've…" She twisted her shoulder forward and slipped down Ry's suit coat jacket.

Never leaned forward and inspected her back. "Really? You're faery?"

"No. I'm human. These things just popped out about an hour ago. I'm sure the healer did something to me. Ry told me the two of them had something going on that didn't end well. You men and your lacking insight on we women. He probably broke her heart. And now she's getting back at him through me. I should go look for her right now." Indi gripped the door handle. "If Ry is busy—"

"He said not to let you go wandering. I don't know

how or why you have the sight, but apparently you do. And a human walking around FaeryTown alone? Not cool. Turn around again and let me take a look at those things. They're like baby wings."

Indi twisted and she flinched when the man touched one.

"Sorry. Shouldn't have done that," he offered. "It's a freaky thing when someone touches your wings, isn't it?"

"What's freaky is actually having wings. Do you have wings?"

"I do. Even though I'm half vampire."

"You are? Ry didn't mention that. But I guess that makes sense, if you two are half brothers of a father who seems to be some kind of faery gigolo."

"Malrick is a slut, no other way to put it. He likes to make half-breeds. Don't ask me why. Not like any of us want to spend time with the old man in Faery."

"You don't visit him? Go to Faery?"

"Hate that place. Hate the man. Try to avoid it as much as possible. Just like Ry."

"Ry never mentioned why he has such hatred for him. Just that he and his father do not get along."

"Malrick is... The dude has been around forever. He is king of the Unseelies."

"I didn't know that."

"Yeah? And Ry is the Unseelie Prince, or so Malrick would make him that if he would go to live in Faery."

"A prince." Indi clutched the back of the seat and laid her head aside it. "First I learn he's a freakin' billionaire. And then that he's a werewolf."

"With a bit of faery mixed in," Never added.

"And now a prince. And he also has a penchant for playing Batman by slaying wicked creatures from another realm."

"And now his girlfriend is turning into a faery. Mighty strange, all around."

"Do you really think I could turn into a faery? Is that possible? Where does that healer live?" Indi opened the door and shoved out a foot.

She had to get some answers before she fell asleep and Ry returned to take her home. No more waking in the morning beneath a coffee table without memory of the previous night. She would not leave FaeryTown tonight until she knew what was wrong with her.

As she stepped out of the car, Never shuffled around the front of the hood. He was as tall as Ry but leaner. And the Goth look did not intimidate her. It was just a fashion choice. And she knew her fashion.

"Move," she said. "Or help me."

The man put his palms on her shoulders and bent to study her eyes. Yes, his eyes were eerily beautiful, and yet she didn't feel a sense of safety by looking into them. But not fear, either. More a tense sort of expectation.

Finally, he nodded. "Ry will kill me, but I want to find out what's up with you, too. Let's go find Hestia and get some answers."

Chapter 13

Le Grande Sidhe was the official title for the Seelie faery called Riske. It was a pompous title, and Ry didn't recognize Faery politics or their ways. Hell, this was the mortal realm. But he could respect those from whom he needed answers. And since he was the leader of a powerful Mafia-like organization, Ry did strive to keep the waters as smooth as possible between them.

When he entered a hazy room filled with what he recognized as opioid smoke, he bowed to the man sitting on a pile of tufted pillows on the other side of the small room. It resembled an opium den, decorated in bohemian colors and fabrics. Weird music played, which could only be Faery in origin.

The man's legs were crossed before him and his palms cupped each knee. He wore a black pinstriped business suit. Yet on his head was splayed a massive headdress consisting of tiny bleached skulls, feathers—not mortal realm in origin—and quills.

Riske watched as Ry stood there, acclimating himself to the summery smell of the smoke. It filled his lungs with a swelling that felt like drowning. A wide line of white dashed the man's face from ear to ear. Probably wasn't paint, Ry figured, for many faeries had markings or sigils on their skin, in all colors. Never had a few on his ribs and legs he'd once shown him. They were infused with faery magic.

The sigil on Ry's hip didn't seem to do much more than annoy him that it was there, always reminding him that he was not what his werewolf father wanted him to be. And, of course, made him dust during sex.

"Grande Sidhe," he said to prompt conversation. A slight bow of his head felt necessary.

He was in a hurry. Didn't want to leave Indi sitting in the car with Never too long, and in her state. But he'd focus and get the answers he needed while he had this opportunity.

"Never says you've been asking about stolen human babies," Riske stated simply. No airs in his voice, nor accusation. He gestured with a hand, the iridescent markings on his skin glinting, to a stack of pillows to his left.

Ry sat, awkwardly. The pillows were wobbly, and he was too big and bulky to rest comfortably. He settled by leaning onto his knees and sitting back partially on the pillows.

"Malrick's chosen son, eh?" Riske said.

Ry gave a noncommittal wobble of his head. The label sounded more like an accusation than an accolade to him.

"Your werewolf is stronger than your wasted faery will ever be. Why don't you allow the sidhe in you to rise and embrace both of your natures?"

"Listen, I didn't come here to discuss me. There's a

situation in FaeryTown, and I'm not sure you're aware of it."

"While my business operates out of this thin place, I have been spending much time in Faery of late. Never says you've been slaying sidhe? There are consequences."

"Only out of necessity. And if anyone wants to punish me for taking out the collectors, then I challenge them to stand before me and take me out."

"Not many would accept that challenge, I'm sure. Collectors?"

"You're obviously not aware someone has been sending collectors into this realm to steal human infants."

Riske tilted his head. Black-tipped white quills framed his vibrant violet eyes. "It is our right. Is it not?"

If one followed Faery convention. And Ry knew the line between both worlds was smeared, at best, in places like this where they both existed.

"It is a Faery right that harms the humans," he offered carefully. "But it's only ever been a right when a changeling has been left in the stolen infant's place."

That got Riske's attention. He leaned forward, pressing his fingertips together before his lips.

"They are not leaving behind changelings," Ry said. "Every night, at midnight, the fabric between our worlds is breached by one or two collectors intent on assuming a human's soul for the time required to steal an infant and take it back to Faery."

"But that's not how it is done. We take something away. We leave something in its place. It is how the two realms have coexisted over the millennia. And it is how humans can live unaware of our kind. Should an infant go missing, without a changeling left in its place there would be questions. Panic. We don't create ripples."

"Yeah? Well, someone doesn't care how big a ripple they stir. You had no idea this was happening? You don't know who's behind it?"

"I do not. But I will learn. As you should continue to take out the collectors nightly, if what you tell me is true. But why have they stopped bringing changelings to this realm?"

"I don't know. The sacrifice is too great?"

"That doesn't make sense. It throws everything off balance. Besides, changelings are bred for such an exchange."

Ry winced at that statement. Changelings were born to be used as a replacement for a stolen infant? It sounded not cool for the changeling. But he also knew a changeling rarely had memory of its life in Faery, and easily assimilated into the human realm.

Riske suddenly pointed to Ry. "You must ask your father about this. Malrick knows all that occurs."

"In the Unseelie realm. I have no idea where the command to send in the collectors is originating from."

"But you can learn by asking Malrick. I insist you do."

"With all due respect, Grande Sidhe, you don't get to tell me what to do. I'm a free agent. Just trying to look out for the interests of innocent human children."

"Then even more so you should be eager to learn the truth. How long can you continue to slay the collectors without results? Without end to the infiltrations? Someone is sending them here. Collectors are mindless things that need direction."

"I know that." Ry caught his forehead against his palm. He'd hoped for, at the least, a lead from Riske. "So no clue whatsoever?"

"I'm sorry. But whoever is behind this is taking business away from my pockets."

"How so?"

"There is a tariff for bringing a changeling into this realm. It's been...perhaps human decades since it last occurred. I had thought the practice abandoned. Which may explain why this sudden resurgence has gone unnoticed by myself and my staff. Perhaps I'll send Never into Faery to ask around."

"I don't think Never will agree to that. He's not too keen on Faery."

"If the half-breed doesn't do as I ask, there will be consequences."

Ry reached for the sword that should have been at his back, and instead clasped a hand onto his shoulder and rubbed. Damn it.

"You mustn't worry about one insignificant half-breed faery, Sidhe Slayer."

"Never is my brother."

"Half brother."

"No difference to me. Family is those you trust and care about."

"Is not Malrick one of those you trust or care about?"

Ry stood. "I think this conversation is over. I appreciate your time, Grande Sidhe. But please, send one of your more devoted employees to ask around in Faery. I can utilize Never's help here in FaeryTown."

"I wouldn't bring him along when you speak to Malrick," Riske said.

"What makes you think I'd ever purposely speak to the Unseelie king?"

Riske stood now and he was taller than Ry, which surprised him. The smoke in the room seemed to coil toward him and slink along his outline. Ry felt the power hum from him like a cruel summer wind.

"All the answers you seek can be gotten from the Unseelie king."

"You don't know that."

Riske shrugged. "A lifetime of slaying collectors, or a fast resolution to what you deem a problem to the humans and their infants? It's all in your hands, Ryland Alastair James."

Ry winced. He hated when faeries used his full name. There was magic in repeating a person's birth name. And he took Riske's use of it as a threat. But the man didn't know his complete name, so he was safe.

Without another word, he exited the room and stomped down the dark hallway. Once outside, he grabbed his sword and stalked back toward the car.

He didn't get far before a crowd of faeries milling about what sounded like a shouting match between two women made him pause. Ry shook his head and cursed under his breath. He recognized both women's voices.

Pushing through the crowd, Ry stopped beside Never, who stood with arms crossed over his chest, and was watching as Indi dodged to avoid Hestia's swinging fist.

"What the hell?" Ry asked. "I thought I told you to keep her in the car."

"She wasn't in a mind to listen. But I came along with her. I'm keeping an eye on her, eh?"

"I don't consider allowing her to get into a cat fight with Hestia keeping an eye on her."

"Hey, a man learns quickly enough not to get between two women when their claws are out."

"And why are they out?"

"Hestia insists she's not to blame for Indi's wings."

Indi yelled and slashed her fingernails across Hestia's shoulder. The faery hissed at her and lunged. Indi, clad in the black-and-white ball gown with elegant makeup and a certain carriage, going against the stealth and feline healer, whose wild beribboned hair glittered with the promise of her faery magic soon to be unleashed.

It was when Hestia lifted a hand and prepared to blow dust at Indi that Ry decided enough was enough.

He grabbed Indi around the waist and swung her away from the flurry of dust that would likely have landed in her face and eyes. Her tiny wings fluttered across his face as he struggled to contain her.

Hestia lunged for Indi, and Ry yelled, "Grab her, Never!"

"She's lying," Indi shouted. "And she insists you two were lovers."

Ah, hell. He did not need this tonight, on top of all the other things that had decided to tilt his world upside down.

"He was!" Hestia howled. "And he's taken a step down in that department by screwing you, filthy human impostor."

"I am not an impostor! What's she talking about, Ry?"

"Never!" Ry gestured for his brother to get Hestia.

"There's nothing to see here!" Ry called, making eye contact with a few of the residents who were watching eagerly. Some slunk away, others remained defiantly standing ten to twenty feet away.

Never managed to wrangle Hestia and shove her inside the front door to her shop, while Indi settled enough that Ry trusted letting her go. She tugged at her skirt and adjusted her blond curls.

Ry eyed those who still stood watching. He swung out his sword before them. "They call me Sidhe Slayer for a reason!"

The horrified gawkers fled.

And Ry turned to find Indi was no longer standing

beside him. He saw her froth of skirt disappear into the healer's shop.

"And here I thought she was tired and wanted to go home to have a good cry."

He dashed inside the shop and encountered Never, standing before Hestia, arms out to stop Indi's approach. Ry grabbed Indi about the waist. The tiny wings whisked at his shirt and chest while her arms pumped, as did her scrambling legs.

"Would you settle down? We can talk about this like civilized people."

"Civilized? She's the one who tried to turn me into a faery!"

"I can do no such thing!" Hestia shouted back at her. "Ryland, I healed the cut she received from the collector. You saw that! And that is all I did! You know I cannot change a human into a faery."

"All right, ladies, can we all take a breath and settle down? Talk about this?" He looked from one to the other. Never shrugged, still holding his position between the two of them. "Indi?"

Sniffing and crossing her arms, she stomped over to stand beside him. "She's still got it bad for you. She's not going to tell the truth."

"I've never known Hestia to lie," he reassured both women. "And she doesn't…" He exhaled and cast Hestia a look, but he'd expected her to sneer, and instead she glanced away. Was Indi's guess correct? Did the healer still have feelings for him?

"Then how did this happen?" Indi thrust a hand over her shoulder. The wings fluttered madly. Had they grown bigger since he saw them in the car but half an hour earlier?

Ry looked to Hestia.

"I didn't do it!" she insisted.

"I believe you, Hestia. But can you help us here? Since the night you healed Indi, she's been feeling bad. And the pain in her back has grown worse. And now tonight, not two hours ago, those wings popped out."

"Impossible. If she's human."

"Are you saying she's not human?"

"Oh, come on!"

Ry managed to catch Indi about the waist as she stepped forward, arms swinging for a punch. "Princess, holster those claws."

"Princess?" Hestia scoffed. "You've changed, Ry. Never thought you'd go for a poseur like her. You once told me you could see the gold diggers coming. What's with the stupid ears, huh?"

"These ears are my bestselling product," Indi countered. "And they haven't changed anyone into something they are not. Unlike your products. What did you use on me? Some nasty magical herbs? Faery dust?"

Hestia slammed her hands to her hips. "Educate her about faeries, Ry."

"I'm not up on the whole faery lexicon, Hestia. But if you say a human can't be changed to a faery..."

"Not in the mortal realm," the healer said. "But if you take a human infant to Faery, it grows into sidhe. And vice versa— That's it! She's a changeling!"

At that suggestion, Indi stepped back and landed her shoulders up against Ry. He slid an arm across her chest, holding her trembling body before his. The sensation of her wings against his pecs disturbed him. A changeling? That would mean she had been switched at birth. And Riske had said changelings had not been brought to the human realm for decades.

Indi was over a few decades in age. Could it be true?

"She's lying," Indi said quietly. "I was born to Claire and Gerard DuCharme twenty-seven years ago right here in Paris. I've never known anything about faeries or seen…" She gasped, pressing her fingers to her mouth.

Ry recalled her saying she'd seen faeries in her garden. For sure, she had the sight. But that didn't imply she should grow wings because of it.

"How can we learn if that's the truth?" Ry asked Hestia.

She shrugged. "No clue."

"Hestia, come on. Give me a break here, will you?"

"I don't need to help you anymore, Ry. We're paid up. Remember? I saved your ungrateful girlfriend's ass from death."

"And I paid you a million euros."

"A million…?" Indi gasped.

Hestia gestured furiously toward Indi. "And now she dares to come into my home and accuse me of something so heinous?"

"I'm sorry," Indi offered suddenly. She turned to Ry and slipped her hand into his. "Can you take me home? I want to get out of here. Please?"

He nodded. "Sorry, Hestia. Never, can you—"

"I'll hang around until everyone is feeling fine," Never offered.

Indi wandered toward the door while Ry held Hestia's gaze a bit longer, seeing her pain. She was hurt. Indi should never have attacked her. But Indi was at odds and out of place.

And he was stuck in the middle.

"Thank you," he said. "I promise I won't bother you again." He turned to leave.

Outside, he followed Indi's swift pace to the Alfa. She slid into the passenger side, and he dashed up to tuck in her dress before closing the door for her. He'd take her to his place tonight. Because he didn't want her to be alone. And because whatever had happened to her, he felt to blame.

He had a new mystery to solve.

Chapter 14

Indi's eyes fluttered open. Sunlight beamed through windows that stretched diagonally to the ceiling above the bed. She spread her hand across crisp sheets. They didn't smell of lavender like hers at home. Where was she?

She sat abruptly, and didn't recognize the bed or the room. But the slanted windows were the same as the ones she'd seen in Ry's living room the one time she was at his place.

"I gotta stop waking in this guy's apartment unawares."

She was still clad in her black taffeta dress, and the tulle underskirt cushed as she rolled her legs off the side of the bed. But the notion to get up and wander didn't appeal. Yet something had woken her. A dream or memory.

She'd been sitting in a sports car with a man wearing far too much guy-liner and he'd said something to her...

"He's a prince?" she whispered.

Ryland James was a prince. Of Faery. His weird Goth brother had definitely said that to her.

And where was Ry? He'd driven her...

Well, she'd lost track of the ride home from Faery-Town because she must have fallen asleep. Exhaustion had literally attacked. But she'd never forget her squabble with the bitch faery healer.

Falling onto her side, her head hitting the über-plush pillow, Indi slid a wrist across her forehead and stared out at the brightening sky. The faery woman with strangely pink skin had been downright vicious. She'd snapped at Indi, claiming she wasn't going to talk to Ry's whore. In her lifetime Indi had never been called something so terrible. And who cared if she was dating Ry? The only reason the healer should have been angry about that was if she was still seeing him.

Was Ry two-timing her?

He'd been cagey about his relationship with the healer, but Indi did not think the man would be so cruel to her, another woman.

Yet the argument had only escalated. Incensed, Indi had been the first to swing out with a smack to the woman's face. That was so not her. She'd never fought another woman—except that one time in high school when Amelie Theroux had screwed her boyfriend under the bleachers after a lacrosse game.

That Ry had come along and torn her away from the faery healer was humiliating. What was going on with her? She wasn't herself lately.

And for reasons that had plunged out of her back and now crinkled against the sheets.

Indi didn't know anything more about her condition than she did earlier. She rolled carefully to her back. Her body weight crushed the wings. It didn't hurt, but it didn't feel comfortable, either; they tugged for release, a bit like long hair stuck under the pillow when she tried to shift from side to side.

She rolled back to her side.

The healer had accused her of being a changeling. The word, issued with a sort of hissing hexlike tone, had shivered over Indi's skin. And thinking it now gave her a shudder.

How could she be a faery and not know it? That was the most ridiculous thing she had heard. She'd been raised by loving parents, and had grown up in Paris. In the mortal realm. She'd never once thought about flying or that she might have lived in another place or realm. Nothing in her life could point toward suddenly sprouting wings.

Though she did see faeries in her garden. But that wasn't at all related. Was it?

"I should give Mom a call."

Indi made a point of calling her mom once a week, and visiting her once a month. Claire DuCharme traveled a lot, and seemed to have a new boyfriend every time Indi checked in. The fifty-five-year-old socialite was enjoying her retirement and Indi couldn't offer a single argument against her plunge into adventure and freedom. Claire had always worked hard and after she'd divorced Indi's father, had worked even harder to prove she could survive on her own. Although she'd never snub alimony. And Indi knew her father's monthly payments were footing the bill for his ex-wife's adventurous lifestyle.

Could she tell her mom about the wings? That would freak her out. Claire DuCharme was solidly a nonbeliever. She actually went to church every once in a while and believed in Heaven and Hell. Catholic-girl guilt, she'd once said to Indi, whom she had raised nonreligious simply because by that time Claire hadn't the time or interest in tending to her daughter's religious education.

But maybe Indi could ask about her childhood? Infancy? Had Claire and Gerard DuCharme ever noticed that their daughter was…weird? Not right? Was she crazy to even consider asking such a thing?

She was not a faery!

And yet how had she been able to walk into Faery-Town and see other faeries? She had seen the collectors Ry had insisted a common human could not see.

Maybe she had that thing he'd also mentioned. Seeing? The sight. That was it. Because all her life she had seen faeries in the garden. Of course, she'd never told her mother about those, either. Claire would have laughed and offered her a Xanax. But seeing tiny beings flit amongst the roses did not explain the wings on her back.

Closing her eyes, Indi felt her mind humming busily. Sliding her hand across the crisp white sheet, she wished Ry was lying next to her, and then wondered why he was not.

He'd witnessed her in a chick fight. And he'd had to physically remove her from the ridiculous encounter. Probably wanted to give her some space. Would the man still want to date her now that wings had popped out on her back?

He didn't seem so happy with his own faery side, wasn't willing to tell her much about it. There were things about Faery that offended Ry, she could tell. And until she learned what they were, she wasn't sure where she stood with the man. And she wanted to stand beside him and before him. In his arms.

Because, despite only knowing him a short time,

she felt certain she was falling in love with the mighty werewolf warrior. And that was not a faery tale.

Using a thick towel, Ry sponged out most of the water from his wet hair, then popped his head into the bedroom. Indi was sitting on the opposite side of the bed, her back to him. The wings were— They had definitely grown larger. They had been about the size of his hand last night. This morning? Twice as big.

"Hey," she offered over her shoulder. "Thanks for tucking me in last night. You could have taken me home."

"I wanted to be around for you. I hope you don't mind. I turned on the towel warmer in the bathroom. The shower is all yours."

"Thanks. A shower will feel great. Do you think I can get these things wet?"

"Uh…" She was asking about the wings. "Of course. Faeries do all the time."

She nodded, head bowed.

What Hestia had suggested last night must be weighing heavily on her mind. It was bothering him. How did one discuss with a relatively new girlfriend the fact that she had just sprouted wings? And that she could be a changeling?

"I ordered breakfast from the bistro down the street," he said. "They make a mean goat-cheese-and-asparagus omelet. It'll be here in half an hour. I'll leave you to do your thing. Uh, you can steal some clothes from my closet. I'm sure I have a few T-shirts that you could wear like a dress."

She nodded again. Not talkative.

Ry closed the door slightly and left her to herself. Five minutes later he heard water patter on the marble walls in the bathroom, so he snuck into the bedroom and dropped his towel in the hamper. Pulling on a pair of jeans and forgoing a shirt, he grabbed his iPad and headed out to the living room. It was a workday, and while he didn't expect Kristine to be in the office today after last night's encounter, he figured he should text her and let her know to take the day off.

Everything had been tilted on its head last night. Or at least, one very important thing. And it hurt him as much as it must hurt Indi. What was up with her? And for as much as he trusted Hestia, had she lied to him? Could she have done something to Indi when she healed her?

He opened a browser and tapped into the para-net, which was like a dark net except it was exclusively known to paranormals. When investigating possible charities and clients, he occasionally visited a board that was open to any and all questions.

In the chat room labeled Sidhe he posed the questions: What can you tell me about changelings? Their origins? Can a human who has only lived in the mortal realm suddenly become faery?

He figured that was enough to garner many replies, so he set the iPad on the coffee table and, just about to put up his feet, jumped when the doorbell rang. He buzzed up the delivery guy, tipped him ten euros and then unpacked the steaming breakfast onto two plates. A side of bright orange papaya and juicy kiwi made his mouth water.

As if on cue, Indi wandered into the living room, flipping her wet hair over a shoulder. She wore one of his gray T-shirts, and it was loose and long, hanging to her thighs. But it was just short enough to make him look to see if anything would be revealed with each step. Nope. Maybe? Ah! The tease!

Ry whistled. "If I knew my shirt was so sexy, I'd wear it every day."

"I prefer you sans shirt." She slid onto a chair before the kitchen counter, which hugged the stovetop and sink area. "That smells great. Madeleine's? Me and my mom used to go there in the summers. You have good taste. Hand me a fork."

"You want water? Or I've got some funky aloe-vera juice stuff."

She lifted an eyebrow.

"I have a personal shopper who gets my groceries for me once a week. She tends to sneak in a new thing once in a while. It's good, but chunky."

"Chunky juice? I think I'll go with water. Don't stand on the other side of the counter. Come sit beside me."

Ry joined her and they ate in silence for a few minutes. Because again, how to casually discuss what seemed to stick out like a pair of wings? The T-shirt bulged across Indi's back where the soft fabric wasn't heavy enough to weigh down the wings.

Out of the blue, she asked, "Do werewolves need blood to survive?"

Her mind must be tracing all the weirdness she'd encountered since first meeting him. Had she not wandered into FaeryTown that night and been attacked by the collector, would she have wings now?

"You mean like vamps?" he asked. "Hell no. We have a distinct disgust for blood. Unless we're in wolf shape, that is. We don't kill for the thrill of it. Only for sustenance."

"Good to know. I think dating a vampire would freak me out."

"Are we dating?" he asked. The label hadn't come

up, and he realized he'd probably asked that a bit too quickly.

"Can we be?" she asked with all the sweet innocence of a summer flower.

Ry bowed his head to hers and kissed her lips. She smelled like his brisk male shampoo, which seemed to be mostly cinnamon and clove scents. "I hope so," he said. "I like you, Indigo."

"I like you. Even if it's been a wild ride since meeting you."

"I like my rides wild, if that's any consolation."

"Apparently, I'm growing wilder by the day. Do you think the wings got a little bigger?"

He shoved a forkload of food in his mouth but managed a confirming nod.

"I thought so, too. I can't see them well in the mirror. You don't have a hand mirror to hold up to look at them. Oh, Ry… What am I?"

"I'm not sure, Indi. But I'm going to help you find out."

"Thanks." She squeezed his hand. "I feel lost. My world was so normal and moving along swimmingly. If you consider ball gowns and tiaras normal. Which I do. But now?" She sighed.

Again, he was compelled to kiss her. To be close. To feel her against his skin. He eased his temple beside hers and said, "I hear normal is not what it's cracked up to be."

"I suppose. But at the very least, I would have liked to have a choice in the matter. Do you like asparagus?" She shoved her plate forward on the counter. "I'm not so hungry. Sorry."

"It's all right, Princess. You've had a crazy night. You want some more fruit?"

She plucked a half circle of kiwi from the plastic container it had come in. "I'll just pick at this."

He smiled then and collected their plates, placing them in the sink.

Indi suddenly slapped the counter and exclaimed, "What's this about you being a prince?"

Ah, hell. Really? "That's the last time I ask Never to do me a favor. Did he tell you that?"

"He's kind of strange," she said, inspecting the cut kiwi, "but nice enough. I don't know how it came up— Oh, yes, he was talking about your dad and mentioned you were a prince. Really? I mean, you're a sexy werewolf faery. And a billionaire. And a superhero. And now I learn you're also a prince? I think I've just stepped into the latest romance novel. *The Werewolf Faery Billionaire Prince's Wild Life.*"

"Is there a book with that title?"

"No, but I could write one."

"Then the werewolf faery billionaire..."

"Prince," she said, helping him.

"...*prince's* girlfriend would have to be a gorgeous Princess Pussycat with wings."

"That's getting too complicated for a title. And I am not a princess. I just play one in your dreams."

"I have very good dreams about you."

She turned on the chair and leaned an elbow onto the counter. "Does it involve vibrators?"

"You know it."

"You're avoiding the question. Which you have a talent for. But my talent is recognizing that sly move. Tell me about this prince thing. I need all the deets if you're going to be my boyfriend."

"Come here first." He gestured for her to follow him over to the living area, and he sat on the back of the sofa.

Indi sailed across the room and into his arms. This kiss was long and deep and involved as much of their body parts crushing against each other as possible. She felt like a piece of brightness that had escaped to shine on his world. And she tasted like fruit and giggles because she ended the kiss with a laugh.

"What's that about?" he asked.

"The laugh? I've been reading romance novels since I was a teenager. And paranormal romances are some of my favorite. Who would have thought I'd find myself in my own paranormal romance?"

"That's a thing?"

"A very big thing. Women dream about having love affairs with vampires or witches or shape-shifters."

"Really? That's…huh. Have *you* dreamed about it?"

"Not really. I mean, I love the stories, but I know what's real and what isn't."

"I'm real."

She hugged up against his chest and nuzzled her nose along his neck and up to his ear, where she dashed the lobe with her tongue. "I know it. Every bit of you is real and hard, and…if this is a fantasy, I don't want it to end."

He slid a hand up her back, remembered her wings and stopped. "Feels great with your hard tits hugging up against me."

"You're avoiding the question, lover. Now spill." She sat up on his lap, yet thrust forward her chest and winked. "Then I'll let you touch my boobs."

"I can be bribed." He lifted her, and in the process spun over the back of the sofa and slid down, landing with her on his lap, both of them facing the windows. The day was growing bright. Clasping her hands in his lap, Ry explained, "I'm not a prince. I mean, I guess I

am. My faery father, Malrick, named me a prince because…" He sighed.

"Never said the guy's an asshole."

"That he is. I don't know him all that well. I told you
about the money."

"Right, the leaves that change to cash. I wish I had
that problem."

"No, you don't. Malrick thinks by bribing me he'll
win me over and I'll move to Faery. I don't want to live
in Faery. I was born and raised in this realm and it is
my home. As good a home as it'll ever be."

"But you were raised in a pack?"

"I was. I was seventeen when my father, Tomas—my
werewolf father—asked me to leave the pack because
it wasn't right, a half-breed staying on."

"That's awful. And he had raised you as his son?"

"He thought I was his son. As I did. This sigil—"
he tapped his hip "—only appeared when I was seventeen. My father saw it—and another thing, I'd started
to dust—and he knew something wasn't right. And it
all went to hell after that. My mom confessed her affair with Malrick and then fled. And Tomas ignored
me for weeks after that. Stewing. And then he told me
to leave."

"Just like that?"

He nodded.

"I'm so sorry, Ry. I can't say that I can understand,
but it must have been difficult for you."

"That's when Malrick stepped in with his magical
leaves and promises of making me a prince should I
move to Faery. I'm thankful I was resistant to it. I only
wanted to get away from them all, Tomas and Malrick,
and start new. Which is why I'm in Paris now."

"The city suits you."

He shrugged. "I miss the country. I want to go out running every day. It's an innate thing."

"Could you go to your cabin more often?"

"I try to, but I've been so busy with the finances. It seems the more money I give away, the more it grows. It's madness. Some days I want it to stop. And then other days I know I can do so much good with that money, so I admonish myself for feeling sorry for myself. So many have it so much worse than I do. Hell. I don't have it bad at all."

"And you've a good heart, which makes your situation even more impressive. Never stop giving the money to those in need, Ry."

"I won't." He kissed her nose. "Did that answer your question?"

"Are all Malrick's sons princes? You said you had hundreds of half brothers and sisters. Why doesn't he ask some other sibling to move to Faery?"

"Because I am his only werewolf son. And supposedly that makes me his warrior prince, as he calls me. Most desired. Strong and capable of…"

She turned on his lap. He knew she was looking into his eyes, but he avoided meeting her gaze. Finally, he said, "Capable of taking over the reins when Malrick dies and assuming the Unseelie throne."

"You mean like king of the Unseelies?"

Ry nodded. "I don't want that. It's not my place. But Malrick won't make the offer to any other of his by-blows. So he continues to try and seduce me over to Faery."

"Have you ever been to Faery?"

"Once. Briefly. I visited Malrick's kingdom after he'd first introduced himself to me. I didn't know him well then and was curious. I learned my lesson. The Unseelie lands are beautiful and malicious. Faeries are…

well, they're not the fluttery sweet things you read about in the children's tales, that's for sure."

"The ones in my garden flutter, and I think they're pretty sweet."

"Be cautious," he warned. "Faeries are never what they seem. And yet they are fierce and strong. I would never judge one too harshly. I talked to Riske last night and he suggested the only way to figure this stolen-baby thing out is to talk to Malrick. I don't think I can do that."

"The Riske guy didn't have any answers for you?"

"He was unaware of what was going on in Faery-Town. In fact, he's kind of pissed about it and is going to send someone to Faery to check in to things."

"Do you really have the time to wait and see what he learns? Ry, if you miss one night, those collector things will take another baby. Oh, my God..."

She slid off his lap and leaned forward, catching her head in her hands.

"What is it, Indi?"

"Was *I* one of those babies? Or rather, was I a faery put in a human infant's crib? Why do they only take babies? Why not adults?"

She subtly shook now and Ry pulled her back onto his lap and hugged her tightly. It hurt him to feel her fear and pain. Her unknowing. How could he reassure her when even he didn't have answers? There were days he felt as lost in the world as she probably did right now.

"They take babies because then they grow into sidhe. Much as the changeling then grows into a human. Yet adults who get lost in Faery remain human, no matter what. No matter what you are, Indi, I've got your back. Promise. You don't have to go through this alone. We're going to figure things out."

"Thank you. I do need the support. I feel like if you let me go I'll fall into a deep pit."

"Never let that happen." He kissed her. Deeply. It was like falling with his arms outstretched and he did not fear landing. With Indi he could be himself. Almost? He would get there with her. He wanted that.

"I need to go home and get changed and…" Indi sighed. "Stare in the mirror a while at these things. I have to call Janet."

"The BFF?"

"She's my bestie. And my business partner. She moved to New York three months ago and is currently setting up a new office for Goddess Goodies. We plan to open that branch before the holiday season. But I can't tell her about this. Not yet."

"Not ever." He waggled a finger at her. "It is never wise to tell humans about what they believe to be myth and fantasy."

"Humans? Am I no longer in that category?"

"Oh, sweetie."

All he could do was hug her. Ry felt her confusion. Her utter inability to accept what had happened. Hell, he was as confused as she was. He didn't know what to say, so he nuzzled his nose against her hair and hugged her even tighter. She felt so good curled on his lap.

When she slid a hand over his abs, he winced as his erection took notice. Didn't take much to get horny with this woman close. But it didn't feel like the time was right…

"You're so hot," she said against his throat as she slid her hand up higher.

Was she in the mood? Because if she was…

"It's hard to walk away from you," she said. "Last night should have been a night to remember. We danced. We kissed. Then we should have topped it off by coming home and making love. Can we do that part that didn't get done last night?"

"The making-love part?" He shifted his hips, and her hand dropped to stroke over his jeans. Not much room left in them now. "If that's what you want?"

"You're thinking it's strange now with these wings on my back?"

"Not at all. I want you, Indi. I just don't want to take advantage of you if you're in a weird place."

"It is a weird place, but I need you to stay beside me in that place. More so, I need to feel you inside me. To just...lose myself right now."

She kissed him, shifting her body as she did, so she straddled him. Sitting fully on his lap, she pumped her mons against his erection as her tongue danced with his.

Ry moaned and set aside any reluctance over having his way with a confused woman. She wasn't mixed up right now. She knew exactly what she wanted and needed.

They'd moved to Ry's bed, and Indi now sat on top of him, his cock seated deep within her. She rocked on him, drawing up his moans. The man was lost in the moment, and yet he still hadn't forgotten that she liked it when he put pressure on her clit. His thumb altered from a firm to a soft touch right there. And when she increased her rhythm, he read that as a sign to touch her harder, longer, and jitter that touch to milk the burgeoning orgasm.

She felt like a goddess sitting upon him, demanding worship from her follower. And while she knew the strange wings on her back were there, she didn't need to think about them now. Ry's other hand found her breast and teased at her nipple. She tilted back her head, gripping his thighs behind her, and groaned as the intensity of their connection grew her feminine power. She'd never felt more wanted, more desired.

The man gave to her always. And she would take what he offered.

"So close," he said through a tight jaw. His hips bucked up against her thighs. "You almost there?"

"Oh, hell yes." She pressed her hands to his shoulders and met his deep brown gaze. The wolf lived within those irises. She could see his wild, and feel it in his tight muscles and his panting breaths. "Worship me," she whispered.

"Oh, my princess, always."

He suddenly gripped her wrist and dragged her hand to his mouth. His kissed her palm and bit gently as he came forcefully within her. With a squeeze of his fingers at her clit, she went over the edge along with him. Her body tightened and then loosened and she bowed her head to his chest as their combined magic moved through her and burst in a brilliant shimmy of satiation.

And with a glance down, Indi saw the faery dust glimmering about their hips. Something amazing had bonded the two of them.

Now to survive this new adventure without chasing him away.

Chapter 15

After Ry dropped her off at home, Indi strode straight to the bathroom and pulled off his shirt and dropped it to the floor. She stood naked before the vanity mirror to stare at a woman she wasn't sure she recognized anymore.

She could just see the tops of the clear, iridescent wings over her shoulders. They didn't move, but they had made reflexive movements when she pulled off the shirt.

Why was this happening to her?

Or was that the wrong question to ask? It had already happened. She needed to know if they were merely temporary or if she'd have to adjust to having them for the rest of her life.

Wincing, she reached for the hand mirror on the vanity. She turned around and held the mirror high. There were two sets of wings on each side of her spine. They resembled bee wings. The top one was a little larger than the narrower bottom wing. And they grew from her back in a narrow jut and formed a sort of elongated teardrop in shape. They were clear, and looked like delicate paper that could be easily torn if pierced or even bumped. A twist at her waist caught the light in the fabric of the wings and flashed in pinks, blues, emeralds and a deep violet.

Indi sighed. They were pretty. But they did not belong on her.

Sucking in the corner of her lower lip, she wondered how she would ever disguise them. They were already about a foot long. And she hadn't even had them twenty-four hours. Would they grow as large as a real faery's wings? How big were a faery's wings? She'd never be able to hide them if they stretched many feet beyond her body.

Real faeries could put away their wings, yes?

"I have no clue," she muttered. "Is that what I am? Could I really be…?"

She couldn't say the word: changeling. It felt wrong. Not at all like anything that belonged in the comfortable world she knew as her home.

Picking up her phone, she googled *changeling*. The first definition that came up read: "a child believed to have been secretly substituted by faeries for the human parents' real child in infancy."

The entries that followed were similar, yet they were all linked to folklore and myth.

"Not real," she whispered.

And yet proof glimmered just behind her shoulders.

Her phone suddenly rang and it startled Indi so much she almost dropped it. Janet was calling? It had to be middle of the night in New York. Or…maybe early morning. It was past noon here.

"Janet!"

"Hey, chickie baby, what's up?"

"Oh, the usual." She bit the corner of her lip. Ry said she couldn't tell anyone about this. And why was her hand suddenly shaking?

"Oh, yeah? How did the date with tall, dark and billionaire go last night?"

"Great. You know I'm in my element at fancy balls."

"Hence, your business. But I don't care about what you wore or if you chatted up the movers and shakers."

Indi pressed her shaking fingers to the vanity and leaned forward, eyeing herself in the mirror. "Are you kidding me?"

"I kid you not. I want to hear all about the sexy man."

With a sigh, Indi smiled at her reflection. She could do this—chatter with Janet about Ry and not bring up the fact that she had suddenly sprouted wings. She loved her best friend, but Janet would never believe her. She was also a card-carrying Catholic schoolgirl. The one time Indi had mentioned to her she'd seen a faery in her garden, Janet had laughed and then snorted until she'd started hiccupping.

"This man is one in a billion," Indi said. "And the sex!"

"Ooh! You must tell me all."

"I will." She turned off the bathroom light and wandered into the bedroom to plop down, stomach-first, on the bed. "Where should I start? With his steel abs that could support a ten-story building or with his nice long, thick—"

"The nice long thick one!" Janet insisted.

They always shared the intimate details about sex because it was a BFF privilege. For the next twenty minutes they talked sex, abs and orgasms. And Indi didn't once think about the wings fluttering at her back.

* * *

Ry gave Indi a call as he headed out of the office. She was in her backyard, basking in the sun…naked. He wished he could be there for that. The woman was a nudist? He could get behind that. And in front of her. Hell, all over that sweet-smelling skin.

She'd given her mother a call, thinking she might ask her what she'd been like as a baby. Kind of feel her out without actually asking if she suspected her daughter was a changeling. Claire DuCharme was headed out on a midnight flight, but she'd said her daughter could stop in before she left this evening.

Ry had offered to go along, and Indi had appreciated that.

His girlfriend was turning into a faery. Or she already was one. Or…he didn't know. It would be fine by him if she was a faery and had wings. He had no prejudices against any from the paranormal realm. Except maybe witches. Just a little creeped out by witches.

And okay, to get real with himself, *did* he have a preconception against faeries?

"No," he muttered.

Any prejudices toward faeries were directed toward the one pompous Unseelie king. Because he'd had the fling with Hestia. That hadn't bothered him. Of course, he'd been heavily drugged at the time. But for sure his eye had been turned by more than a few female faeries while wandering FaeryTown. He could deal with someone not like him. Because he knew what it was like to be different than most.

If the changeling theory was true, Ry wanted to help Indi get the answers she needed. He knew what it felt like to live your life one way, and then to suddenly be told you were not the person you thought you were.

Why had his mother kept that information a secret

from him? Because she'd thought he'd tell his father? The man who wasn't actually his blood father, but merely a stepfather.

Never *merely*, Ry thought now as he slid into the Alfa and fired it up.

And yet Tomas LeDoux had been able to push his stepson out of the pack with little concern. And Ry had only heard from him twice since leaving when he was seventeen. Once, right after Ry had left, Tomas had sent him a message through another pack member inquiring if he was doing well. And then years later, he'd sent that same pack member with a message that he'd seen him on the news and was proud of his philanthropy. He'd made something of himself!

If Tomas only knew that money was from his real father. Would he be as angered over the faery king's attempts at manipulating the one person he'd spent nearly two decades believing was his son? Tomas had seemed to shuck Ry from his life as easily as pulling off a shirt and tossing it aside.

There was a time when Ry had been close to his werewolf father. Immediately after his first shift, around twelve years of age, Tomas began taking Ry everywhere with him, out for runs through the forest in wolf shape, to secret pack enclaves where only the males showed and where they fought one another for rank in the pack. Tomas had been the only man Ry had to look up to and model himself after as he was growing up. And he'd loved him.

As for his mother? He had no clue where Lisa LeDoux was or if she was even alive. After she'd confessed the affair to Tomas, Ry had woken the next morning only to be told his mother had slipped out in the night, taken a few personal things and hadn't left a note for him. He'd mourned her for months, until his father had finally stepped up to tell him Ry was no longer welcome in the pack.

Everyone he'd thought cared about him had run away or shoved him out of their lives. It wasn't an easy truth, but it was his reality. Now he did the best he could, and tried not to let anyone get so close again. Kristine was truly his only confidante. He hadn't any close male or female friends.

But Indi was another matter. She had insinuated herself into his life without him even noticing. One moment he'd been standing alone in FaeryTown facing down the collectors; the next moment he'd been curled up in bed with a woman and her newly sprouted wings, thinking she was the best thing that had ever happened to him.

And tonight he was going to meet the mother.

He had definitely stepped out of his comfort zone with Indigo DuCharme.

Claire DuCharme was leaving Paris on a midnight flight to New York, but she was always thrilled to give Indi a few minutes of her time. *Minutes* being the key word. Indi didn't mind the brief visits with her mother. They chatted on the phone. And they had never been a huggy-kissy, let's-all-go-to-the-cabin-and-do-the-nature-thing family. Her father always traveled for business, and Claire was also a businesswoman.

Hence, Indi's desire to do the same. Start her own business, that is. It had been natural. Entrepreneurship was in the DuCharme blood.

But faery wings were not. So she'd put on a blue blazer over her white lace sundress before leaving with Ry for her mother's condo. The wings were now so large that they gently folded around her back and halfway toward her chest when flattened. Wearing the blazer gave her the feeling of being strapped down, confined.

"Do you think," Indi said to Ry as they waited for the maid to answer the door buzzer, "if these wings become a permanent thing, I'll be able to make them go away when need be? I can't function in this world if they are going to be a constant." She felt her confidence shrink.

"Faeries do it all the time." Ry's sudden clutch of her hand caught her before she sank too far, and she lifted her head to meet his gaze. "You'll learn to live with them."

The reassurance felt genuine to her, and his hand in hers lifted her spirits.

The door opened and instead of the maid, Claire answered, with champagne goblet in hand. She didn't like flying so always juiced up before leaving.

"Darling! My limo just called and it's going to arrive early. He'll be here in ten minutes. Do come in, come in! I've got champagne!"

Indi followed her mother's clicking footsteps into the vast kitchen decorated in stainless steel and rare violet quartz her mother simply had to have for the countertops. She never cooked and always ordered in or her chef prepared the meals.

"Oh?" Claire stepped around and focused her blue gaze on Ry. With a tap of her real gold fingernails to her lips, she turned on her patented flirtatious grin that didn't annoy Indi so much as confirm her playful yet persistent need to toy with people's reactions. "And who is this handsome piece of hunk and muscle? Indi, you didn't tell me you were bringing along a model. Oh, please, tell me he's more than just a friend. It would be a terrible crime to let all this muscle and pretty go to waste."

Controlling the urge to roll her eyes, Indi squeezed Ry's hand and he stepped up beside her. "This is Ryland James, Mom. This is my mom, Claire. She's already half-wasted. A necessary condition before she boards any plane."

"Not even close to half-wasted," Claire admonished. "I am perfectly sober. Mostly." She tilted back a healthy swallow of champagne. "So, you must have something important to talk about if you couldn't wait until I got back, or talked about it on the phone. Oh, please, Ryland, come sit here on the stool. Would you like champagne?"

Ry looked to Indi and she could sense his discomfort. "No, thank you, Madame DuCharme. Your place is gorgeous. I love the stone for the countertops."

"Oh, he's a charmer." Claire tilted back the rest of her goblet, then nodded toward her six suitcases, packed and ready to go by the door. "If you play your cards right, I'll let you carry down my bags. We'll save the driver a trip, eh?"

"We'll both help," Indi said as she sat on the stool next to Ry.

Claire combed her fingers through her long bleach-blond hair and held her chin just slightly higher than was comfortable. It disguised the wrinkles on her neck, she'd once told Indi. While she wasn't afraid of the plastic surgeon, she hadn't gone quite that far with the adjustments and tightening. Yet.

"What's up, darling mine?"

"Mom, I went in for a regular checkup with the doctor." Indi started on the story she'd decided would be not so terrible a lie, and perhaps get the information she needed from her mother without asking her straight out "Am I a faery?" "Nothing's wrong with me. Just haven't been in for years. You know."

"You really need to go in regularly, darling. Do you want my surgeon's name? It's never too early to consider Botox. That line between your eyebrows will only get deeper."

Indi pressed a finger between her eyes. She had a wrinkle there? She hadn't noticed anything.

"I think Indi is beautiful as she is," Ry said. "When I first met her, it was her eyes that attracted me. Bright, bold and gemstone-blue. Just like yours."

Claire preened her fingers down her hair and thrust up her breasts, wiggling appreciatively at the compliment. "He's a keeper, Indi. Why does your name sound familiar?" she asked Ry.

He shrugged. "I do some charity work. You might have read about it somewhere."

And if Claire discovered the man was worth billions, her flirtations would only intensify, so Indi rushed to save Ry from that deluge and steer the conversation back on track.

"Mom, I need to know about early childhood stuff for the doctor's records. Do you still have my vaccine records? How was I as a baby? Everything cool? No major sicknesses?"

"Oh, darling, that was so terribly long ago. You're not getting any younger, you know."

"Mother."

"I'm just saying, darling." She winked at Ry. "Though men certainly take on a certain seasoning with age, don't they? Not that you're old, Ry. Mmm, that name."

Indi leaned forward on her elbows, blocking Claire's sight of Ry. "Was I a good baby, Mom? Everything… cool? Nothing, you know…weird?"

"Of course not! Well…" Claire tapped her lips.

"*Well* what?"

"You did have your father and me worried right after you were born. Those first few weeks. Oh, the dramatics!"

"What? I'm not dramatic. Am I?"

"You were, darling. You cried constantly. Day and night. I swear, I thought I would go mad. And I didn't have a nanny then. Your father insisted I had the time to take care of you myself. You were determined to make my life miserable. At least until that one night."

Ry leaned forward and his clutch on Indi's hand tightened. "That one night?"

Claire poured herself another full goblet of champagne and fluttered Ry another wink over the rim as she sipped. "It was the craziest thing, but I'm so thankful it happened."

"Tell me about it," Indi insisted. "I was a crazy baby?"

"Not crazy, just... I never knew what was wrong with you. You burst into this world crying, and didn't stop. I was a walking zombie. I don't think I slept more than twenty minutes at a time those first few weeks. Talk about a need for Botox! And your father wasn't very hands-on. He was always away for business.

"Anyway, that one night I woke, and I couldn't figure out what it was that suddenly jarred me awake. Because there was no crying. I mean, you were always wailing. I was constantly checking for pins or needles in your clothes or weird things in the diapers. There I was, sitting up in bed, thinking maybe something was wrong. Had you died? You know that SIDS thing is a real worry when you're a parent. There's no explanation for it. Babies just suddenly die."

"Mother. Get on with it. What was wrong with me?"

"Right." Claire finished the champagne and grabbed the bottle but didn't pour again. "I rushed into your nursery and there you were, in the crib. Quiet. It was so odd."

Indi and Ry glanced at each other.

"You were completely naked," Claire continued, her gold fingernails rapping the bottle. "Your onesie was on the floor. And a clean diaper lay at the end of your crib. All I could think was I had truly gone over the edge. I'd somehow forgotten to put your diaper on during the last change, and your clothes! Isn't that crazy? That's what sleep deprivation will do to you. I'm sure my hair was a mess that night."

"Mother, continue!"

"You're very testy today, Indigo Paisley. What's up with you?"

Ry pushed the champagne bottle toward Claire. "I think you need a refill, Madame DuCharme."

"Oh, aren't you delicious?" she cooed as Ry refilled her goblet. Claire took a long sip before tapping her lips. "Where was I?"

"I was lying in my crib naked and quiet," Indi prompted.

"Yes, naked as a baby bird. I think that's when your nudity thing began. She's a bit of a nudist, you know?" she said to Ry.

"I've—"

Indi rushed a hand over Ry's mouth. Her mother didn't need the salacious details, and she would never hear the weird truth about her as a baby if they didn't keep Claire on track.

"What happened next?" Indi asked.

"Hmm… Oh, I leaned over to make sure you were all right and you just beamed up at me. It was the weirdest moment. The light from the baby lamp shone across your cute little face and it was as if you were smiling at me. Sort of reassuring me." Claire placed a hand over her heart. "I'll never forget that moment. I cried. All the anxiety and uncertainty whether I was a good mom over the past weeks melted away. I put your onesie and diaper on you and sang a little tune until you fell asleep. And then I didn't wake until morning. That was six hours later. You'd never slept that long. I couldn't believe it."

"What was that about?" Indi asked. "Did I start crying all the time again?"

"No. After that night you suddenly became the perfect baby. I told your father it was as if you were a different baby. The doctor suggested you probably had gas or some unresolved issue from the birth that finally worked itself out. You've been the perfect child ever since. Though you do still have a tendency toward dramatics. Oh, and the nudity."

Indi's mouth dropped open, but she didn't know what to say. Her mother had thought she was a different baby. Because she had been? Had that wailing, crying baby not been her? Had a faery taken her to this realm and placed her in the crib while whisking away the crying infant? Was she even related to Claire DuCharme?

A sickening feeling curdled in her gut and she swallowed down the need to gasp, to cry, to clutch at her chest and scream.

"That must have been difficult for you," Ry offered to Claire. "Babies can be a handful. Your daughter grew up to look just like you. A stunner."

"Oh, darling, if you keep that up, you'll have to come along with me to New York. I know my lover enjoys threesomes."

"Mother!"

Claire chuckled and this time took a chug of champagne directly from the bottle. Her cell phone rang and she checked the rhinestone-studded monstrosity.

"The driver is here. I'll text him to wait while I have my daughter's studly boyfriend bring down the bags."

"I'm on." Ry stood and squeezed Indi's shoulders from behind. He whispered to her, "You good if I do that?"

She nodded. "I think I've heard what I needed to hear. We'll be down in two shakes."

Ry grabbed a bag, then another, then another, and managed four of them without so much as a wince of struggle.

"Where did you find him?" Claire asked as the door closed behind him.

"I ran in to him the night Todd broke up with me."

"Oh, a rebound man. I love it!"

"He's not a rebound. I like him, Mom. I want to keep him around for a while."

"I second that idea. Sorry. Do you think I flirted too much?"

"No need to apologize, Mom. If you hadn't flirted with him I would have thought something was wrong with you. Thanks for telling me about how I was as a baby."

"You can tell your doctor there's nothing at all wrong with you. You were such a good child. Never once got sick. Seriously. Not even a sniffle."

Indi nodded. She had been remarkably illness-free over her lifetime, and had often wished for a cold or flu just to miss some school. Yet another twist to the bizarre scenario that had suddenly become her life.

"Darling, where did you get that awful blazer? Is that cotton?" Claire shuddered. "And really, when did you start wearing blazers?"

"I'm cleaning out my closet, seeing what fits and what doesn't work."

"Well, that shroud does not work. Toss it in the charity bin. Your man does charity work, huh?"

"He's…" If she let Claire know Ry's financial status, the woman would hire the wedding planner right now. And if she let her know he was a werewolf faery? No amount of champagne would ever get the woman to stop laughing. "He's a good man."

"And sexy as fuck. Grab my purse. I think I can manage another goblet of champagne on the elevator ride down." Claire poured the remainder of the bottle into her glass and then pointed to the remaining two suitcases as she opened the door. "You got those, too, darling?"

"Yes, Mom. Right behind you."

Chapter 16

Ry pulled the car in front of Indi's place, then leaned over to cup the back of her head and kissed her. She'd been a little off since they left her mother's home, and for good reason. The things Claire had told her about Indi's sudden change in behavior really did lean toward a changeling being placed in a crib.

He held his mouth against hers, lingering in her sweet warmth, her pistachio-and-almond scent, then kissed her nose and each of her eyelids. "Can I come back and crawl into bed with you when I'm done with the big bads?"

"Will you have strange black sparkly stuff all over you?"

"I can take a shower."

"Deal. I'll leave the door open. I'd love to roll over and find your warm body lying next to mine."

He dipped his head and nuzzled his nose against her ear. "Please be naked."

"That's not going to be a problem. Apparently that was a thing for me right from the start."

He kissed her again, then asked, "Are you okay?"

She shrugged. "Probably not. My mom just laid some heavy information on me. And there's only one way to take it."

"Don't forget what I said about being here for you. I promise you that, Indi."

"Why are you so good to me?"

"Do I need a reason?"

"Maybe."

"I can't *not* be nice to you. It's not how I am. And you're so cute and cuddly. And you've got those pretty new wings that I find very sexy."

"You're just saying that to make me feel better."

"No, I mean it. You're not up on faeries and their wings, are you?"

"What do you think?"

"Would it make you feel a little better if I found someone for you to talk to? A faery? How about Never?"

"Like ask him questions about faeries and their wings? Maybe. I still need to confirm this changeling thing. Because much as it all seems to point in that direction, I'm the sort that needs a solid."

"I thought you believed once you saw something."

"Right. And I can see them. I just…"

He understood. It had been difficult for him to accept he wasn't completely werewolf in those days following the upset in his family. "We'll take things slowly. But I think it might not hurt for you to chat with Never. Just let me know if you want to."

"Thanks, lover. You'd better get going. It's eleven thirty."

"See you, and all those vibrators, soon."

"If you don't hurry," she said as she got out of the car, "I might start without you!" She blew him a kiss and wandered up to the front door.

When she was inside, Ry pulled away from the curb and headed toward the eighteenth arrondissement.

Had he been truthful by telling her the wings appealed to him? He wasn't sure. He'd denied his faery heritage all his life. At least, ever since he'd found out he wasn't full werewolf. Being ousted from one's pack by the man he thought had been his real father was not something a guy took lightly. Or could ever forget.

He did everything he possibly could to push down his faery attributes, and was thankful he didn't have wings. That would cement the fact that his life was not what he'd expected or wanted it to be. He was not the wolf he'd thought he was.

Stopping at a light, Ry had the sudden realization that Indi must feel the same way. Her life had been going fine and dandy up until those wings had popped out. Then…wham! Life as she knew it would never again be the same, and the life she had led had all been a lie.

They were two alike. They could share things no others could. The realization was so immense he could but sit there at the light, not driving forward, as he choked back a heavy swallow and bowed his head.

He'd never felt like this about a woman before. Was he falling in love with the Princess Pussycat who wore wings and rhinestone ears?

Indi rolled over in bed, and her hand slapped against a hard, hot stretch of skin that then moved and growled in a seductive tone. Without opening her eyes, she snuggled up against Ry's body, her body reacting like a magnet snapping firmly to iron. She was still drowsing in dreams, but the closer she snugged to him, the quicker some parts of her body strived to come awake.

"You smell like you got into my body cream," she whispered, and kissed the body part closest to her mouth, which pulsed once under her lips. "Mmm, now I know why you like it so much. I could eat you up." His stone-hard pectoral muscle felt like steamed rock. She dashed out her tongue and landed it on the tiny jewel of his nipple.

"You want to sleep?" he asked on a whisper.

"No. Do you?"

"Couldn't sleep against your beautiful body if I tried."

His hand glided down her side, pushing the sheet below her waist and exposing her skin to the warm summer breeze that sifted the sheers before the open window. Indi arched her back, pressing her breasts against his chest, and he urged her forward by the hip. They entwined legs, and a crush of his hard-on against her pussy started her engine.

Now she was awake.

She kissed his neck and nuzzled up against the stubble that shadowed under his jaw. He felt like an inferno and she wanted to burn herself out within him. Against her mons, his erection tightened and he pumped it slowly, wantingly; the heavy head of it tugged at her clit.

"Mmm…" His growl crooned to her like dirty song lyrics.

Entwined in kisses, and skin hugging, Ry embedded himself deep within her. They barely moved yet managed to find a slow pumping rhythm that fed the exquisite spin of burgeoning orgasm in her core. It felt like she could come, and then she did not because it seemed ungraspable. And she fed that sensation because it teased and promised and tempted.

"I could stay inside you always," he whispered. "Indi, you're a new home I want to keep only for myself."

"You can stay. I'll never ask you to leave." Their clasp slowed even more until their bodies were still, yet she squeezed him inside her with pulses of her muscles. "Feel that?"

He nodded against her forehead. His hand released hold of her hip and slid upward until she felt a strange shimmer course through her system. It was as if her whole body was her clitoris and he'd licked it lavishly. She gasped.

"That okay?" he asked. "If I touch your wings?"

"Oh, yes, please, Ry, that makes everything… Oh…"

The next stroke of his fingers lightly gliding along a wing scurried all sensation directly to her core. Crashing into bliss, Indi cried out and came powerfully, her muscles tensing and relaxing and tensing again. She clung to Ry's body, her fingernails clutching into his skin as she gritted her teeth. Wave upon wave of pleasure rolled through her body and shivered her system in a joyous surrender.

Ry moaned out a low cry of triumph as he, too, came. His hips bucked against hers as he filled her.

"What the hell was that?" she gasped against him as they settled into a panting, elated loose embrace.

"That was what happens when you touch a faery's wings," he offered.

"I think I don't mind these things so much if that's going to happen when I have sex."

Ry chuckled and lifted himself to lean onto an elbow. Pale light from the bathroom shone into the room and barely lit the bed, but she could see his face and his glistening skin. He studied his hand, then slid it along her hip.

He slicked his fingers along his softening erection, then showed them to Indi.

"Is that from you again?"

"Actually," he said in a gentle tone, "I think you're starting to put out dust. My dick is sparkling. Heh!"

"Does that mean I've got a glitter pussy? Oh, my God, that's…"

"That will be our little secret. The half faery and the changeling." He turned to sit up on the bed and ran a hand over his hair. "Be right back."

Ry wandered into the bathroom and Indi slid her fingers between her legs. Sparkle orgasms?

"This is crazy," she whispered.

Ry didn't turn on the bathroom light. His vision was honed so he could see shadows of his reflection in the vanity mirror. And the glints of dust sparkled on his skin in a weird rendition of the collector's sparkly skin, only his was in shades of gray.

He winced and bowed his head. He'd come with her before and the sheets had sparkled softly afterward. But not quite so much as tonight. It had startled him in a surprising way. He hadn't wanted to upset Indi, but seeing the dust had instantly shot him back to that night at the pack compound.

Seventeen and randy as hell, he had dated a few human females but hadn't been able to tell them he was werewolf, so he'd been eyeing the one eighteen-year-old female in the pack, yet she had been his friend since they were kids. He'd wanted to keep their friendship and not complicate it with sex. And yet there had been only so much a guy could do to stave off those feelings of desire.

That night he'd jacked off and had been startled when his hand had sparkled. Had that stuff come out of him? What the hell?

He'd not had a moment to consider what was up when he heard footsteps, and scented his father's approach. Tomas had laughed at catching his son in the act, then had punched him on the shoulder. It was something men did. Wasn't anything to be ashamed of. Except...his father's eyes had veered to Ry's shaking hand.

"What the hell is that?" Tomas had asked. "You're sparkling like some kind of..."

"I don't know. It's never happened before."

"Don't tell me." Tomas's jaw had tightened and he'd turned to face the compound, half a mile off through the forest. "That bitch!"

Ry had followed his father back to the compound but had found him arguing with his mother. Only then had she broken down and confessed that she'd had an affair with a faery and that Ry was actually that man's son.

The betrayal and shame Ry had felt that night to learn such a thing had tightened his throat and dropped his heart to his gut.

And he felt the same thing now. He gripped his chest and looked out toward the bedroom, where Indi was lying on the bed, glittering with faery dust.

Could he do this with Indi? It was bringing up all this...stuff. Issues. Bad memories from his past, which wasn't really his past but something that he had to face very day. And his life had been going smoothly until recently, when he'd started slaying the collectors. Everything had been cool. He'd had no worries.

A man shouldn't run away from the trouble that reared its head and defied him to step up and change and evolve. But how to resolve the big empty hole that had formed in his heart that night he learned about his real parentage? And then, months later, when he'd been ousted from the pack by the man he had only ever known as his father?

"Ry? You okay in there?"

"Be right out," he called.

He closed the bathroom door and took a piss.

It was either walk away from Indi right now, mark it off as a great time and focus on stopping the collectors, or face the shame that still clung to him and teased with the sigil at his hip.

He pressed a hand over the sigil. It warmed. Faery magic? If he used it, he was submitting to the reality that he had never been a son of a werewolf.

Chapter 17

Ry woke early to head into work today. Indi still slept and he was inclined to let her bask in the soft morning light showering her half-covered body. Hair strewn across her face and wings spread over her bare back, she looked like a fallen faery someone might have batted out of the sky.

He wiped a hand over his abdomen where some of the faery dust had settled. His dick no longer sparkled. Most of that had rubbed off on the sheets. He wasn't going to dwell on the dark feelings that had attacked him last night. At least, he would try not to.

He collected his clothes and wandered into the bathroom to dress. On the way out, he took a moment to glance out the patio door.

Indi had told him this place had been in her family for centuries. She had probably been raised in this house. Or rather, if she truly was a changeling, she'd have been brought to this very house and placed in the crib of that wailing baby Claire DuCharme had told them about. And if a faery had come into this home, that meant there could be a thin place nearby.

Sliding on his sunglasses, he opened the patio door and walked out. The sun heated his face and he tugged back his hair, wishing for something to tie it away from his face. He wandered along the pool edge, focusing his senses to the air, the smells and the pressure of the world falling against him. Felt like a backyard to him. He smelled the roses growing wildly along the fence and shrubs. That was Indi's innate scent, and he smiled to realize it came from her garden. Earth and grass sweetened the air. And a neighbor must have cats, because he smelled the fur and urine of a marked territory close by.

Cats. They were so obstinate.

He followed the pool around to the long and narrow yard and toward the copse of frothy chestnuts at the back. Suddenly a tug of something stopped him. He spread out his arms and closed his eyes, sniffing and noticing the waving vibrations in the air.

"A thin place," he whispered.

It had to be. It felt as it did when he entered Faery-Town. An ineffable tug at his musculature, and then the awareness that the air was lighter and…then it was gone.

He stepped back, feeling the tug as if he was stepping out of what could be a portal. Indi might have been brought through this very area twenty-seven years earlier.

And if a guy wanted to communicate with a particular faery, he might call him out here. Not that he wanted to. But it was good to know this place existed.

Ry turned and marched back into the house, made

sure the patio door was locked and quietly left through the front door.

He glanced back to the house before getting into the Alfa. He might have to use that thin place. Like it or not.

Working on the spreadsheet for the vibrator samples, Indi had narrowed it down to three. Even with all the data, she still felt she was missing something. A factor that wasn't terribly important to most vibrator users, she felt sure, but she wanted to discover anyway. The data point regarding usage with a male partner. Ry had seemed interested in helping her. But it hadn't come up last night.

The wing sex had been amazing enough. That she'd gotten a shock of sensation when he touched her wings was stunning. It had served like a supercharge to her orgasm.

Did all faeries experience such when their wings were touched?

She'd ask Never that question when he stopped by tomorrow. Ry had called her to let her know his half brother was willing to talk to her and she agreed. While she was still freaking about it, the smart thing to do would be to learn as much as she could about being a faery.

Because all evidence pointed to that truth.

It was weird. It was awful. It was horrifying.

Yet at the same time, it was wondrous. It was interesting. And it was kind of cool. She had wings! Did that mean she could fly? Could she change to a small size like those faeries she had seen in her garden? And the faery dust during sex. What was that about? Would she start to sparkle and glitter constantly? And would she ever be able to make her wings disappear so she could go out in public and act like a normal human woman?

After a long afternoon and into the evening, Indi texted Ry that she would make him supper if he was interested. He had a late meeting with the man he'd spoken to the other night at the ball, so he took a rain check.

Gathering up the vibrators she'd decided were unworthy of inclusion in the catalog, she packed them away. Three remained.

"Guess it's just us tonight, folks. A movie and then an orgasm? Sounds like a plan."

The next morning Indi flitted about the house, straightening up and dusting. So many questions, and she was eager to have them answered. Ry's brother was stopping by today. Normally the faery would insist she come to him, but Ry had mentioned she had a pool. Apparently his half brother loved to swim, so he was bringing his trunks and would be here soon.

Thinking she should prepare a snack or drinks, she veered toward the kitchen, and set to making a welcome feast for a faery. Grocery shopping was tops on her list after seeing all she had was some cheese, crunchy baguettes in need of the garlic she didn't have and a box of Pierre Hermé's macarons that had been in the fridge for a week.

"So much for a welcome spread," she muttered. "Maybe he doesn't eat normal food. What do faeries eat?"

Yet another question to add to her list.

When the doorbell rang, she panicked and checked her hair, then tugged at her skirt. The long, flowy maxi skirt was the same color as the roses out back. And she'd panicked over which shirt to wear to top it off, and had settled for a T-shirt from a Soundgarden concert she'd been to years ago. Not quite her style, but the Goth faery might appreciate it.

She'd met Never before, but for some reason inviting a faery into her home felt momentous. A concession to the reality she had found herself shoved into.

"You're so weird," she muttered as she approached the front door. "Get over it. Your boyfriend is werewolf and faery. It doesn't get more awesome than that."

She opened the door with a big smile and was greeted by a somber, sulking dark faery. Streaks of guy-liner stretched out from the corner of each eye. Coal-black hair was spiked all over his head and had begun a party-in-the-back shag. Dressed all in black and sporting a nose ring, he dangled a pair of bright red swim trunks from his forefinger.

"Let's party," he said, and wandered inside her house.

Indi set a tray of lemonades and macarons on the table by the lounge chair and then settled in. Never toweled off and stretched his lean figure, which was surprisingly muscled. A doggie-style shake sent water flying from his skin and hair in all directions.

"That was awesome," he announced. His guy-liner had washed off and the hair was spiked about his head at awkward angles, until he rubbed the towel over it, making it even more awkward, yet strangely appropriate for his style. "I need to get a place with a pool. Or rather, a girlfriend with a pool. Ry really made out by hooking up with you."

"You don't think Ry can afford his own pool if he wanted one?" she asked as he sat on the edge of the double lounge chaise. She handed him a lemonade, which he tilted back. "Or even ten pools, for that matter."

"He gives all that tainted money away. My brother lives very spare, save for the sports car and that fancy watch. This is good. What's it called?"

"Lemonade. It's a popular human drink," she said, unable to prevent the mocking tone.

"Really? You think I don't know what lemonade is, changeling?"

"Don't say it like that."

"Like what?"

"Like it's an accusation." Indi pulled up her knees and propped her chin on them. "Sorry. I was teasing about the lemonade. You're…different."

"Way to compliment a guy."

"I mean… I've not been around your sort much. I'm not sure how to act."

"My sort? Is that the faery sort? The vampire sort? Or the Goth sort?" He snorted. "You and Ry make the perfect pair. Silver spoons and limousines."

"I don't think Ry was born with a silver spoon."

"Doesn't matter. He's got the bucks now."

"Are you jealous?"

"No. Yes." He shrugged. "I thought we were talking about you."

"We are. All right, here goes. Is being a changeling a bad thing?"

"No. Maybe. I don't know." He settled beside her and stretched out his legs before him. "Depends on who you ask. Doesn't bother me. I pretty much hate everyone until I get to know them. You're cool. If Ry likes you, I like you."

"Despite the silver spoon?"

"You got it."

She met his lemonade glass with a *ting* and they both drank.

"Hand me that plate of cookies," he said.

She did and his movement flicked water across her face. She wiped it away and said, "I've never seen a man enjoy the water so much."

"Maybe I've got a bit of mermaid in me, eh?"

"Ry mentioned mermaids are real and vicious."

"Every myth, fable and legend is real. Including unicorns. And mermaids are assholes, so avoid them."

"You mean they're not like Ariel?"

"Who's that chick?"

She dismissed bringing a fictional character into a conversation she wanted to be real and honest. She sat next to a man who was half faery and half vampire. "Tell me about yourself. The half stuff. You're a faery and you have wings, and…fangs?"

He took a bite of a macaron, then opened his mouth to reveal fangs lowering amongst the pink crumbs. "That I do. And one of the advantages of not completely being vamp is I can eat human food. These cookies rock. They're crunchy but soft. Funky."

"I can't believe you live in Paris and have never tasted a macaron."

"I live all over. But when in Paris I spend most of my time in FaeryTown. Macaron, eh? Nice."

"Do you bite people and drink their blood?"

"I do not." Never leaned against the back of the chair. He set the plate of macarons on his bare abs. The man's skin was pale. Indi suspected a flash of sun might instantly burn him. "Human blood makes me sick. It's the iron in it. It fucks with the faery side of me. Faeries and iron do not mix."

"How so?"

"Meaning, iron can kill us if it's in the proper form and we consume it or it's stabbed into our organs."

"Will it harm me?"

"I don't know. If you're just coming into the whole faery thing, it could be gradual. Or not. Who knows?"

She would like to know for certain. But if he couldn't tell her what she was, she could at least get more information from him.

"Then if you're a vampire don't you need to drink blood? To survive?"

"I drink ichor."

"What's…isn't that like the blood of the gods?"

"Could be. It's what we faeries call our blood. But our blood isn't red like humans'. It's clear and sparkly."

"Really? That's kind of cool. And that's coming from a woman who lives for the sparkle."

He smirked and downed another macaron. "Ichor tastes great. But I don't need it as often as a vamp needs blood. Maybe once a month. And the weird thing? Full-blooded vampires can't drink faery ichor. Or they can, but ichor is addictive to them. It's like a drug. Faery-Town is where dust addicts go to get their fix. But for some reason it doesn't have that effect on me. Which is good, but also so wrong. I'd like to know that high."

"Sounds complicated. And a little twisted."

He delivered her a smirk that told her all she needed to know about how he felt about twisted.

"I thought vampires couldn't go in the sun."

"A myth. Mostly. The sun will burn a vamp, slowly, but it's not an instant thing. I myself love the sun."

"You'd never know."

"I can't tan. Maybe that's a faery thing."

"No worry of skin cancer, then."

"We don't get human diseases."

"That's one less thing to worry about. What about wooden stakes and crosses?"

"A wooden stake through the heart will pretty much kill anyone or thing. But there's a legend of a vamp who got staked and the thing was left in. Slowly, over weeks, the stake worked its way out and he survived. Freaky. And crosses? They can give a vampire a serious life-threatening burn *if* the vamp has been baptized. Me? No sacraments were ever said for me. Bless whatever freakin' god or goddess for that."

"So if I have a vampire chasing me, I should ask if he's been baptized before whipping out the cross?"

"If you have a vampire chasing you I'd suggest running faster, not pausing to chat."

"I suppose so. So that's the vampire side of you. Tell me about faeries. About…me. I mean, I think I'm still human, but I'm not sure. But just in case I'm not, I need to know what to look for, to recognize. Oh. Just tell me what you can, please?"

"You know I'm doing this as a favor to Ry? I don't normally spend my afternoons drinking lemonade with a fancy woman and answering all her probing questions."

"I need this, Never. I'm trying to figure out what I'm becoming. Or have I been this all my life?"

"If you're changeling? You've been that way all your life. Changelings are born in Faery and taken to the mortal realm. As I understand it, the changeling, when left in this realm, becomes like human. But once a faery always a faery. I wonder if Hestia's healing did something to awaken your true self."

"Maybe?"

"Herne knows what the hell kind of herbs that bitch healer used on you. It's a good thing Ry didn't hang around her too long."

"Were they close?"

He shook his head. "Just a quick fuck, as far as I understand. Couple nights, then so long, see ya later. Heh. Sorry."

"I'm a big girl. You can say things to me."

"Yeah, but you're shivering, sweetie. You're not cool with all this, so don't get too big for your britches. How are you adjusting to the wings?"

She reached over her shoulder and stroked the top of one. "They're getting bigger every day. Will I be able to control them? Put them away? I can't live with wings, Never. I couldn't go into a store again. Or an event. I have business meetings I need to attend. Fashion shows to watch. Negotiations with designers to make. I don't see showing up with wings as a positive."

"All faeries have control over their wings. Unless you're a sprite. Those things have wings out all the time. And they are nasty little critters. Mark them on your *stay-away* list, too."

"Sprites and mermaids. Check. Now tell me how to control my wings."

"You should be able to fold them down and put them away so they furl into you. It's hard to explain, but you sort of think them away and then think them back out."

She cast him a doubtful look.

"Want me to show you?"

"Please."

He nabbed another cookie and stood, then checked the sides of the yard. "Any neighbors watching?"

"The neighbor to the right is on vacation for the summer in Austria. The neighbor to the left is an invalid and lives on the lower floor. She can't see over the fence and shrubs."

He lifted an eyebrow.

"I walk around naked out here all the time. There's nothing to worry about."

"Naked. Nice. Did I mention Ry found himself a good one?"

"You did. Now back to the important stuff."

"All right. Prepare—" he splayed out his arms in a showman's pose "—to be dazzled."

With a dramatic stomp of his foot and thrusting back of his shoulders, wings suddenly unfurled at Never's back. They were huge and elegant and...black. They resembled bat's wings to Indi, yet they gleamed with a silver and violet iridescence and were much finer and more delicate than a leathery wing.

"Nice, huh?" He winked at her. "Tell me you're dazzled."

"Very fitting for a vampire faery," she said. "I am dazzled."

"That's faery vamp. My faery nature is most prominent. And unlike Ry, I'm not afraid to admit that."

His wings stretched behind him, then spread wide. Then he curled them forward to hug about his arms and they wrapped across his thighs.

"You've got such control over them. Can you fly?"

"Of course I can fly. What good are wings if you can't take to air?"

The man leaped up and the wings flapped. He soared over the pool and to the back of the yard, then circled and landed back before her. "Never wise to fly in the city. Someone could see. And I don't trust that your little old lady might not spend her days with a spyglass."

"Do you think I can fly?" She stood, reaching back to touch the wing that seemed to shiver. Clasping at the thin fabric, she felt it slide through her fingers like fine silk.

"Maybe. They probably need to grow to full size first. Those are baby wings."

"How big will they get?"

"Big as mine? Bigger? Smaller? Every faery is different. But look. Once you learn to control them—" he folded down his wings so they dusted the tiled deck floor "—you'll be more confident. And you should be able to put them away, too." As he gestured with one arm in display, suddenly his wings curled toward his back.

Indi walked around behind him. His back was bare of wings or any sign he'd had them out. "That's amazing."

"You should be able to fold yours down now and put them away. You just have to concentrate."

"Concentrate on what? You said it was a feeling. That's so vague."

"Maybe think to yourself 'wings down' or 'wings away'? I don't know. I've been doing this all my life. I was born this way. It's like trying to explain how to breathe to someone."

She nodded. "I'll try it. But can you turn into a small faery like the ones I see in my garden?"

"I can. But I don't do it often. Takes a lot of energy. That's another thing you have to feel to do. And you will get control over your dust, if you have any. Faeries put out dust at all levels and amounts. Some put out a lot, others not so much. Like me. I'm stingy with my dust. And that works fine for me."

"What about when you have sex?"

"Ah, so we're getting into the true confessions now?"

"When Ry and I have sex…there is dust."

"Ry *is* half-faery."

"Yes, but he thought it came from me last night. Is that something I'll be able to control?"

"Not when the orgasm is good," Never said with a wink. "Have your wings started reacting to touch?"

"Oh, my god, yes." Indi realized that was an overly enthusiastic answer and pressed her fingers to her lips.

Again, Never winked. "It's only a good thing. That's why I'd never invite you to touch my wings, and vice versa. You should not allow anyone you don't trust or feel intimate with to do the same."

"This is so much to take in." Indi sat heavily on the end of the chaise.

Never joined her and gave her knee a friendly nudge with his. "You've got Ry on your side. And me, I guess. Any friend of Ry's is a friend of mine. Even if me and the half bro aren't best buds. I wish we were closer. I like the guy. He's one of the good ones."

"He is. You're not so bad yourself."

"Don't go letting people hear that. I do have a reputation to protect. Mad, bad and slightly crazy faery vamp. I work for le Grande Sidhe and do some questionable things, let me tell you."

"I don't want to hear about them. I want you to be the guy in the red swim trunks with a greedy penchant for macarons."

He caught his head in his hands and shook it. Then he looked up. "Yeah, I suppose. But don't tell anyone I was wearing red. It would shatter my rep. You have any more questions?"

"Is there any way to confirm that I was brought here when I was an infant? That I'm not really Claire and Gerard DuCharme's real daughter?"

"I don't think you should go down that path. I mean, listen." He took her hand and met her gaze. "Parents are the people who raise you, right? Doesn't matter who gave birth to you or how you ended up in this life. What does matter is who took care of you, who loved you, who caught you when you fell and encouraged you when you wanted to race."

"That's very profound coming from a mad, bad and slightly crazy faery vamp."

"Don't tell anyone, okay?"

"You have a lot of secrets to keep. But deal. Thanks,

Never. I do believe that family is and are the people who care about you. I care about you. So that makes us family."

"Don't get all mushy on me."

"I won't. But you're Ry's family, so I'm going to adopt you as mine as well. I have more macarons in the kitchen if you're interested?"

"Promise you won't tell Ry I like the pink ones?"

"Yet another secret!"

Chapter 18

The next day, Ry called and said he was bringing over something for supper, so when Indi opened the front door she expected to see her tall, handsome lover holding some takeaway bags. Instead, what she saw was a huge burst of red and violet roses. There must be dozens.

"Oh, my gosh." Overwhelmed by the lush colors and fragrance, she stepped back.

The flower spray moved a bit and she heard Ry's voice. "Are you okay? Indi? Can I come in? These are getting heavy."

"Oh, yes, come in! Ry, these are so beautiful. I've never seen so many."

"I bought all the florist had. Didn't want any other woman getting them but you. You like them? They're the colors I see in your wings."

She absently reached for the bottom of one of the wings that she'd had to wear a low-cut sundress for so they didn't rub against her clothes. "Really? I thought they were sort of shimmery clear."

"They are deepening in color. They're pretty." He managed a kiss to her cheek while holding the massive bouquet. "But not as pretty as you."

The gesture was so amazing Indi wanted to hug him and tell him she loved him. But that felt abrupt. And was it true? Did she love him? Not that fast. Maybe?

"You are the best boyfriend a girl could have. I might have a vase big enough to fit these."

"You don't need one. They threw a vase in for free. It's in here, hidden by all the flowers. Let me set them on the coffee table before I drop them."

He set down the bouquet and then ran out to retrieve the food he'd left in the car. Cucumber and dill filled the air as Indi unpacked the food and plated it. She kept looking at the roses. They were more lush than those small ones she had climbing the fence in her garden, and their perfume filled the entire living room and kitchen.

As Ry stood up from searching her fridge for some beer, she lunged into his arms and wrapped her legs about his hips and kissed him. "Thank you, lover. You really know how to make a girl feel special."

He turned her against the fridge and held her there, kissing her deeper and longer. A cold beer pressed against her thigh, but the shiver was sexy cool. When he finished she sighed and let her fingers toy with the ends of his hair, which fell against his chest.

"Let's eat fast, then have sex in the pool."

He raised an eyebrow at that. "Didn't my brother go for a swim yesterday?"

"He did. I don't think I've seen a grown man more excited about swimming. He's a character."

"Did he answer all your questions?"

"Some of them. Others he gave me a lot to think about. I'm going to practice folding down my wings and maybe I can make them disappear."

"Not forever. I do think they are gorgeous. And I'm not saying that to make you feel better."

"Thank you." She kissed him again, then shuffled down from his clutch to sit by the counter. That compliment she would accept without argument. Goddesses were strong like that. It would take a while to accept this big life change, but Ry made it easier. "So, about the sex?"

"I'm in." He sat next to her and popped open a can of beer. "But first…"

He stopped speaking for so long, Indi bent to study his face, bent over the plate, fork lifted high. "Ry?"

"Right. I need to do something when we're done eating. I, uh, checked out your yard the other morning before I left."

"For what?"

"I was thinking about what your mother said. And I guessed that you were probably raised in this house?"

"I was. I told you this property has been in the family a long time. I did a total remodel a few years ago when the place officially became mine."

"I was thinking that if a faery came through with a changeling baby twenty-seven years ago, there had to be a portal or a thin place close by. And after walking around in your yard I found one back near the trees."

"A thin place? Like FaeryTown?"

"Yes. It could be a portal even. It's a very small, concentrated area."

"What does that mean? A portal?"

"It means it's a spot where faeries can enter and leave this realm. And… I can make contact with my father from there. I think it's time I did. Last night four collectors came through from Faery."

"Four?"

"Yes, they are increasing in numbers. And I almost let one get by. It was a close call. I need to end this, Indi. And as much as I don't want to talk to my father, he seems the only option. Someone who might have information."

"Sounds like a good plan to me. So, you just stand in the thin place and call him out?"

"Basically. If I'm correct about that area of your yard, then it should work. I'll run out in a bit. But would you do me a favor and stay inside when I do so?"

"Oh."

"I don't want Malrick getting distracted. And whatever is said is something I need to keep between the two of us."

"Oh, sure. I'm good with that. I have some work on my spreadsheets to do. Though I'm still missing some important data for making a decision on which vibrator the catalog will feature."

He cocked his head her way and grinned that sexy charmer smile.

"Yes, it involves getting a man's assistance."

"Well, I have offered to assist."

"I'll put it on the schedule for tonight?"

He winked. "Let's be crazy and spontaneous about it. Why not? Like maybe later after I've talked to my dad."

"Spontaneous it is. Now, tell me what this is I'm eating."

"That's a falafel. Made with chickpeas."

"It's very good."

"It's even better with cucumber sauce." He handed

her the little plastic sauce container and she gave it a try. "Yeah?"

"Num. Do werewolves have a cultural or traditional meal?"

"Raw meat," he said without a blink. When Ry looked to her, his jaw dropped. "Sorry. It's a wolf thing."

"All righty, then. Promise not to invite me along on any forest-foraging excursions, 'kay?"

"Deal."

Ry strode through the yard close to the area he'd noticed as a thin place. He brushed against it, feeling it tug. Rubbing an arm, he vacillated over what he intended to do. He'd never thought he would ask Malrick for help. And he suspected there would be strings attached.

"Hell. In for the dive, right?"

He stepped forward. The air about him lightened. His heartbeat raced. His fingers clenched and unclenched by his sides as his breathing quickened.

Inhaling a deep breath, he found his calm. The wolf inside him didn't like the Faery air, and he growled as if warning an approaching predator. Shoulders stiffening, he attempted to quell his anxiety.

The last time he'd spoken to Malrick, the man handed him the leaves and told him he was always welcome in Faery.

It could never be his home. It was just the place where his biological father lived. The man was a mere sperm donor. His contribution to Ry's existence had probably taken all of five seconds. Over the years, he'd reasoned it was truly those who raised a man who were his parents, blood or not. His mother had been blood.

And the pack leader, Tomas LeDoux— Ry tried not to go there. It was too painful.

Tomas had turned his head away the day Ry walked away from the pack. He had told him he wished him well and knew he would succeed on his own, but then had merely shaken his hand. Not a fatherly hug. Not that Ry had expected one. Though he missed that final contact now. Something to show him all those years had been real. That Tomas did not regret raising him as his own.

He'd never have the answer to that question. Because much as he did not want to go to Faery, the idea of returning to his pack was even more outrageous. He hadn't been banished, permanently marked as an unwanted, but it felt much the same.

Glancing back to the house, he couldn't see if Indi was peeking out the kitchen window. It wasn't that he didn't want her to see him talking to Malrick, he just didn't want her to get upset. Because if anyone could piss off another with a few words or even an obstinate look, it was the bratty Unseelie king.

Exhaling heavily and shaking his arms loose at his sides, Ry nodded decisively. Tilting his head from side to side, he worked up his courage. And then he blew out a few huffs and planted his boots on the grass.

And quietly, ever so softly, he whispered, "Malrick."

Because it wasn't as if he was overly excited about this plan.

Before he could second-guess his decision, the air shook in waves and the fabric between worlds opened to allow a tall man with black hair and silver eyes to walk through. Dressed in a tailored green suit that sported beading along the sleeve cuffs and hem, and which had been cut to allow his massive silver wings freedom, he bowed his head to Ry.

"My warrior prince has finally called for me. I am honored, Ryland Alastair James LeDoux."

That Malrick knew his full name did not sit well with Ry. But he'd not used it to control him. Yet.

"I have a few questions for you, Malrick. Don't get all excited. I'm not coming for a visit."

The man's upper lip twitched, but he maintained decorum. He wielded a cane that looked fashioned from a dark yet clear crystal, and which was capped by metal that probably wasn't silver but something faery in composition. Many rings hugged his long, graceful fingers, and one glinted fluorescently. At his neck, violet sigils curled up and back into his dark hair.

"You do know what's been going on in FaeryTown every midnight, yes?"

Malrick turned his head to face the wind and it blew his hair to reveal his skeletal bone structure. Some faeries were alien in appearance to Ry, and his father was one of them. His eyes were silver. They didn't exactly glow, rather they glinted like chrome, and it disturbed Ry to look at them. Most faery eyes were violet. Only the eldest's eyes turned silver with age.

With a splay of one beringed hand, Malrick finally said, "Enlighten me."

Ry had a hard time believing the man—a king of the Unseelie—was naive regarding the goings-on, but if that was what he had to do, he'd spell it out.

"Someone is sending collectors to this realm to steal human babies and take them back to Faery."

Malrick shrugged. "It is what is done."

"Not without leaving a changeling in its place. And even then, it's just wrong."

"There is no right or wrong, son. Only perception."

"Don't go New Agey on me. You know about this situation. That is apparent."

"No changelings, eh? That is…a novelty."

Ry narrowed his gaze at the man. He wasn't lying, but he wasn't telling the truth, either. He could feel it as his werewolf growled warningly within him.

"Settle your wolf," Malrick admonished. "I don't like it when your sort sniff at me like I'm a strange being."

"My sort? I thought you favored werewolves."

"I do. You are the strongest and the bravest of all my children. But I don't abide any who would treat me as something they must fear."

"Somehow I think that's exactly what you enjoy. Without others to fear you, what power would you have?"

Malrick's smile was so tiny it barely curled the corner of his mouth. "Why won't you come to Faery and assume the title of Unseelie prince, as you should? I need you there, son. I won't live forever."

Ry scoffed. The sound almost turned to full-out laughter, but he toed the grass and shook off the sudden urge to show his disgust. "You've got many centuries ahead of you, I'm sure. And in Faery years that's a long time."

"What if I told you I was dying?"

"That would be a lie spoken in an attempt to manipulate me."

Malrick tilted his head down. His upper lip flinched. When he looked at Ry, the man's power seemed to creep out and grasp Ry by both shoulders and hold him in an aura of fierce enchantment. He could not look away from Malrick. Didn't want to. He did honor his position as a great king of Faery. Despite his rumored wicked ways.

On the other hand, weren't all faeries wicked? At the very least malicious or mischievous to a fault?

"It is my doing," Malrick announced boldly. "The collectors. The Unseelie have developed a need for human offspring to populate our dying numbers. We are fading, Ryland. You must believe me. There's something wrong with the Unseelie. Perhaps too much inbreeding over the years? I cannot know. Much as it belittles our great race, we require the infusion of human blood into our species to keep it strong."

"You have no right to steal innocent human babies."

"Should I resume the practice of leaving a changeling in its place? Tit for tat? The human families are never the wiser. Although…we've no longer the resources for those nasty changeling beings."

"Changelings aren't—" Ry stopped himself from giving the man too much information. Stuff he didn't need to know about. "Stop sending your collectors. Now. Or I will come after you if that's what it takes to stop it."

Malrick's wings unfurled with a hiss, stretching at least eight feet out on each side of his body and glistening in the sunlight. The high cartilage along the tops of each of the four-sectioned wings gleamed like steel, and perhaps it was solid and adamant with age. The sheer silver fabric reflected the light and made Ry blink.

"Do not threaten your father, boy."

"Your ichor might run in my veins, but my father was the man who raised me, Tomas LeDoux. You will never earn the right to call me son!"

The faery lashed out and gripped Ry by the throat. His fingers seemed to stretch all the way around until his nails clicked together at Ry's nape. The faery king lifted his feet from the ground with ease, yet Ry did not struggle. Let him power-play. He wouldn't condescend to such theatrics.

"You do not want to make an enemy of me, Ryland,"

Malrick said, looking up at him. "I can accept your faulty mortal-realm beliefs about parentage, but know that indeed my ichor runs in your veins, and you will be called to your homeland. Sooner, rather than later."

He set down Ry and his wings swept up to a snapping close behind his back. "Is that all you wanted from me?"

"I want you to stop," Ry insisted. "I can go out every night and slay those mindless idiot collectors forever if I have to. But that will get neither of us where we wish to stand. Can we come to terms on this, Malrick?"

"You're not listening to me, boy. The Unseelies need the infusion of human DNA. And if you had ever the time and interest to visit, as I've requested, you would see how we are failing. Another few winters and we may simply fade away."

"Impossible. The Unseelie lands are vast. Or is it just your kingdom you are focused on?"

The Unseelie king lifted his jaw at that statement. Ry's guess was correct. The man was only concerned for his subjects and closest of servants, surely.

"What do I have to do to make you stop?" Ry asked, knowing what the answer would be, but hoping the man might surprise him.

"Come to me in Faery. Sit on the throne beside me."

As he'd suspected. "Never."

"Ry!"

Turning at the sound of Indi's voice, Ry hissed an oath. Malrick opened his wings wide at her approach and put up his cane to stop her from approaching too closely.

"Who is this one?" Malrick asked.

"I'm sorry, Ry. I had to come out here," Indi said. "I realized your father could be the one who can verify for me what I am."

"What you are?" Malrick sniffed. His upper lip curled. "You mean a nasty changeling?"

Indi's jaw dropped open. She caught her palms against her chest.

Ry stepped toward her, but she took two steps back.

"Is this your woman, Ryland? You would choose a changeling?" Malrick's lips crimped. "She is beneath you. Changelings are dirt. Meant to be cast away for a more valued prize."

"Enough, Malrick. Be gone with you!"

At that powerful entreaty the faery king took a step back. With a *whoosh* of his wings, he swept backward through the portal.

Indi dropped to her knees in the grass, catching her face in her hands. "Is it true?" she asked on a wobbly voice.

"Princess, no." Ry kneeled before her. "I told you Malrick is an asshole. He said that to you because he's mean. It's what he does best."

"But he knew what I was. That confirms things. Am I…less than dirt?"

"That is merely the opinion of a stupid, pompous king speaking from his position of false power. Don't listen to him. You are valuable and beautiful and I care about you, Indi."

"Can you care about me even though you hate the faery part of yourself?"

"I—" He'd never told her that about himself. Had she gleaned as much from him?

"Indi, faeries are…they are a fearsome breed. Strong and powerful. Warriors. You should not be afraid that you are one."

"I'm not afraid. But you are. Why do you try to hide that part of you? Why not talk to your father more? If the only reason you hate him is something your parents did—because none of that was your fault—then you might be missing out on something that could be truly amazing."

He'd never heard it put that way before. Yet it had been his fault. His mother had fled because his father had learned that Ry was not completely werewolf. And then when he hadn't been what Tomas had expected, he'd been kicked out of the pack. If his father had never stumbled on to him that night, he might still be in the pack.

"Ry?"

He pulled Indi into a hug and caught her soft sobs against his shoulder. This had gone over as well as he'd expected. The faery king had confirmed his worst nightmare about the source of his struggles. And he'd given his girlfriend the truth, which was that in Faery she could never be viewed as anything but the lowest of the low. Truly, she had been born to be cast out for something more valuable.

But this was the mortal realm. And he didn't subscribe to Faery beliefs. He only hoped Malrick's words would not sink too deeply into Indi's psyche.

Chapter 19

Indi curled up in a ball on the couch. Ry had walked her inside after Malrick had left, but then had wanted to return to the thin place and speak a few words to cleanse the area. She'd left him to it.

What that awful faery king had said to her. Was it true? Changelings were dirt, the lowest of the low, abandoned here in the mortal realm?

But this was her realm. Her home.

Or was it?

Now she was more confused than ever. And she didn't know how to process it all. And with the overwhelming scent of the roses Ry had given her filling the air, she felt dizzy and not at all on balance with the world.

Closing her eyes, she thought she should be crying about this, but the tears didn't fall. Instead, a heavy emptiness filled her chest. And the crush of her wings against the back of the sofa annoyed her, so she stretched out to lie on her stomach.

"Stupid wings," she muttered. "Stupid changeling. I hate this! I want it to all go away."

But she knew that could never happen. She'd lived her life thus far as something she was not. Only now was she turning into what she really was. And was that a despicable thing?

Despite Ry's comforting words, it was difficult to grasp hope.

"It's starting to rain," Ry announced as he walked into the living room. "Hey, Princess, you going to be okay?"

"No," she answered flatly.

He kneeled before the sofa, their faces inches apart. "You get to pout about this for the rest of the night. It's a lot to take in. Then tomorrow morning you're going to lift your head and accept it. This is you now, Indi. There's no going back."

"I know that. But what about you?"

"What about me?"

"When are you going to accept your faery side?"

He bowed his head. She knew this was something he'd been dealing with for a long time, and she could never relate to being literally kicked out of house and home by a man he'd once believed was his real father. But Ry had told her faeries were fierce and strong. The description fit him to a tee. If he wanted her to believe that she could weather this storm in her life, then he'd better help her by showing her he could do the same.

"You've given me something to think about," he finally said. "You're right. And I don't hate faeries. It's a manipulative father that makes accepting the idea of them difficult."

"I'm sorry your werewolf father wasn't more supportive when you needed him most," she said. "I'm very lucky to have loving parents. Even after they divorced, both have remained key in my life." She slid a hand into his. "Maybe we can do this together?"

"I'd like that," he said.

"But I still get the night to pout?" She jutted out her lower lip.

Which he kissed. "Absolutely. You're going to start practicing folding and putting away your wings tomorrow, too. Promise me?"

She nodded.

"What do you need, Indi?"

"What do you mean?"

"I don't know. Most women like ice cream or chocolate when they're depressed. Kristine goes for the vanilla mochi. I'll get you whatever you need to wallow in."

She had to laugh at that one. What a sweet man. He was trying to make her feel better. And he wasn't doing a terrible job at it. "I do have a tendency to drown my sorrows in fig jam."

"That sounds…weird. You want me to get some?"

"I have ample stores in the kitchen. And it does sound good slathered on some crunchy shortbread. Do you have to leave soon?"

"It's still early." Ry sat on the floor, his back to the sofa, and tapped the rose petals that hung lowest in the bunch.

"Malrick is not a nice man. Faery." Indi toyed with Ry's hair, which spilled down his back. "What did you learn from him? If you want to tell me."

"He's behind sending the collectors to this realm. He gave me some excuse about needing humans to repopulate the dying Unseelie race."

"Are they dying?"

"I don't know. Doubtful. I suspect Malrick is merely populating his inner circle. Of course, he agreed to stop if I move to Faery."

"Oh."

"I'm never going to live in Faery. It is not my home. And he can't force me to do anything."

"But then the collectors won't stop coming. And eventually one or more of them will get past you. Especially if they start arriving in greater numbers."

"I'll figure something out. It's going to be a fight. But I'm up for it." He kissed her forehead. "Those flowers are full of fragrance."

"Yes, they're making me dizzy. I might fix myself some fig snacks and go out to the patio for fresh air. I think I need to be alone tonight, Ry. Is that okay?"

"Of course. But will you call or text me later to update me on how you're feeling?"

She nodded. He was made that way. Kind and caring. A warrior protector to her Princess Pussycat.

"I'll see you tomorrow," she offered. "Maybe I'll stop by again with lunch for you and Kristine. I just need the night to wallow and feel bad about myself."

"Fresh start in the morning. The both of us. Promise?"

"Agreed."

He stood and she tugged at his jeans. "Ry?"

"Yes?"

The words *I love you* sat on the tip of her tongue, but they didn't quite trip out. "Thank you."

"I'll see you tomorrow." He started toward the door. "Don't forget to call before you go to bed!"

He closed the door behind him and Indi sat up, wiping away the tears that had fallen. He was right. She was pouting about something she couldn't change. But she was allowed a good pout. If not, she'd never be able to move beyond.

She headed to the kitchen to prepare her sad-girl supplies and then headed outside to the chaise, where she devoured half a jar of fig jam. And when the sun was completely below the horizon, lightning bugs glinted in the roses climbing the fence.

And Indi had to wonder if any of them were faeries. And if so, were they like her? Or rather, was she like them?

Ry took a hit to his back, right in the kidney. It never ceased to amaze him that the collectors, which appeared as if made of mist and a substance of blackest black, could deliver a physical blow. He swung around, battle sword sweeping the air, but the sudden twist felt as if something punctured inside him. He dropped to his knees, clutching his side. Blood oozed over his fingers. Had one of those bastards managed to stab a talon into him?

He'd slain three collectors—as had Never—and two remained. Malrick was increasing their numbers.

His brother aimed a small, specially designed bow loaded with arrows toward a collector. Direct hit in the heart. The thing spun and yowled silently, clawing the air. When it soared above Never's head, the dark faery thrust up with his other arm, slashing a small sword across the collector's throat, and succeeded in decapitating the nasty thing.

Never turned to pump his fist, yet Ry pointed behind him, and yelled, "That one! He's almost out of FaeryTown!"

Pulling himself up, yet staggering, Ry winced at the incredible pain in his kidney. He might have internal bleeding, but his werewolf nature usually allowed for rapid healing. As Never turned, and with a flap of wings took to flight after the collector, Ry staggered down the cobblestone street. Neither was swift enough to catch the creature before it exited FaeryTown.

When the collector broke through the skein that demarcated FaeryTown from regular Paris, the creature's body glittered like millions of stars and then soared down the street.

"It's going to latch on to the first human it sees," Ry said.

Never landed near him, shoving the sword back in a holster on his thigh. He wielded the crossbow at the ready. "Let's do this!"

Both ran full speed after the thing.

Ahead, a nightclub blasting techno tunes began a long stretch of clubs, theaters and sex shops. The streets teemed with partiers, both residents and tourists. While Ry and Never could see the collector, they knew a human would not see it. And if anyone saw them, running down the street with swords wielded high, the police—who, he noted, were parked a few blocks ahead—would be on them swiftly.

"How we going to do this?" Never asked as he shoved the crossbow at the back of his waistband. He glanced to Ry's side, where he bled, but didn't comment.

Ry sheathed the sword at his back. "We don't have much choice but to follow the thing. It's going for that man in the red shirt. We'll never make it—"

Both Ry and Never stopped as they witnessed, fifty yards ahead of them, the collector insinuate itself into a particularly burly man standing in line, holding a drink and chatting and laughing with a circle of men and women. He suddenly handed his drink to the person next to him, made a gesture like he was going to take a leak, then strode off, down the sidewalk, away from the nightclub. Purposefully.

"Do we grab him?" Never asked.

"I don't know." Ry increased his strides, wincing at the pain in his kidney. "We can't kill the human. We'll have to wait until it leaves the body."

"Then I guess we're going to play follow the leader."

Heartbeats thundering, Ry crossed the street before oncoming traffic, following the human body that was no longer human in thought. The collector controlled it completely, yet the body functioned as a human and couldn't fly or run any faster than a normal man, so this would be an easy follow.

The thing wove through the streets, focused as it headed toward the Seine and the main island. When it paralleled the river and headed east, the destination became obvious to Ry.

"I think he's headed to the Hôtel-Dieu," he said.

"The hospital?"

"Where else to find a baby?"

"How the hell can a creature from Faery manage to steal a baby in a place like that? There's security. Cameras, and maybe even tracking ID technology."

"I'm not sure."

But he was going to find out.

Soaking in the bathtub filled to the steaming surface with bubbles, Indi decided to take what Ry had said to heart. She got to pout about the whole changeling thing for a little longer. The rest of this night. But then she had to pull herself up and move forward. It was what she did. She'd not established a successful business by wallowing over her defeats.

Besides, they were not defeats, but rather challenges.

And her new condition was not something that was going to suddenly change. She. Was. A. Changeling.

The Unseelie king had confirmed that fact.

Now what was she going to do about this challenge?

When life got tough, she put down a couple goblets of champagne, cried about it, then moved on. Just as she had with Todd.

She had moved on. In a very strange way.

If she had never been cut by the collector that night, and Ry had not taken her to be healed, might she still be the same old normal human she'd once been?

"But you've never been human," she reasoned with a blow at a handful of bubbles.

And besides, had she not been healed that night, it sounded as though she would have died. So the result had been to uncover her truth—and live. Which she should be happy about.

And she would get there. As soon as she figured out how to control her wings.

She had to admit, this hot bath made her wings feel great. It was as though they channeled the heat through her system like a luxurious spa treatment. She'd never felt so relaxed.

Grabbing her cell phone from the shelf beside the tub, she texted Ry, thinking he was probably finished with tonight's slayage, but just in case he wasn't, she didn't want to interrupt him while he was busy with a call.

Doing much better. Taking a bath, then heading to bed. See you tomorrow, my sexy werewolf lover.

She set aside the phone and settled deeper into the water and bubbles. Sitting on the edge of the tub was a pink silicone vibrator designed for use in the water. She'd get to that soon.

For a woman who had easily accepted that the man she was dating was werewolf, she should find accepting her wings as easy. She wanted to see Ry in all his werewolf glory. To meet that part of him that he kept from this crazy rat race of a world. She'd love to go to his cabin and watch him dash through the fields and forest in wolf form.

While in that shape, would he know she was his girlfriend? Or would he be more like a wild and feral animal?

He'd said something about being in his animal and human mind at the same time when he was werewolf. And two werewolves could have sex? That was interesting. As well, he'd said something about a werewolf having sex with a human. Even more interesting. Also, squicky.

She wouldn't judge. She did have wings. And that could prove very weird in bed. Sparkles flying every time she came?

She smiled to remember Ry's dick glittering with faery dust. That was not something he'd ever let his male friends know about. But she thought it was spectacular.

Apparently, there were some good things that came with being faery. And from this point forward, she intended to embrace and accept them.

Her phone rang. It was Janet. Indi still wasn't ready to tell her bestie about learning that she was a changeling. But that didn't mean they couldn't discuss Janet's date last night with the drummer from a minor yet known rock band.

Indi connected and said, "Tell me everything."

"Oh, girl!"

Ry and Never followed the collector inhabiting the human's body in through the ER doors at the Hôtel-Dieu, a city hospital located in the shadow of Notre Dame. Ry had not been inside a hospital before. He'd no need because wolves didn't get human ailments, and when they were injured the rapid healing process negated any need for a doctor.

And if the wound was serious? He knew a certain healer in Faery who— Nope, he had to stop considering Hestia as a convenient fix for his problems. He had hurt her. Unknowingly. Best he stayed as far from her as he could. For her emotional healing.

While the wound on his side still pained him, he knew it was healing from within, and he should be top form soon enough. He wore a dark shirt, so the blood wouldn't be noticeable. The faery dust was another issue.

Did anyone notice his subtle sparkle? Wasn't making it any easier for him to embrace that side of himself, that was for sure.

The antiseptic smells in the ER hit him hard. He dialed down his senses, then noticed the strange look Never got from a patient seated on one of the waiting-room chairs.

"We stand out," he muttered.

"You think?" Never ran a hand along his thigh holster. "I give it two minutes before we're forcibly tossed out for the weapons alone. He's going right."

They picked up their pace and followed the man, who, as he neared a nurse walking toward him, paused to ask her a question. He touched her arm, and the nurse's eyes fluttered. She clutched a clipboard to her chest. The man stepped back, leaned against the wall and shook his head in bewilderment. The nurse turned and walked with purpose in the direction from which she had come.

"I think it just switched bodies," Never said.

"Me, too. Don't lose that nurse."

As they passed the man who had initially been standing outside the nightclub, he muttered, "Where am I?" and then he wandered down the hallway.

"He'll be okay."

"If we take out the nurse," Never said, "we kill the human as well."

"We're not going to harm any humans today. Don't let her out of your sight."

The nurse walked through a ward painted soft green and Ry smelled the sweetness of innocence and new life. And anxiety. This was definitely the maternity ward. The nurse walked into a nursery and he and Never stopped in front of it. Behind the glass viewing window were two neat rows of babies in cribs. The nurse walked up to one wrapped in a blue blanket, cradled it in her arms with no emotion, then walked out.

"She can't walk out of the building with a baby in arm."

"I'm not sure," Ry said. "Can humans see her? I don't know."

"They can see the human baby."

"Maybe. The collector might have some enchantment to conceal the infant. We let her get outside, then grab her. You take the baby and I'll take care of the collector," Ry commanded.

"Why do I have to grab the kid? I don't know what to do with a baby."

"I don't know, either," Ry said testily. "Just bring it back inside. Hand it to someone in the ER. But don't drop it."

"You think I'd drop a baby?" Never swore. "Maybe.

I haven't touched one of them before. They look so… delicate. She's heading outside!"

Once the nurse broached the outside, Ry saw that she began to shudder. The collector was leaving her body, forming in black mist all about her, still clutching the baby.

"Now!" Ry ordered.

Never ran up and grabbed the baby from a swirl of black mist. The nurse screamed. And the collector swept toward Ry. It slashed its talons, catching him across the jaw. Bending and twisting at the waist, Ry spun around, dragging his sword through the collector's torso. Its maw opened in the toothy silent yowl and it dissipated.

"What are you doing with that baby?" the nurse cried.

"She's in her body. Give it back to her," Ry said.

Never shoved the infant into the nurse's arms. "It belongs in the maternity ward. You took it out for a walk."

"That's not something I would—"

But Ry and Never did not wait around for an argument. They ran across the street, insinuating themselves into the shadows caressing the buildings, and didn't stop until they reached the river.

"That was close." Never jumped onto the concrete balustrade before the river and sat, legs dangling.

"Yes. But how many will Malrick send tomorrow night?" Ry eased his fingers along the cut healing on his jaw. "We won't be able to hold off the invasion for long. I have to make Malrick stop this."

"You said he wanted you to sit the throne beside him in Faery? You cool with that to save some human babies?"

"No. But what other choice do I have?"

Chapter 20

Ry was on the phone in his office when Indi arrived with lunch for the threesome. When Kristine suggested they head to the nearby park, Ry nodded that he'd follow as soon as he got off the phone.

The Jardin des Plantes was a massive garden that had existed for four centuries. It consisted of many themed gardens devoted to various flowers, insects, a zoo, a gallery of mineralogy and geology, even a labyrinth.

Kristine, marching like an Amazon goddess on her six-inch bright yellow pumps, led Indi to her favorite lunch spot in the garden of bees and birds under the shade of a chestnut tree. She kept a blanket at the office for such adventures. Indi settled next to her and opened her salad.

"Ry has been distracted today," Kristine said after they'd eaten for a few minutes. "He actually growled at me when I asked him how things went last night."

"Really? I haven't had a chance to talk to him since

he left for FaeryTown last night. I hope everything went all right. Has he, uh, told you about…me?"

"Your wings?" Kristine made a show of peering around Indi's back, but she'd put on the blazer again today and figured she'd only get another few days' use out of that before her wings stretched below the hem. "He told me the day after the ball. What's up with that, sweetie? You a faery?"

Kristine leaned against the tree trunk and crossed her legs at the ankles. Her skintight dress matched the shoes, and she accessorized with copper jewelry. Against her dark skin tone, she worked it.

"A faery," Indi said. "Maybe? Probably." She set her lunch on the blanket. Ry trusted Kristine, and even though Indi knew her not at all, she could use some girl talk. She could not talk to Janet about this. "I met Ry's father yesterday. It was not a happy event."

"Really?" Enthralled, Kristine munched a carrot stick while granting her a rapt ear.

"Ry found a thin place in my backyard, which is where he suspects I was brought through when I was a baby. And then his father, Malrick, confirmed it. He said I was a changeling. He also called me nasty and lowest of the low."

"I've heard that sparkly-lipped king is an asshole. I wouldn't take his opinion on anything for gospel. A changeling, eh? That's interesting. That means you get to keep the wings forever?"

"I guess so. Seems whatever that healer did to me she must have awakened my true self. I'm trying to accept it. It's just… Kristine, all my life I've thought I was one thing, and now I suddenly learn I'm not that at all. I'm not sure who or what I am anymore. And Ry can relate, having always thought he was full were-wolf, only to learn about his crazy family background.

Though I think he struggles with his faery side more than he'll let me know."

Kristine tutted and wiped her lips with a napkin. "You paranormal sorts. So mixed up. I think the only one of us who has a firm grasp on who she is, is me. And who would have thought the transgender chick would ever say that?"

Indi laughed. "You do have it all together. Any advice for someone who has had it all pulled apart?"

"Don't look at it that way, sweetie. This is just you, progressing. Moving forward. Hmm…" She tapped her lips in thought. "Look at it like this. You're emerging from a chrysalis the mortal realm wrapped around you when you were brought here as an infant. Now you're spreading your wings."

Indi liked the sound of that. Of a butterfly emerging to spread her wings.

"You've got to grow into those wings and become the faery you were born to be," Kristine said. "You're pretty and smart. Ry tells me you have a million-dollar business that caters to goddesses?"

"It's called Goddess Goodies. It's focused on renting used designer gowns to those who might not be able to afford a dress for prom or an event. We only charge for shipping and cleaning. We make the money to buy those gowns from my accessories line. We also buy vintage gowns, which I and a handful of seamstresses fix up and resell. Those we sell for the big bucks."

"Ooh, I'm all about the dresses and goodies."

"I'm excited about the accessories line. I want it to encompass all the things we women want and need to feel good about ourselves. Like the cat ears I wear. They're one of my best sellers."

"I love those cat ears. I need some leopard-print ones myself."

"I have those. I'll bring you a pair next time I stop by."

"Ooh!" Kristine wiggled the toes of her shoes glee-fully. "Oh, here comes Ry. He's got his pouty face on."

"Ladies." He sat on the blanket and opened the un-touched boxed lunch. "What did I miss?"

"Just girl talk," Indi said. "Things not go well last night?"

He sighed heavily and stabbed his fork into the sau-sage-laden pasta Indi had figured he'd prefer over a girlie salad. The man was a carnivore, after all. "Mal-rick sent eight collectors last night, and Never and I missed one. It escaped into the mortal realm."

Kristine and Indi exchanged wide-eyed looks before they said in unison, "What happened?"

"We followed it to the Hôtel-Dieu and watched it kidnap a baby. The collector can assume the body of any human it touches, and it took over a nurse's body. We stopped it. The baby is safe. I'm not sure Malrick is going to let up, though. He's going to send more and more, and I'm just one man. Even with Never's help, we won't be able to hold them off in numbers for much longer."

"Don't you dare succumb to your daddy's bribes," Kristine said. "We want you here in this realm. It's the only home you've ever known."

"I want that, too, but I'm not sure how to get around it." He stabbed at the pasta. "Can we...not talk about this right now? I've got a headache trying to sort this all out."

"Of course. You want this?" Indi offered him an olive on the end of her fork and he ate it.

"Did you see the invitation that I left on your desk this morning?" Kristine asked.

"Invitation?" Indi searched Ry's face.

He shrugged. "I did. I'm not sure about it."

"Another ball?" Indi asked hopefully.

He smirked at her enthusiasm. "A Midsummer's Eve masked ball. I'm not sure about attending if I'm going to be busy slaying collectors."

"It's an early party," Kristine offered hopefully, with a wink to Indi. "Starts at seven."

"Oh, Ry, can we go, please? You know how much I love a fancy party."

"I do know that."

"And costumes!" Indi cooed. "You know, I do have a nice set of wings I could wear."

He lifted an eyebrow and exchanged a look with Kristine. "Why don't the two of you go?"

"Why not all three of us?" Kristine offered. "I'd love to arrive on the arm of a handsome man. But I can share." She fluttered her lashes at Indi. "You okay with that?"

"Of course! Oh, please, Ry? Taking two women to a costume ball? We don't have to stay long. And you can ditch out early to fight the big bads while Kristine and I close the place down."

"Now you're talking." Kristine met Indi with a fist bump.

Ry shook his head and laughed. "I know when I'm outnumbered. Fine. But it's not for another week or more."

Indi clapped and squealed. "That'll give me time to put together a costume. What are you going to go as, Kristine?"

"Probably something feral, like my heart." She curled her claws at them and purred. "A sexy wildcat."

And Ry laughed, though Indi sensed he wasn't completely on board with the idea. He was worried about

saving the world. Or at the very least, a bunch of innocent babies. The man was honorable.

And she was falling in love with him.

Ry took the rest of the day off. It was near quitting
time by the time they finished lunch. He wasn't about
to drop off Indi at home, either. She breezed into his
apartment, wings shimmering at her back. When she
turned and fluttered her lashes at him, he quirked his
gaze at her.

"I brought something along we might like to play
with." From her purse she pulled out a hot pink vibrator.

Ry took the intriguing object, clicked it on to a
steady rhythm, then waggled his eyebrows. "Let the
games begin."

With a giggle, Indi turned and raced toward his bedroom, sundress dropping in her wake. She jumped onto
the bed and crooked a finger at him. She was in a good
mood. And with a humming vibrator in hand, he was
the man to oblige her anything she wished.

"You know how to operate one of those things?"
she asked as she dropped to her knees. Her pale skin
lured him closer and the glint of the sun in her wings
appealed.

"Can't say I've used one before." He held it up before him, going cross-eyed to look at it. "But I'm willing to learn."

"Then shut it off for now. First, we warm up."

"Oh, I'm warm, Princess."

She unbuttoned his dress shirt and shoved it down
his biceps. Ry cast aside the vibrator to the pillow and
dropped his trousers. The grip of her fingers about his
erection made him hiss.

"You're more than warm," she cooed.

He slipped his fingers between her legs, where she

was as hot as he was. "I don't think a warm-up round is going to be necessary."

"Probably not." He bowed to suck her nipple in between his tight lips, and her wanting moan dripped with need. "Oh, mercy, you make me go from zero to ten like that."

"I think I saw the controls on this thing only go to three." He leaned aside to grab the vibrator, without leaving her breast—he did have talent—and blindly clicked it on. He teased it over her wet nipple. "Is this where you like it?"

Her gasp was accompanied by a rotating maybe-yes-maybe-no head shake.

"You're going to have to speak up," he said, moving the vibrator about the tightly ruched nipple. "Or I'll figure this thing out on my own."

"Oh, yes, please. You…do that."

She clutched his shoulders. The scent of her arousal wilded him. Ry wanted nothing more than to push her back onto the pillows and bury his face between her legs to sup at her heat. But her sudden inability to speak a full sentence intrigued him.

"That's…" She bowed her head over his as he licked at her other breast. "Wow. Uh-huh."

"Did your spreadsheet cover this kind of usage?" he asked, looking up to catch her open mouth and closed eyes. So beautiful. And completely at his command right now.

She shook her head and sucked in her lower lip.

"Hmm, this one is getting all the attention." He laved his tongue over her nipple, then placed the humming pink vibrator over the wet bud. And Indi groaned deeply.

He kissed her there at her throat, where her pleasure found voice. And when he leaned in close, his chest connected with the little vibrator and it played over his nipple. He jumped, and then…leaned in closer. Whew! That *was* interesting.

Indi managed to find her senses and she kissed his neck, then under his jaw, where he kept his beard trimmed close. "Lower," she whispered. "Please."

He trailed the vibrator down her abdomen and as he did she leaned back and sat, opening her legs for him. Displaying herself like a lush goddess.

"Not inside," she said quickly. "I don't like that. Just…everywhere else!" Her last syllable ended on a high note as Ry touched the vibe at her clit.

Nestling his face between her breasts, he licked and kissed and suckled at her while playing the vibrator all over and along her delicious edges and folds and rises and swells. She moved so lusciously beneath him, undulating and moaning. The wings swept the sheets, fluttering rapidly at the tips. He was so hard, and could come—but he needed to watch her, to hold her as she shook in his arms. To own her.

He noticed she liked it when he let the nicely weighted vibe rest outside her swells for a while, and it seemed to get her off even more. Her body began to pulse. He heard her heartbeats quicken. Her fingers clenched and unclenched at the sheets. And…then she gave herself to him.

Powerfully. Unabashedly. Sweetly. And with a cry of utter pleasure that invited him to finally let go as well. As he clutched at Indi's arm and buried his nose against her neck, his body tremored. The bedsheets were dusted.

And his heart surrendered.

Indi rolled over on the bed to face Ry's back. It was broad and suntanned and his ab muscles curled around his torso. Like a sculpture. She stroked his skin, devouring the warmth radiating from him.

At the center of his back, she traced where she decided wings would sprout were his faery side more prominent. Her own wings were folded down against the mattress, a skill she was proud of. Now to master putting them away so they wouldn't hamper her everyday routine. Like shopping. Going out and about. And sex.

Ry had mastered the use of a vibrator like a pro. Whew! That model was going on the website for sure. And she noticed sparkle on the sheets and Ry's skin. Not like a nightclub glitter disaster. Just a glint here and there. Imagine how much money she'd save on glitter now.

That was a bright side to suddenly learning one was a faery, yes?

There were plenty of bright sides. And she had to start moving toward them instead of always going with the negativity. Because, yes, there was the sex. And she might be able to fly someday. That could be cool. If she was out in the country with no one around to witness such an odd thing as a grown woman flying. If Ry shifted to wolf shape and she flew, they could race through a forest together. That was a weird yet intriguing goal to set. But why not?

Ry stirred and rolled to face her with eyes closed but a smile on his face. She slid a palm up his abs and leaned in to kiss his chest. "You get in late last night?"

He yawned mightily. "There were so many of them."

"Did you get them all?"

"Thanks to Never's help, yes. Hell, this has got to stop. I'm going to take a shower and brush my teeth before I kiss you." He rolled over and sat up. His hair spilled down his back and Indi just managed to brush her fingertips over the tops of his buttocks before he stood and wandered into the bathroom.

He was outnumbered, fighting the collectors. And it was his father's doing. The mean old faery king. Indi wished there was something she could do to help. Could she wield a sword and stand beside him every midnight? She might have to give it a try because the man could not fend off the denizens without a crew of his own.

She rolled to her back and shook her head. Weeks ago she would never have had thoughts about faeries and denizens of evil come to steal human children before getting slain by a heroic werewolf whose half brother faery vampire stood by his side.

What a wild ride her life had become.

And…it was a ride she wanted to stay on. So she'd grip the reins and see where it took her.

Ry wandered back to the bedside. He was naked, and he smelled like toothpaste.

"God, that's so big," Indi said, eyeing his hard-on.

He rocked his hips, setting the sizable attribute to a swing.

"Really?" she said. "Do that again."

He obliged her by pumping his hips again. "It's what I've got to offer. But, uh…maybe you prefer that?" He nodded toward the vibrator sitting on the nightstand.

"You're skilled with it, but I do prefer how you operate your own equipment to an auxiliary device any day."

"I am familiar with its operation." He waggled his hips, setting his erection to a bounce.

"I want to gain more experience operating that tool." She patted the bed. "Come here, wolf."

Chapter 21

Ry parked in front of Indi's place and walked her up to the door. He had intended to slip into the office this afternoon, but when she took his hand and led him inside, he abandoned that plan without another thought.

The woman dropped his hand and wandered ahead of him, dropping her dress in her wake. She never wore a bra or panties, and her heart-shaped derriere wiggled as she strode toward the patio doors. With a glance over her shoulder at him, and a wink, she went outside.

Pulling off his shirt, he tossed it on top of Indi's dress as he stepped outside. He unzipped and shuffled down his jeans. She hadn't jumped in the pool. Where was she? Kicking off his pants, he wandered out naked, searching the yard. When a woman whistled from behind him, he spun to find Indi sitting on the lounge chair, one hand between her legs, and a coy smile inviting him closer.

* * *

"If you wanted to go to Faery," Indi said as she stretched out her bare limbs on the lounge chair, her hair falling across Ry's thigh, "could you go from my yard? Through that thin place?"

"Yes. But I'll never go there. I have no desire to be a prince."

"Sounds like a good time to me."

"Not if I have to sit on a throne next to Malrick."

"You think he actually has a throne?"

"I know he does. Never has visited. He told me about the palace and the throne and the servants. Many servants. And his courtesans."

"Sounds so eighteenth century."

"Fashion-wise and social norms-wise, Faery is a weird mix of human centuries. You know they say that time is happening all at once? And if there's a good example of that, it's Faery."

"I'd love to see it someday. Just for a visit."

He stroked her hair. They lay on the chaise longue naked after some exhilarating sex and a quick dip in the pool. Indi tilted her head to check his expression but couldn't read his face, for he stared off across the backyard.

"I fear if I go," he finally said, "there will be no return. This mortal realm means too much to me. I have friends and family here. And even if my never going to Faery means Malrick stays pissed and continues to send the collectors through? I'll fight those bastards forever if I have to."

"I want to help. You know, I took a fencing class when I was in high school. I was actually good at it."

"Is that so? You think you could wield a broadsword against the collectors?"

"I'll give anything a try."

"My sword is out in the car. You want a lesson?"

"Yes!" She flipped over on the chaise and propped her chin on his thigh.

"But not naked." He kissed her forehead. "You don't want to damage any of these pretty parts I love so much."

"I'll get dressed."

"I'll run and get my sword."

Indi had changed into a slim-fit sundress, and Ry had protested her choice of attire. Didn't she have a pair of jeans or leggings? When she insisted that her standard wear was a dress, and if she was ever going to be enlisted to fight with a sword she would likely be wearing one, he acquiesced.

The broadsword he showed her was long and heavy, and the blade was slightly curved and featured some pretty etching.

"It's enchanted to kill sidhe," Ry explained as he held it before her to inspect.

Indi ran her fingers along the smooth, cold blade. "But doesn't that include you? And me?"

"It's also focused to the wielder's intent. I couldn't harm myself with it if I tried."

"But someone else could?"

"No one is going to lay their hands on this."

"Except me?" she asked with hope.

He winked. "Except you."

Initially, he showed her some correct grips, and helped her to balance the heavy sword, but it only took her a few minutes to get a feel for the weapon and now Indi swung it through the air with expertise. At least, she was going to claim expertise. She'd hacked off a section of the rose shrub, but had told Ry that was on purpose, though she suspected he knew the truth.

"All I have to do with the collectors is thrust and drag, right?" She performed the move in front of her while Ry stood back a good fifteen feet.

"You need to stab them in the chest, where I think they have a heart. Not positive on that one, but seems to be the sweet spot. Either that, or decapitate them."

She swung the sword over her head, both hands to the hilt, and slashed an imaginary head off a wicked sparkling villain. "Gotcha!"

"You do have some skill, Princess Pussycat."

"I have my secret talents. This sword is heavy, though. You got anything lighter?"

"I've a few weapons at home. I have an épée that would be perfect for you. The blade is three-sided. An excellent but light weapon. I'll bring it over next time I stop by and you can give it some more practice. How's that?"

She performed a giddy jump, then handed the sword over to him.

"I have never seen someone so thrilled at the promise of a weapon." Ry sheathed the weapon in the thin leather holder. "You never cease to surprise me."

"I wouldn't want you to become bored by me." She spun and when her twirl took her into a strange-feeling area of the yard, she suddenly stopped and put out her hands as if to balance. "What's that? Is this the thin place? Ry, I can feel it."

"Yeah?"

"It's…lighter? And…" She shook her shoulders and her wings trembled. "I feel like I could fly."

"Can you?"

"No. I tried this morning. I try every morning."

"I think they've still a bit of growing to do."

She sulked. "I have to learn how to put them away. I need a shopping fix. And I cannot march into Hermés with these things sweeping the security guards as I make my entrance."

"Did Never give you the lowdown on how to do that?"

"He said it was just a feeling."

Ry swept her into his embrace with one arm across her back. His fingers traced the bottom of one of her wings. "Like this feeling?"

The sensual strokes arched Indi's body forward against his. "That is so good. Never said I shouldn't let anyone touch my wings."

"No one?"

"Not unless I want to have sex with him."

"Then I hope I'm the only one you'll ever let touch these pretty wings." He kissed her. "If you want to visit Faery someday I'll…see what I can do about that."

"Really?" She bounced in his embrace. "As long as I could return here. I wouldn't want to stay. I'm like you. I have a home and family here."

"Do you wonder about your family in Faery?"

"I have a little. Did my mother have me merely to send me off to another realm? That sounds callous. But maybe she needed to? Did she get paid for it? She might have needed the money. That's all I've thought about it. Not sure I'd ever want to meet her. I mean, my human parents are my parents. No matter what."

He kissed her. "You've accepted this, haven't you?"

She nodded. "Mostly. I'm moving forward. And it's my new reality, so I'm starting to put my arms about it. I wish you could accept your—"

He kissed her again. "It's getting late. I should get a move on. I have to run by the office before heading to FaeryTown. See you later?"

"Of course."

* * *

Days later, Indi put a pair of leopard-print cat ears in a gift bag, along with the Girl Power enamel pin, which was a Goddess Goodies bestseller. She'd give it to Kristine next time she saw her.

Ry had left an hour ago for another meeting. He was not looking forward to it because the man was a celebrity and he expected cameras to be flashing. But the celebrity was also half-vampire, so he knew the drill. He owned a charity devoted to blood diseases that Ry wanted to contribute to.

Now she stood before the dressmaker's dummy, which she'd been using to work on her costume for the masked ball. She'd started with a vintage McQueen chiffon gown in violet and soft rose and had shredded the four-level hem. It now looked like something Tinkerbell would wear to a summer faery bash. Rhinestones and moiré ribbon added the perfect touch here and there.

"And I have just the pair of wings that'll go with it."

She folded down her wings and then took great delight in stretching them out wide. She'd become talented at the tuck and fold, yet the complete putting away of wings was still out of her grasp.

"Not something I need to worry about for the ball. But I may never get invited to another brunch again if I insist on sporting wings and claiming them a new accessory for my business."

She touched the delicate chain around her neck where the tiny silver paw hung. She was the werewolf's girlfriend. The billionaire werewolf prince's girlfriend.

Ry's riches didn't matter to her. She was a self-supporting woman. She didn't need a man to take care of her financially. Never did she want to rely on a man for that. She invested wisely and had started a nest egg from her trust fund.

What she really wanted from a man was closeness and companionship. Trust and honesty. And toe-curling sex. Which she got in spades from Ry. He was the perfect man. And even his faults—always having to leave for midnight slayings, unsure about his faery side, camera-shy—were lovable enough to overlook.

So why did she feel a weird twinge of anxiety that this was all too good to be true? As if she was standing on the outside looking in at a world of creatures she might never be a part of. How to truly belong?

"I need him to embrace his faery side," she said, thinking out loud. "Maybe?"

Leaving the dress, she decided to head out and bask in the setting sunlight in the garden. Plucking her gardening gloves from the drawer at the end of the kitchen counter, she also grabbed the small pruning shears and headed out the patio doors to check on the roses. The spent blooms needed deadheading.

Surrounded by lush perfume and the golden glow of the setting sunlight, she got lost in the mindless task of snipping and dropping the flower heads to the dirt bed to compost. Fat, furry bees hummed about the flowers, and an emerald dragonfly flitted by, its wings glinting.

Indi felt the sun on her wings move through her body in a warm rush. They were a part of her. Maybe being a member of the faery race simply required her to say *yes*?

"Yes," she said with resolution.

When something much larger than a dragonfly but smaller than a bird fluttered close, Indi didn't make a sudden move. She focused on beheading another dead blossom while aware the tiny faery landed on her shoulder and stood there, perhaps observing her work.

"Hey, friend," she said quietly. She supposed such a small creature might feel as though she was blasting its ears if she spoke in a normal voice. "Suppose you noticed those fancy wings on my back, eh? No wonder I've always been able to see you. I just wish I could learn to put them away."

The faery on her shoulder alighted and hovered to a stop above a thick rose bloom. The tiny thing was shaped as a human, with a diaphanous petal dress she must have fashioned from these very roses. Her pink hair stuck out straight from her head like a spent dandelion bloom, and she fisted her tiny hands at her hips and made a face, as if concentrating. Of a sudden her wings furled and disappeared, dropping her to land, legs straddling the rose bloom. She looked to Indi and spread her arms as if to say "See? I can do it."

"You can understand me?"

The faery nodded.

"Oh, I wish I could hear you speak. Then you could teach me how to do that."

The faery tapped her temple and furrowed her brow.

"I know. It takes concentration. A feeling. Easier said than done."

Standing, the faery unfurled her wings and buzzed up and around Indi's head. With a wave, she fluttered off, leaving a faint trail of faery dust glistening in her wake.

"That was cool," Indi whispered. That they were communicating with her meant they must realize she had changed and was one of them. The acceptance felt immense.

Closing her eyes and dropping her hands to her sides, Indi curled her gloved fingers about the cutting shears as she focused her thoughts toward where her wings met her back. Imagining them and the blood, or was it ichor, that flowed through them, she folded them down with ease. And then she unfolded them but tried to pull them in. And…of a sudden they did just that.

Indi sucked in a gasp as she felt as if the wings entered her back and became a part of her. "I did it?"

She reached over a shoulder and couldn't feel any part of her wing. "I did it!"

Jumping and pumping the air with a fist, she performed a hip shimmy. And in her excitement, her concentration faltered. With a sudden tug and a whoosh, her wings unfurled to full glory.

But she had managed it for a few seconds.

"I am so good."

Turning to twist into another victory dance, Indi stopped abruptly at sight of the silver-eyed faery staring snidely at her from five feet away. Dressed in purple velvet with a silver lace cravat, he shook his head and sniffed.

"Changeling," Malrick said. "You disgust me."

Chapter 22

Indi sucked in a breath and stepped backward. A rose thorn scraped her elbow and she flinched. Folding down her wings, she felt the action as a tremble that shivered through her body, and the feeling did not relent.

"Why are you here?" She'd had to muster the courage to ask the question to the imperious faery standing before her. "Ry's not here. He doesn't want to speak to you anyway."

"You have not the right to speak for my son. Do not besmirch his integrity by attempting to do so."

She puffed up her chest and lifted her chin. The man was intimidating, but she wasn't about to shrink before him. "What do you want? If I disgust you so much I can't imagine why you would waste your time standing in my air."

"It is a rather interesting air." Malrick stretched out an arm to the side, palm curled over the cap of his cane, which regally displayed his physique. Even beneath the hippie velvet, he was long and built, most likely a force that could bring a strong man to his knees. "The enchantments in this little yard are many. Curious."

Indi looked about. Sure, the roses grew rampant and she rarely found a weed to pull. And there were the faeries. But enchanted?

"I wonder over your parentage," Malrick said. His silver eyes were hard to look at. They were metallic and reflective. "Most changelings are born to their fate." He narrowed his black eyebrows and tilted his head as he took her in with a sniff of disdain. "There's something more to you."

"You mean I may not be the disgusting changeling you claim me to be?" Was there hope that the wings were temporary?

"Oh, you're a changeling, no doubt."

Indi's shoulders dropped.

"But what I wonder is this—were you born to be brought to this realm or were you taken away from one who would have preferred you remain in Faery?"

"I don't understand."

Malrick sighed, and in two seconds he stood but a foot before her, looking down into her eyes. He hadn't moved his legs, but had rather flown toward her. Indi inhaled his sweet perfume. Citrus, vanilla, pepper, a softer hint of something unnamable. He was…alluring. Like a creature of myth that one might only dream to see. To possibly touch.

His eyes darted over her shoulder, taking in her wings. "They have a distinct color to them," he said. "The violet on the upper wings and ruby on the lower. Much like…well, hmm…"

"Tell me what you're not telling me."

"No." He stepped back and with a flick of his wrist

the cane slid up his grasp until he held it by the black crystal center. He turned it to shove the silver head against her chest. "You are not fit to be my son's menial maid, let alone his consort. And I will not allow this silly romance to continue."

Indi shoved away the cane. "You don't have a right to tell me what to do. Or to decide what is right for Ry. He's a big boy. And he seems to have done quite well for himself in life."

"With my donation."

She'd forgotten about the gift from Malrick that Ry was constantly trying to give away. But she had no intention of rocking the boat. She had no idea of what this man—a faery king—was capable.

"Ry gets to choose whom he dates. Right now? That's me. You don't like it? It's not as if you've ever given your son any of your time, or showed him that you care. Go back to Faery."

"Strong words, which you cannot stand behind, foolish changeling. In this instance, it is you who must be the one to step away and allow my son to resume his life in the manner which it was proceeding before he met you."

She crossed her arms and defied him with a stare. Janet called it her don't-fuck-with-me look. A girl had to hone that talent to survive in the business world. She could stand up for her words, but she sensed the minute trembles in her wings would give her away, so she quickly folded them back and away.

"My son fights valiantly to rescue human babies," Malrick said.

"Because of you! You are the one sending the collectors to steal the babies. You can stop it. Why don't you?"

"I am sure Ryland has told you my reasons."

"To repopulate your kind?" Indi shook her head. "Pitiful. Don't you have enough babies by now?"

"Indeed." Malrick again shoved the cane head against her chest and she gripped it but could not push it away. "I offer you a bargain."

"Which is?"

"I will stop sending my collectors through Faery-Town. You need only do one simple thing."

"And what is that?"

"Walk away from my son. Break his heart. End the relationship."

"But I—"

Malrick lifted a beringed finger before her. "It's entirely up to you, Indigo Paisley DuCharme. Make sure my son never wants to see you again. The moment that occurs, I will cease to send in my collectors."

He pulled the cane from her grasp, and it seared her skin as it slipped away. Indi hissed and clutched her hand against her heart as the faery king turned and strolled away, alongside the pool, and back toward the thin place. When he appeared to walk through the sky and disappear, Indi finally let out a gasp of pain.

She looked at the cut on her palm, which sparkled with faery dust and…her red blood had lightened. It was becoming ichor. As she watched, it healed. A shiver of relief softened her wings and they fluttered forward around her arms as if to provide the hug she desperately needed.

"Break up with Ry?" she muttered. "To save the babies."

Her heart thudded double-time. Indi fell to her knees, there before the roses. Tears spattered her cheeks, and she realized just how much she loved Ryland James.

* * *

Ry returned home after a long day at the office spent confirming many donations. When his doorbell rang and Indi's voice asked to be let in, he couldn't get to the door fast enough to buzz her up. When she reached his floor he rushed out to embrace her and lift her into his arms. Her legs wrapped about his hips and she met his kiss with as much passion and hunger as he felt.

"I miss you when more than a day passes that I see you," he confessed. And it didn't feel weird to admit that neediness. The woman had gotten into his veins and he didn't mind that at all. "Want me to take you out and wine and dine you?"

"No, I want you to pull off all my clothes and have sex with me."

"The second option sounds much more appealing."

He closed the front door and didn't set her down. As he veered toward the bedroom, Indi pulled off her top. And as Ry held her there before the bed, he realized something.

"Where are your wings?"

She beamed and kissed him quickly. "I mastered the art of putting them away. It really is a sort of feeling, like Never explained to me. And I can keep them that way. At least for a few hours. Pretty cool, huh?"

"That's awesome. But I do love your wings. They are like your hair or your eyes and your soft lips. They fit you. And they look right on you."

"You're a sweetie." She curled her fingers over his shoulder and he felt her nails dig in. "Let's see if I can bring out your wild. I'm horny, wolf. And your hard pecs against my tits feel so freakin' good."

Ry laid her on the bed. She spread out her arms, closing her eyes and tilting forward a hip. She seemed to revel in her newfound ability to put away her wings. It had to be an accomplishment that bolstered her confidence. And it was evident as she arched her back, lifting her breasts in an irresistible tease.

He kissed one luscious breast and laved his tongue over the rigid nipple. He loved teasing them about in his mouth, toying and playing with them. Sucking them as if she could feed him life and brightness and love.

Love? Where was his mind heading? It wasn't love. Not so fast. Maybe?

Ry leaned over and sucked in her other nipple, while tweaking the wet one he'd left behind. She squirmed and rocked her hips beneath him. His erection strained for escape and she pushed up his shirt to under his pits. Pausing from the delicious feast of her breasts, he pulled off the shirt and tossed it aside.

Meanwhile, Indi unzipped her miniskirt and shuffled it down to reveal she wore no panties beneath.

"Either you dressed fast today," he muttered as he shoved down his jeans and boxers, "or you planned ahead."

"I'll never tell," she said with a wink and a grab for his cock. "Oh, yeah, bring that big boy back down to me. It's so hot and hard. And it's all mine."

Being claimed had never felt so awesome. Ry leaned over Indi and she took control of him with a masterful clutch about his cock. She was in a hurry as her actions lured him between her legs. Using him as a sort of paintbrush, she rubbed the head of his erection against her folds. Mmm, so hot and already wet. He groaned and pushed harder, showing her his impatience to get inside her.

Yet she kept him firmly in hand and slicked him up and down over her clit. So he let her play, knowing she was feeding her desires. Bowing to her chest, he kissed her throat, then nipped his way down to tease each of her nipples. If he bit a little too firmly she squeezed his cock, which he didn't take as a warning but rather a reaction to the intensity of what she was feeling.

She had wanted to see his wild.

Sunlight threatened to spoil a good sleep, but Indi resolved to surrender to the day. She spread her arms across the sheets, hearing the shower shut off in the other room. Ry was an early riser. Of course, the man was a philanthropist who took pride in his work. She was thankful that her job could be done from her home or anywhere she could get Wi-Fi.

She rolled to her stomach and closed her eyes. Last night after he'd returned from slaying the collectors, she'd heard him muttering how they were still increasing in numbers. It was getting harder to stop them. He needed help. He needed to do something to make it stop.

And she could do that for him.

Malrick's bargain had not been forgotten. She'd come here last night with intent.

"Hey, Princess." Ry breezed into the bedroom, buttoning up a pale green dress shirt, then found his shoes and stepped into them. "I'm late. Have an early meeting today with a client, so I gotta run." He bent and kissed the crown of her head. "Text me later, okay?"

She nodded as he was leaving the bedroom. A lump formed in her throat, but she forced herself to call after him, "Goodbye, Ry!"

"'Bye, Princess!"

She heard the front door open and close.

And Indi sat up on the bed and began to bawl. That had been their last goodbye.

Chapter 23

Ry swung by the flower shop on his way home from work, but they had already closed.

No flowers? He tugged out his phone and texted Indi. Done with work. Want to go out for Italian?

It took her a minute to reply: Sorry. Not home. Business issues. Will be busy...all night. Rain check.

"Rain check," he muttered.

He texted back. I can wait for you in your bed?

He reached the Alfa and slid inside. Three or four minutes passed and still no reply from Indi.

"She must be really busy. All right. This wolf can deal."

He'd pick up something on the way home and make it bachelor's night. Time to give a good think to how he was going to resolve the collector issue. Last night, he and Never had let another slip through to the mortal realm. If they ever let more than one slip, they'd not be able to track them both, and thus rescue the baby before the collector could bring it back to Faery. It was a two-man job.

Was it time to consider Malrick's plea that Ry abandon his only home to live in Faery? He was no prince. And even if Malrick's days were numbered, Ry had no desire to become king of a bunch of faeries. He didn't do king. He didn't want to do it. He just…did not.

His phone rang and he answered. "Kristine. What did I forget?"

"Your briefcase with the file you were supposed to read tonight and fax back before you come in to work tomorrow morning. I've scanned the file and will email it to you."

"What would I do without you?"

"You'd be living in that sweet castle, making babies with your faery princess and not having a care about all this real-world stuff."

"Someone's gotta give that money away, Kristine. It's not going to happen by itself."

"I have a pretty good handle on it, Ry."

She did. Ry knew his foundation would do just fine if he left it in her capable hands a day or two.

"Take a vacation, why don't you?" she suggested. "Why not after the ball this weekend you head up to the cabin? It is the full moon that night."

"It is? Shit." He hadn't realized it was coming up so quickly. This past month had been a whirlwind. He couldn't go to a ball on that night. Could he?

"I figured you forgot, otherwise you never would have agreed to take us out that night."

"I'll have to make it an early evening."

"Bring Indi along with you to the cabin, *mon cher.* I mean it."

"Maybe."

It would present a good time for him to show her

his true colors. Make that fur. But there were also the collectors to worry about. Damn it. The night of the masked ball was going to be a challenge.

"You two have plans this evening?"

"Indi is…busy. Just me and a frozen dinner from Picard."

"I could pick up some sushi and head over to your place with the documents that you need to sign."

"Sounds like a plan. Thanks, Kristine. See you in a bit."

He hung up and veered toward his place. Full moon this weekend? And still the collectors to deal with. Could he get a break?

On Thursday morning Indi stood before the dressmaker's dummy staring at the costume that she would never wear. Pastel chiffon hung like the softest feathers in dagged tiers to form a long and flowing skirt. The ivory-beaded bodice was strapless and laced up in the back to the point where her wings could comfortably rest on top. Overall, tiny rhinestones—which she had added—glittered on the skirt. And she'd imbued her own dust—possible with a shake of her wings—into the chiffon to make the entire creation shimmer.

It was so pretty. She hated to take it apart.

"I could sell it. Never sold costumes before. Could be a test and trial. Maybe."

Though it was certainly a beautiful dress that could be worn as a noncostume. She stroked her fingers over the skirt. Ry would have loved to see her in this. And while she didn't know what his plans were for a costume, it didn't matter now. He could be a wolf, a superhero, or even a regular guy and he'd win her heart.

A heart that was cracking open wider and wider.

She'd lied to him last night in the text about being

busy with work. And what would she say to him today when he texted or called?

"You have to do this before Saturday," she said. "Rip off the Band-Aid. Just do it so the man can be free of the responsibility of trying to save so many."

With a nod, and a wince, she decided. Despite every inch of her body screaming against it, she would officially break it off with Ryland. But she didn't want to do it face-to-face. How could she? Yet the thought of being so unfeeling only reminded her of how cruel Todd had been to her. She wasn't that person.

"You have to be."

Because if she saw Ry again she wouldn't be able to go through with it. She'd wrap her arms and legs about him and kiss him and forget there were more important things in this world than her happiness.

Wings falling to hang behind her, Indi could but shake her head. Yeah, it was like that.

When her cell phone rang she grabbed it, but then stared at the screen. It was him.

"I can't do this."

Another ring vibrated the phone in her hand.

"I have to do this."

One more ring and it would forward to messages... Indi clicked on. "Hey, Ry."

"Indi. Princess. How'd work go last night? I missed you. Me and Kristine ate Indian food and watched reruns of *Game of Thrones*."

"You and Kristine are awesome together."

"She's my sis. So when can I come over? After work? I want to take you to a new place in the seventh. It opened last month. Supposed to be organic, fresh from the farm to table kind of food."

"Ry, I..."

"Please don't tell me you're busy again. I will come

over there and physically pull you away from your work if I have to."

"Ry, stop."

"Uh...okay. What's up, Indi?"

Her fingers dug into the back of the sofa, and her heart dropped to her gut. The subtle shivers she'd experienced when facing down Malrick returned and her wings trembled against the backs of her thighs. It was all she could do to speak clearly and not burst out into tears.

"Ry, it's over. You and me? It's not going to work."

"What the—"

"Just listen. I'm so sorry. You are the nicest man. Truly, an amazing person. But I'm not right for you. You've got things to concentrate on, like protecting innocent babies. And... Batman never had a real girlfriend. Not for long, anyway. That man could never settle down. And for good reason. So much hero stuff to do. I'm holding you back."

"No, you're not. Indi, where is this coming from?"

"From my heart, Ry." She sucked in a breath as she felt something stab mercilessly at her heart. "I'm trying to do this fast and as painlessly as possible. I care about you, but...it won't work. I'm going to ask that you don't come over here. Just...please, try to walk away from this. Love you."

She clicked off and tossed the phone to the sofa. Then she pressed her fingers to her mouth. She'd ended by saying she loved him! What the hell?

"I don't. I can't. Do I?"

Her heart knew the truth, and that sent her running for her purse and car keys. She had to get out of the house. Away from the possibility that he might hop in his car and head over here to talk to her. Because he would. She'd just delivered him the worst dump of all. He deserved more from her.

But she didn't know how to do that convincingly.

Fleeing her home, she had no idea where to go or what to do, but she couldn't sit and wait for him. Her heart wasn't that strong. She left the phone on the sofa, locked the front door and with tears blurring her vision, ran for the car.

Ry raced up to Indi's front door and rang the bell. He peered through the side window but didn't see any movement inside. The silhouette of a dressmaker's dummy stood before a far window. He glanced down the street and didn't see her car. She wasn't home.

Turning and kicking the door behind him, he cursed none too quietly. He'd missed her.

How could she have done that to him? Break up with him over the phone? It hadn't felt right. Like she had been forcing the breakup. She'd spoken so quickly and hadn't given him a solid reason why she didn't want to see him again. He was too good for her? What a load of crap.

Batman had a girlfriend. Vicki Vale and Catwoman and...so many others. All right, so the man had never truly settled down.

Why the hell was he thinking about Batman anyway?

Something was up with Indi, and he wasn't about to walk away without talking to her face-to-face.

He kicked the door again and marched down the sidewalk to the Alfa. He could sit in it and wait for her return, but he had no idea where she was. She wasn't replying to his texts. And if he sent another one he'd tilt over into stalker column.

Gripping his fingers at his temple, he squeezed them through his hair. "What did I do wrong?"

Seven texts, each asking for her to meet him so they could talk. Indi set down the phone after she'd returned to the house. After dark. And with a slow drive down the street to make sure Ry wasn't parked out front waiting for her. The last text had been sent half an hour ago.

He wasn't giving up.

Which only deepened her love for him. He didn't want to let her go easily. And much as that would prove difficult for her to stand against him and do as his father demanded, she had to. For Ry's sake.

She wasn't doing this to make the faery king happy. She was doing it to make life easier for Ry. And to save the babies.

When she tossed the phone angrily across the room, it hit the dressmaker's dummy and bounced off, landing on the floor. Indi headed upstairs to run a tub. If Ry came over, she would not answer the door. She couldn't. It hurt too much to do this, but she had to be strong.

Chapter 24

Ry had fallen asleep on his sofa, phone in hand. After waking, the first thing he did was check his messages. No return texts from Indi.

She'd really done it. Walked away from him. And he couldn't figure it out.

"What did I do?"

His foot slid across the hardwood floor, shoving the broadsword under the coffee table. He'd gone to Faery-Town last night, as usual. And…nothing had happened. Not a single collector had come through. He'd stayed there an hour beyond the time they normally arrived. Never had joined him in searching the sky for the tear between the realms that would signal their arrival.

Had it finally stopped? It didn't feel right to Ry. Mal-rick would never stop sending the collectors. He was too greedy. The old man had simply missed a night. They'd be back tonight.

Ry would hope for the best. That it truly was the end.

The phone rattled in his grasp and, answering quickly, he said, "Indi?"

"Sorry, *cher*, it's just me. You bringing in those signed forms today?"

"Right." After he'd signed them, Kristine had forgotten to bring them back with her. "Yes. I'll be in soon." He hung up and tossed the phone aside on the sofa.

Summoning the energy to rise and take a shower and eat something was a monumental task. He felt defeated. Not in control. And as if, once again, he'd been rejected by someone he'd thought had cared about him.

It wasn't like when his werewolf father had told him to leave the pack, and yet his heart hurt the same way it had then.

Had he fallen in love with Indi?

He needn't consider the answer. He knew it without question.

But life continued to move and exist around his aching heart and romantic entanglements. He did have to bring in those forms. He'd drop them off, then immerse himself in work. Maybe Indi needed a few days to work out whatever had scared her away from him.

He nodded but wasn't buying his logic. It was the best he could manage right now.

An hour later Kristine stood in the doorway to his office holding the forms he'd handed her. She wasn't about to move aside and let him through. And he recognized that steely glint in her brown eyes.

"Something's up with you, Ry. And I think it has to do with Indi. Tell. Or I'm not letting you into your office."

"Not today, Kristine."

"It's that bad, is it?" She cocked a hip to the right, effectively filling up the whole doorway. "Talk."

* * *

Around eight in the evening, Indi checked her text messages. Ry had texted three times today, and the last one had been over six hours ago. He must be busy with work.

Or he had finally given up.

It had only taken him twenty-four hours to accept their breakup.

She wasn't sure how long it would take her. Forever felt about right.

Catching her face in her palms, she sniffed back tears. Out the corner of her eye she spied the pile of tissues that had collected during the day as she paced, sat and wept, paced some more, went out to the backyard to curse the faery king, cried some more, tried to do some work, then ultimately ransacked the fig jam and now had a terrible stomachache and sore eyes. At her feet, the discarded tissues glittered with ichor.

Swiping a finger along her eye, she studied the tears wetting her finger. Faery dust sparkled in her pain. It was dreadfully pretty, and only made the lump in her stomach all the harder. Who would help her to understand and grow into the faery she had become now that Ry was out of her life?

Could she do this alone? Janet might be able to understand. Eventually. But Indi thought of Ry's insistent warnings that she tell no humans about them. She needed a Paranormal 101 class to know how to function now that she had become one of the myths.

When the doorbell rang, she froze, her flight-or-fight instincts begging her to crawl behind the sofa and hide.

Of course Ry wouldn't give up on her. Not so fast.

She could not look into his beautiful brown eyes and then not fall into his arms and confess her deep love for him.

"Indi?"

He'd sent his secretary to talk to her?

"Indi, we need to talk," Kristine called from behind the door. "Ry doesn't know I'm here. Come on, sweetie, open up. I brought mochi."

With a sigh, Indi waded through the tissue piles and opened the door. When Kristine saw her red eyes and tousled hair, the woman bent and pulled her into a hug.

"I knew this would require mochi."

Half an hour later, and after a lot more tears, Indi was done dodging Kristine's questions about why she'd broken up with Ry. She couldn't do it anymore. She had to tell the truth.

"I love him, Kristine."

"Oh, I know that, sweetie. And he loves you."

"He does?"

"Of course he does. He hasn't told you yet? I can smell it on the two of you when you're together. All flowery and hope and romantic pink sparkles. I've never seen Ry fall so hard so fast. And look at you with your puffy red eyes, trying to convince me you don't care about the man. You are a terrible liar. And you definitely need to clean up all these tissues."

Indi plucked another mochi ball from the container Kristine had brought along. She'd not tried the sweet balls of dough-wrapped ice cream until tonight, and oh, they were delicious.

Kristine nudged a tissue aside Indi's cheek, then showed her the sparkle. "That's some serious dust, sweetie."

"Who would have thought such heart-deep pain could be so pretty?"

"Oh, don't do this to your heart. You two deserve each other. Can you tell me why you don't want to see Ry anymore?"

"No. Yes. Oh!" She needed to spill everything. Faery king, be damned.

"Okay, here's the truth," Indi said. "But if you tell Ry I swear I will come for you. I will sneak into your house and break all the heels off your shoes. And don't even get me started on the Chanel I've seen you wear."

Kristine gasped. She crossed her heart with her forefinger. "Girl's honor. I'll stay mum. But I can't promise not to convince Ry that you're worth going after."

Indi sighed and her shoulders dropped. "You can't do that. Or the collectors will start coming again."

"Say what? Ry told me he went out on the hunt last night and not a single collector came through. Can you believe that? Maybe it's over?"

"It is over. Because of me. Kristine, Ry's dad came to me and told me if I wanted it to stop all I had to do was stay away from his son. To break his heart. Malrick hates me because I'm a low-life changeling. I'm not good enough for his prince of a son. So…as much as I adore Ry and know I really do love him, I couldn't imagine him fighting those things forever. And if I can help him by walking away from him?"

Indi quickly grabbed another tissue and caught a stream of tears with it.

"Daddy dearest blackmailed you? The asshole. You did the right thing. I mean, not really. You broke Ry's heart. But you did stop the baby stealers. That was unselfish of you."

"Thanks. I hate myself for it. Because I had to be so cruel to Ry."

"You were. He's suffering. But, sweetie, do you really want to stand back and let Malrick tell you what to do? Don't let him control you like that."

"But…you said the collectors have stopped."

"Do you love Ry?"

"Yes." Her response came out much quicker than Indi imagined it would. But she nodded, following up with another firm and very true "Yes."

"Then tell him."

"I can't! Malrick will send back the forces to collect more babies."

"We'll stop that when it happens."

"No, that's— It's impossible. Ry was having a tough enough time as it was holding them off. He can't fight them forever. And I've put an end to it by breaking up with him. Done deal."

"It sounds good. In theory." Kristine fluttered her spangled manicure before her. "Oh, this is a tangled mess. You're damned if you do and damned if you don't. I hate to see two people with broken hearts like this. It's not fair."

"Maybe Malrick is right. Maybe I'm not good enough for Ry. He's an important man. He's got a billion-dollar business."

"It's charity, sweetie, and you know how he loathes that money."

"Even better reason for him to give it away. He needs to do that as a means to slap his father in the face."

"True. Oh, what are we going to do?"

"There's nothing to do."

"The ball is tomorrow night."

Indi shrugged. "The two of you go and don't think about me. I'll be fine."

"Sure, but that dress—" Kristine gestured over her shoulder "—is stunning. A dress like that demands you make an entrance."

"There are more important things to consider than how I look in a dress. Although, I confess, it makes me feel like a faery princess."

"I bet it does. Aggh! This is crazy. Are there any more mochi left?"

"Sorry, I ate the last one. Those are the best."

"My go-to for breakups and missed seasonal sales. Always picks me up."

Indi slid sideways across the back of the couch, landing her head against the woman's muscled shoulder. "Kristine, do you think you can convince Ry to stop thinking about me? To let it go?"

"I'll do no such thing. But I won't encourage him to go after you, either. As promised. This is between the two of you. I'm glad I have both sides of the story, though. I was starting to hate you for being mean to my big brother."

"I hope we can stay friends, but I'm afraid that would keep me too close to Ry. I can't ever see him again, Kristine. It's too hard on my heart."

"It'll get easier. With time. I should probably go. It's past eleven! Wow. I want to call Ry later and see how it went in FaeryTown. If he doesn't find any critters to slay, then we know that old asshole of a father has kept his word. Oh, sweetie, I wish you could come to the ball tomorrow night. Ry was worried about it, but I think he figured out a plan."

"A plan?"

"You know it's the full moon tomorrow night. Midnight chimes and he doesn't turn into a pumpkin but rather a raging werewolf. He was going to whisk you off with him to the countryside."

"Really? I dreamed about going to his cabin with him." Indi touched the delicate silver wolf's paw dangling about her neck.

"You do know that cabin is actually a castle, right?"

"I didn't know that. Wow." Indi put up both palms. "Don't tell me any more, Kristine. I'm going to donate the dress to Goddess Goodies and be done with it. Paris is a big city. Ry and I can both live here and not ever worry about seeing each other. If only it weren't for—" She sighed. "Maybe I'll find myself a place out in the country, where I can run my business and not worry about people seeing me walking around with wings."

"Hiding from the snoopy people. Just like Ry and the paparazzi. Did I mention you and Ry were meant for each other?"

"Enough!" Indi stood and picked up Kristine's red leather Gucci purse. "It's time for you to leave. I don't want you to leave. But this is another Band-Aid I have to rip off."

"I hate that bastard Malrick for doing this to the two of you."

"Me, too." Indi wrapped her arms around Kristine, and the woman's hug nearly squeezed the breath from her. "I love you, Kristine. Take care of Ry. Promise?"

Tears wobbled at the corners of her eyes and the woman tipped her red-lacquered fingernail to catch one. "Promise. God, you make your own sparkles now. That is so crazy. Oh! I love you too, Indigo DuCharme. If I text you, promise you won't block me. It'll be hard walking away from you."

"Nonsense. You've got the swagger, girl. Just put one of those five-inch heels in front of the other and keep doing it." She opened the front door and watched as Kristine left. Waving, she sniffed back tears.

The woman was going to tell Ry everything.

And secretly, Indi was relieved for that.

Chapter 25

Ry charged through the office doorway and bypassed Kristine's desk. Last night had been almost perfect. He'd waited in FaeryTown until well after 1:00 a.m. No collectors had shown. Again. Malrick had stopped sending them. Hallelujah!

The only thing that hadn't made it perfect was that Indi had broken up with him. And much as he'd wanted to go to her house after waiting for the collectors, he'd had to force himself to return home. Alone.

He wasn't done with her. But he wasn't sure what was up with her, either. It killed him to stay away from her, but something inside him told him to give her the space.

He'd slept fitfully. And this morning an old friend from Ireland had rung him. That call had knocked him off his short-lived confidence regarding the baby trafficking. So much so, he'd checked in with another friend from Berlin. And one in California.

What the hell was going on?

"I'd offer to brew you a coffee, *mon cher*," Kristine said, "but I don't think any amount of caffeine is going to chill that anger vibe you've got going on. Is it Indi?"

He almost slammed his door on her but then decided she didn't deserve to feel his anger. When she clicked into his office on a pair of towering red heels, he could but sit in his chair and shove the laptop across the desk. Kristine caught it before it could slip off and land on the floor.

"Talk," she said simply.

Ry grasped the air before him, imagining his fingers clutched about Malrick's neck. He shook his hands, then growled.

"That bad? I know you're in love with her, but—"

"This is not about Indi. And I'm not in love."

"Oh, yes, you are." She tapped her lips and shook her head. "But we'll table that discussion for the more pressing concern. What's got you so tight and angry?"

"It's happening everywhere, Kristine. The collectors are coming through all over the world."

"What? Are they back in FaeryTown?"

"No. Last night was calm and collector-free. I don't know why they've stopped coming through in Paris, but I'm glad for it. And I was thinking, at least something was going right in my life until a friend called me this morning. He knew I was having trouble with collectors here and wanted to compare notes. Seems they are coming through in Ireland. And Berlin. And I verified the same with another friend in the States. They are coming through all over, Kristine!"

"Shit. That is so not what Malrick—" Kristine pressed her lips together and her eyes grew wide.

Ry stood and leaned across the desk. "Malrick what? What do you know?"

She shook her head, then closed her eyes tightly, then dramatically let out a breath and dropped her shoulders. "Oh, the girlfriend code just can't apply now. I have to tell you."

"Tell me what?"

"Ry, I went to see Indi last night."

"What? Why would you do that?" Then he straightened. "What did she say? Is she okay? How does she look? Did she give you any clue what is going on with her and me?" He thrust up a palm. "No. Sorry. It's not my business if she told you things in confidence."

"She did, and I do respect the girlfriend code made over emergency mochi and tears."

"You brought her mochi?" He couldn't help a small smile. He wanted to hug Kristine for that one.

"Of course! I raided my secret stash for her. Let me tell you, that girl had so many tissues scattered about I could have swum through them. Her tears sparkle, you know? It was such a pretty mess. Anyway, whatever is spoken in confidence from one girlfriend to another must be kept sacred. But, Ry. Now that I know about collectors coming through everywhere else?" Kristine made a show of looking over her shoulder, then directly back at him. "I have to tell you what Indi told me. She didn't dump you because she wanted to. She thought she was helping you. And your father lied big-time to her. That asshole!"

"Malrick talked to Indi?"

Kristine nodded and brushed her fingernails against the lapel of her white business suit.

"Shit." Now he was beginning to understand. If Malrick had spoken with Indi, the faery king must have convinced her to stop seeing his son. A son he deemed unworthy of a lowly being such as a changeling. "Why didn't I make that connection? Malrick must have threatened her."

"It wasn't a threat he made, but a promise. Which he's not upholding if the collectors are coming through everywhere but here."

"I don't understand."

"Sit down, *cher*. What I'm going to tell you is for information about fighting the good fight only. What you and Indi do romance-wise is between the two of you. But you have to promise me you won't go running back to her. That would betray the trust she has for me."

"But if she didn't want to break it off?"

"Just sit. We'll figure this out. You need to know exactly what a sleazeball your father is."

On Saturday morning Indi stood in the kitchen staring at the front door. The doorbell had just rung, and she'd heard footsteps walking away, followed by the roar of a delivery vehicle. Something had been dropped off on her stoop. Or...? Ry could be out there, waiting to talk to her.

She wanted to see him.

She couldn't see him.

Kristine had verified to her that the collectors had stopped coming through in FaeryTown. Malrick had upheld his part of the bargain. She would uphold hers.

With a nod, she went back to unloading the dishwasher. A mindless task that she hadn't taken care of for days. She'd been so busy with...

No, she wouldn't think about him. But how not to?

Another glass placed in the cupboard. Another plate...

"Did he eat off this plate the night he brought over takeaway?"

She clutched the plate to her stomach, then turned to

eye the front door. Three minutes had passed. Setting the plate aside, she decided no one was out there, and made a beeline through the living room. She opened the door to find a flat white box tied with a pale green ribbon sitting on the step. Her name was lavishly scrawled on a thick ivory card tucked under the ribbon.

A mystery present left on her stoop? That was too fabulous to resist. Even though she suspected it could be from Ry. No one else would be so generous. And she'd not heard from Todd since that fateful night. Not that he'd ever been generous with gifts or surprises.

She carried the box inside and sat on the sofa. She'd yet to clear away her tissues, so she had to wade to get there. What a pitiful case she'd become. Time to call for a one-day maid touch-up on the whole house.

The card was just that. No message on the back. She tugged the ribbon loose and then pressed the soft satin against her cheek. Ry hadn't kissed her for days. She missed the heat of his mouth against hers. Of feeling it glide over her skin as he devoured her want and need and gave to her so easily. Unconditionally. He was a man who would never ask her to do something for a favor in return. He was not his father.

Tears threatened, but she shook her head. She was a big girl. And she would get through this. But whatever was inside the box, she suspected it was because Kristine had talked to Ry.

Indi had been hoping she would.

Inside, under a folded layer of pale green tissue paper, lay a gorgeous engraved invitation for tonight's costume ball. It was for Ry's plus one. She picked it up and rubbed it against her lips. The paper was satiny and smooth and emitted the slightest scent of clove. Nice.

But she wasn't going to the ball. She'd already packed the faery costume in a box in preparation to send it to the warehouse for a photo session and to ultimately sell online.

"Has to be done," she said decisively.

Why had her heart become so involved? She had managed to forget about Todd in less than twenty-four hours. Ry? She felt sure she'd never shuck his presence from her heart.

Ready to set the invite back in the box and toss it away along with the flood of tearstained tissues, she noticed a piece of white blue-lined paper at the bottom of the box and pulled it out. Torn from a notebook and written on with blue ballpoint pen. In Ry's handwriting.

Her wings shivered. She didn't want to read it. But she couldn't crumple it up and toss it aside. He hadn't called her. He'd respected her enough not to do that. This was his way to communicate with her.

Sighing heavily, she read the note.

Talked to Kristine. Malrick lied to you. More on that later. What's important is that I get to see you one more time. It can be the last time we see each other. If that is what you want. But please, Indi, allow me one last moment with you. One last dance. One last hug. One last kiss.

Please, be my faery princess tonight.

I'll be waiting at the ball.

Tears streaming down her cheeks, Indi shook her head and clutched the note to her chest.

It was what she wanted more than anything: one last hug, one last kiss. One last moment.

But if he touched her again, could she walk away from him? If his mouth kissed hers, how then could she manage to turn away from him? If she felt the heat of his body up against hers, how to push away and deny that deliriously delicious sensation?

And yet… She reread the second line he'd written. Malrick had lied to her? What was that about?

"Oh." She leaned forward, eyeing the invitation. "You're only asking for heartache if you go, Indigo. You know that. You and fancy balls lately. Nothing good ever seems to come of them."

And if she was to tell Ry how she really felt about him—that she loved him—that would break her bargain with Malrick. The collectors would return to Faery-Town. Ry's nightmare would begin again.

But she wanted to see him this one last time. Maybe that would make the end easier? She didn't need to tell him she loved him. She could go to the ball, give him that one last dance and then confirm that the break-off was indeed what was best for them. Let him kiss her. And then walk away.

"Aggh!"

Indi wished she'd never opened the front door.

Chapter 26

It hurt Ry's heart to be the one standing at the ball, alone, wondering if the girl would show up. Would Indi walk in and stand at the top of the stairs, looking for him? All eyes would land on her and everyone would wonder who that beautiful woman was. And why was she alone?

He should have sent a limo for her.

But no. Ry had wanted to give Indi the *option* of showing tonight. He hadn't wanted to force or cajole her into coming. It was entirely her choice to show up. And if she did? He prayed it would be for that last kiss he'd requested.

Or it could be for much longer. Dare he hope?

He checked his watch. Sixteen minutes, two seconds after 10:00 p.m. It was getting late. Tonight he needn't dash out at midnight to check for collectors; he had backup. Never was standing watch right now. Because things could go many ways tonight. And Ry had prepared for one or two of those instances.

Would she show?

Feeling as if his heart was a heavy lump in his chest, he pressed a hand over the crisp white tuxedo shirt. Most of the men wore tuxedos to these fancy costume balls, along with masks or other accessories to make the costume part. The focus was on the gorgeous women and their elaborate costumes. Ry wore a quarter mask that covered his left eye and was furred like a wolf and had one wolf's ear. It was all he'd wanted to do for a costume. Kristine had called it understated but sexy.

And where was Kristine right now? She, in all her glorious leopard-print girl power, had wandered off to find champagne.

And Ry had never felt more vulnerable. Sure, he could stroll about, find some familiar faces to chat with, laugh at some jokes. But…no. He didn't feel right tonight. And he would not unless and until she showed.

"She's not coming," he whispered as he clenched his fingers near his thighs. Were people staring at him? Why did he feel as if he stood alone in the center of a vast ballroom with all eyes on him? He hated this feeling.

Indi had felt that way when he had arrived late for the Grand Palais ball. The night her world had changed and she had sprouted wings.

"A faery," Ry whispered to himself.

That word had only ever been a cruel judgment against him—faery. But how could he think that when seeing Indi in all her glory with wings spread and smile beaming, and dust glittering in the air about her?

He would never have wings. But he did dust and he knew some faery magic lived within him. What sort of magic, he wasn't sure. He'd always denied it and turned his back on all things Faery.

If he embraced his faery side, would Indi come back to him? He had never been a man to make measures to win other people, to change in hopes of gaining the advantage.

And yet…how could it hurt to truly explore that weak part of him that might only enhance his life? Magic? What man wouldn't want to tap into a little of that now and then?

Ry winced. Was this what desperation felt like? Forming concessions in hopes of a more positive outcome?

"Champagne!" Kristine announced grandly.

Saved from his dark thoughts, Ry spun to take a goblet from his catty assistant. She wore a long leopard-print gown that was slit up to the thigh to reveal some crazy tall heels. Her nails were black and sharpened to points, and on her head of bouffant hair she wore leopard-print cat ears that Indi had given her.

"You want to take a spin around the dance floor, *cher*?"

He probably should. To get his mind off the fact that he'd been jilted. For real. And for reasons that tore him apart. Indi believed Malrick's lies.

"Oh, Ry, she might still show."

He tried a smile, but it came out as a straight line. "I don't deserve someone like Indigo DuCharme."

"Why would you say something so ridiculous as that?"

He shrugged. "She's an independent woman. Smart, talented. She doesn't need a man."

"Needing and wanting are two different things. And I happen to know she wants you. You feeling sorry for yourself? You? The man with all the looks, charm and money?"

Kristine's indignant flare of nostril and that judgmental side-eye always clued Ry he needed to climb down a step. Or two. She was his compass, and he was wise enough to know that.

"You're right. As usual. I've never been on the getting-dumped side of a relationship before. It hurts."

"Oh." Kristine's eyes suddenly widened and she smiled widely. "The hurt is about to go away. I do believe the faery princess has arrived."

Ry followed the gesture of her long, wicked nails. Turning, he glanced up the staircase. And standing at the top, looking down over the crowd, was a faery princess in pastel silks with wings that swept in lush waves of color behind her.

Ry handed the champagne goblet aside, blindly letting it go, and didn't care if anyone caught it. She had come for him. He took the stairs two at a time, but stopped on the one stair below the main floor, putting him eye level to the beaming princess who had stolen his heart.

"You came," he whispered. It was the stupidest thing to say, but he was happy and relieved and…in love.

Indi's smile beamed. "A girl can't miss an opportunity to wear a pretty dress, can she?"

"It's the prettiest dress in the whole room. But you are prettier." He tilted his head, taking in her blue gaze, which… "Your eyes are violet." The color had deepened. Had they become the color they were when she had been born in Faery? And everywhere, her skin sparkled with natural faery dust. "My gorgeous faery princess, you are truly in your element tonight."

She bowed her head shyly, and Ry felt compelled to touch her under the chin and gently tilt up her head.

"And some sparkly cat ears to finish the look," he said of the rhinestone-studded ears she wore. "You've stolen my heart, Indi. I want you to know that. Whether you've come to give me a final kiss or a kiss that'll last forever."

"Actually, I'm not sure what I've come for," she said.

"You don't have to know. I'm just thankful you're here. Can we… Would you like to dance?"

"More than anything."

Offering her his arm, Ry escorted Indi down the stairs to the dance floor. By luck, a waltz began and he swept her along with the other fancily clothed couples. Beneath the twinkle of a half-dozen chandeliers, the room and the mood of the partiers alchemized into a wonderland. And Ry, the reluctant prince, had found his princess. He might never take her to Faery, but he would love and honor and care for her here in the mortal realm. If she would give him a second chance.

Yet she had said she wasn't sure why she'd come. To dump him or to take him back? He'd leave it to her. And he'd have to accept whatever decision she made. He wouldn't try to influence her. Right now he wanted to enjoy her in his arms. For the short time they had. Because before midnight, this wolf had to get the hell out of here. Collectors or not, the moon was high and full. And his wolf was already champing at the bit for release. FaeryTown would be his best bet to make the shift without being noticed by humans, and that was his plan.

"You've mastered the wings," he said as they slowed to spin about the curving end of the dance floor. "They move as if dancing with you."

Indi beamed at him. "They are mine now. They are no longer some strange appendages I must learn to accept. I'm a faery. And I'm cool with that. About ninety percent cool with it. I've still got a lot to learn. Your costume is perfect. Only revealing a little bit of yourself, right?"

"I'm not big on costumes. I prefer to see what's behind the mask. No secrets."

"Some secrets are necessary. How's your wolf doing?"

He squeezed her hand, leaned close and whispered, "He's ready to run, but I'm good. I won't howl in the middle of this tony crowd."

"I was surprised when you sent the invitation," she said. "Kristine told you she stopped by, didn't she?"

"She did, but she didn't tell me everything you two talked about. She invoked the girl code. Or so I was firmly told that some things are sacred."

Indi laughed, and Ry took the moment to spin her toward the center of the floor, where it wasn't so crowded with dancers. She felt like air and light in his arms. He desperately wanted to kiss her. But he didn't want to share that moment with others.

"You understand I had to do it, then?" she asked as they slowed while the music segued to something more like a rumba.

"I do," he said. He slid his hand around to her back and rested it at the base of her back, where the flutter of her wings brushed his skin.

"Malrick said I'm not good enough for you. You're a prince, after all. I'm just a fake faery princess. I'm not even a princess. That's just a name you call me."

"What Malrick said was a whole lot of fiction. There's something you need to know about the Unseelie king. But I don't want to talk about it now. I want to hold you, Indi. To feel your heart beating against mine. Because I'm not sure if this will be the last night I get to do this."

She stepped up to hug him and they swayed to the music. As she tilted her head onto his shoulder, her hair tickled the underside of his jaw.

She said softly, "I remember the first time you kissed me. I forgot my name."

He recalled a moment of losing memory of his name when looking at her as well. An amazing feeling, actually.

"I'm going to make sure I don't forget a moment of tonight," Indi added.

Ry slid his hand up her back and when he touched her wings they flinched, then folded over his hand. And he hugged her until her heartbeats pounded against his chest. Nothing felt more right. Or more frightening.

He couldn't lose her.

When Indi looked up at him, tears quivered at the corner of her eyes. The teardrops sparkled. "Ry…"

He bowed his forehead to hers. He didn't want to hear what she was going to say. Damn his father for making that awful bargain with her!

She gasped and pushed her hands up to clutch at the back of his neck. "I don't want this to end."

"It doesn't have to."

"It does. Kristine told me the collectors have stopped coming through in FaeryTown. I made a bargain with your father."

"She told me about the bargain. It's a bargain Malrick didn't keep."

"What?"

He'd not wanted to get into this during these precious moments he had with her, but it was now or never. And the clock was ticking closer to his need to pull a Cinderella.

"Come with me." Ry clasped Indi's hand and walked her off the dance floor. He weaved around a massive marble column and behind it found some quiet, though partiers were everywhere.

A woman dressed as an Egyptian goddess leaned close to Indi and said, "The wings are stunning. And they must be animatronic. Gorgeous costume!"

"Thank you," Indi said, then bowed her head.

Ry lifted her head with a tip of his finger under her chin. "Be the goddess you are," he said.

She smiled. "I do feel amazing in this dress and with these wings. And on your arm." She snuggled up aside him. "But I'm freaking about what you just said. How has Malrick lied to me?"

Ry leaned in, putting his hand to the marble column above Indi's head, closing them in a private moment. He said quietly, "I learned this morning that Malrick has been sending collectors through portals and thin places all over the world. He's stopped sending them in Paris, but not everywhere else."

"I don't understand. There are collectors stealing babies elsewhere?"

Ry nodded.

"That bastard. We had a deal. I—I walked away from you because I thought it would stop things."

"Please walk back into my arms, Indi," he said. "These past few days without you have been the worst. I need you in my life. I love you."

"Oh, Ry, I love you, too. But…if we get back together, Malrick will send the collectors through Faery-Town."

"I'm ready for that. It'll happen tonight. Malrick knows everything about me and what I'm doing. He'll know if I kiss you and make you mine. Are you willing to stand by my side and accept whatever comes because of our feelings for each other?"

"But those poor babies…"

"All across the world. Not just Paris. Indi, your sacrifice did not stop a thing."

"I feel like such a fool. But, oh, Ry." She pressed her hands to his jaw and tilted up to kiss him. "I want you back."

Her mouth fit to his like nothing else could. They were made for each other. Two strange souls thrust into this realm and led to believe one thing, then surprised with something else. He could accept his faery side with Indi to support him. Because he wanted to help her accept her life just as much. He would do it. He needed her.

And he hoped she needed him.

"I love you so much, my werewolf prince."

"Will you be my faery princess?"

She smiled against his mouth. "That's not a proposal, is it?"

"Oh, uh…"

"Because it's too soon for that."

And he hadn't meant it as that, either. Whew!

"Just be my girl," he said. "My lover. My faery. My Princess Pussycat." He pressed his hand against her bodice, over her breast. "My heart."

"I can do that."

And with a tug up of her skirts, she jumped to wrap her legs about his hips and they kissed all through the next song, and the next. Lost in her was the best place. A place Ry never wanted to leave.

When Ry's cell phone buzzed in his inner pocket, his heart dropped. It was a call he'd been expecting. He'd kissed Indi. He'd sealed their fates. Malrick knew. The time was eleven forty-five. He answered Never's call and was told exactly what he'd expected to hear.

"I'll be there as quick as I can," Ry said, and tucked away the phone.

"What is it?" Indi asked.

"Never just slayed a collector in FaeryTown. And we don't expect one or two or even a dozen tonight. Malrick will send multitudes. I've got to go."

She grabbed his hand. "I'm going with you."

He didn't argue because he wanted her by his side so he could protect her, and know that she was back in his life. "You better believe you are. I'm going to need all the backup I can get. Good thing we trained for this." He kissed her forehead and scanned the area for a quick escape.

Kristine spun as Ry approached and she saw the fierceness in his demeanor. "Got the call?"

"You know it."

"I'm right behind you." Kristine fell in and the threesome left the ballroom and headed for the rental Ry had picked up earlier.

"This car is not yours," Indi said as he held the passenger door open for her and she got in.

"Needed something with a bigger trunk," he said, and closed the door, then held the back door open for Kristine. "Time to go kick some collector ass!"

Chapter 27

"It's the full moon," Indi said as Ry parked the car close to where FaeryTown merged with the mortal realm. "You can't be here, Ry."

"Once in werewolf shape I'll go unnoticed in Faery-Town. And I will shift. Just a warning. You should probably stay in the car."

"Oh, hell no. You're not leaving me alone."

"Hey!" Kristine called from the back seat. "I know you two are in love and all, but look beyond those rose-colored glasses, faery girl. I am here!"

Ry spoke up before a girl fight could break out. "I need you both. If you're willing?"

"Hell yeah!"

Ry looked back at Kristine in the rearview mirror. "You use that ointment I gave you to see faeries?"

The woman tapped the side of her elaborately made-up eye. "Mixed it in with the eye shadow. I can see your sparkle, big boy. And Indi's, too."

Indi, surprised by that, gave Ry a good once-over. Sure enough, he did sparkle. But was that from her touching him or his innate faeryness? She was starting to see as a faery now? Cool.

"Everyone out!" Ry swung around to the trunk and opened it to display the contents.

Indi leaned over to inspect the assortment within. "Wow. You really did plan ahead. No wonder you needed a bigger trunk."

Inside the trunk were swords, knives, a battle-ax with spikes on it and even a whip. Ry grasped a sword that hummed when he pulled it out, and the whip.

"What is that?" she asked.

"It's my sword."

"But I've never heard it hum." Indi turned to Kristine, who shrugged because she obviously hadn't heard it. And the realization struck Indi. "I'm totally faery. I can hear swords!"

"It's got a song, that's for sure." Ry sheathed the sword behind his back. "Now for you, Miss I Took One Brief Lesson on Swordfighting, I think this will be perfect."

He handed Indi an épée that wasn't at all heavy. The hilt sat nicely in her grip and it felt like an extension of her arm as she gave it a practice thrust. "I like it. Feels right."

"Good. It's perfectly balanced. It was made by a friend of mine from the States, Malakai Saint-Pierre. You won't have to work very hard with that one. It knows what it's meant to do. And that is slay the big bads."

"Works for me."

Kristine perused the collection, her fingernails fluttering over the remaining assortment. Finally she grabbed the battle-ax and a short-blade sword.

Ry glanced down at Kristine's shoes. "You might want to slip into something a little less...precarious."

"Are you kidding me?" Kristine pointed out a toe of her glossy black shoe. "*Cher*, I wear shoes bigger than your dick. I can run a mile in them, top speed, and kick your sorry ass to the curb." She tilted the sword blade against her shoulder and looked askance at him. "What's your super power?"

Indi looked to Ry, who blanched, but then nodded in concession. "Knowing when to hold my tongue." He bowed before the two of them. "Ladies first."

"Oh, you know it!" Kristine marched forward.

And with a wink to Indi, Ry asked, "Are you ready for this?"

"Dressed in faery finery and reunited with the man I love? Hell yes. I want to poke some sparkly bad guys with a sword."

"Remember to avoid their talons. And stay close to me. I'll protect you."

"I know you will. What about when you shift to werewolf? Will you...know me?"

"I will. But don't expect me to be able to speak. Just...trust me?"

"I do, Ry." She kissed him. "I do."

They arrived in FaeryTown to find Never battling three collectors, a short sword in one hand and a loaded crossbow in the other. He signaled to Ry, then pointed toward a mass of darkness oozing through the torn fabric in the sky.

This was going to be a battle. And Indi wasn't so much scared as pumped with the adrenaline racing and stirring in her wings. So much so that her feet lifted from the ground, and as Ry gave the battle charge, she soared toward the approaching collectors.

* * *

Ry kept an eye toward Indi as he slashed his way through the horde of collectors that blackened the sky. She was flying about a foot off the ground. Never for more than a few seconds, but those wings at her back were certainly trying. And she dodged more than a few lunges from the taloned collectors with a swift beat of wing. Good girl.

Never winked at him and pointed toward Indi. "I've got her in my sights as well. We can do this, man!"

They could do this. And as black mist hailed about them with each collector death, Ry surrendered to his werewolf and shifted, gripping the weapons in each paw with fierce determination.

It was not easy swinging an épée while wearing a ball gown, but Indi found that with a leap she was able to flutter her wings and fly briefly, which freed her from getting tangled in anything on the ground.

Another dash of the blade straight up into one of the creature's chests rained down black sparkly ash over her head. She remembered the cut that had almost killed her, so she closed her eyes and mouth so as not to swallow any of it. But she didn't stay unaware for long. Swinging about, and with a battle cry that pushed up from her very soul, Indi charged toward a pair of collectors that were giving Kristine some difficulty.

The creatures blackening the sky came at him swiftly and with teeth exposed. The werewolf, who experienced it all in his most primal state, and yet also with the sharp cunning of a man, used the enchanted sword in one paw, and its claws on the other paw to bash through the enemies.

It howled at the moonlight. It howled for the release

and freedom in this shape. And it howled because it knew it was fighting for a good reason, and not for some means to satiate a hunger.

But it needed something more. And the burning at its hip answered that need. With an innate sense of what it must do, the werewolf allowed the faery power to course through its system. It tightened in its muscles and expanded its chest. It made his growl deeper and more forceful. And with a glow of faery dust surrounding it, the mighty creature marched forth, leading its troops toward victory.

What seemed like an hour later, but was probably half that time, the black dust from slain collectors settled in a strange, sparkling mist about them. Indi took stock of their motley crew. Never, covered in ichor and with shirt torn and blade dragging the cobblestones beside his foot, stood with his head tilted back, eyes closed, lungs heaving.

Kristine wiped the ichor from her blade and toed the heavy base of the battle-ax. Her dress was torn, or possibly sometime during battle she'd turned the long gown into a mini. Her legs were streaked with black dust and glittering ichor and her cat ears were tilted to one side of her head. But her mascara was intact and so was her lipstick. Tired, and defeated, she still looked like a million euros.

Indi inspected her damage. Her wings hung heavily, and she sensed one of them was torn from when she'd dodged a collector but had swerved toward Kristine's sword. It hurt, yet she also sensed a strange tingling. Perhaps it was healing.

She'd kicked off her Louboutins. The dagged hem of her chiffon skirt was tattered and stained with black dust and ichor. She didn't want to know what a mess her makeup looked like. The long cut down her calf was from her sword, not a collector, so she didn't worry about having to face the jealous healer again. Her blood was pale pink and...it sparkled.

She touched the cut and rubbed what must be a mixture of blood and ichor between her fingers. "This is me," she whispered. "And I'm ready for it."

To her side, huffing and taking things in as she did, stood a mighty werewolf. A tattered white dress shirt hung from one furred and muscled shoulder, while the black trousers barely clung and were still belted on. His body was shaped like a man, for the most part, covered in fur, and übermuscled. His chest was wide and heaving, and Indi had witnessed him howl more than a few times. It had been spectacular.

And...something had happened to Ry's werewolf amidst the calamity. In one moment, Indi had glanced over her shoulder to spy the wolf surrounded by a cloud of bright dust, its arms outstretched as it howled the deepest and wildest call to the night. His faery had joined the fight. She knew it as she now innately knew she had been born faery.

Ry glanced at her with his wolf's head, the long maw revealing rows of vicious yet white teeth. His wolf's eyes were gold and his ears twitched, perhaps to disperse the collector dust that had covered all of them, like soot. The faery sigil at his hip glowed brightly, a beacon to her confused and wanting heart.

Indi dropped the épée with a clank, wandered the few steps over to Ry, and reached out. She wouldn't touch him. And much as she wasn't afraid to touch him, she didn't know how he would react. She knew he was thinking with both a man and an animal mind right now. He was instinctual and reactive, also predatory.

However, as she stood there, the werewolf did something remarkable. He turned and held the sword horizontally before him, then bowed to his knee and laid it down before Indi's feet. Then he nudged her leg with the crown of his furred head, as if marking his territory. The wolf rose and stopped in a partial crouch when its eyes were level with hers.

"My werewolf prince who has, this night, owned his faery heart," she whispered. She glanced her fingertips over the glowing sigil on his hip. "I love you."

The werewolf stood tall and proud and thrust back its head as he let out a long and wild howl. Then Ry took off on a lope down the cobblestoned street.

Never walked up behind Indi. "He needs to run it off. The werewolf. He should be safe in FaeryTown."

"He let out his faery tonight," she said.

"I think so. I've never seen Ry so strong and focused before. And he does sparkle like never before. Good for him. How are you? Your leg is bleeding."

"That was me." She tugged aside the torn chiffon to reveal her bleeding leg. "Trying to get a handle on fighting in a freakin' dress. I'm good." She picked up the sword that Ry had said was enchanted to slay the sidhe. It hummed in her grip. And it didn't feel comfortable to hold it. "How about you?"

"I'll survive. There's some wicked energy coming off that thing. You'd better leave it for Ry to claim."

"I was going to take it back to the car, but yes, I feel the warning vibrations. It knows I'm faery."

"And that blade does not like faeries. Leave it here on the street. Seriously, Indi, that thing is screaming for Ry."

She quickly placed the sword back on the cobblestones. It gleamed and a single discordant note shivered in the air.

"Kristine!" Never wandered over to Kristine and bumped fists with her.

"It's not over." Indi felt compelled to say the words as she looked over the carnage. Because it didn't feel over.

They had defeated the hordes Malrick had sent this night. Dozens upon dozens, surely. Yet apparently the Unseelie king was sending them all over the world. Somewhere, in some part of the world, one or many of those vicious black creatures had gotten their hands on a human baby and whisked it away to Faery to be raised and bred as a slave to the Unseelie.

Was there no way to stop this horrible crime against the innocent?

"How can we stop this?" she whispered.

"It ends tonight," Ry called as he strode toward them. He'd shifted back to man form. His trousers hung at his waist and were shredded, but a few larger shreds covered the most important part. Otherwise, he was naked and gleamed with sweat and faery dust. His sigil no longer glowed.

Slowly, the curious inhabitants of FaeryTown, who had watched from behind windows, now slipped out onto the street, some flying cautiously at a distance, others still clinging to the shadows.

Ry picked up the sword that he'd laid on the street and thrust it above his head. "Malrick!"

Indi stepped over to stand beside Never and Kristine while Ry stood in the middle of the street, waiting. He filled the air with his presence, his utter masculine power and strength. Indi wanted to rush over and jump into his arms and kiss him. The elation of having participated in a battle—and survived—pulsed in her veins. But now was no time to interfere.

And in a glimmer of blinding silver and faery dust,

Malrick stood before Ry. The faery king was dressed in silver finery that gleamed as if sewn with silver threading. His long black hair glinted and his eyes were wide and eerie. As the king surveyed his fallen minions, his expression took on a hint of mirth. And when he unfurled his wings, the crowd standing about gasped and stepped back into the shadows.

"My werewolf son calls?" Malrick asked casually. As if he had not a clue why the bother.

"Enough, Malrick." Ry spread his arms to encompass the piles of extinguished collectors that dirtied the cobblestones about them. "You've had your fun and games. I ask that you cease this insanity. You've taken more than enough human children for your own, and without reciprocation of a single changeling. You've changed the rules. I'm going to guess that won't go over well with those higher than you in Faery."

Malrick smirked. "Higher than me? You jest."

"I don't know much about Faery, but I'm guessing the Seelie king might have an interest in your untoward ways. But most important?"

Malrick crossed his arms and lifted his chin in defiance.

Ry glanced over his shoulder to Indi before turning back to his father. "You made a bargain with Indigo DuCharme. A bargain which you did not uphold."

"I did not specify I would cease sending collectors in areas beyond Paris," Malrick stated flatly. "And besides, she's also broken her half of the bargain. She was to stay away from you."

Ry approached his father with a growl. Any lingering observers scuffled behind doors. Ry lifted his hand to grip Malrick about the throat but at the last moment clenched his fingers and swung his arm out, away from the pompous faery king. "This ends right now. And if you cannot agree to that, I will come to Faery."

"You will? But that is all I want!"

Ry stepped to his father until he was but inches from his face. "I will come to Faery and sit the throne. Your throne. You won't need it. Because I will end you."

Malrick tilted his head with a sinister smirk. "You dare to threaten your own father?"

"That I do. And I don't care if traveling to Faery traps me there forever. It will give me great satisfaction to rip out your throat for all the pain you have caused others not even of your realm." Now he did grip Malrick's throat. "Take this as a warning and step back and cease. You've obtained great spoils for your wicked collection of human breeders."

He shoved Malrick away but did not relent his commanding pose.

"You'll not come after such spoils?" Malrick asked.

"Much as I would love to rescue all the human babies your minions have stolen, I don't see how it is possible. Not on my own. Nor with my resources."

Malrick lifted his chin, appearing to give it some thought. His glance swerved to Indi and she felt his disgust crawl over her limbs. But she didn't shiver this time. She had stood strong beside Ry and defeated Malrick's collectors. There was nothing she couldn't handle now.

"I suspect that changeling was not bred for such a fate," Malrick said quickly to Ry. "She may not be as pitiful as I first guessed. I suppose there are worse *things* for my son to associate with. And besides, it's probably a fling. You and your human ways tend to jump from affair to affair."

"Just like you?" Ry interjected. "You've no authority

to pass judgment on relationships, Malrick. How many half brothers and sisters do I actually have?"

Malrick shrugged and flicked his beringed fingers before him as if shooing a bug. "Thousands?" He smiled, his silver eyes beaming. "I am quite a prolific lover."

"A fact best kept to yourself."

"The interesting fact is…" Malrick's gaze swerved to inspect the sigil at his son's hip. "You've welcomed your faery this night. I can feel my blood coursing through your veins now. You will become such a powerful ruler in due time."

"I don't wish to rule anyone. Ever. But the faery in me… I will no longer shun it."

Ry stretched out his hand in offering to his father. "Will you give me what I ask? In return I…well, I would like to visit you on occasion in Faery."

"You…would?" Malrick studied his son's hand while his face went through a remarkable series of emotions. And for a moment Indi thought his irises changed to violet. "You would come to visit me?"

"If I can be assured it would merely be a visit and that my return would be of my free will."

"Of course," Malrick agreed. He clamped his hand into his son's. "We have a bargain. That I will uphold. I swear it to you. I shall cease to send out collectors. Everywhere. You are right. We've collected quite a menagerie of bleating infants from across the world. That should give us a good start on repopulation. Will you visit soon?"

Ry squeezed his father's hand and then dropped it. "Maybe."

"Before your mortal winter?"

"Don't press your luck. But…it's possible."

Malrick nodded effusively and then it appeared to

Indi as if his eyes watered. The man truly did love his son. She suspected it was deeper than surface and the need for someone to take the throne after he died. Despite being king, he must be very lonely. Perhaps he craved a connection to the vast and sordid family he had created.

Indi wondered about her faery family. Had they really had her only to then give her away? And then she dismissed the idea of learning about them. For now. She'd been raised by two amazing parents and would never consider anyone else family.

Unless his name was Ryland James.

Malrick looked over Ry's shoulder to Indi and he bowed his head to her. "Forgive me, Indigo Paisley DuCharme. I know you do not require it, but I grant you my blessing. And should you ever wish to learn about your sidhe family, you may come along when my werewolf prince son visits me."

She nodded but didn't know what to say. It wasn't necessary.

With that, Malrick stepped back and unfurled his wings. In a glint, the faery took to flight and passed through the fabric between worlds.

Indi rushed up to Ry and hugged him from behind. He reached back and slid a hand over her arm. He filled her arms with strong, hot muscle and smelled like those nasty collectors and sweat and wild and salt and air. And she never wanted to let him go.

"Well, that was better than a whole season of *Game of Thrones*!" Kristine announced. "And I'm bushed. I need to go home and burn this dress and soak these calloused fingers, sweeties. My manicurist is going to complain."

"I'll drive you home," Ry offered. He turned and Indi did not let him go, continuing to wrap her arms about his bare torso. "Just keep clinging, Princess. I might need the protection should what's left of my pants fall off."

"Oh, we want to see that," Kristine announced as she clicked by them in her heels and tossed her sword up against her shoulder.

Ry released Indi and shook hands with Never. "Thanks, brother."

"No problem. Are you serious about visiting Malrick?"

"Yes. I mean, I'm not overexcited, but…maybe the guy deserves my unbiased and open mind for once. You know?"

"He's an asshole, but his place is a nice bit of real estate. And you are the prince."

"I'm not a prince. I'm just Ryland James. You need a ride anywhere?"

"Nope. I'm good. I've got a friend down the block where I can stop in to clean up and…" He winked and then bent to take Indi's hand and kissed it. "You and my brother make a great team. And you are handy with a sword. Watch your back," he called to Ry as he wandered off.

Ry collected the enchanted sword along with the épée Indi had been using.

And Indi jumped into Ry's arms, wrapping her legs about his hips and kissed him. "I wouldn't have you any other place," he said to her. "Wrapped tight about me with your lips on mine. Never is right. We're good together."

"We are."

He walked down the street to the rental car, where Kristine was sorting through the inventory in the trunk. Half an hour later they dropped her off and headed to Ry's place. They raced to the shower and shared a long hot soak.

Indi slicked her hands down Ry's wet abs and kissed his chest. "You don't need to shift to werewolf any more tonight?"

"I'm good. But there's tomorrow night. The nights before and after the full moon I'll have the desire to shift. I'm going to head out to the cabin."

"Kristine tells me your—" she made air quotes "—*cabin* is more like a castle."

Ry shrugged. "You want to come along and decide for yourself?"

"You know I do."

Chapter 28

Ry stood at the top of the castle tower, watching, as three stories below Indi practiced flying with her red and violet wings. She was a marvel. Every so often she looked up and waved to him. She couldn't get much higher than about three feet off the ground. He suspected her wings still had a bit of growth to go before they were complete. They were beautiful, soft and shimmery. Like her.

He swiped his fingers over some faery dust that he noticed on his wrist. Must be left over from sex this morning. His werewolf had no need to come out last night with Indi in his arms to sate that craving. And... he lifted his shirt to see the sigil that had only ever been a pale marking now did not glow, but it definitely had darkened.

He'd surrendered to his faery while in the midst of battle, and the burst of strength had been immense. From now on he would not deny that half of him, and looked forward to exploring exactly what this welcome part of him could offer.

Before coming outside, he'd called Kristine to tell her he intended to take a few days off, maybe the whole week. She had squealed and said all would be well at the office.

He knew that it would be.

When he turned to go down the spiraling stairs of the ancient castle, he was shocked to find Malrick sitting in one of the spaces of the stone crenellations, leg up and elbow resting casually on his knee.

"Do you have to do that?" Ry said sharply.

Malrick shrugged. "Do you wish to bell me like a cat?"

"Just because I agreed to the occasional visit doesn't mean we've suddenly become best friends or—"

"Or family? I understand. Believe me, I am honored at the concessions you've made and look forward to welcoming you to my home. Even if for a visit. But I did a little asking around after last night's adventure, and thought it would behoove me to fill you in with a few details on your not-so-graceful changeling below."

"She's still learning."

"She is terrible. Her wings are not ready to support her heavy mortal realm bones. I suspect she's changing both inside and out, and it'll be a while before she becomes completely sidhe."

"Is that what you came to tell me?" Ry shrugged. "Fine. I'll let her know to be patient."

"I was wrong about her being born a changeling. Indeed, she was taken from her crib to this realm and used as a changeling. But…"

Ry raised an eyebrow.

"She was never bred to be a changeling. She is…" Malrick sighed. "A princess."

"What?"

"I suspected something about her after noticing the distinct color of her wings, and so I asked around, sent out some assistants. She is Unseelie. And her mother is Touramire, queen of the Crystal Lands."

"I don't understand. Her mother is a faery queen? Why would she send away her daughter?"

"She did not." Malrick swung his legs around and jumped to stand before Ry, resting the heel of his palm against the tower wall. Simple black togs today made him slightly less imposing. "Seems Touramire had a vicious argument going on with a troll, who, in order to teach her a lesson, stole her child and sold it as a changeling to Riske. You do know Riske. I believe he takes a toll on all changelings brought to this realm. He used to buy and sell them in the days when the changeling practice was more common."

Ry tightened his jaw. The bastard had lied to him. In a manner. He had mentioned the toll part. And if he was doing brisk business, Indi might have been just another bleating infant to him.

"So Indi was born a faery princess?" Ry couldn't help a broad smile.

"Indeed. Tell her if you wish. But I'm sure she's fixed her life and memories to her human family. How will learning her truth change anything?"

"It's none of your concern."

"It is if my son should someday marry the missing Crystal Lands' princess. Until this winter, my son."

With that, Malrick winked, then jumped up to the crenellated wall and took a step backward. Ry could hear his wings whoosh out and he soared low, right over Indi's head, before disappearing through a tear in the fabric between realms.

"Hey!" Indi pointed to the sight.

Ry waved to her and called that he'd be right down.

"Was that Malrick?" Indi asked when Ry walked out into the grassy courtyard behind the castle. Yes, the man lived in a castle. And he was looking extra sexy today. No shirt, just some loose jeans hugging his hips, and all that glossy long hair blowing in the breeze.

"It was. You're looking good with the flying skills."

She shrugged, but dropped her wings so the tips treaded the lush emerald grass behind her. "I can't get very high. I don't know what's up with that."

"Malrick suggested you're still changing. Faery bones are light. I think they're like honeycomb. Your bones, which developed in this realm, are slowly changing back into what they were. Once that happens you'll be able to fly so high."

"And then will I be able to get small?"

"Maybe? I'm not sure, but I wouldn't doubt it. You want to go for a swim in the falls later?"

"There's a falls around here?"

"About a mile through the forest there's a clearing and a crystal-clear falls. My wolf always heads there when I'm out here."

"I could fly there?"

"We'll race."

She jumped into his arms, wrapped her legs about his hips and kissed him. "Why was Malrick here? Are you two buds now?"

"I don't think that'll ever happen. He, uh…" Ry set her down and clasped her hand. "Had some information for me that he thought I should know. And I think you have a right to know it."

"What do you mean?"

"Come inside. I'm hungry. We'll dive into the cheese and charcuterie we brought along and I'll tell you everything."

An hour later, they lazed before a fire crackling in the hearth. Ry had eaten all the meat and grapes, and Indi wished they'd picked up more wine. The man owned a castle, and yet he had no wine cellar? She would see to changing that.

And he had told her everything.

"I'm really a faery princess?" Indi rolled to her back. Her wings she furled up and out of the way, and she dragged her bare foot along Ry's bare chest.

He clasped her ankle and kissed each of her toes. "That you are, Princess Pussycat. What do you think about that?"

"I feel badly for my faery mother. But I'm not sure if I do want to meet her. I will always feel like Claire and Gerard are my real parents."

"They are. That doesn't have to change."

"It would be interesting to visit Faery and meet my mother. Queen of the Crystal Lands? How cool does that sound? Do you think she'd remember me?"

"I'm sure she would."

"A troll stole me. That's crazy. Thank you for telling me that. Malrick thought you'd keep it to yourself?"

Ry shrugged. "Malrick's an ass."

"But he is your father."

"Not my real father. Tomas LeDoux was the only man I've ever known as my real father."

She leaned in and kissed him. "Maybe someday the two of you can reunite."

"That would mean a lot to me. But I won't hold out hope."

"You should always have hope. But I'm thinking you and Malrick might hit it off."

"Don't get crazy."

"Okay, how about mutual respect?"

"I'll settle for mild interest."

"It's a good start." She crawled on top of him and he flipped to his back. "So you're a prince and I'm a princess. Kind of cool, huh?"

"You've certainly mastered the title. You in your faery finery and tiaras."

She touched the wolf's paw at her neck. "I'd trade it all for a simple life in this realm with my werewolf lover."

"I love you, Indi. I'm glad you stumbled drunkenly into my life."

"Never thought I'd be thankful for a drunk, but me, too. Now I want to get drunk on you. It would be a shame to let this fire and this warm wool blanket go to waste."

Ry shoved the food tray aside and pulled her down to kiss. He slipped her dress strap from her shoulder and kissed her there. "Here's to a normal life filled with not-so-normal experiences."

She tapped the sigil on his hip. "Like faery dust and wolf howls?"

"Just like that."

* * * * *

Karen Whiddon started weaving fanciful tales for her younger brothers at the age of eleven. Amid the gorgeous Catskill Mountains, then the majestic Rocky Mountains, she fueled her imagination with the natural beauty surrounding her. Karen now lives in north Texas, writes full-time and volunteers for a boxer dog rescue. She shares her life with her hero of a husband and four to five dogs, depending on if she is fostering. You can email Karen at kwhiddon1@aol.com. Fans can also check out her website, karenwhiddon.com.

Books by Karen Whiddon

Harlequin Nocturne

The Shadow Agency

The Texas Shifter's Mate
Finding the Texas Wolf

The Pack Series

Wolf Whisperer
The Wolf Princess
The Wolf Prince
Lone Wolf
The Lost Wolf's Destiny
The Wolf Siren
Shades of the Wolf
Billionaire Wolf
A Hunter Under the Mistletoe (with Addison Fox)
Her Guardian Shifter

Visit the Author Profile page
at Harlequin.com for more titles.

FINDING THE TEXAS WOLF

Karen Whiddon

To all my "family" not related by blood ties. You know who you are, always offering help or a smile, or a shoulder to cry on. Many of you are my friends, but oh so much more than that. I appreciate you, I love you and I'm grateful you're in my life.

Chapter 1

The heavy oak door, scarred and weathered, looked like something out of a medieval castle. Above, a simple sign. No words, just a rusted iron bar from which hung two chain links, each half of what had once been whole. There were no lanterns, not even a streetlight to illuminate the shadows. The entrance sat near the end of a dead-end alley, innocuous enough that no soul, human or otherwise, would give it a second glance. Unless, of course, one knew what lay inside.

Maddie Kinslow usually preferred to take her time. Her slow and steady approach, sometimes viewed by others as reticence, enabled her to take full notice of her surroundings. When in her human form, her eyes were her primary tool, and when she shape-shifted into her wolf form, her nose took precedence over her other senses.

Tonight, with the moon a perfect sliver in the cloudless sky, she walked a little faster than normal, intent on reaching the dead-end alley that led to Broken Chains, the Galveston bar where only others of similar ilk were welcome. She, along with two of her best friends, had recently formed The Shadow Agency, a private investigative firm catering exclusively to Shape-shifters, Vampires and Merfolk. They'd recently successfully closed their first case and she'd gotten a lead that someone might be in the bar tonight who wanted to set up a meeting about becoming their second client.

Since Maddie lived and breathed her goal of making The Shadow Agency a success, her eagerness to meet with this individual had her practically running.

Until she stumbled over the bloody and beaten man halfway up the alley.

She tripped, caught completely by surprise, screamed once and fell. Right on top of the unfortunate human, who let out a guttural groan.

Naturally, she scrambled up, away from him. "What happened to you?" she asked, not even sure he could answer her. He appeared to have been on the losing side of a run-in with a semi truck. Digging her phone from her pocket, she realized she couldn't call 911. Not from here, so close to the unmarked door. By spell or by due vigilance, it would never open, not for humans and not without potential death. To be safe and prevent any unnecessary curiosity, she needed to get this poor man out of the alley.

"I was beat up," he said, his voice clear, despite the fact that his lip had been split. "Two big guys."

"Were you robbed?"

"No."

She watched in disbelief as he managed to heave himself off the ground to his feet. With one eye swollen shut, he squinted at her with the other.

"They went in there," he said, pointing at Broken Chains' unmarked door.

Heart pounding, she shook her head. "In where? There's nothing around here but some old abandoned warehouses."

"Lady, come on." He swayed slightly as he took a step toward her. "You know exactly what I'm talking about. I've been watching this place. I've seen you here before. What I want to know is what's going on behind that door? People come and go all night. I don't know what they do to get inside, but they do. I've tried, but no one will let me in."

He had no idea what kind of danger he'd placed himself in. A human, trying to gain entrance to Broken Chains? Now she understood. A couple of the bouncers must have taken exception to him pestering them. In light of that, he was lucky he'd only been beaten rather than killed.

"You need to go somewhere else." She didn't even bother to try to hide the urgency in her voice. "It's not safe here for you. Go away and forget you ever saw this door."

Judging from the way he perked up, her heartfelt warning only made him more determined to stay. She eyed him—as far as human males went, he looked tough, with his broad shoulders and muscular build. But even the most fit human had no hope of fighting back against a Shape-shifter or Vamp. Both had power reserves of at least ten times those of any human.

Which explained why this guy's swollen face made his features unrecognizable.

"I'm not going anywhere." He crossed his arms, exposing purpling bruises and several small cuts that still oozed blood. In addition to the split lip and black eye, and judging from the multiple bruises and swelling, he'd been pummeled. Again, lucky to be alive, even if he didn't get that. "My name is Jake Cassel. I'm an investigative reporter."

"You can barely stand," she pointed out. "I'd think you'd want to get yourself some medical assistance."

"Good idea. I'll dial 911 and when the paramedics arrive, I'll ask for them to also send cops. I'm sure they can find out what's behind that door."

Exactly the situation she hoped to avoid.

"It's not safe for you here," she reiterated. "How about I walk you to my car and drive you to the ER?"

Her offer appeared to confuse him. "What? Why? You don't know me. What if I turn out to be a predator? You'll be alone with me."

Of course she had no answer for that. She wasn't about to tell him that as a full-blooded Shifter she knew she'd be safe. "I'll be fine," she finally replied. "I might even be willing to tell you what I know of that door."

That finally got his attention. "Seriously?"

"You sound skeptical. I don't blame you." Somehow, she managed to keep herself from glancing at the still-closed door. "But I should also let you know that I expect those guys to come back at any moment." And she did. "If they attack you again, which they will if they find you still here, they'll kill you this time."

While she had no idea if he believed her or not, he shuffled forward. "Give me your word," he demanded. "Give me your word that you'll tell me the truth about that door."

"I'm Maddie Kinslow. You have my word." And she would tell him. Because one thing she'd learned was to be very specific when relaying what one wanted. This human had asked for information about one item only—the door. She knew where it had come from, when it was installed, what kind of wood it had been made of and how often it was painted.

And a careful reciting of those facts was exactly what he'd get.

Driving as fast as she could without breaking the speed limit, Maddie soon pulled up in front of the ER at UTMB Health John Sealy Hospital. Despite his best efforts to remain alert, her passenger lost consciousness before they arrived. Well aware of how these human hospitals worked, she hoped Jake Cassel had his ID and an insurance card on him.

After leaving him in the car, she rushed inside and up to the triage window. "I found a man beaten on the sidewalk," she said. "He wouldn't let me call for an ambulance, but he allowed me to drive him here. He's outside in my car, now unconscious. I need help getting him inside."

If she expected a medical team to jump into action like they did on TV, she was wrong. The nurse simply nodded and told her she'd send someone out with a wheelchair in just a moment.

Eventually, after what felt like an eternity but was in fact four minutes, an orderly appeared with a wheelchair. She led the way out the double doors to where she'd left her car parked, with the injured human in the front seat.

But the front seat was empty.

Cursing under her breath, she spun around. "He couldn't have gone far," she promised. "He was pretty beat up. And he lost consciousness on the way here."

The orderly squinted at her. "Okay," he said. "Come and get me when you find him." And he turned to head back into the hospital.

He had a point. There really wasn't anywhere to hide. The helipad sat behind a metal rail, and the tall palm trees dotting the landscape didn't provide much in the way of shelter.

"Wait," she ordered, stopping the orderly in his tracks. "The man can barely walk. I was inside for under five minutes. He really can't have gone far."

"Is that him?" He pointed to the covered bus stop near the road.

A lone figure sat on the bench. A quick calculation revealed that maybe, just maybe, Jake Cassel could have made it to there.

"I think so," she said, letting her excitement show in her voice. "He's wearing the same color shirt. Come on, help me go get him."

"I'm sorry, I can't." The orderly appeared apologetic. "I'm not allowed to leave the ER grounds."

Of course he wasn't. The way this day was going, she'd begun to wish she'd never set eyes on the beat-up human. "May I borrow the wheelchair?" she asked.

"I don't know." Clearly wavering, he looked uncomfortable. "I'll get in trouble if you steal it."

"I won't," she assured him. "I just need to retrieve that patient."

"I think you might be too late," he said, pointing. "The bus is coming. Your guy might not be able to walk too well, but he apparently doesn't want to go to the ER. I'm guessing he's getting on the bus."

Calculating, she knew even if she started running, she'd never make it in time. Instead, she watched as the bus pulled up and as Jake, doubled over in pain, managed to climb on board.

Cursing, she turned and sprinted back to her car instead. She knew the bus would continue down Avenue D to 22nd Street, where he'd have to get off and switch buses or ride back to the hospital. She planned to be there either way.

Because what he'd done didn't make sense. Jake Cassel had been severely beaten. He needed X-rays and possibly stitches, definitely pain meds. He wouldn't have fled unless he had something to hide.

And Maddie had never been able to resist uncovering the answer to a good puzzle. The trait was what made her such a doggedly good PI.

She managed to catch up to the bus after its first stop. She watched as the two elderly women who'd gotten off slowly crossed the street.

Next up would be the 9th Street stop. The bus slowed, but continued on. It made several more stops, but he didn't disembark. Finally, at 22nd Street, it turned into the new downtown terminal. Her heart sank. If he got off in a crowd, she'd never be able to tell if he got on a different bus. She could only hope his slow and painful movements would help her locate him.

As she drove past the terminal entrance, her luck held. There. Jake. Arms still wrapped around what had to be an aching middle, he shuffled down the sidewalk as the bus rumbled off.

Where could he be headed? If he'd driven to Broken Chains and parked, his car was in the opposite direction. It would have been much easier to reach from the hospital. Perhaps he had friends in this area or, even better, lived nearby himself.

Instead of immediately confronting him, she decided to follow him and see where he went. She hoped his destination would give her some answers.

She got caught at a streetlight. While she waited, she kept her eyes on him, aware that at his pace he wouldn't be able to get too far ahead of her. There were only two cars coming from the cross street. One continued past, but the second—an older model black Lincoln with dark, tinted windows—pulled up alongside him.

Jake lifted his hand in greeting and carefully got in.

The Lincoln took off, past City Hall, making a left on Avenue M. It disappeared in traffic before her light changed. Though she drove as fast as she could, by the time she got to heavily congested Seawall Boulevard, she had to concede that he'd lost her.

Worse, she realized she'd stood up Carmen. They'd agreed to meet at Broken Chains to discuss strategy for their next Shadow Agency case. Maybe she wasn't too late. She swung the car around and headed toward Harborside Drive. Most likely, Carmen was still there.

Earlier that night, when he'd been in the alleyway by the door that wouldn't open, Jake Cassel hadn't seen the two large men until he turned and saw them right behind him. Since the alley was a dead end, they must have come through that door. He cursed silently, moving aside to get out of their way.

But instead of pushing past him, they stopped. Too late, he saw the anger in their faces. Hostility radiated from the jerky way they moved to their clenched fists.

"I mean no harm," he began, about to offer them his wallet and his watch, whatever they wanted. But when one of them punched him, followed by the other, raining down blows so swiftly he barely saw them move, he realized this was not a mugging. No, this was a beating, and he'd be damn lucky to survive.

Though he could hold his own in a fair fight, not only was this two against one, but they were built like linebackers. So he curled himself into a defensive ball and tried not to make a sound, hoping eventually they'd leave him for dead and he wouldn't be.

The next thing he knew, the redheaded woman was tripping over him. She let out a little scream as she fell, the sound letting him know he'd somehow survived. He must have lost consciousness, because the last thing he remembered before that was the two men whaling on him. They'd even gotten in a couple of kicks, catching him right in the ribs.

He wasn't sure he could breathe, never mind stand, but somehow, he managed to push himself to his feet. This woman had been here before. He'd watched the alley for weeks, and she'd visited at least twice. Maybe three times. Since he could only watch the entrance to the alley, he assumed she'd gotten the door to open for her. Because she'd gone into the alley and hadn't come out for hours.

He'd observed all kinds of people heading into that dead-end alley. From suit-wearing business types, to hipsters, to the grunge-slash-metal crowd. They never came out immediately. Whatever they were doing in there, behind that mysterious door, had to be interesting.

The wondering consumed him. Every single journalistic instinct he possessed kicked into overdrive. Whatever went on behind that door had to be a story. A big story. Not just mildly interesting.

Because one night when he'd been staked out watching the alley, he'd seen a man emerge, unsteady on his feet, clearly inebriated. The guy had walked to where the alley met the street, looked left and right and, right there on Jake's cell phone video, began to shimmer. His form had wavered, too, changing from human to something definitely wolf-like, before going back to human once more. Then, the man shook his head, adjusted his clothing and walked away.

Not believing his own eyes, Jake had watched the video several times. He'd uploaded it to the cloud, knowing he couldn't take a chance of losing it, though he kept the copy on his phone.

This, if he could prove it, would be the story of the century. Because based on what he'd witnessed, he just might be able to prove to the world that werewolves truly existed.

If he could manage to live through this investigation, that is.

A groan slipped from his lips as he attempted to take a step after standing. She came to him then, using her slender shoulder to brace him, uncaring of the fact that his blood would stain her pretty dress. As she helped him move toward the street, she muttered under her breath.

"Did you just say *'Damn humans'*?" he asked, careful to hide his excitement.

"I don't know," she said, her voice cross. "If I can get you to the sidewalk, we can call for an ambulance."

"No ambulance," he insisted.

"We need to get you to the hospital. How else do you propose we do so?"

"My car is parked over there," he told her, pointing with an unsteady hand. "The keys are in my pocket." Somehow, he managed to dig them out. "Here. You can drive."

Though his pain level had been off the charts, Jake had known he'd have to ditch the redhead. Though he wasn't sure why exactly, he knew the reason would reveal itself soon enough. He'd learned to always trust his gut instincts. Always.

She'd been kind. Interested, even. And beautiful, the kind of beauty that once would have sent men off to war. While her beauty lured him, he didn't trust her. She knew things he didn't. Since she'd done everything in her power to hustle him away from the dead-end alley, she had no intention of sharing any of her knowledge with him.

He'd seen her go in the door. That damn door. What had started out as idle curiosity had become a full-blown obsession. So much so that he'd put his own life in danger.

The salt-scented, humid breeze made the cuts on his face sting. He thought he could make it back to his car, but he'd begun to second guess the instinct that had made him flee the hospital. While the woman—Maddie Kinslow—had put on an outward show of compassion, she was part of whatever secret lay behind that door. Call him overly paranoid, but he couldn't help but wonder if she'd been sent to finish the job the two thugs had started. He wasn't prepared to risk finding out.

Still, she'd been right about one thing. He needed medical attention. He suspected he had, at the very least, a couple of broken ribs. If not broken, then bruised.

An older black Lincoln pulled up alongside him. "Hey, man," a familiar voice said. "You need a ride?"

Wayne. One of the guys he played basketball with every Saturday. Jake had never been so glad to see someone in his life. "I do," he said, lifting his hand in greeting.

"Climb on in."

Jake did. When Wayne got a good look at his face, he whistled, low and furious. "What the hell happened to you?"

"I got jumped over by Harborside."

"By the cruise ship parking lots?" Wayne wanted to know.

"Yeah, sort of."

"What were you doing over there?"

Since his friend knew exactly what Jake did for a living, he told the truth. "Following a lead. I got a little too close for someone's comfort."

"Let's go to the hospital," Wayne suggested.

Since Jake felt dizzy, like he might pass out again, he agreed.

This time, he made it inside the ER under his own power. Though Wayne had offered to stay, Jake told him no.

Three and a half hours later, Jake learned his ribs were bruised, not broken. By some miracle, his most serious—and painful—injury was a dislocated shoulder. They gave him some muscle relaxers and a shot of something, and the doctor manually worked it back into place. When he did, it hurt like hell. Perspiring, trying not to swear, Jake managed to stay conscious.

When they were finally done and the doctor came to discharge him with a prescription for more pain pills and some antibiotics, he asked Jake if he had someone to drive him home.

"No. But my car is only a couple blocks away," Jake said, his tongue feeling thick in his mouth.

"You can't drive," the doc said firmly. "You need to call someone to come and pick you up. We gave you some strong narcotics. No driving for at least twenty-four hours."

"I'll find someone." He dug out his phone. Maybe he could talk Wayne into coming back and picking him up.

"No need," a cool, feminine voice said from the doorway. "I'll take you home."

The redhead. Maddie Kinslow.

"Perfect," the doctor said, smiling. "Take him straight home, make sure and fill these prescriptions, and force him to get plenty of rest."

"I sure will." Now she sounded positively cheerful. He turned to stare at her, wondering how she'd known to come back here looking for him.

"I'll send a nurse to wheel you out to the car," the

doc continued. "Hospital regulations," he added when Jake began to protest.

Jack nodded. He waited until the doctor had left the room before confronting Maddie. "Are you stalking me?"

"No." She frowned, looking both hurt and angry. "I will say I was concerned, especially when you took off like you were afraid to go into the ER. Why was that? I wondered. Do you have a warrant out for your arrest?"

"No. And no. As you can see, I haven't been arrested. Where do you come up with this stuff?"

"I'm a PI," she retorted. "It's part of my line of work."

"A private investigator?" At first surprised, the more he considered, the better he felt. Ms. Maddie Kinslow might not realize it, but she'd just given him an idea.

She started to respond, and then closed her mouth. Lips a tight line, she looked away. Whatever she wasn't telling him, she clearly had no intention of saying anything else about her work. Which was okay with him. She'd said enough.

Luckily for her, a cheerful nurse arrived with a wheelchair. She ordered Maddie to get her car and pull up right outside the entrance. Once Maddie had left to do that, the nurse wheeled him out front to wait for her.

When Maddie had parked, the nurse helped Jack out of the wheelchair and into the passenger side. He was able to buckle the seat belt, wincing.

"Are you all good?" she asked, her candid gaze searching his face.

"Yep. Better than good," he replied. "I'm actually really glad to learn you're a private investigator. As it turns out, I want to hire you."

Judging by her sudden intake in breath, he'd shocked

her. "Um, my agency is specialized. We wouldn't be a good fit."

"Yes, we would," he insisted. "Plus, you're the only PI I know. I'll pay whatever your going rate is. And I promise, you'll find my job to be a simple one, easily completed."

She shifted into Drive and pulled away from the hospital.

"Well?" he pressed once she'd exited the parking lot. "What do you say?"

"I'm thinking. Give me a minute."

He gave her more than a minute. She followed his directions, pulling in to the driveway of his small home on San Jacinto. Once she'd put the car in Park, she turned in her seat to face him.

"What's the job?" she asked, her expression professional. "I really can't commit my resources until I know what is involved."

And here came the part she wouldn't like. He told her anyway. "I want to hire you to find out what's behind that door on the dead-end alleyway. The one where you found me all beat-up."

Chapter 2

Inside Broken Chains, Carmen Vargas sat back in her chair, took a sip of her drink and surveyed the smoky room. As always, every table had been taken, and those without a seat stood shoulder to shoulder. Carmen had arrived early and claimed her usual prime spot near the back, close enough to have a view of the dance floor, but not so close that the loudness of the band would make any attempt at conversation impossible.

Her friends Maddie Kinslow and Shayla Dover-Cantrell usually met her here, but Shayla had recently gotten married and was just getting back from her honeymoon. The three of them had formed a supernatural private investigative agency and had recently successfully closed their first case. Carmen imagined Maddie had already gotten busy hustling for a second. Still, she was very late. Not like her. Carmen figured she'd give her a little bit longer before calling her friend's cell phone.

"Have you got a minute?" The low growl of a masculine voice to her left had her betting he'd be a Shapeshifter. With a lazy movement, she swiveled her head to look. Damn. She, who never was shocked, sucked in her breath. Talk about hot. This guy had to be new. His aura revealed she was correct. Shape-shifter. And a damn good-looking specimen, too.

Exactly her type, if she'd had one. Tall, close-cropped dark hair, bright blue eyes, broad shoulders, narrow waist and muscular arms. He looked like a cop, or some other straight-laced profession. She'd learned from experience that those kinds of men were almost always the most fun in bed.

She let herself experience a delighted shiver before responding.

"Of course," she purred, indicating the chair next to her. "Have a seat."

He pulled out a chair and sat down, his bold stare frank and assessing. Confidence. She liked that in a man.

This evening had just gotten a thousand times more interesting. After so many centuries on the planet, Carmen rarely felt an overwhelming attraction like this.

"I work for the government," he said. No surprise there. "And I've been talking to the Pack Protectors. They let me know about your Shadow Agency, operating right here in Galveston."

A job. He wanted to discuss a job with her. Years of practice enabled her to hide her disappointment. She simply eyed him calmly while waiting for him to elaborate.

Instead, he glanced around. "Is there somewhere quieter we can talk? This is classified, so not information I'm comfortable shouting."

She took a moment to consider, enjoying the way

his gaze traveled over her. "Maybe later," she finally said. "I'm waiting for a friend and I don't want to lose our seat."

His gaze narrowed and his mouth tightened. "This is a matter of national security."

Though intrigued, she pretended not to hear him at first. Only when he leaned close, his mouth against her ear, and repeated himself, did she nod. "Perhaps you should make an appointment with our office. I'm certain you don't want to discuss such a weighty matter in a bar."

Instead of putting him in his place as she expected, a flash of annoyance sparked in his eyes. "This is urgent. I don't have time to make an appointment. If you don't want the job, just say so. I'm sure I can find someone else."

Rueful, she conceded. "Wait. I'm interested. If you could just give me a few minutes until my friend arrives, I'll find a quieter place where the two of us can talk."

"Five minutes," he said. "No longer."

Clearly, he was the kind of man used to giving orders. She found this incredibly arousing. Most men were too intimidated by her frank and blatant sensuality. They tended to fall all over themselves trying to please her.

"Five minutes," she agreed, smiling. Maddie had a tendency to run late, but never extremely so.

The allotted time passed. Still no Maddie. Handsome Guy eyed her and she knew he meant to leave.

"Come on," she said, getting to her feet. "They have private rooms in the back. Let me see if I can secure one and we'll go there and talk."

He followed as she strolled to the bar. One glance over her shoulder showed no less than six people had rushed the table the instant she'd left. They'd have to duke it out among themselves over who ended up with it. Or share.

As luck would have it, she was able to rent a small room for half an hour. She sent Maddie a quick text to let her know where to go once she arrived, and then led the way through the double doors to the private part of the bar. She'd heard stories about some of the goings-on in these private rooms.

Stopping at room number 7, she used her key to unlock the door. "Here we are," she said, entering. Handsome Secret Agent Man brushed past her and began looking around. As in, seriously searching for something. Fascinated, she watched, realizing he must be checking the room for recording devices.

When he finally finished, he turned to face her. "I'll need your cell phone," he said, holding out his hand.

"Thanks, but no thanks," she replied. "I'm not handing that over to a total stranger, just because he's cute."

Her choice of adjectives made him blink, but that was his only reaction. Disappointed, she pulled out a chair and sat. "You were about to tell me why you needed to hire me?"

"Not until I know for certain that you're not recording," he countered, stoned-faced. "At least put your phone on the table."

"Are you serious?" she asked, even though she knew he was. With a sigh, she retrieved her phone from the depths of her Prada bag and placed it on the table.

"May I?" he asked, as he reached for it.

"You can look at it," she replied. "But I want it back on the table once you're done." Though she had no idea what she'd do if he decided to drop it into his pocket. By virtue of being a Vampire, she had the elements of superspeed and strength on her side, but he was some kind of Shape-shifter, which made him a much more even match than, say, a human would have been.

Finally, he finished checking out her phone and placed it back on the table.

"My name is Rick Fallin," he said. "I'm a member of a covert intelligence agency within the FBI. Our country is being threatened by terrorists and we need the help of someone with your credentials."

"My credentials?"

"Yes. You are one of the top biowarfare scientists."

She nodded. "True. But you could have approached me at the lab. Why here? Why ask for help from The Shadow Agency?"

"Because we need you for one other reason. You're a Vampire. And as such, you'd be immune to a deadly, human-created virus."

"You're a Shape-shifter," she shot back. "And if you're full-blooded, you're also immune."

"We're not sure about that," he replied. "Let me explain. This is a completely new virus. We're not completely sure of the effects it will have on the paranormal population."

"Now I'm really intrigued," she drawled. "I can't wait to get a look at this thing."

Though several of his colleagues had warned him that he'd take an immediate dislike to the Vampire woman, Rick Fallin discovered they were all wrong. Instead of the usual revulsion his kind normally felt around those of her ilk, he got a jolt of attraction every time he looked at Carmen Vargas instead. Which he struggled mightily to do as seldom as possible, aware he needed to focus on the job and only the job. This was far too important to mess up.

"A terrorist group has developed a new disease,"

he said, once he had her full attention. "Not a known group, either. They call themselves Sons of Darkness. This one appears to be newly formed. We're not even sure what kind of ideology they possess."

"Sons of Darkness," she mused, a flash of interest in her eyes. "Sounds like possible Satanists. Do you have proof of this disease?"

"Yes. I don't know if you heard about that junior senator who died so mysteriously a couple days ago?"

"I rarely watch the news anymore." She gave a delicate shrug. "Unless it pertains to my work or my friends, I'm content to keep my world knowledge as compact as possible."

Made sense. While he had no idea of her actual age, he'd always heard Vampires lived centuries. He imagined anyone would get a bit jaded after watching so many humans come and go.

"Let me fill you in then. Samuel Jansson was infected with this virus. We're not sure how or when, but most likely it was in a bar on the hill where he frequently stopped for a drink after work. He died a horrible death at home in his bed less than twelve hours later."

She whistled. "That's a fast-acting virus. But how do you know that's what killed him?"

"The terrorist group contacted us shortly before his body was discovered. But even then, we had the same doubts. We rushed an autopsy."

"And?"

"What killed him was a virus never before seen. We have no antidote."

Another flash of interest lit up her face. "What do they want in exchange? I'm assuming it must be something big, right?"

"Oh, it is. It is." He'd been instructed not to tell her

if at all possible, to gain her assistance without doing so. Once he'd completed a full read-through of her dossier, he'd wondered what his boss had been thinking. A rational, intelligent, professional scientist like Carmen Vargas would want to know everything. If they needed the best, they'd have to give her 100 percent of the info.

"They want our country to go to war," he said slowly. "Unless we obliterate the entire country of West Latvia, they'll unleash this virus on our general population. It spreads through the air and kills fast."

"West Latvia?" She frowned. "Why?"

"They trade heavily with Russia. Whoever these terrorists are, they want something Russia gets instead. They haven't specified what exactly. We have people working on finding that out."

"You say this senator was found dead?" she asked. "What about the people who found his body? Have they been placed in isolation to avoid contamination?"

"Yes. The terrorists claim it's only active while the body is alive. We've got people working around the clock to verify this."

She nodded. "As you know, I'm a damn good scientist. I assume you want me to join one of your research teams?"

"Possibly. Though that's not the entire reason we need your Shadow Agency—and you. Many on my task force are full-blooded Shifters, too. As you know, only a silver bullet or fire can kill us. Normally."

Tucking away one wayward blond strand of hair behind her ear, she eyed him. "You aren't sure if this virus might be another thing that can take your kind out, are you?"

"Exactly."

"Since I'm already dead…" Her slow smile made his heart skip a beat.

To cover his unwanted reaction, he looked down, pretending to be lost in thought.

"Hey, it's okay." When she reached out and covered his hands with hers, he felt a jolt straight in his groin. His inner wolf, startled awake, sat up and took notice.

"I enjoy being useful," she continued. "What I need to do is get you a full printout of our rates. We charge by the hour, plus expenses. There's a flat fee—a retainer—that's payable up front and is nonrefundable."

Slowly he slid his hand out from under hers. "None of that matters. You're dealing with a well-funded covert government operation. If you agree to assist us, we can pay you this." Though doing so felt a bit melodramatic, he opened his briefcase to get a better look at the neat stacks of bills inside. "Twenty-five thousand dollars cash, up front. Another twenty-five once the mission is successfully completed."

If he expected her to gape, he was doomed to disappointment. She looked coolly from the money to him. "This is most unusual," she said. "I'll have to consult with my partners."

But he refused to accept this. "I happen to know your private investigative business is a start-up. You've only had one case, I believe. Cash flow has to be important. You can't afford to turn this down."

Stone-faced, she stared at him.

"And this is important," he continued. "It's not just a case. It's your chance to make a difference."

Watching her, he swore he saw that same flicker of interest in her eyes.

"Fine," she finally said. "I'm in. Representing The Shadow Agency." Her chin came up and she held his gaze. "But not just because of the money. I've always wanted to make a difference."

Admiration warred with attraction. He nodded, closing the one briefcase before pulling a manila folder from the other. "We've taken the liberty of having a contract drawn up in advance. I'll need your signature in three places."

Though she accepted the pen he offered her, instead of immediately signing on the dotted line, she began to read through the contract. "No," she said abruptly. "This part here is unacceptable." She stabbed her long, bloodred fingernails at the page. "I refuse to keep my partners in the dark about this job. We're in this together. Otherwise, you're not hiring The Shadow Agency. You're just hiring me."

Somehow, he sensed this minor issue would be the one thing that could make her walk away. As far as he knew, they didn't have a backup. "I agree," he conceded. "Strike through that part and initial it. I'll do the same."

Once she'd done as he'd suggested, she finished her read-through and then signed. Handing him back the papers, she held out one elegant, pale hand.

"I should have told you," Rick said, after neatly filing the contract in his briefcase. Then and only then did he slide the briefcase full of cash across the table toward her. "You and I will be partners for this case."

She stared. "I work better alone. Plus, I already have two partners."

"Not on this case, you don't. You might want to put that somewhere safe," he added, gesturing at the briefcase. "Once you've done that, you'll need to let your partners know that you have to disappear for a while."

"Disappear?" She didn't really protest. "They'll be used to it. It's kind of what we Vamps do."

He laughed, the full, rich sound filling the room.

"I just need to let Maddie know," she managed to say, sticking to the topic at hand. "She's the one I was supposed to meet here tonight. She's probably out there right now, anxious about where I am even though I texted her."

"Let's go find her, then. After that, you're coming with me."

"Okay. Enjoying this, are you?" she drawled. "You might be pretty, but this is serious business. I don't need a distraction, and believe me, I could see you becoming a big one."

To her annoyance, rather than fluster him, her remark made him laugh. "Nice try, Vargas. But it'll take more than that to make me go away. I'm going to be stuck to your side like glue, so get used to it."

"Fine, whatever." She gave in sullenly. "I was thinking I'd start in the lab first. I'm assuming you plan to provide me with tissue samples so I can begin to analyze the thing."

"That won't be necessary," he said. "We've already got teams of the best scientists working on that."

He'd managed to surprise her, and not in a good way. "I am one of the top biological specialists."

One corner of his mouth quirked up. "True, but there are others. We've got them in the lab working feverishly for answers."

He could see she didn't like that. "Then why do you need me? Honestly, if you want to develop an antidote, I'm of the best use to you in the lab."

"We need your help to neutralize the terror group. Time is of the essence. While the president has been fully briefed and continues to be, he's not sold on the idea of declaring war on West Latvia."

She nodded, watching him closely. "Have they given you a time frame?"

"Yes. Seven days. If war is not declared and troops deployed, they plan to infect Houston. If they release this virus into the general population, we'll lose a couple million people in one day. No, Carmen Vargas. We need you in the field. You and I are going to try to infiltrate the terrorists. Our job is to unmask them and take them down from the inside."

She nodded. "This job is sounding more interesting by the minute. How do you propose to do that?"

When he grinned, the flash of his white teeth made her fangs ache. "I have my ways. We've got people who've been working undercover. You and I are going to pose as people interested in joining the terrorist cell."

"I thought you didn't know who they were affiliated with."

"We don't. Not yet. They may be part of a larger group, or might have splintered off from one."

"With a name like Sons of Darkness, I wouldn't be surprised to find out it's a bunch of teenaged kids," she said. "Except for the virus."

"Except for the virus," he repeated. "I think we can pretty much rule out teens. Even if one of them turned out to be some sort of genius, I'd think they'd want cash rather than war declared on some small European nation sandwiched between Estonia and Lithuania."

"West Latvia," she mused. "I believe some of my ancestors came from that area, but I've never been there."

Though he nodded, his mind was elsewhere. When he looked up to find her watching him, he grimaced. "Sorry. I've been going over the plans. Are you ready to get started?"

She nodded. The rush of anticipation that filled her was unlike anything she'd experienced in centuries. "I am. Tell me what you want me to do." She frowned. "But first I need to check on my friend."

If he hadn't known better, Rick would have thought Carmen was stalling. He stayed with her, right on her heels, as she proceeded to search the bar for her missing friend. They made two complete sweeps of the crowded place, upstairs and down, before she finally admitted defeat.

"This is so not like her," she said as they walked out the door. "She's really reliable. Always where she says she's going to be. I hope she's all right."

"Try calling her," he suggested.

"I have. Several times. Calls are going straight to voice mail. I left her a message—well, two now."

"That's worrisome."

"Maybe." She lifted one shoulder in an elegant shrug. "And maybe not. Maddie's always forgetting to charge her phone. It's entirely possible that it's dead and she has no idea."

He spoke without thinking. "She sounds like a scatterbrain."

"She's not." Rushing to defend her friend, Carmen sounded fierce. "We all have our own little character flaws. It's not such a big deal."

"Maybe not," he agreed, glancing at her sideways. "What's yours?"

His question appeared to puzzle her. "Mine?"

"Your little character flaw. I'll tell you mine if you'll tell me yours." He couldn't believe he was flirting with her, but then again, how could he not. They needed to get past this awkwardness with each other for the undercover roles they were going to play.

"I don't have any flaws," she snapped. A second later, she appeared to realize what she'd said. "I'm pretty damn near perfect," she elaborated, laughing. "As I'm sure you are, too."

As he gazed down into her smiling face, something shifted inside him. Damned if she wasn't alluring.

He hadn't expected this sudden craving to hit him so strongly.

Outside in the alley, he led the way across the street to where he'd parked. "Do we need to move your car somewhere?"

This made her chuckle again. "No. I walked here."

Her statement almost gave him pause, considering that some of the neighborhoods nearby could be dangerous late at night. But then he remembered she was a Vampire. Anyone messing with her would get the shock of their life.

She settled into the passenger seat of his black Tahoe, even using the seat belt. He couldn't help but notice how her every movement contained a sensual sort of grace. "What now?" she asked. "Where do we go from here and what's the plan?"

Now was as good a time as any to tell her. At least they weren't inside the crowded bar. "We're posing as a married couple," he said, starting the engine at the same time.

"Married?" One elegantly arched brow rose. "That's the one thing I have absolutely no experience with. I'm not sure I can be convincing."

He glanced at her and grinned. "Just follow my lead, darlin'. That's all you have to do."

From the momentary look of confusion on her face, he guessed she wasn't sure how to react to the endearment. He hadn't called anyone *darlin'* in years, not since his fiancée had died. But since he and Carmen were going to pretend to be spouses, he figured using it would be particularly apropos.

"Sounds good, sugar plum," she drawled, dead-faced.

He laughed—he couldn't help it. It had been a long time since he'd been around a woman who could make him laugh. Pity she was a Vampire. But then again, he wasn't looking for a mate. "I think we'll work fine together," he finally said.

When he glanced at her again, her beautiful face wore a ghost of a smile.

"Here's how we're playing this," he said, all serious again. "Word has gone out in a certain group of people that the Sons of Darkness are looking to hire someone with a biology background. They're willing to pay big bucks. You happen to perfectly fit the bill."

"A biology background?" she snorted. "That's putting it mildly."

He continued on as if she hadn't spoken. "Your credentials and employment are right there for them to look up. You've never done any work with law enforcement, so there's no reason they'd suspect you."

"Maybe not, but what's my motivation? I'm well paid. I like my job. Why would I want to join their organization?"

Bracing himself, he gave her a sideways look. "You've just lost your job. That's your motivation. Plus, we've set it up so that anyone looking will believe you're massively in debt. You need to find work and find it fast."

"Lost my job?" She might have become a statue, she went so still. "Are you serious?"

"It's only temporary. We've got someone who pulled a few strings to make this happen. I'm sure you'll be fully reinstated once this is over."

Glowering at him, she sighed. "I'd better be. I love my job and I'm damn good at it."

"I'm sure you are. But look at it this way," he said. "You've got a chance to save the world. How many can say that?"

Chapter 3

Maddie could only stare. This guy, this *journalist*, had no idea what he'd just asked her to do. She couldn't, she wouldn't, and she needed to figure out a way to tell him that wouldn't arouse suspicion. Betraying her own kind, not to mention the other paranormal beings who frequented Broken Chains, was an act punishable by death.

"Jake," she said, swiveling in her seat to face him. "I can't. The private investigative agency I work for specializes. Your particular request doesn't qualify."

His jaw clenched. Slowly, he shook his head. "First off, I don't believe you. Second, I'm well aware you know what's behind that door. I've seen you go through it. With or without your help, I will find out what's going on."

Though she knew he had no idea of the magnitude of the danger he'd be placing himself in, she couldn't help but admire—just the teeniest bit—his dogged determination. Even though it completely mystified her.

"What is it with you and that door?" she finally asked. "Do you honestly think whatever is behind it is worth you being beaten within an inch of your life? Because I can promise you, if you keep pursuing this, that's what will happen again. Or worse."

"Wow." He stared at her. "Whatever the secret is that you're hiding, it must be something big. I can't believe you're threatening me."

"Not threatening. Warning." She let her gaze roam over him. Even with his battered and bruised face, he was still handsome. His angular features and the light brown tint to his skin made his brown eyes stand out. She liked his lean muscular build and narrow waist. In fact, if she'd met Jake Cassel under different circumstances, she'd have dated him.

Even now, despite him ditching her earlier and then stating he planned to continue on his dangerous and foolhardy course of action, she felt a twinge of attraction.

A jolt of awareness struck her. She realized she had to do whatever it took to keep the truth hidden from him—and by doing so, keep him safe.

"Jake, look." She swallowed. "I'll do it. I'll take the job."

Instead of making him happy, he narrowed his eyes. "Why?"

That made her laugh. "What do you mean, why? I thought you wanted my help."

"I do."

"Yet you're still frowning."

"Because I can't shake the thought that you're somehow playing me."

Good instincts, though of course she couldn't say

that out loud. Instead, she shrugged. "Up to you. We don't come cheap. I completely understand if you've changed your mind."

He tilted his head, eyeing her as if honestly trying to read her mind. "Do you have a card?" he asked.

"Of course." Luckily, she'd just printed up a batch. She kept several in the console, so she pulled one out and handed it to him. "You can call me if you change your mind."

He accepted it, put it in his pocket and stared straight ahead.

"Where to?" she asked. He gave her an address in a neighborhood near hers, but a few streets away. She drove silently, efficiently, keeping her concentration on the road. When they finally pulled up in front of a small yellow frame house, she parked. "I hope you get to feeling better soon," she said.

"Thanks." Still avoiding her gaze, he slowly and painfully climbed from the car. "I'll be in touch."

She watched him walk up his driveway, waiting to pull away until he'd disappeared into the house. Then, because it was her habit, she made a note of the address on a small pad she kept in her console.

As soon as she got home, she called Carmen. Her friend didn't answer, which made Maddie suspect the Vamp harbored some resentment over being stood up. Maddie apologized over voice mail, said she needed to talk to her about a potential new case and hung up. No doubt Carmen would disappear for a day or two, as was her wont. When Maddie and their other partner, Shayla, called her on it, Carmen always simply shrugged and told them to get used to it, because that's what Vampires did.

Simple chores, like pouring herself a glass of wine and reheating a leftover bowl of pho she'd picked up for lunch yesterday, brought Maddie a measure of calm. A creature of habit, she liked things to happen as planned and in a particular order. This made her feel secure.

Tonight she'd agreed to meet Carmen for an early drink at Broken Chains. Everything had spiraled out of control before she'd even reached the iconic door. And while she hadn't intended to spend so much time tracking down Jake Cassel, she knew in her core that she'd done the right thing. There were procedures put in place—some of them primitive and violent—by those who protected their kind from discovery. Jake was lucky he'd only been beaten.

In fact, Maddie knew she actually had an obligation to uphold. Sipping her soup, she deliberated. If she made the call to the Pack Protectors—or, most likely, her brother, since he worked as one—they'd send people to round up the reporter. It wouldn't be pretty, it wouldn't be kind, and she wasn't a hundred percent sure Jake would survive.

Though calling her brother might be the right thing to do, she couldn't. Not yet. Instead, she'd keep an eye on Jake and try her best to protect him from harm. And from getting too close to the truth. If he'd actually hire her, that would make her task a lot easier.

She poured herself a second glass of wine and rinsed her bowl before putting it in the dishwasher. Carrying her wine to the living room, she clicked on the TV just in time to catch the evening news.

An ominous red banner was displayed across the scene. Breaking News. Apparently, there had been an explosion in one of the warehouses down near the pier. No one had been killed, there were three people injured and the police were looking for the suspects. It had not yet been called a terrorist attack and motive had not yet been determined. The warehouse had been believed to be empty, but firefighters said it was not.

When the camera panned the crowd, Maddie let out a little yelp of surprise. That woman in the group over to one side—tall, blonde and elegant—looked like Carmen.

Maddie hit the pause button on her remote and went back. Yep. She paused again. For whatever reason, Carmen was down near the pier. And from the looks of things, she wasn't alone. She stood arm-in-arm with a ruggedly handsome military-type man. He gave off a dangerous yet sexy vibe. He'd have to, she thought, to keep up with Carmen.

No wonder her friend hadn't answered her phone. Maddie couldn't say she blamed her. Jake made Maddie feel the same way—like going off the grid and getting to know him.

She found herself grinning when she thought of Jake. He didn't realize it, but she'd only told him the truth. While she knew what she was planning on doing walked a fine line as far as Pack law, she'd be careful. If, at any moment, Jake got too close to the truth, she'd talk to her brother, but right now she thought she could redirect Jake to some other story. The only problem was that she'd need to find one first.

In the years since moving to Galveston, Maddie had been on a lot of dates, especially when she'd worked as a police dispatcher. Human men, Shifter men, and even a Merman or two. Not a single one of them affected her the way Jake did.

Because she had an analytical mind, she sat down and tried to figure out what specifically attracted her to him.

It could be his dark good looks, but she'd dated many handsome men. She didn't know him well enough for it to be his personality or sense of humor, which brought her an odd sort of relief. Physical attraction was easily dealt with. She certainly wasn't ready for anything stronger.

The next morning, Maddie set to work. Taking her time, she snapped a camera phone pic of the sheet she'd printed out with The Shadow Agency's rates. She'd actually had to print out an amended list, as she couldn't send Jake the one that listed items like "Undersea Investigation," which was Shayla's area, since she happened to be a Mermaid.

After she'd sent the text to Jake, she tried again to call Carmen. She went straight to voice mail, which meant her Vampire friend had disappeared. With a sigh, Maddie left another message, knowing Carmen wouldn't call until she'd finished with whatever it was that she did when she disappeared.

Next, she phoned Shayla. Though her Mermaid friend had just returned from her honeymoon, Maddie really needed someone to talk to about this entire Jake situation.

Shayla answered and sounded delighted. "I was just thinking about you," she exclaimed. "I told Zach I needed some girl time with you and Carmen."

"Carmen's gone on one of her disappearances," Maddie said, relieved. "But I'd love to meet up with you for a drink at Broken Chains when you have time. I need to talk to you about something."

"I hope that's not as serious as it sounds," Shayla teased. "Either way, you know I'm full of advice, whether needed or not. Can you make it tonight around eight?"

"Perfect. I'll get there early to snag our usual table."

After ending the call, Maddie felt like a heavy weight had been lifted from her chest. Even though

her friend wasn't Pack, Shayla understood all too well
the intricate nature of keeping their truths hidden from
humans. Heck, Maddie wouldn't have minded if Shayla
brought Zach, her husband. Since Zach was also Pack,
Maddie would definitely welcome his input, though she
wouldn't have been able to speak as freely if it were
just her and Shayla.

Trying not to look at the clock too often, Maddie
caught up on housework, went grocery shopping and
checked her email. She heated up leftover pizza for her
dinner, reapplied her makeup and tried to decide what
outfit to wear. In the end, she went with a simple black
skirt and light green sheer top over a black camisole.
Though she usually wore ballet slipper–type flats, she
tried on a pair of heels. In the end, she discarded them
and slipped on her usual comfy shoes.

Dangly silver earrings and several cute bracelets
and she was out the door an hour early. As was her
habit, she parked near Pier 21 and walked back in the
direction of the bar. The salt-scented sea breeze felt
warm and familiar, reminding her how long it had been
since she'd visited the beach. Now that tourist season
was over, she needed to go. Fall was always a good
time, even though her favorite time to meander down
the sand was winter, when the colder water kept even
most locals away.

As she strolled toward the bar, she found herself
wondering where Jake hid when he did his surveillance. He'd claimed to have spent weeks watching the
dead-end alley, but for the life of her she couldn't see
where. This time, she'd pay special attention to her surroundings and see if she could spot him.

When she reached the alley, she slowly pirouetted.
Regular protocol demanded those entering the alley
check left and right, making sure no humans were in the

vicinity before proceeding to the door. Now, in addition to that, she realized the abandoned warehouse across the street still had numerous windows that had not been boarded up, some with shattered glass. It would be a simple thing for someone like Jake to gain entrance and set up a camera in one of those windows. In fact, for all she knew he might be there right now.

Refusing to wave, she finally made her way down the alley, knocked on the weathered door and waited. After a moment, it swung open and she stepped inside, then waited until it closed automatically behind her.

Because she was Shifter, the smells hit her first. Smoke and beer and whiskey, along with the various scents of other bodies. Next came the noise. Even though the band had not yet started playing, there was the low hum of voices, the clinking of glass and silverware, the scraping of chairs on the old wooden floor.

She sighed with pleasure. Of all the places she frequented on the island, this bar felt the most like home.

Wending her way through the crowd, she smiled when she saw Jason, her favorite bartender, had placed a small Reserved sign on her favorite table.

Waving at him, she took a seat. Immediately, he brought her a tall glass of wheat beer, her usual. She told him Shayla would be joining her, but not Carmen, and he nodded, whistling cheerfully as he walked off.

A shadow fell and she looked up, smiling. Her smile faded as she realized it wasn't her friend. Instead, a tall, muscular male Shifter stood glowering down at her.

"I'm not interested," she started to say, then gasped when he grabbed her arm in a painful grip.

"We need to talk," he said. "You've been seen with that human reporter. I'm a Pack Protector. I don't think I need to warn you of the severity of your crime against the Pack if you've revealed anything to him."

* * *

Nothing could have prepared him for the way Maddie affected him. After all, Jake considered himself like a bulldog. Once he fixated on a story, nothing got in his way. Nothing.

Not even a sexy redhead with a smattering of freckles across her nose. Then why couldn't he stop thinking about her?

When he'd asked to hire her, he hadn't expected her to eventually agree. After all, he knew she had secrets and they were tied in with whatever was behind that damn door. If his investigative reporting uncovered something illegal, something dangerous, he had to be prepared to take her down, too. This knowledge made his stomach churn.

Especially since he knew it could be worse than he'd originally suspected. When he'd seen the news of the explosion in a warehouse near Pier 21, he'd immediately thought of *them*, the mysterious group of individuals who met behind that strange old door.

Especially when, without any proof, the anchorman speculated that this might have been a terrorist attack. He'd said this as casually as if speaking about the weather. Sloppy reporting, Jake knew. Yet of course, this possibility made him wonder. Terrorists. What if a local cell of them met in that place along that dead-end alleyway? That would explain the reason for refusing to open the door and for the two men to jump him there.

No. He refused to play a guessing game. His journalistic integrity demanded facts. Without them, he had nothing.

The more he thought about it, the more he realized Maddie Kinslow might be his best chance at getting an actual lead.

He pulled out the business card she'd given him. *The*

Shadow Agency was emblazoned across the top. Underneath that, *A specialized private investigation firm.* And then simply her name and phone number.

Specialized. In what? He turned the card over in his hand. To be fair, she'd tried to tell him her company handled only a certain type of clientele, though she hadn't been specific.

Deciding, he pulled out his phone and dialed her number. His call went straight to voice mail. He left his name and number, nothing else. Now to see if she'd actually return the call.

When his phone rang five minutes later, his heart leaped in his chest. "That was quick," he said after answering.

"Yeah, well… I've been worried about you." She made the confession in a husky voice that had his body stirring.

Ruthlessly, he tamped down the desire. "Don't," he snapped. "I'm fine. I just need a little time to heal and I'll be back to normal."

To his surprise, this statement made her chuckle. "I'll never figure out what it is about men that they think they have to be so tough. You forget, Jake. I was there. I saw you."

Instead of replying, he let his silence speak for itself.

"Okay," she said when he didn't respond. "What did you need? Why did you call me?"

Though he'd already begun to doubt the wisdom of his decision, he decided to go through with it. "I want to hire you."

Now she went quiet. He waited her out.

"For the same reason as before?" she finally asked. "Because you want me to help you find out what's behind the door?"

"Yes."

She sighed. "Are you absolutely certain you truly want to continue to pursue this? Because I can tell you this—it's dangerous. As in, you could lose your life, dangerous."

Deep down, he'd suspected as much, but hearing her confirm it made his gut twist. "Are you involved in whatever it is?" he asked.

"I can promise you, whatever you think you know is wrong," she said, without answering his question.

"Then enlighten me," he urged. "I've been watching that place for nearly a month. I've seen all the people coming and going. I've see you there numerous times, Maddie Kinslow. And you went inside. Why play games? Just tell me what you can and I'll find out the rest."

Again she sighed. "I wish I could, but then I'd have to kill you." She laughed, but he couldn't shake the feeling she wasn't kidding. "While I can't reveal the truth to you, even though it is such a minor thing, I can help you get a fabulous story."

"Are you offering me a bribe? Because it sure sounds like it." Now it was his turn to laugh, though without humor. "I have to say, the fact that you're actually doing that makes me even more eager to uncover the secret."

Silence.

"This is a bad idea," she finally replied. "Forget I ever offered my services. I wish you luck, Jake Cassel. Believe me, you'll need it."

She ended the call.

He cursed. He'd gone too far and lost his chance. The beautiful Maddie Kinslow would be avoiding him now. What a shame, because he truly would have enjoyed getting to know her. Maybe it was all for the best. With such strong attraction sizzling between them, she'd probably have been too much of a distraction. Now he could focus solely on the story.

His phone rang again. "It's me," Maddie said, the sexy sound of her voice sending a shiver down his spine. "Look, I like you, Jake. I really do. But there is too much at stake here. People's lives, homes, families. Are you sure you don't want to at least consider my offer?"

"How can I when I don't even know what I'd be giving up?" He used the most reasonable argument he had. "Tell me what's behind the door and let me decide."

She hesitated. "Fine. There's a bar behind that door. Access is granted only to certain individuals. See? No story. Not even interesting."

"A bar?" He didn't bother to hide his skepticism. "What would possibly be so secretive about a *bar*?"

"The clientele. It's imperative that no one but certain...people are allowed in."

He had to give it to her. Her story had enough intrigue in it to interest him. And he knew it had to be—whatever, if any, part of it was true—the tip of the iceberg.

"Well?" she prodded after he didn't respond. "What do you think?"

Now he knew he had to play it cool. While he didn't entirely buy her story, in the end she was the best and only lead he had. If he "hired" her, eventually she might slip up.

"If your rates are reasonable, I'll definitely consider it," he finally said, trying to sound as disinterested as possible.

This time, he hung up first.

Pretending not to notice the man who'd been parked in the expensive car across the street and watching his house, Jake limped down his sidewalk to get the mail.

The sun had begun to set and the breeze carried the smell of the sea. Bruised and battered didn't begin to describe how he felt today—more like he'd been run over by a large truck loaded with cement.

Late-model Mercedes, navy blue. Dark tinted windows, no plate on the front.

While he had no idea who his shadow might be, he figured it had something to do with that dead-end alleyway and the door that wouldn't open for him.

Back inside the house, he glanced at the clock. If he planned to continue his surveillance, he'd need to head downtown soon. He'd taken great pains to ensure his point of entry into the abandoned warehouse would be hidden from any inquisitive eyes. And now he had no doubt they'd be looking.

He opened his laptop and checked his email. Finally, he really examined the message from Maddie detailing her company's rates. While he had no idea if these prices were competitive or not, it wasn't like he had another option. Maddie knew what went on behind that door. He just had to figure out a way to get her to tell him.

As dusk began to arrive, he knew if he wanted to leave his house, he'd need to shake his tail. If he got into his car and drove, the guy would certainly follow him. Normally he'd simply go out the back door, climb the fence that separated his yard from the guy behind him, and walk out onto the next street over. From there, it wasn't too long a walk to reach a bus stop, or if necessary, he could call for a taxi. But his bruised and battered body simply wasn't up to it yet.

Instead, he needed to get rid of the stalker. First, he called Maddie. But the call went straight to voice mail. Okay, he could understand that. It was after hours and he hadn't yet become her client.

Next up, he dialed the Galveston Police Department's nonemergency number. "I'd like to report a suspicious vehicle parked outside my house," he said. "I was jumped and beaten up the other day and I think the same individual has come back to try to finish the job. Could you please send someone?"

The dispatcher rerouted him to 911. After he repeated his situation, he was told to stay inside the house and wait for the police to arrive. She asked him to stay on the line, so he did.

A moment later, a police cruiser turned onto his street and pulled up behind the parked Mercedes. The officer got out and walked up to the driver's-side window. He stood there a few moments, clearly talking to the driver. Jake hoped he'd asked for a driver's license and registration. If he at least had a name, he could do more research.

Finally, the policeman stepped back, lifted his hand in a friendly wave and watched as the luxury car drove off. One it had turned the corner, the officer walked up Jake's sidewalk and rang the bell.

Ending the call with the dispatcher, Jake hurried to answer the door. "Thank you so much, Officer," he began.

"You're welcome. But I wanted to let you know, there was no reason for you to be concerned. That was the mayor's son. He works for the City Planning and Zoning Department. He was parked on your street for business."

Though his insides froze, Jack managed to nod. "Good to know. Thanks again for coming out, Officer."

"No problem. I'm glad I could put your mind at ease." The policeman peered at him. "They did a hell of a job on you, didn't they? I hope you saw a doctor."

"I did."

"Good."

Finally the patrolman left. Jake closed the door behind him and made sure he locked the dead bolt. The mayor's son? Just how high up did this story go? If anything, this made him even more determined to get to the truth.

Moving as fast as he could, Jake hurried to his car. But before he even reached it, the navy Mercedes turned back onto his street and parked in the exact same spot.

Chapter 4

Carmen hid her surprise when Rick took her to the pier. Once the shrimp boats came in, sometimes the men would get together and drink and play cards or dice. An occasional prostitute worked one corner. Mostly, both tourists and locals avoided this place. It was nothing like Pier 21 with its popular restaurants and fish markets, close to The Strand. It wasn't even like Pier 19 or 20, with Sampson and Sons and Katie's selling seafood right off the boat.

No, this was further down, past a few abandoned, dilapidated buildings with cracked sidewalks and weeds. An overall sense of decay permeated the place. Once, smugglers had hung out here, with illegal gambling and gin joints and a whorehouse or two. Now, most of that was only a memory, though Carmen had been here once or twice during its heyday.

These days, this was where men went when they wanted to do things in secret, where the dim lighting and sense of anonymity made them feel at ease. It was an area she sometimes frequented when the craving for fresh, warm blood grew too strong. She'd become quite a pro at extracting just enough to make her target pass out, but without serious harm.

"Here." Rick's gravelly voice brought her back to the present. "In a moment, there's going to be an explosion. It will bring the rats scurrying from their holes."

She swung around and stared. "Why?"

"It's something I promised to do, as a sign of good faith. There's an illegal shipment of guns in one of these buildings. The Sons of Darkness needed a distraction so they could get them out. This will be a big one." He got out his phone and prepared to punch in a number. "Are you ready?"

"Sure." This got more interesting by the minute.

"Here we go." He dialed a number. A second later, a loud boom sounded and the ground shook. Someone screamed and someone else swore. Several people staggered toward them, some of them drunk, others in shock.

"I'm calling 911," Rick told them, holding up his phone. She watched, wondering if he really would since he didn't appear to be in any hurry to punch in the numbers. Maximizing time for the distraction, she guessed.

Someone else must have called, though, because sirens sounded in the distance, getting closer. The occasional straggler came down the sidewalk, one or two of them appearing shell shocked. Thick black smoke billowed from somewhere behind them, appearing to almost follow them as they fled.

"Do you think there were any injuries?" she asked.

"No one was seriously hurt," Rick assured her, sounding positive even though she didn't see how he could be certain. "The bomb was in a locked warehouse where we stacked some dry hay and bundled newspaper. Just enough to start a good fire with possible building collapse. It's far enough from the warehouse with the guns that no one will spot the crew moving the cargo. A perfect plan, if I do say so myself."

Since he sounded so pleased with himself, she felt the need to point out what seemed to her an obvious flaw. "But you destroyed a building. Most likely a historical one."

His jaw tightened. "That kind of collateral damage is better than people. Millions are at risk unless we do our job and get inside this group. I hope you understand that."

"I do." Before she could say anything else, the sirens grew closer. Lights flashing, two patrol cars pulled up the next street over. A moment later, a fire engine and ambulance arrived. Along with a growing crowd of people, they watched as Galveston PD cordoned off the street and sidewalk.

Soon a KHOU 11 news van arrived, which seemed awfully quick since they were out of Houston. They set up a reporter with her back to the mayhem, handed her a microphone and began filming.

"You do know in a few minutes that reporter is going to start asking people what they saw?" she said drily.

"That's good. We want to be seen. How else can I make sure Sons of Darkness know I was there?"

"You seem to have thought of everything." She shook her head.

"That's my job," he countered. "And I'm damn good at it."

Before long a couple of the other news stations sent their own crews. The crowd of onlookers continued to swell. News cameras panned the area. Rick grabbed Carmen's arm and made sure they were front and center, virtually guaranteeing them a spot on one, if not all, of the stations' evening news programs.

Since she'd spent most of her long, long life avoiding the spotlight, Carmen struggled with this. While she managed to keep her outward appearance cool, calm and collected, inside she battled the urge to step back and disappear into the large group.

But Rick's plan, she concluded reluctantly, actually made sense. If this was what was needed for them to gain entrance into that group, so be it. The idea that she—Carmen Vargas, Vampire—could make a difference in this world intrigued her. Plus, if she were totally honest, as she always was, she ached to get her hands on a microscope and take a close look at this new virus. Because of her expertise, the CDC had even contacted her several times, wanting her to come to Atlanta and work with them. She'd been tempted, but she'd come to value her friends and life here in Galveston, so she'd declined. Since they were no doubt involved closely in this case, she had a feeling that was how her name had been mentioned. For that, she considered herself lucky.

"Okay," Rick said, tightening his grip on her arm. "Time to go."

This time, she let him pull her away without questioning. He led her through the thick throng of people, up the sidewalk and to the still-crowded Pier 21 area. A couple had just gotten up from a bench along the walkway, and he hurried them to it.

"No matter what happens," he told her sotto voce, "show no expression. Just go along with it."

"No worries. I'm a master at that."

They sat. He put his arm around her shoulder, drawing her close. She let herself relax into the curve of his arm, liking the solidity of his muscular body. They pretended to be people watching. Despite the commotion going on a few blocks over, most of the ones strolling by her were fixated on having a good time.

"Mind if I join you?" The tall man wore a baseball cap pulled low over his eyes. Carmen eyed him coolly but didn't speak.

"Sure," Rick said, pulling Carmen closer to him so there was additional room on the bench. "Have a seat."

The stranger sat, staring straight ahead and ignoring him. Every sense alert, Carmen pretended not to be hyperconscious of him.

"Are you the biologist?" he finally asked, low-voiced.

Widening her eyes, Carmen nodded. "I am. Actually, I'm an infectious disease specialist. And this is my husband, Rick." The instant she spoke, she realized she hadn't asked if they were using assumed names or not. Most likely not, at least for her, since these people no doubt had wanted to verify her credentials.

"Rick." The man nodded, his gaze skittering from her to Rick and back again. "I'm Landers. The shipment was moved without a hitch. Thank you for your help."

"No problem." Rich shrugged, both his demeanor and his voice casual. "I did what you requested, and here we are. Are we in?"

"You're in." Landers stood, glancing left and then right. Finally, he focused on Rick and grinned. "Just so you know, we have several other guys who can do what you can do, but only one other biologist in our employ. Your wife is infinitely more valuable to us than you could ever be."

Carmen exhaled, recognizing the tactic. Divide and conquer. Except she knew this wouldn't work, not this time. "It's okay," she said, her tone lofty. "He likes that I make so much more money than he does. He jokes about being a kept man."

"Really?" Landers shook his head. "Well, there's none of that around here. Every single one of us has to earn our keep."

"And I will, I swear." Shooting Carmen a cross look, Rick shifted his weight from foot to foot. "You won't regret hiring me, I promise you."

"We'd better not." Was that a flash of pleasure across Landers's face? Carmen thought so, which meant she'd been correct. For whatever reason, Landers wanted to put a wedge in between her and Rick.

If that's what he wanted, she'd speak to Rick privately and make sure that's what he got.

"He follows orders well," she drawled, just for the hell of it. "Ask me how I know."

Rick flushed but didn't respond. This prompted another snorting laugh from Landers. "I'll bet he does," he sneered, leering at her.

"Now, can we possibly get out of here?" she asked, pretending to be uneasy with their location. "There are too many people around. If someone hears, they might have questions. Questions for which we will not have answers. I prefer to avoid collateral damage whenever possible."

Landers stared. "As if you've done this sort of thing before," he scoffed.

For an answer, she only lifted one perfectly shaped eyebrow.

Instantly, the other man's demeanor changed. "If you'll come with me," Landers said, "I'll take you both to meet the others."

"Lead the way," Carmen pronounced. "I'm looking forward to getting started."

Keeping his arm around Carmen, Rick followed Landers to a black Escalade with dark tinted windows.

With shiny chrome accents everywhere, it was not the most inconspicuous vehicle. Who knew? Maybe they wanted it that way.

As they approached, the driver stepped out and opened the back door, motioning for Carmen to get in first. Moving with her usual fluid grace, she climbed inside. Rick followed her, trying unsuccessfully to avoid staring at the gleaming length of shapely leg her short skirt displayed.

Once the door closed, Landers got up front, riding shotgun. "It's about a thirty-minute ride, depending on traffic," he said.

"Off-island?" Carmen asked, frowning.

"Not too far, but yes. La Marque."

This surprised her, Rick knew. Surprised him, too. La Marque was a small town. Building a quality lab and running an operation of that size without attracting unwanted attention would be more difficult in a place like that.

As they drove, Landers turned around several times, making innocuous comments about the passing landscape. His frank stare assessed Carmen, as if weighing what options he had as far as trusting her.

Feeling the need to reassert the fact that he and Carmen were a team, Rick took her hand and clasped it firmly. Though he felt her briefly tense, her expression remained smooth and unruffled. And beautiful. He couldn't blame Landers for repeatedly checking her out. Hell, even Rick fought a constant battle to keep from staring at her.

Finally, they exited 45 and turned left, passing under the freeway and by the single motel, eventually leaving pavement for a gravel road. The houses here were small frame structures, and the flat landscape and sparse vegetation made everything visible.

For the first time, Rick wondered what they'd gotten into. He squeezed Carmen's hand, telling her silently to be ready in case this was some sort of trick. She squeezed back, cutting her gaze to connect with his to let him know she'd thought the same thing.

One more turn and they found themselves surrounded by pasture. Cattle grazed and vultures circled in the cloudless sky above. They continued on until they reached a black wrought-iron gate, which was closed. The driver punched a code into a keypad and the gates swung slowly open.

After turning in, they continued on to a low-slung stone ranch house. Nearby were several outbuildings, one of them a well-constructed barn that appeared to be new. There were black burglar bars over the windows.

Which meant that had to be the lab.

As they rolled to a stop in front of the house, two armed men stepped outside to greet them. Though inside Rick tensed up, he kept his posture and expression relaxed.

Again, the driver jumped out and opened the door, this time on Carmen's side so she could get out first. And she did, with an impressive display of leg. Her sky-high heels made her look both dangerous and sexy. Exactly his kind of woman, except for her being a Vampire. Too bad.

Head high, expression cool, she looked both of the newcomers up and down. Rick hid his smile.

Landers came around and told them to follow him. Once they'd gone up the steps onto the porch, someone pushed open the screen door and stepped out of the way. Rick reached for Carmen's hand as they went inside.

The small room had been sparsely furnished. Three men looked up as they approached, though they all remained seated. Eyeing them, Rick wondered which of the three was the leader. Landers made the introductions in a clipped voice. The short, wiry man with the long white beard was Tommy. The bald guy who looked like a linebacker gone to seed was called Holt. And the thin, pale dude with the flat dark eyes was Gus.

They all dipped their chins in greeting. If Landers found it odd that no one spoke, he didn't show it. He motioned that Rick and Carmen should sit, so they took the empty spot at one end of the soiled couch.

"We got the shipment," Landers announced, filling the others in on the explosion Rick had engineered as a diversion. They listened carefully. Rick couldn't help but notice the way their gazes continually went to Carmen, as if they hadn't seen a woman in too long. For the first time since meeting her, he was glad she was a Vampire. At least he knew she could defend herself against any human male's unwanted attention.

"She's the biologist," Landers finally said, gesturing at Carmen.

"I'm thinking Sheldon's not gonna be real happy about her," Holt said, scratching his double chin.

"Maybe not," Landers replied. "But he could use the help. And look at her. What red-blooded man could stay mad in the face of such beauty?"

Though Rick's stomach twisted hearing this, he pretended not to care.

Carmen, however, apparently had heard enough. "I'm right here," she said, her voice clear and hard. "I can hear you, you know."

While Tommy and Holt fidgeted, each appearing embarrassed, Gus simply continued to stare. The hair on the back of Rick's neck lifted. Something was off with that one. He bore watching, in case he turned out to be especially dangerous.

Landers laughed. "True. I'm sorry, sweetheart. I'll try to do better."

"I'm not your sweetheart." Yanking her hand free from Rick's, Carmen pushed to her feet, eyeing them with clear disdain. "I've changed my mind about helping. I don't see anything here that makes me think you could actually pull off engineering something as complicated as a new virus."

Damn. What the hell was she doing? Did she really think these people were going to just let them go? Not likely, especially since they'd now seen their hideout.

"And," she continued, "even if this Sheldon person is some kind of biology genius, I fail to see how you could use something like this to your benefit. Thanks, but no thanks."

Though he had to tamp down his alarm, Rick stood, too. He hoped Carmen knew what she was doing. "Well, the boss has spoken," he drawled, while keeping his eye on the others to gauge their reactions. "I guess this means we're out."

"Not so fast." Landers placed himself squarely between them and the door. "It's too late. You can't quit now. You know where we are and you've seen all of our faces."

Rick decided he'd take a chance. "Maybe so, but none of that matters. We haven't laid eyes on your boss, so I'm thinking we're good to go. If you'd just pay me for the explosion, we can call it even."

Landers narrowed his eyes. "What do you mean, you haven't seen the boss? You've been dealing with me all along."

Unsure whether to laugh or take the other man seriously, Rick realized it would be prudent to play it safe. "You're in charge here?"

Immediately, Landers nodded.

"No, he's not," Carmen put in, her voice cool. "It's the quiet one, Gus. He's the leader here."

Landers froze. Judging by the panicked look he shot Gus, Carmen was right. Good instincts.

"Grab her," Gus ordered, his tone bored though his expression seemed furious. "Put her in my bedroom. It's time she and I had a private, one-on-one chat."

Rick stiffened, ready for whatever might happen next. To his relief, Carmen allowed Landers and Tommy to manhandle her, leading her from the room. The glint in her eyes told Rick she was actually enjoying this.

Rick started after her, but Holt, moving surprisingly fast for such a large man, blocked his way. "You wait with me. The boss will let us know when he's finished."

There was nothing Carmen loved better than taking down a power-hungry idiot who thought he could dominate her. While she knew she had to be careful so she didn't blow this important mission, there was no way in Hades she'd let this Gus person push her around.

His two henchmen shoved her into a large bedroom, dominated by an ornate four-poster bed. She pretended to stumble, but pivoted on her feet, ready to face the leader of the Sons of Darkness. As if. If only they had an idea of what a real son of darkness could be. Silly humans. They had no clue, nor would they ever.

Gus strode into the room and gestured at the other men to leave. Once the door closed behind him, he crossed his arms, his flat gaze hard. "Why are you here?" he demanded.

Since this line of questioning was not at all what she'd expected, she took a moment to choose her reply. "For money," she said. "As I'm sure you're aware, I was let go from my job."

He continued to glare at her, as if by the force of his gaze he thought he could compel her to be truthful. Such a stunt might work on humans, but since she was a Vampire, she had to suppress the urge to laugh in his face.

"That's what I've been told, but I don't believe it." There was the slightest hint of a challenge in his even tone. "I've looked up your credentials," he continued. "You're one of the top three leading biologists in the United States."

In the world, she thought, but didn't say it. "I didn't believe it, either," she said, her voice sullen. "They accused me of stealing narcotics." Spur of the moment, but she thought it sounded realistic. "Among other things," she added, just in case. "None of it is true. I'm a damn good biologist." After all, she'd had centuries to hone her skills.

Looking her up and down, he grimaced. His flat eyes reminded her of some really ancient Vampires she'd met once. But this one was only human; she could smell the coppery scent of his blood and hear the steady thump of his heart.

As the silence stretched on, he continued to stare at her, no doubt trying to make her uncomfortable, but she refused to allow this. Instead, she stared right back and waited.

"Do you know what we're developing here?" he asked.

This time she didn't have to feign her interest. "Yes. A new virus. I admit, I find that fascinating. I'd love to be part of research like that."

"It's not research," he corrected her. "We plan to use it if we have to. Unless we receive what we want from the US Government."

Now they were on tricky ground. Rick hadn't told

her how much of this she was supposed to know. "What do you want?" she asked, even though she already knew the answer.

"War with West Latvia," he immediately said. "I want that country's trade wiped off the map."

"But why?" And this truly was the part she didn't understand. "What are your reasons?"

"Russia." He spoke the name as if saying it should be enough. Still, she waited, not sure what he meant.

He sighed at her lack of reaction. "Russia trades heavily with them. It's a way to buy myself power."

"But why would you want power with Russia?"

This time, he laughed. "How about you just stick to biology? I don't have time to explain the intricate nature of politics to you."

His condescending tone had her clenching her teeth. But she kept her annoyance in check, aware the stakes were far too high for her to blow it on something so trivial.

"Money can buy power," she finally said. "I'm guessing you're aware of how much something like this would fetch on the international market?"

"We're exploring all options." He waved his hand in dismissal. "I can see how someone like you might be valuable to my organization. Your husband, though— I'm not sure I need him."

Alarm prickled along her spine, though she took care to show no reaction. Straightening, she tilted her head and eyed him the way one would look at a particularly noxious rodent. "My husband and I are a team. You can't have me without him."

He laughed. "You're not running things here, sweetheart."

This human was damn lucky she'd had centuries to learn how to control her anger. Even so, she felt that familiar flash of rage and wanted to crush him. Which she easily could, right here and right now, without blinking an eye.

"Again, I'm not your sweetheart," she drawled. "It's me and Rick or neither of us. Now, do we have a deal or not?" Bracing herself for Gus's reaction to her declaration, she knew she had to come up with a quick plan in case he decided to simply kill them. He had no idea he couldn't—the only thing that would end Rick was a silver bullet or fire. As for her, a stake through the heart. Beyond that, they were invincible. They could be hurt, true. But Rick's kind had supernaturally fast healing powers. She couldn't bleed if she hadn't been fed enough blood.

Instead of yet another staring contest, Gus laughed again. She detected a slight note of unease hidden in his pretend mirth. "You're a tough one," he said. "I will agree to take both of you—on one condition."

She nodded.

"No drug use while you're in my employ. Either of you. If I find out you indulged, I will kill you."

Finally, something that actually made sense. "Agreed," she replied. "As long as you leave my husband to me. I will need him at the lab, working as my assistant. He follows my orders really, really well. If he doesn't…" She lifted one shoulder delicately, letting her meaning sink in. "There are consequences to pay."

Chapter 5

Maddie stared up at the man, shocked at first. "How dare you," she said, her expression turning icy. "Do you know who my brother is?"

"Lady, your brother could be the President of the United States for all I care," he responded. "My job is to protect our Pack from discovery. You've been seen with that human who's been snooping around here."

Shaking off his hand, she spoke her brother's name. "Colton Kinslow," she said. "My brother is also a Pack Protector. Why don't you ask him if his sister would ever endanger the Pack?"

He stared at her, his expression still hard. "I'll call him and let him know what's been going on. I expect he'll be phoning you. Just be aware, we have our eyes on Jake Cassel. If we learn you have, in any way, enabled him to gain access to information that is off-limits to humans, you will be arrested and prosecuted to the fullest extent of the law."

Having said that, he turned around and stomped off. Frowning, Maddie watched him go. What the heck had Jake done now? As far as she knew, he'd been caught lurking around Broken Chains and beat up for it. Was there more he hadn't told her?

As if he knew she'd been thinking about him, her cell phone rang and the caller ID showed Jake's number.

"Well, well, Jake Cassel," she answered. "Were your ears ringing?"

"What? Never mind. Just call off your dog."

Perplexed, she wondered if he'd taken too many painkillers or something. "I'm not sure I follow," she replied. "Maybe you should just lie down and get some rest."

Silence. For some reason, she could picture him dragging his hand through his hair. "Fair enough," he finally said. "I'm guessing you have no idea what I'm talking about."

"None whatsoever." Taking a long sip of her beer, she rolled her shoulders and tried to relax.

"Someone's parked outside my house, watching me. If I get in my car and drive anywhere, I know he'll follow me."

"Really? Have you tried it? How do you know for sure?"

Then she listened while he told her about calling the police and who the person claimed to be. When he got to the part about the stalker returning once the police had left, a shiver snaked up her spine. That and the fact that the Pack Protectors were actively interested in him meant there was more going on than she knew. Much more.

"I'm guessing you haven't told me everything," she said. While she couldn't inform him about the confrontation with the Pack Protector, she knew there had to be more to this than a case of a persistent reporter continually coming down the dead-end alleyway and trying to get Broken Chains' door to open. Other humans had tried in the past to no avail. No one paid them any mind, at least that she knew.

So what was so special about Jake Cassel? She got that he was a reporter, but he had no story. Even if he managed to make it inside Broken Chains—which he wouldn't—all he'd see was a bar with a bunch of people drinking and dancing. Like a private club. A human couldn't tell from looking at someone that they were a Shifter or a Vampire or a Merfolk. That was why all those different species were able to live side by side with humans, undetected.

And Broken Chains belonged to them, the nonhumans. It was their place, one of the few where they could go and relax and simply be themselves.

Sure, she found Jake Cassel attractive. It happened often. Shifters dated humans, Vampires dated Shifters, etc. Heck, her friend Shayla, who happened to be a Mermaid, had just married Zach, a Shifter. She was allowed to date Jake Cassel if she wanted. She wasn't permitted to let him find out her true nature unless they were in a serious, committed relationship.

One thing Maddie Kinslow believed in was following the rules. Though other private investigators might bend them once or twice, her father had raised her differently. He'd proven she could be a great PI without breaking the law. Did the Pack Protectors truly think she'd break Pack law and betray her own kind?

The silence had stretched out for so long she thought he might have hung up. "Jake? Are you there?"

"I am," he answered. "Just thinking. Where are you? Judging from the background noise, I'd guess a bar or restaurant. Do you mind if I join you? I need to get out of the house."

She nearly laughed out loud at the irony of that. "I'm sorry, but I already have plans. I'm meeting a friend. But even if I weren't, I think you really should consider staying in tonight and getting some rest so you can heal. Oh, there she is. I can see her crossing the room right now, so I'd better go. We'll talk later."

Not sounding very happy about that, Jake agreed and hung up.

"Shayla!" Maddie pushed to her feet, grinning from ear to ear. Every single man in the place watched as her stunning Mermaid friend made her way toward their table. With her silky mane of long black hair and her heart-shaped face, Shayla Dover-Cantrell tended to draw masculine attention. Even the large wedding ring on her left hand did little to deter their pursuit. Their other friend, Carmen, had a similar effect on men.

Reaching Maddie, Shayla enveloped her in a hug. "I know it's only been a couple of weeks, but it feels as if I haven't seen you in forever," she said, taking a seat.

"I know. How was the honeymoon?"

For the next several minutes, the two women caught up. Their waiter brought Shayla a glass of chardonnay, her usual beverage of choice, and a second beer for Maddie.

"What's he like, this Jake guy?" Shayla asked, eyeing her friend. "You really seem to like him."

Startled, Maddie had no choice but to laugh. "I do, you know. He's human and stubborn, but he seems to have a good heart. Plus, he's cute."

Her comment brought a grin to Shayla's face. "Too bad on the human part, since he can't come here."

Maddie hesitated, and then decided what the hell. "I might as well tell you everything," she said. "He wants to hire me. For some reason, he's obsessed with getting inside Broken Chains."

As Maddie explained, Shayla listened, her expression changing from incredulous to dismayed. When Maddie finished up with how the Pack Protector had threatened her, Shayla shook her head. "You need to dump him," she advised. "Jake Cassel might be cute, but I don't think he'd be worth all that trouble."

"But don't you see?" Maddie protested. "He hasn't done anything that other humans haven't done over the years. You know as well as I do that we get at least one per month, wandering down the alley and trying to open the door. Yet he was beat up, probably by Pack Protectors, and left for dead. Now someone is staking out his house. I've clearly been seen with him, and now I'm being threatened. None of this makes sense."

Shayla tilted her head. "You're not going to back off, are you?"

"Of course not," Maddie scoffed. "How could I? You know me. I can't let a puzzle go unsolved, and that's what this is."

Shayla laughed. "Just be careful," she said, taking a sip of her wine.

"Always." Maddie noticed her friend glancing at her watch. "What's up? Is there somewhere you need to be?"

With a sheepish grin, Shayla shrugged. "Not really. I'm just missing Zach."

"You could have brought him. I wouldn't have minded."

"Really? He wanted to come, but I told him it was girls' night. I thought it might be good for us to come up for air." Shayla blushed, leaving no doubt as to what she meant.

Maddie pushed away the twinge of jealousy. "Someday," she told her friend, "I hope to find a guy who makes me feel the way Zach does you."

"Oh, Maddie." Shayla jumped up and hugged her. "You will. Wait." She pulled back, peering into Maddie's face. "Are you thinking Jake might be that guy?"

"Who knows?" Maddie took a drink of her beer to hide her confusion. "I suppose anything is possible. Maybe. Maybe not."

"Gut instinct." Eyes narrowed, Shayla watched her closely. "Let me hear what your gut instinct says."

Because they were such good friends, Maddie gave serious thought to the question. "I'm attracted to him," she finally answered. "Intrigued by him. I don't know how much of that is because of the mystery, though. To be honest, I wouldn't mind having an intense fling with him as well as getting to the truth of why he's considered so dangerous to the Pack. Beyond that?" She shrugged. "I don't know."

Apparently, her answer satisfied Shayla. "Fair enough," Shayla said, raising her wineglass in a toast.

They sat and chatted another hour, each having one more drink, until the band began to play, making conversation difficult. Finally, their glasses were empty and they settled up the tab. Arm in arm, they walked to the door and outside.

At the end of the alley, Shayla stopped. "Now what?" she asked.

"Now I walk you to your car or to get a cab, like always," Maddie replied. As a Mermaid, Shayla couldn't defend herself like a Shifter or Vampire could. Therefore, Maddie or Carmen or both always made sure she was never left unaccompanied.

"Oh, that…" Shayla blushed again, just as an SUV pulled up. "I texted Zach so he'd come and get me."

"That was quick," Maddie said, her tone dry. "Let

me say hello to the lovestruck fool and then I'll let you two go on your way."

"Of course. But what are you going to do for the rest of the night? It's still pretty early. Maybe Jake would like some company."

Now it was Maddie's turn to blush. Unfortunately, when she did, she knew her pale skin turned the color of an overripe tomato, not all soft, appealing pink like Shayla's did.

Seeing the blush, Shayla chuckled. "I think you should find out if he would," she said. "Now come say hello to Zach so we can get home."

Maddie walked around to the driver's side and Zach rolled down the window. He tore his gaze away from his new bride long enough to smile at Maddie. "Do you need a lift to your car?" he asked. "I'd be glad to take you."

"Not tonight," she told him, lifting her head and sniffing the air. "With weather like this, I don't mind a walk." And since she was Shifter, she could easily defend herself if someone tried to jump her the way they'd jumped Jake.

Just thinking about him made her blush again. Luckily, Zach and Shayla were too engrossed in each other to notice.

Maddie said her goodbyes and watched as her friends drove away. Then, before she chickened out, she got out her phone and called Jake.

After ending the call with Maddie, Jake looked outside again. The car was still there. He thought about walking outside with a bottle of water and offering it to the driver, but in the end decided against that idea. His bruised and bandaged body and aching ribs warned him to be more careful.

Though he hated to admit it, Maddie was right. He did need to rest and heal. Instead of giving the stalker something to do, he'd let him sit out there with nothing going on and be bored. At least that made Jake's mood improve. More than anything, he hated to feel as if he were powerless. After the childhood he'd had, he'd sworn never to put himself in that position again.

He pulled out his laptop and continued his research about werewolves. As far as he could tell, they were the stuff of urban legend. Lots of people claimed to have seen one, but there existed absolutely no proof. They were beloved by literature and filmmaking, and these days people seemed to regard them with a kind of benevolent fondness rather than any real fear.

Not for the first time, Jake doubted what he'd seen with his own eyes. Of course, he shouldn't. He was a trained reporter. Observant by both nature and calling. It wasn't likely he'd imagine something like this. Especially since he'd never even thought about werewolves at all until the moment he'd actually seen one.

When his cell phone rang, he almost didn't answer. But when from habit he checked the caller ID and saw it was Maddie, he did.

"Are you still awake?" she asked, a smile in her voice.

His heart skipped a beat. "Of course. What's up?"

"My friend had to go. Since it's still early, I was wondering if you still wanted company? I mean, I could come by if you'd like."

"I'd enjoy that," he responded, not bothering to pretend not to care. "We can talk about the case."

She laughed. "You definitely have a one-track mind. I'm not sure whether to be flattered or insulted."

Was she *flirting* with him? He swallowed, stunned.

"Come on over," he said, his voice as casual as he

could make it. "I've got beer. We can order a pizza if you want."

"Now you're talking. Text me the address again, please. I've got to walk to my car and then I can get on my way."

"Walk to your car?" He hoped it wasn't a long walk. A beautiful woman out walking alone made an easy target for some guy looking for trouble.

"Yep. It's not too far now. Just a couple of blocks. I'm near The Strand, so there are lots of people around."

He rattled off the address and ended the call. She'd said she was near The Strand. Had she been near the dead-end alley with the mysterious door? He resolved to ask her directly. After all, he saw no reason why they should play games.

Twenty minutes later, her headlights swept his front window. He hurried to the door, just in case the guy in the parked car decided to try and confront her. To his surprise, the stalker was gone.

"Hey there!" Smiling, Maddie greeted him. With her wavy red hair loose around her shoulders, she managed to look both innocent and sexy in her black skirt and green top, with a sleeveless back tank underneath. He noticed that even though she wore flat shoes, her legs seemed to go on for miles. As she got closer, a jolt of pure lust punched him low in the gut.

"Come on in," he said, stepping aside. As she walked past him, he got a tantalizing whiff of her perfume, which was floral and light. She took a seat on his couch and eyed his laptop, which he'd left open on the coffee table.

"Just doing some research," he told her. "Nothing too serious. Would you like a beer?"

"I'd better not," she said. "I had two at the bar. Just water for me, please."

When he returned from the kitchen, she was leaning close to his laptop, unabashedly reading what was displayed on the screen.

"Here you go," he said, handing her the water.

"Thank you." She flashed a brief smile before returning her attention back to the computer. "You're reading about *werewolves*?"

Something about her tone didn't ring right. "I am," he answered. "Fascinating topic. Do you know anything at all about them?"

She shook her head. "Only that they don't exist. I thought you were a journalist. I wasn't aware you planned on writing fiction."

"Ouch." Taking a swig from his beer, he sat next to her, close enough that if he moved his leg, they could bump knees. "I'm actually considering writing an exposé, attempting to prove their existence. I just need proof."

Now he knew he hadn't imagined that flash of alarm in her eyes. "That sounds interesting," she replied. But her voice contained little conviction.

"You think I'm nuts, don't you?"

"I mean, think about what you just said. Sounds really crazy."

"Maybe, maybe not," he argued. "But if I can get real proof, nondoctored video, people will have no choice but to believe me."

"I don't think they ever will. It's too far in the realm of myths and legends." She met his gaze, her expression troubled. "And even if werewolves were somehow real, what would be the point of making people aware of them? Can you imagine what kind of hellish reaction that would provoke? It'd be the Middle Ages and the Salem witch trials all rolled up into a modern-day frenzy to exterminate them."

Taken aback by her reaction, he wasn't sure how to respond.

"Our country is already divided enough," she continued. "But then you'd have to lobby for werewolf rights. There wouldn't be peaceful protests, because there'd be too much fear. And here in a state where carrying a gun openly is legal, I can see groups being organized to hunt them down and kill them. And for what? Just because they're different than us? Is that what you really want?"

"Wow," he said, scratching his head. "Where did all of that come from? How did we go from proving the existence of a supposedly mythical creature to worrying about protecting them?"

"Because, Jake, you have to think ahead to the consequences of your actions." Her green eyes were full of passion, and he could see her pulse beating furiously in the hollow of her throat.

"Consequences," he muttered. Though he was sore, though bruised and battered, he reached up and cupped her chin in his hand and kissed her. Slowly and thoroughly, exactly the way he'd been wanting to do since the moment he'd laid eyes on her.

He kissed her until she kissed him back, until she shivered. When her arms came up around his neck and she clung to him as if she wanted more, he gently broke off the kiss. Breathing hard, he let his forehead rest against hers. "You're something else, Maddie Kinslow. I've never met a woman like you."

Her generous lips curved at this, making him ache to kiss her again. Instead, he pushed himself back, putting some distance between them so he could think.

"Would you go to dinner with me sometime?" he asked.

"I don't think that would be a good idea," she answered. "Since you're going to be my client. I try not to mix business with pleasure."

"I'm thinking in our case, that's unavoidable." He smiled when he delivered what he knew to be the truth. "Look at how great we are together. Just a simple little kiss…"

"I'm thinking we shouldn't kiss again," she said. The lack of regret in her voice warred with her uncertain expression and her immediate blush. "That would be a simple rule to follow."

"Maybe," he allowed. "As long as I don't look at you, or touch you, or catch a whiff of your perfume."

The hitch in her breath told him how his words affected her. She swallowed, her eyes huge, her pupils dilated. "You make us getting together sound inevitable."

"Eventually. I'm confident of that. Not right now, when I can barely move my chest and stomach without pain. But someday, once I'm healed. Sooner rather than later."

Was that disappointment in her gaze?

"Since we're apparently being candid," she said, "you should know I find your confidence really sexy."

Damn. Another jolt of lust hit him. His body responded immediately and decisively. "And there you have it. Proof. When we do come together, it's going to be gasoline on a flame."

She flushed again. "Okay, I'll take your word for it. But right now, let's talk business. I sent you The Shadow Agency's rates. What do you think?"

"I want to hire you. But honestly, not if my doing so will come between you and me getting together."

"Oh, it definitely will." Even her quiet chuckle struck him as sexy. "So, what you have to decide is if you can be patient enough to wait until the investigation is finished."

Surprised, he considered her. "Knowing what you now do, are you still willing to help me investigate?"

"I think so. Are you still fixated on that door and that dead-end alley where I found you, or have you moved on to somehow proving the existence of werewolves?"

"Both," he answered promptly. "I think the two are tied together."

Rolling her eyes, she groaned. "Are you serious?"

"Yes, I am. I've been doing investigative reporting a long time. I've got a gut feeling that I'm on to something. And I've learned to trust my gut."

"You're not afraid of ridicule? It will happen if you continue to pursue this werewolf thing." Back straight, hands folded in her lap, she studied him.

"I have my reasons." He hesitated. "I'll go ahead and tell you, just so you understand. I don't want you to think I'm crazy, but I know what I saw." He took a deep breath. "After I became interested in that door, I started watching the alley. People went in and didn't come out for hours. Some of them stayed all night."

None of this seemed to surprise her. But then again, he reminded himself, she'd actually been one of those people he'd seen going in through that door. She knew more than she was letting on.

She didn't react when he pointed that out to her. "I can promise you that what's behind that door is infinitely less interesting than you think it is. It's a club, a private club. With drinks and music, just like any other bar. Except only members are allowed. Which is why I can go inside. I'm a member. Nothing nefarious is going on, I promise. You've been wasting your time."

"Have I? Then tell me why those two guys beat the crap out of me in that alley?"

"Who knows? Drunk bullies have been known to do such horrible things outside bars all over the country. They might not have liked the way you looked at them, or—"

"Or my skin color," he interrupted. "I admit the possibility of it being racially motivated occurred to me. But I don't think so. They didn't call me names and the entire time, it seemed clear from the way they attacked me that it wasn't personal. More like they were defending something instead of lashing out."

"You really are observant," she mused. "If you're correct, then why do you think they attacked you?"

"To warn me away. Somehow, they figured out I've been watching them."

"Okay, even if I buy that explanation—which I don't—it doesn't make sense. There's a bar behind that door. Nothing more, nothing less. A private party place for members to go."

"I don't believe you," he said.

Hurt flashed across her mobile face. "Then I guess it's best if I go."

"Wait." Though he'd told himself he wouldn't touch her again, he grabbed her arm. "I have a good reason for saying that."

"For calling me a liar?" She shook off his hand. "Let's hear it."

"I've seen something," he told her, hoping she'd believe him. "I've spent a lot of time watching that alley and seeing people come and go. One night around three a.m., I saw a group of men leaving. They seemed drunk, which lends credence to your claim. They were pushing each other around, loud horseplay, like young guys do."

Crossing her arms, she watched him. "Go on."

"They'd gotten loud enough to cause a disturbance or, at the very least, attract notice to the place. So a big guy—must have been a bouncer—came out and told them to shut it down. That's when it happened."

He took a deep breath, not sure how she'd take what he had to say next.

"One of the young guys changed into a wolf and tried to attack the bouncer. The other two had to pull him off."

Chapter 6

Rick knew in his role as pretend human husband, he needed to act at least slightly upset that Gus had not only taken Carmen to his bedroom, but that they'd stayed so long. Truth be told, he actually did feel a twinge of something—maybe even jealousy. Had playing the fantasy messed with his head? When the two of them finally emerged, he narrowed his eyes. "What were you two doing in there?" he asked, making his voice heavy with suspicion and crossing his arms.

Gus turned away from him, clearly not wanting to quibble. Rick let him go, focusing instead on the beautiful Vampire. "Well?" he demanded.

Expression grim, Carmen only shook her head. "Nothing untoward. We were discussing the terms of my employment," she said. "Needless to stay, we both had differing ideas. But we finally reached an agreement. Now I'm eager to get to work."

"Terms?" he asked, his gaze sliding from her to Gus. "I thought we'd already settled all that."

"No. We hadn't." Gus wasn't smiling, either. Whatever discussion that had taken place between him and Carmen must have been a doozy. But, judging from the way Gus was acting, it appeared Carmen had won. Good.

Then Carmen took Rick's arm and peered earnestly up into his face. "No drugs," she said, imploring.

"What?" He wasn't sure he'd heard her correctly.

"That's part of the deal," she continued, trailing one scarlet-tipped finger down his chest. "Neither one of us can use drugs while working on this project."

Ah. Now he got it. He'd need to tell her later that her acting skills were superb.

For the sake of their audience, he pretended disappointment. "Not even—"

"Nothing," she cut him off. "Or this deal's off. Got it?" Again she used her nail, trailing it up the side of his throat, making him actually shiver. "Don't make me have to punish you."

Punish him? That actually sounded interesting.

Fighting through an unexpected haze of arousal, he nodded slowly. He wasn't entirely sure what Carmen was up to, but he clearly had no choice except to go with it.

Watching them, Gus laughed. "You'll survive," he said, his good humor clearly restored. "I'll even allow the occasional alcoholic beverage. But nothing else. No pills, no needles, no smokes. Got it?"

Rick and Carmen nodded in unison. Rick kept his face expressionless while he worked furiously to get his body under control. He couldn't believe she'd made him hard with just a touch of her fingernail and a few drawled words. Damn.

"Good. Come on." Landers motioned for them to follow him. "I'll show you where you'll be staying for the duration."

Staying on premises? Not good. Rick cursed under his breath, realizing he should have thought of this.

Next to him, even Carmen tensed. Vampires didn't like to be confined, so this would be even worse on her. Especially if Landers put them in a room near his, where he could keep an eye on them at all times.

To his relief, Landers led them out the back door. "We have a small guesthouse set up for your use," he said, winking at Rick. "All our on-site employees have them. We prefer to keep you where we can see you, you know. Plus, the individual structure gives you two some privacy to indulge your little role-playing games or whatever."

Unable to bring himself to wink back, Rick nodded. "Thanks," he said. "We appreciate that."

And then he caught sight of the "guesthouses." Landers had stretched the meaning of the term to describe these. Several tiny buildings the size of storage sheds had been set up on the expansive property. They were at the most twelve by fourteen, made of wood, with a door and one window. For whatever reason, each had been painted a different color. There were yellow, green, red, blue, brown, white, and black.

Landers stopped at the yellow one that sat closest to the main house. "It's not big, but it has everything you need," he said as he unlocked the door. "Come take a look."

Rick and Carmen exchanged a glance as they followed him inside. He flipped a switch and stepped back, gesturing grandly. "See? All the comforts of home."

He wasn't kidding. Somehow, they'd managed to

cram a miniscule kitchenette with a miniature two-seater table, a living area with a small love seat and a TV hung on the wall, and a tiny bathroom with sink, toilet and stand-up shower inside the roughly 168-square-foot building. Talk about a tiny house.

"Wait," Carmen said. "There's no bed. And there's not room on that couch for one person to sleep, never mind two."

"Oh, we thought of that." Grinning proudly, Landers gestured at a wooden wall. "You'll have to push the kitchen table out of the way, but there's a Murphy bed. It pulls down for you to sleep on it and goes back up once you're awake. Perfect space-saver."

One bed. Rick could read the dismay in Carmen's eyes, even as his body practically thrummed. He'd tell her later that he'd sleep on the couch. Unless she, as a Vamp, needed other arrangements. He realized he'd never really considered where or how the undead slept.

On top of that, he knew she'd need a steady supply of blood for nourishment. How the hell would she get that if she was being watched 24/7? He'd have to hope she could figure out a way. She was a Vampire, so no doubt she would.

"This will do," Carmen said, nodding at Landers. "When do I start work?"

"Tomorrow morning, at 0600 hours."

She nodded. If she found it at all odd that she'd be starting work before the sun even rose, she didn't show it.

Finally, Landers left.

"Come here," Carmen ordered, standing and holding out her arms. Heart thumping, he stepped into her embrace, instantly hard and ready. She leaned close, her breath tickling his ear. "They're probably watching and listening to us," she whispered, pressing herself so close to him that he knew she had to be aware of his arousal. "So this is the only way I can tell you what went on in there. They think we're drug addicts. Oh, and also that we're into S and M. I'm the dominant and you're the submissive."

"What?" He reared back, too shocked to think straight. When he realized what he'd done, he wrapped her in his arms and pressed his swollen body against her. Her swift intake of breath was a satisfying reaction. Two could play this game. "Why the hell would you say something like that?"

She smiled, a slow, sensual smile. "To make things interesting, of course. In reality, I needed a way to be able to come and go as I pleased, plus protect you." She licked his earlobe, which made him start slightly. "You may not realize this, but I'm valuable to them. Gus wanted to kill you. By assuring him that I had you firmly in hand, I was able to guarantee your safety."

He wanted to tell her he could take care of himself, or that such elaborate subterfuge was completely unnecessary. But she kept shifting her body, putting friction and pressure on his swollen anatomy, and he could scarcely think beyond the red haze of desire.

What the freakin' hell?

Finally, she released him. Her savage grin told him she knew of his discomfort. "I already informed Gus that I need you to assist me in the laboratory," she pronounced. "He agreed. I said I'd work much better if I'm not distracted by worry about you."

Begrudgingly, he had to admit she had a good plan. At least, that part of it. But there was one thing he felt he needed to make perfectly clear.

Snagging her arm, he pulled her up against him. "Why do you think I'm going to let you be in charge?" he murmured into her ear. Then, telling himself he only wanted to prove a point, he covered her mouth with his, hard and punishing.

She gave back as good as she got, standing her ground. The instant she opened her mouth, giving his tongue access, he realized he'd made a major mistake. She took, he gave, until he found himself so caught up in the taste and feel of her that he spiraled out of control.

Worse, he didn't care. He wanted, he craved, and with his hands tangled up in her hair, he would have given anything to push himself up inside her.

She laughed, letting him know she knew. "Not now," she murmured, her unsteady voice telling him she wasn't as unaffected as he'd thought.

In fact, the desire blazing from her heavy-lidded eyes came close to matching his own. "Checkmate," he said.

To his surprise, she nodded. "We'll need to tend to this fire before it gets out of control."

"I agree." With a savage ruthlessness, he turned and worked at getting himself back together. It had been a long time since a woman had aroused him so strongly. The fact that this woman also happened to be a Vampire shocked him.

His inner wolf, now fully awake and restless, paced and whined. Rick had to spend a few extra moments calming that aspect of himself, as well.

Behind him, Carmen waited silently. Rick sure as hell hoped she was having to pull herself together, too. If not, he definitely needed to up his game. No way did he intend to allow her to have the upper hand. No way at all.

Finally, he turned to face her. "What now?" he asked.

"I think we should go for a walk and explore the

grounds," she said, using a normal voice. "I'd like to check out the landscape of where we're going to be living while working here."

"Sounds like a good idea." He held out his hand. When she slipped her slender fingers into his, he resisted the urge to tug her close. This would never work. He was good at his job, damn good. He refused to let lust be this big of a distraction. As soon as possible, they'd deal with it and get it out of their systems. Things would surely go back to normal after that.

Either way, he knew he'd enjoy finding out.

Damn that Shifter. Though smiling on the outside, Carmen fumed. She'd planned on having the upper hand, using her considerable sexual prowess to beguile and ensnare Rick Fallin. He might be a covert intelligence operative, he might work for the Pack Protectors, or both, but in the end, he was male. When she set her sights on a man, she knew exactly how to reel him in.

Except when she tried it on Rick, she found herself wanting him with an intensity that had shaken her to the core. Actually, she'd come perilously close to losing self-control. Talk about backfiring.

Maybe she'd simply gone too long without taking a lover. That had to be it. Which meant the solution was a simple one. She and Rick needed to have at each other, let loose the desire, and surely both of them would find their clarity of focus restored.

She would have done it right then in their small cabin, but she didn't want them to be on camera for anyone and everyone to view. And while she hadn't taken the time to search for any recording devices, she felt quite certain there were some. An operation as sensitive as this one wouldn't take chances with their assets.

Hand in hand, they walked outside. Rick leaned

close and put his mouth against her ear, again sending a shiver of longing down her spine. "I feel confident this entire place is under heavy surveillance," he murmured. "Just so you know."

She nodded, her mouth suddenly dry. She couldn't tell when the tables had turned, and truly didn't understand why. For most of her long, long life, she'd used sex to control men. She hadn't really thought it would be any different with this one.

Until it was. Now she had two intriguing mysteries to investigate. The science of the new virus and Rick Fallin.

Both promised to be equally pleasurable. For the first time in decades, anticipation filled her.

As they strolled around the huge yard, they passed several other small sheds just like the one they'd been given to occupy. If any of these had inhabitants, no one came out to greet them.

Though at first walking around holding hands with Rick felt odd, eventually she began to relax. They had roles to play, after all, and role-playing happened to be one of her specialties.

Finally, they went past the last of the sheds. Careful to avoid the barn/laboratory, they continued on to where the mowed grassy area ended and the forest began. No one stopped them or confronted them.

"Do you still think they're watching us?" she asked. They'd ducked into the trees and walked to the edge of a fast-moving stream.

He frowned. "I'm not sure. It doesn't seem reasonable, but I don't understand why no one is making sure we don't simply continue walking until we're gone."

"Maybe we're not prisoners," she said.

"Hmph," he snorted. "I imagine security will be a lot tighter once you see what's inside their lab. There's no way they can risk you taking off and selling your information to the highest bidder."

"True." Contemplating pulling her hand free from his, she let it stay. There was something comforting in his touch. While she'd never been one to seek the softness of such coddling, she found she liked it too much to let it go just yet.

"Tomorrow is going to be a big day," he said, still keeping his voice low. "I'm wondering if once you get in there and start working with this virus, you can find a way to disable it."

Since she knew he had no idea how biology worked, she took pity on him. "Clearly, at least from what you've told me, it's already been developed and used. I'd have much better luck finding an antidote."

"That would be helpful, too." Facing her, he smiled. "I should let you know I have several concerns with how this is playing out so far."

She shrugged. "Don't worry about it. I'll try not to boss you around too much. Remember, like you told me, it's all for show."

"That's not what I'm worried about." His smile faded and his gaze darkened. "Think about it. As you pointed out just now, they already have their virus. What do they need an additional biologist for? What exactly are they going to ask you to do?"

"That's a valid question." Again, her anticipation was so strong it almost felt sexual. "Whatever it is, this is right in my wheelhouse. Someone like me could work for years without ever coming across something like this. It's fascinating. Honestly, I can't wait to report to work in the morning."

"You really mean that, don't you?" His serious tone matched the gravity of his expression. "This is really something you want to do."

"It is," she told him. "This is what I've worked for, studied for, reinvented myself for. When I moved to Texas, I went back to school for this advanced degree. I did unpaid internships, whatever it took to increase my knowledge."

Wondering why she felt compelled to share all this, she took a deep breath and continued. "Eventually, I planned to work for the CDC in Atlanta. But since we Vampires live so long, when I met Shayla and Maddie, I decided it wouldn't hurt me to live in Galveston for a few more years. The one thing I have an overabundance of is time."

"I see." He squeezed her hand, his expression thoughtful. "You love your work."

"Yes."

"That's one thing we have in common, then. I love my job, too."

Since she'd just spilled her guts, she probed for him to reveal more. "What is it you do, exactly?"

When he didn't immediately respond, she nudged him with her hip. "Come on, you can tell me. We're partners, remember?"

Gazing down at her, he finally nodded. "I work two jobs in one. With humans, I'm in a specialized division of the FBI. One so covert, on paper it doesn't exist. With my own kind, I'm a Pack Protector. I'm sworn to uphold the safety of the Pack. They were thrilled when I got my other job. They like to have operatives right in the thick of things."

"I'm guessing if I ask you to tell me about what a regular day in your life is like, you're not going to do it."

A ghost of a smile flitted around his mouth. "Probably not," he admitted. "Actually, you'd be surprised at how boring it can be sometimes. Just routine paper pushing."

Skeptical, she smiled back. "I don't believe you."

The sound of shouting came from the direction they'd left. As they both turned, several gunshots rang out. After that, silence.

"What the…" Rick tugged her hand. "Come on, let's get back. That didn't sound good."

As soon as they left the shelter of the trees, they started running. In a clearing between two of the little sheds, several people stood in a small circle. As Carmen and Rick drew closer, they saw one person on the ground.

The scent of blood drifted as they approached, making Carmen's fangs ache. She kept her mouth closed, holding on to Rick's hand so tightly he had to shake his slightly to make her let up.

"What's going on?" Rick demanded. "Where's Gus?"

"None of your business," Landers snarled. Brandishing a pistol, he waved it at the man on the ground, who wasn't moving. "Damn fool tried to blackmail us."

Several of the other men muttered, too low to hear their words, but no one confronted Landers. After all, he was the one holding a weapon.

At that moment, Gus strode out the back door of the house. "What's going on out here?" He paled when he noticed the man lying in a pool of blood.

"Sheldon was trying to blackmail us," Landers repeated. "He was carrying glass vials of his virus, said it had gone too far and he wanted the CDC to see them so they could work on an antidote."

Eyes bugging from his face, Gus pointed at him. "Where are the vials now?"

"Underneath him," Landers replied. Then, as he realized the implications of this, he swayed. "I'm not sure if they broke or not."

At his words, everyone else started backing away.

"Put away the gun, Landers," Gus ordered. "We've got way bigger problems to worry about."

Carmen finally spoke. "Everyone freeze. No one move. This virus. Is it airborne or must there be contact?"

Every single man turned to look at Gus. "I'm not sure," he allowed. "Sheldon handled all that."

Since she wasn't supposed to know that they'd already used it on someone in Houston, she thought fast. "Did you use any people as test subjects? If so, how were they infected?"

Gus swallowed again. Instead of answering, he turned on Landers. "This is all your fault, you dumb ass. We're right in the middle of the operation. Roscoe is going to be so mad."

"Even worse," one of the other men said, "is if this virus kills us all. Then what Roscoe thinks ain't gonna matter."

At the mention of the virus, several of them again started backing away. This time, Gus barked out the order for them to stay put. "If we're already infected, running away is not going to help. It'll just spread it."

"Again, I need to know how this virus is spread," Carmen interjected, her voice cool and steady. "Air or touch?"

This time Gus looked at her, his gaze hard and assessing. "The last guy who died from it had a dose put into his drink."

She nodded. "If that's the case, it's probably not airborne. Therefore, none of you should be in any danger."

One of the men cried out, falling to his knees. "Thank you, Lord." The others all wore similar expressions of relief.

"We need to dispose of the body," Gus said.

"I wouldn't touch him," Carmen replied. "If those vials are crushed under him, whoever moves him will be exposed to the virus."

Gus nodded, eyeing her with newfound respect. "What do you suggest?" he asked.

"It'll have to be controlled, as if working with the virus in a laboratory," Carmen replied. "I'll handle it, if you'd like."

"I would." Gus looked from her to Rick and back again. "Once you have, clean up and report back to me. Since this unfortunate incident, your job duties have changed. The man Landers just killed, Sheldon, was the creator of the virus. You're going to have to take over from here."

Unfazed, she nodded. "Well then, I sure hope he left detailed notes." Though sorry for the human's death, inside she was delighted at the change in circumstances. She'd have complete and utter control over the laboratory. And with no other biologist working with her, no one would have any idea whether she was working on an antidote or something else.

"What do you want to do with the body?" she asked Gus.

Something akin to respect flashed in his eyes. "Burn it. Less chance of contamination," he replied.

"All right. I'll need gloves, bleach, a large tarp and more vials," she told Gus. "Plus some gasoline or lighter fluid. Will you send someone to fetch this stuff for me? If not, I can go search the lab myself, but since I have no idea where anything is kept…"

"Tommy, bring the lady what she asked for. Everyone else, back to work," Gus ordered. "Except you, Landers. You're coming with me. If we have to explain to Roscoe what happened, you're going to have to do it. So you'd better start thinking about it, because if he doesn't like what you have to say, you're a dead man."

Once everyone had dispersed and they were alone again, Carmen eyed the human body and sighed. "Poor guy. All that wasted blood," she said. "And on top of that, if this man really did create a new virus strain, he was a freaking genius. It's a shame his life had to end this way."

Rick nodded. "I agree. That Landers seems a little trigger-happy. He's one we need to watch out for."

Studying the situation, she nodded. About to ask him if he had any idea who this Roscoe person might be, she remembered the possibility of cameras and decided to wait until later. One thing at a time. Dispose of the body, catalog whatever vials of virus were still intact, and then figure out where to go from here.

"How safe is it for you to move Sheldon?" Rick asked. "I know you'll be okay, but what about me? If those vials are shattered—"

"According to what they said, you'd actually have to touch or drink the stuff to get infected. But just in case, maybe you should stand back, too."

He stared at her. She swore she could see his inner struggle. He didn't want to let a woman do such a horrible job alone, yet no one knew yet if the virus could kill a Shape-shifter.

"You forget I'm superstrong," she said softly. "In the interest of safety, I don't want you anywhere near this guy when I move him, okay?"

Their gazes locked. Finally, appearing reluctant, he nodded. "I don't like it, but you're right."

Tommy returned a moment later with everything she'd asked for. Shooting her a plainly hostile glare, he set it on the grass nearby and hurried back into the house.

After putting on the gloves, Carmen spread out the tarp, rolled poor Sheldon onto it and got busy cleaning up the mess. Luckily for everyone, all of the vials appeared to be intact.

Chapter 7

Jake's words hit Maddie like a punch in the stomach. This was worse than she'd imagined. Far worse.

"Let me get this straight," she said, hoping she sounded relatively normal. "You think you actually saw a man change into a wolf?"

"Yes." There was not a shred of doubt in his voice. "Not think. I really did."

Crossing her arms, she tried to calm her racing heart. "How much had you had to drink?"

"Nothing. Coffee is all I drink when I'm on stake-out."

Stakeout. Crud. If the Pack Protectors were to learn about this, they'd take Jake away for what they called reprogramming. While she wasn't sure what exactly that entailed, she knew it involved some form of brain-washing.

And then they'd try to locate the Shifter who'd been

foolish enough to risk the discovery of their entire species. His punishment would also be severe.

"You do realize how crazy that sounds, right?" She kept her voice gentle.

He shrugged. "I don't care. If there are actual werewolves walking around among us, people need to know."

Once again, she had to tamp down the urge to argue, to explain what kind of chaos would ensue if people believed this. Her own kind, her *people* would be exposed and their lives placed at risk. Maybe she should wash her hands of this and call her brother, let the Pack Protectors take care of the problem.

Except she liked Jake. More than she should. In fact, the intense level of her attraction to him had once again resurrected her old hope that she wouldn't always be alone. That she might have found that special someone. *Mates*, her kind called them. Members of the Pack believed firmly that everyone had a true soul mate, someone who had been placed on this earth specifically to join with them.

Sometimes, when she looked deep in Jake's velvety brown eyes, she wondered if he might be hers.

Fool. It was way too soon to tell. And she refused to squander the possibility, especially when she thought she could convince Jake to give up on his desire to out her own kind. If she could figure out a way to make him believe it had been some sort of magic trick, sleight of hand, change in lighting and costume. All said, such a thing would make much more sense to a human than a werewolf. She shuddered internally at that word. Shapeshifters despised being called werewolves. It was considered insulting, reducing their complicated natures to nothing more than base instincts and superstition. Of course, Jake had no way of knowing that, nor could she explain. If they ever became serious, true mates, then she'd reveal her true nature, trusting that he'd love her enough to understand.

Love. Not yet. But perhaps. The possibility shimmered before her, a bright hope for the future.

She had to give them a chance. Maybe she could be a big enough distraction to cause him to lose focus. Because the alternative—Jake having his memory wiped clean—would mean he wouldn't remember her, either. They'd be over before they even got a chance to begin.

While she'd been lost in thought, he'd started pacing. "I know you probably think I'm crazy, but I haven't gotten to be an award-winning journalist by ignoring my instincts. I truly believe this could be the story of the century."

"Or you could lose any journalistic credibility you might have," she pointed out. "Look, I'm not trying to be harsh, but listen to yourself."

"I know what I saw." Judging from the stubborn set of his jaw, he wasn't going to budge on this. "If I can just get some video or even a few still shots…"

Before replying, she shook her head. "No one would believe it was real. They'd think you doctored the video. Have you considered that possibility? That what you think you saw was some magic trick or something? Involving a costume and just the right lighting."

Expression incredulous, he stared. "Not possible. You weren't there. This guy dropped to all fours. There were a bunch of sparkling lights, like fireflies, swirling around him. When the lights dissipated, his clothes were tattered and a huge, shaggy wolf stood where he'd been. It was unreal."

Whoa. Her heart sank even more. He'd just described exactly what happened when her kind shifted. She went on the immediate attack. "That sounds even crazier. Sparkling lights? Maybe whoever used lights masked the switch. For all you know, someone was filming that thing. It could have all been an elaborate production, of which you were an unknown observer."

For the first time since introducing the subject, doubt flashed across his face. "I thought of that," he said. "I've already asked around to see if someone was shooting a movie, even a small independent film. I thought that would go a long way to explaining everything I saw."

Her momentary flash of triumph went up in smoke. "I take it you didn't find anything?"

"Nope. Not even a whisper. And you know how those film people are. Any media coverage is good coverage." He met and held her gaze. "Plus, they would have been members of whatever club you say is behind that door. They went in. They came out. Maddie, I'm an investigative reporter. It's natural that I'd try to explore every potential angle rather than immediately settling on the most difficult."

"Of course," she murmured. Still, she thought it couldn't hurt if she got someone to put out a fake story about filming a werewolf flick, even after the fact. At the very least, it would provide her with a better basis for arguing against Jake's confidence in what he'd seen.

"Anyway, whether you want to believe it or not, that's where I'm going to need your help. Surveillance. With two of us working on this, we have double the chance of catching it on film."

Seriously? "Nope. That's not going to happen," she said. "I'm sorry. But I withdraw my offer of assistance. I can't work with you. You originally asked me to help you find out what's behind the door and I did. I told you the truth. But this? Werewolves in Galveston? No. The Shadow Agency has a reputation to uphold."

He swallowed, looking down. "Those are all valid points. Maybe you're right. Perhaps I should rethink this idea."

Though she didn't know him well yet, she understood him enough to guess he didn't mean a word of his last few sentences. He had no intention of giving up on his quest. He just didn't want her getting in his way.

Which of course was exactly what she'd have to do. She just needed to figure out a plan. Otherwise, the next time the Pack Protectors got ahold of him, he'd lose his memory.

Why did everything have to be so hard? Just once, why couldn't she meet an attractive man, go out on a date or two, have amazing sex and have a normal relationship?

"I think reconsideration is a good idea," she told him, aching. "In fact, I hope you do. I'd really like to see you again. But if you keep on with all this insane werewolf talk, I don't know that I can."

Their gazes locked. Her breath came faster. She could feel her entire body yearning for him, craving his touch, his kiss. She looked down, afraid of what her eyes would reveal.

"How about this?" he asked, coming to stand right in front of her. "Please. Look at me, Maddie."

She raised her gaze to his. Again, her heart skipped a beat. She didn't understand how it could be possible to desire a man she'd just met as much as she did. What if he didn't feel the same way?

But the warmth glowing in his brown eyes hinted that he did. "Don't give up on me."

"I…"

"How about I prove my theory to you?" he said, his expression intense. "If I can do that, will you help me prove it to the world?"

More than anything, she wanted to say yes. But she couldn't bring herself to outright lie. She knew if, by some miracle, he was able to gather enough information to actually prove he'd seen someone shape-shift, she'd have no choice but to call her brother or one of the other Pack Protectors.

Betraying him would be a thousand times worse if they got involved.

The truth of what she knew she must do felt like a knife stabbing straight into her heart. She had to give him up, cut all ties. And then, if he continued on this dangerous path, she'd have to report him to the Pack Protectors. For the safety of her people.

But first, she thought she'd be allowed one indulgence. Just once, she wanted to make love with this amazing, beautiful man. One time, with him moving deep inside her body, holding her close with those strong arms.

She'd have to wait until after he'd healed, of course. But she'd give herself one night of lovemaking with Jake before breaking things off.

"You know what?" She pushed to her feet, wrapping her arms carefully around his neck, mindful of his bruises. "I'd really rather our relationship be personal rather than business anyway. You do your thing and I'll do mine. We won't talk about this werewolf stuff anymore."

His gaze darkened. "Personal sounds good."

Right before he kissed her, she felt a twinge of unease, wondering if she'd be strong enough to do what needed to be done when the time came. But the instant he covered her mouth with his, her doubt vanished.

This was what she'd waited for her entire life. She'd never known a man like him. His touch, the press of his mouth on hers, and she went up in flames.

She leaned into the kiss, into him, careful of his battered rib cage. She would have given much to have met this man under different circumstances.

"Nice try," he said against her mouth, grinning. "I have to admit, you're really good at distracting me."

She grinned back. "I like you," she told him, surprising herself. "A lot."

"Ditto. I think we should go out sometime. Like for drinks."

Drinks and sex, she thought, though of course she kept that to herself. One time and one time only.

"Sounds good." It took a lot of effort for her to sound casual. "Once you're feeling better, let's make plans."

"Soon, then?" A glint of mischief flashed in his eyes. "Like tomorrow? I'm sure I'll feel much better after a good night's rest."

"Will you?"

"Definitely."

Pleased that he seemed as eager as she felt, she smiled. "You just let me know when you're ready." In fact, it might just be the shortest date on record. A glass of wine and then they'd head to his place and go straight to the good part. A buzz of pleasant anticipation filled her.

"I will," he said. "I know exactly where I want us to go. Since you're a member, I'd like to visit that bar you told me about. The one behind the secret door. Surely members are allowed to bring guests."

Poof. Just like that, her giddy mood vanished. "We'll see," she said, unable to hide her disappointment. "I'd hoped we could move on beyond all that. Maybe start over, as if running into each other in the alley never happened."

"You don't want to go to that bar."

Throat aching, she shook her head.

"Hey." Hand under her chin, he raised her face to him. "I'm guessing you can't."

She took a deep breath. "No. Only members are allowed." If only he knew.

"What does one have to do to become a member?" he asked. "Unless it involves shelling out thousands of dollars, I'll do whatever it takes."

Since she couldn't tell him the truth, that one had to be born a Shape-shifter or Merfolk, or made into a Vampire, she could only shake her head. "And here we are again, with me stuck between a rock and a hard place."

Releasing her, he narrowed his eyes. "You can't even tell me the criteria of becoming a member?"

She sighed. Best to stick as close to the truth as possible. "It's sort of based on lineage. You have to be born into a certain family."

"You're kidding me, right? You're saying membership in a bar situated behind a beat-up old door on a dead-end alley surrounded by a bunch of run-down, abandoned warehouses in Galveston, Texas, is based on heritage, like some highbrow country club?"

"Yes." Gathering her things, she got ready to go. "I shouldn't have come here. This was a mistake. It's been nice knowing you." Her throat clogged up. Horrified, she hurried to the door. Damned if she would let him see her cry over something so silly as the loss of a potential relationship that had died before it could really even begin.

He let her go. At least, he followed her to the front door, but he didn't try to stop her or even walk her to her car.

The other vehicle was parked across the street from his house.

As Maddie headed toward her car, the other vehicle's

driver's-side door opened and a man got out. Under the glow of the streetlight, she could make out his features. A jolt of recognition had her hurrying to get into her car. Jake's stalker was the same Pack Protector who'd accosted her inside Broken Chains earlier.

Watching Maddie leave, Jake caught his breath when he realized the man stalking him got out of his car as she walked down the front walk. If that guy even made a move toward her, Jake would have to do whatever he could in order to stop him.

He grabbed the baseball bat he kept in his hall closet and returned to the front step. Since he didn't own a gun, the bat was the best he could do. At least he could use it to buy enough time for Maddie to get away.

Glancing at the other man, who remained by his car, standing partly in shadow, Maddie quickly got in her own vehicle and started the engine. As she backed out of Jake's driveway, her headlights illuminated the other car. She drove away. The man still stood there, swiveling his head to stare directly at Jake.

"What do you want?" Jake shouted, still clutching the bat.

Instead of answering, the man got in his car and hurriedly drove away, traveling in the same direction as Maddie.

Dammit. That creep was following Maddie. He had to warn her. Closing his front door, Jake dug out his cell phone and called her number, praying he'd catch her.

But she didn't answer. Immediately he tried again, cursing under his breath. This time, he went straight to voice mail, which could mean she deliberately wasn't taking his call.

Despite this, he tried a third time. When she finally

picked up, he didn't waste time on pleasantries. He told her what he suspected. "I think he's following you."

"That's possible." She didn't sound surprised or even alarmed. "There are headlights right behind me."

Suddenly suspicious, he took a deep breath. "Maddie, do you know that guy? Is he your boyfriend or your ex?" Or worse, her husband? After all, how much did he really know about Maddie? Not a whole hell of a lot.

"I don't know him. Not personally," she answered. "And I don't have a boyfriend or an ex. But I have seen that guy before. Don't worry, I'll deal with it."

"You can't go home," he warned her, hating the fact that right now, he was completely powerless to help her. "Drive to the police station, or some other public, well-lit place. I have no idea what he's after. I never suspected he wanted you rather than me."

"I don't think he does." Her enigmatic reply started his imagination again. "But I'm guessing I'm about to find out," she continued.

"What are you going to do?" He prayed she wouldn't try anything foolish. She was a short, small-boned woman and from what he'd been able to see of the stalker, that guy had both height and breadth. If he was crazy enough to follow a woman, who knew what else he might do?

"I'm going to have to let you go," she said, her calm voice at stark odds with his heartbeat hammering in his chest. "I'll call you when I'm home safely."

"Don't hang up," he urged. "At least leave your phone on so I can hear."

But he quickly realized he was only speaking to dead air. Maddie had already ended the call.

The next several minutes moved slowly and felt like an eternity. Jake hated being this powerless. The pain pill he'd reluctantly taken earlier made him feel woozy and dizzy, and he sure as hell figured he'd better not drive.

Yet what kind of man would he be if he left sweet Maddie alone to deal with that stalker? Debating, he realized he actually had no idea where Maddie lived.

He didn't even know whether she'd turned left or right after she'd left his street.

Still, he couldn't sit here and do nothing. Pain pill be damned. He had to at least try.

On his way to locate his car keys, the room spun and he had to sit down. Dammit. Masculine pride aside, he was in no condition to drive—he could potentially harm others.

Maddie was smart, he told himself. She wouldn't do anything foolish or put herself at risk.

When his phone rang twenty minutes later, he had to take a deep breath before answering.

"I'm home," she said, sounding cheerful. "Thanks for worrying about me."

"What happened?" he asked, keeping his voice level and calm. "Did you confront the guy?"

"No. I didn't see the need to. Instead, I just drove around. Went down the Seawall, which is still packed with tourists. Once I was absolutely positive that I lost him, I came home."

"That's a relief."

"It is," she agreed. "Now, if you don't mind, I'd like to get off the phone and chill for the rest of the night. And I saw how that pain pill affected you, so you probably could use some shut-eye, too."

"Where do you live?" He blurted out the question, wincing slightly as he did.

He could hear the laughter in her voice when she answered. "On Galveston Island," she said. "I wasn't Born On Island, but I got here as quickly as I could."

One of the first things he'd learned upon relocating here was how seriously the islanders took that status. BOI—Born On Island—was a source of great pride among them.

Her meager attempt to distract him might have worked if he hadn't been so focused on her safely. "I figured you lived on the island," he told her. "I'm asking for your specific address."

"Why?"

"Because tomorrow I'm not going to take a pain pill, no matter what. I want to come by and see you. And make sure your home is secure." He almost didn't add the last, but figured he might as well tell her the truth. "I'm worried about you, Maddie. Men who do that kind of stalking aren't right in the head. I'm not sure what he wants, but you need to understand he could hurt you."

She went quiet. "Thanks for your concern," she finally said. "I appreciate that you care enough to worry about my welfare. But I have lived alone a long time and I promise you, I can take care of myself."

Though the reporter in him wanted to press for specifics—did she own a gun, had she taken self-defense classes—he could tell from her cool, remote tone that she wouldn't appreciate him grilling her.

And maybe, just maybe, she had a valid point. Maddie was a competent, self-sufficient woman who ran her own business. She also, he reminded himself, had membership in the secret club that met behind the old door. He couldn't help but wonder if the stalker had ties to that place, as well.

"I'm sorry, but I have to go," she said. "I just wanted to let you know that I made it home safely."

"No contact with the stalker?"

"None. I made sure he didn't follow me home. Good night, Jake."

"Good night." After ending the call, he grabbed a pad of paper and a pen and started doodling. This technique helped free his mind, which he sorely needed to do right now.

Every gut instinct he possessed told him this was all connected. The guy he'd seen change into a wolf, the men who'd assaulted him, the "club" behind the door and the stalker. And perhaps even Maddie. For the first time he wondered if she'd been sent as a distraction.

While part of him scoffed at this notion, he couldn't discount it entirely. After all, she had happened upon him immediately after he'd been attacked. And she, a beautiful, sexy woman, was a hell of a diversion.

But then again, he thought, sketching the alley and the strange sign with no words and the door, she had refused to work with him if he tried to catch a werewolf on video. He'd think if her purpose was to negate the story, she'd have agreed and then done everything in her power to make sure he never got the opportunity.

Finally, with his brain growing even fuzzier, he knew he had to sleep. The effects of the pain pill threatened to propel him into unconsciousness there at the kitchen table, and he'd much rather be in his bed.

The next morning, Jake woke, the lingering after-effects of the narcotic making him still feel fuzzy. A shower and a strong cup of coffee did much to remedy that. Once he'd scarfed down some instant oatmeal, he made a second mug of coffee and carried it into the den. He booted up his laptop and logged into one of the chat groups he'd joined under a pseudonym. This one was comprised of people who'd claimed to have seen a werewolf. Jake had not yet posted his experience. He wasn't sure he ever would.

Reading some of the recent messages, he had to acknowledge Maddie had a point. Some of the comments bordered on mentally unhinged. Others spouted ideas ranging from conspiracy theories to alien invasion.

This was Jake's third time logging in. He'd hoped somewhere in the mishmash of random craziness, one or two nuggets of rationality would emerge. Apparently, this was not to be the case.

He logged out of the chat group and next checked his email. There were two legitimate employment offers, both needing articles written about a certain subject. One required photos also. The other did not. The fees listed were reasonable, so he accepted both of them. Knowing he now had legitimate work made him feel better about continuing to pursue what increasingly appeared to be an insane story.

Except he knew what he'd seen. He hadn't imagined it or dreamed it. There'd been no special lighting or costumes or tricks. A man had—somehow, someway—become a wolf. And then, after remaining a wolf for a moment or two, changed back into a man.

While logically such a thing didn't seem possible, Jake figured maybe all the legends about werewolves just might have originated in reality.

If he could obtain proof—real, solid, indisputable proof—such a story would be groundbreaking. He could change the world.

Except... He frowned, trying to picture a future in which werewolves were known to exist. Would fear and paranoia run rampant? Mass incarceration, people making accusations about anyone they didn't like? Werewolf hunts, people being made into second-class citizens just because they happened to possess a special ability?

In his line of work, he'd seen the face of much of humanity, and it wasn't pretty. Still, being a journalist was all about uncovering the truth. In this situation, that was what he intended to do.

Starting with what really was behind that door.

Chapter 8

As Rick watched the self-assured competence with which Carmen worked, a chill went through him. He'd known female special operatives who moved like that, all efficiency of movement, intent upon their task. They'd taken pride in claiming ice ran in their veins, and none of them had been a Vampire. Carmen put them all to shame.

He felt like a fool. Despite knowing exactly what kind of being Carmen Vargas was, he'd deluded himself into allowing the intense sexual pull of her to make him forget. No doubt she'd be excellent in bed, but he needed to remember it could never be anything more than that. Vampires were notoriously adroit at avoiding emotional entanglements. Perhaps because they had no beating heart.

Still, he liked her. Gutsy, smart and beautiful, all in one.

Once she'd carefully moved all the unbroken glass

vials to a safe area, she finished rolling up the dead man and secured him in the tarp.

"For this, I need to be careful," she said, her voice low. "While I can easily drag him off by myself, if anyone sees me, it'll raise questions."

"Good point." A human woman of her size and shape would have difficulty moving a large, inert dead man. "Since nothing broke, I think I'll be okay helping you drag the tarp. Where are we going with him?"

"There's a fire pit in an area away from the little sheds and houses. I noticed it when we were walking earlier. It's not huge, but I think I can utilize it to burn this body."

Again, her clinical, remote tone gave him pause. Something must have shown on his face, because she shook her head.

"Would you rather be dealing with a hysterical, crying female?" she asked him drily. "When you live as long as I have, the one thing you're not afraid of is death. It's a shame, what happened to this man, but nothing I can do will change that."

"Point taken." He matched her tone. "Let's get this done."

"Do you mind grabbing the gasoline and the lighter?" she asked, pointing to where Tommy had placed the items on the ground.

"No problem." He grabbed the gas can with his right hand and stuck the lighter in his pocket. Then he took hold of the tarp, his left hand next to hers. When he gave a sharp tug, he could barely make the poor, dead Sheldon move.

Carmen shot him a look of disbelief. "Allow me," she said, and began effortlessly dragging the tarp away. To his chagrin, Rick could barely keep up with her pace. Of course, he was also carrying a five-gallon can of gas.

"Better slow down," he muttered. "Only a Vampire could move this fast."

Immediately, she complied. "Damn, you're right. I'm sorry. But look, we're almost there."

And they were. The fire pit sat less than twenty yards to their right. With a few more moves, they maneuvered the body into place. At her signal, Rick doused the tarp with gasoline.

"Hand me the lighter," she asked.

He almost declined. Almost. But then, because for whatever reason he didn't want to be the one who set a man he'd never known on fire, he passed the lighter to Carmen.

"You might step back," Carmen pointed out quietly. "You know what fire does to your kind."

Jaw tight, he didn't move. "Just do it," he said. "I'm far enough away."

With a shrug, she picked up a dry stick, dipped it in the gas and lit one end. Once she had a flame going, she touched it to the edge of the tarp and dropped it, simultaneously stepping back. There was no wind, so at least neither of them had to worry about that.

The blaze burned hot and furious. The awful smell made Rick want to gag, but he managed to maintain his stoic expression. Carmen turned away, as if to say she'd finished with this, but when he touched her arm and she looked at him, he realized tears streamed down her face.

Stunned, he froze.

"Sorry." She sniffed, swiping at her cheeks with her fingers. "This man had a brilliant mind. While death doesn't usually upset me, sometimes I just hate the complete and utter disregard humans have for life. If they only understood what a precious gift it is to be alive…"

Stunned, he nodded. Clearly, Carmen Vargas wasn't nearly as heartless as he'd thought.

They stood and paid homage to a man they'd never known, waiting until the flames settled down into embers, glowing amid the thick ash. Soon, with nothing else to use as fuel, those glowing bits of heat would fade also.

"We should have asked for a shovel," Carmen said. "I'd prefer to bury the ashes once this is over."

"I can go back and get one," he offered.

She jerked her head in a nod.

Once at the house, he started up the porch steps, intending to knock on the door. Instead, Tommy came outside and met him. "What's up?"

Rick explained what he needed. Tommy grunted, told him to wait there and went to the garage to fetch it. When he returned with two large shovels, Rick thanked him and started back toward Carmen.

"Do you need any help digging?" Tommy called after him.

Noting that the other man had waited until Rick had gone a fair distance, Rick told him no.

Once he reached Carmen and handed one of the shovels to her, they made short work of digging a hole. It didn't have to be that deep, because wild animals didn't go after ashes.

"There," he said, tossing the last shovelful of dirt on the mound and tamping it down. "That's done."

Expression solemn, she nodded. "Thanks for understanding a bit ago. Let's go for a walk. I need to move. Something, a bit of a distraction."

Since he could well understand this, he nodded.

"Come on. The woods are waiting. I feel better when I'm among the trees."

On impulse, he held out his hand. After a second's hesitation, she took it. He didn't know about her, but right now he needed skin-to-skin contact.

Though it hadn't been that long since he'd shape-shifted, his inner wolf recognized the earthy scent of the forest and grew restless. Rick couldn't help but think about what a relief it would be to change into his lupine self, and run and hunt until exhaustion chased all thoughts from his head. Obviously, he couldn't, and wouldn't, not while the fate of the entire human race hung in the balance.

He imagined Carmen felt similar, in her own way. Vampires enjoyed their own form of hunting.

"That was unusually rough for me," she said once they were far enough into the forest.

"You took that guy's death harder than I expected."

"Maybe." She lifted one shoulder. "Humans come and go. Usually, their passing doesn't affect me much. But this..." Clearing her throat, she looked away. "While I didn't know Sheldon personally, I was looking forward to learning from him. He clearly had a brilliant mind. I wanted to find out what steps he followed in his creation or discovery of the new virus. I'm hoping at least they preserved his notes."

Intelligent and vulnerable. His heart squeezed. Damned if she didn't keep surprising him, making him like her even more, deepening the strong sexual attraction he felt into something he didn't dare guess at. Too dangerous.

Hand in hand with her, walking through the leafy shadows of the trees, he could almost pretend they were a normal couple, out for a stroll. Since this—being normal, with a regular life—wasn't something he'd ever wanted, much less thought about, the odd direction his mind had taken concerned him. Had to be because his libido seemed to be working overtime where Carmen was concerned.

He needed to focus on the case. Nothing else. The rest could wait until the unforeseeable future.

They came to a large boulder near the edge of the stream. He squeezed her hand, meaning to help her up. She grinned at him, pulled her hand free and then leaped to the top. Clearly a Vampiric move and one he couldn't replicate unless in his wolf form.

With a sigh, he climbed up the normal way.

"This is nice." Expression serene, she looked around. "I always thought I'd like living in the country, though I haven't, not since I was a small child. I like the lack of people. Plus, these pine trees have a nice scent."

"They do. Where did you live before you came to Galveston?" he asked, genuinely curious.

"All over," she replied, grinning. "East Coast, West Coast and several places in between. I stick to large cities, usually. My favorite is Chicago. And then Europe, before America became so populated. London, Paris, Rome." Her heavy sigh matched her wistful expression. "I really need to get back there someday. I was born as a human in London."

"Exactly how old are you?" he asked, mentally wincing at the brusque nature of the question. "Sorry," he added. "But I really want to know. Idle curiosity."

Where most women would have been instantly offended, Carmen just brushed her hair away from her eyes and studied him. "Why?"

"I'm intrigued. You're the first Vampire I've ever been even remotely close to. Most of what I know about your kind is hearsay."

"Seriously? In your line of work?"

"Sorry." He shrugged. "I'm a Shape-shifter. I work mostly with other Shifters and with humans. I've never worked with a Vampire until now. In fact, I've never even talked to another Vamp."

"You haven't missed much," she said, deadpan. And then ruined it with a huge grin. "Just kidding. Like anything else, being a Vampire has its good and its bad sides. Eternal life is a plus. Having to drink blood is a minus, though you get used to it. I miss real food, especially pasta. And a good T-bone."

"I'd never really thought about that," he mused.

"Most others don't. That's okay. But in case you ever wondered why we Vamps tend to stick to our own kind, there's part of your answer. It's easier being around others who understand where you're coming from."

Though he knew better, he reached for her hand again. "I think we're all like that. Even among my kind, we Shape-shifters tend to stick to our own beast. Wolves hang around with other Pack members, the big cats keep to themselves, and so on."

"Hmm. Maybe we have more in common than we thought." She squeezed his hand, the simple move sending a jolt to his midsection. "What else do you want to know? I guess I don't mind answering your questions."

"How about instead of me grilling you, you just tell me whatever you feel comfortable sharing." The notion that he truly wanted to know more about her worried him slightly, but right now he couldn't make himself care.

"I was thirty when I was made," she said, still smiling, her misty gaze faraway.

He waited for her to elaborate. When she didn't, he pushed. "What year did you turn thirty?"

Her smile faded. "I'm not sure I should tell you. I fear it will make you think differently about me, and I don't want that."

"I already know you're a Vampire," he pointed out. "And judging by what I know of your kind, I'm guessing you're at least a couple hundred years old. I'm just curious."

"Let's just say it's been a while and leave it at that." Gently pulling her hand from his, she fluffed her hair. "Call it Vampire vanity."

He wasn't sure whether he found her reluctance to talk about herself charming or stubborn. In the end, he decided it was a combination of both. "Interesting," he mused. "I never would have pegged you for being vain."

"Vain?" One perfectly arched brow rose. "I'm female. Why wouldn't I be vain?"

Her response made him chuckle. "Point taken. Beautiful women like you are usually vainer than most."

Her lack of reaction to the compliment disappointed him. But then again, no doubt she was well aware of the lure of her beauty.

The thought felt like someone had splashed ice water in his face. What the hell was he thinking, acting like some lovesick teenager who couldn't keep it in his pants? He had a job to do, as did she. The entire human race's survival was at stake.

"I'm sorry, but this is getting weird," he said, making his voice flat and his expression cold. "Whatever this thing is that's simmering between us, we need to put it aside until we've successfully completed this mission. Then and only then, we can explore it."

Her throaty laugh had him clenching his jaw. "I disagree. I think we need to have wild sex immediately and get it out of our systems, so we can focus on the task ahead. Shutting down this virus is going to be difficult enough without me being distracted. What do you say?"

Since it had been years, no, *decades* since she'd wanted a man with this much intensity, Carmen found herself holding her breath. She'd been bold, certainly, but she'd learned life went better if she simply asked for what she wanted. And in this case, she wanted him.

"Ms. Vargas, Mr. Fallin!" Landers's voice, high with panic, echoed through the trees. "Where are you?"

They exchanged glances. "Let's go toward him before we respond," Rick said. "No sense in giving away our hiding place."

Since she agreed with that, she nodded. "Come on." She jumped down from the boulder, smiling when he did the same.

They took off at a slow jog, heading for the path that led back to the field behind the house. Landers called out again. Since they were halfway there, Rick responded. "We're on our way," he shouted.

As soon as they burst into the clearing, the sight of several men waiting for them sent a shudder of warning up Carmen's spine. "Trouble," she murmured to Rick, who'd skidded to a stop alongside her.

"What now?"

Slightly winded, Carmen and Rick jogged to the others. "What's going on?" she asked.

"Where were you?" Gus's narrow-eyed gaze swept over them, his expression drawn and suspicious.

"We went for a walk in the woods." Carmen kept her voice cool. "What's up?"

"What did you do with the vials?"

"I moved them over by that shed." She pointed. They

were no longer there. "I'm assuming Tommy came out and got them after bringing me the supplies I asked for. Why? Has something happened to them?"

Seriously, she hoped not. Those vials contained a deadly virus. How much more incompetent could they be?

Gus stared at her. "Are you lying to me?"

"Of course not. Why would I?" She took a step closer to him, making her own expression fierce. "What happened to those vials? Surely you understood they needed to be put back in a safe location in the lab."

Naturally, Gus looked away. "Yeah, I got that. I asked someone to do that. No one wanted to. They were *scared*," he sneered. "Finally, one of my newer guys said he'd handle it. Ted."

"And?" she prompted, unable to hide her impatience. "What happened?"

"Ted took the vials, got into a truck and took off. No one even realized he was gone at first. He got a fifteen-minute head start on us, but I sent two guys out looking for him."

"Fifteen minutes," Rick said, disbelief in his voice. "I'm guessing they haven't found him."

"Well, no." Fury blazed from the other man's eyes.

Carmen swore, using words she'd learned long ago from longshoremen on leave. "Do you realize what you have done?" she asked. "Do you have any idea?"

"Believe me, lady." Gus advanced on her, fist clenched. "I don't need you to tell me."

With a look, she dared him to touch her. Dared him.

Rick cleared his throat. "What does this Ted want with the virus? Has he asked for a ransom? Or is he planning to stage some sort of terror attack or something?"

Gus spat. "Probably money. He'd heard enough to

know we were sitting on a gold mine. We'd just started negotiations with foreign countries. I'm talking millions." He clamped his mouth shut.

"What do you want us to do?" Once again Rick, sounding like the voice of reason.

"I don't know." For the first time, panic leaked into Gus's voice. He eyed Carmen. "If Sheldon left notes, can you recreate the virus?"

Careful to contain her excitement, she nodded. "I can. But why do you say *if*? Why wouldn't there be notes?"

"Because Sheldon might have destroyed them when he found out what we planned to do with his creation. That's why I had to shoot him, remember?" Landers said.

"Might," she pointed out. "I take it that means you don't know for sure?"

Gus and Landers didn't answer.

Worst case scenario—no notes. And the virus out in the open, in the hands of someone who might not realize the full extent of what he had. If this Ted were to get into an accident, the repercussions would be deadly.

"How much does Ted know?" Rick asked, apparently having similar thoughts. "Is he aware of how much danger he could be in?"

"Like I said, he's new." Gus shook his head. "I don't keep any secrets from my men, but I'm not sure exactly what he does and doesn't know. He was pals with Sheldon. In fact, Ted took his death hard."

Talk about giving them the important news last. Carmen and Rick exchanged a glance.

"When you say *pals*," Carmen said, "do you mean they hung out together after work? Or did Ted help Sheldon in the lab?"

Gus kicked the ground with the steel toe of his work

boot. "Ted was Sheldon's assistant. He was supposed to be yours, too, once you started work. I imagine he knows more about the virus than all of us put together."

Blinking, Carmen closed her eyes. She didn't want Gus to see her fury, especially since Vamps' eyes tended to glow red when they were engaged. Mentally she counted to twelve, tamping down all emotion. When she felt even-keeled again, she glanced at Rick. He appeared stunned.

"It appears we've got one hell of a mess, gentlemen," she said. "If any of your men even remotely considered Ted a friend, they need to start working on contacting him immediately."

"What for?" Tommy asked. "Ted ain't stupid. He knows he'll be a dead man if he comes back here."

"Shut up," Gus ordered. "She's right. At least we have to try. Who was friendly with Ted?"

Though more than one man shifted his weight uncomfortably, no one responded.

Of course, this lack of response had Gus erupting into a string of curses that rivaled Carmen's earlier outburst. "Come on, now. At least one of you had to be friendly with the guy."

"Not really." Tommy again. "He hung out with Sheldon. He didn't talk much to anyone else. He even slept up at the lab like Sheldon."

Which meant Ted probably knew more about the virus than anyone else. She swallowed hard as a thought occurred to her. "Is Ted a biologist?"

"No. Before he came to work for me, he was a trash collector for the city of Atlanta, Georgia."

Atlanta. Where the CDC happened to be located. Coincidence? Carmen didn't believe in coincidences.

"Let me take a look in the lab," she said. "Now.

Hopefully, I can find something to reveal the methods Sheldon used to create the virus."

Rick glanced at her and nodded. "I'll help."

They both knew in order to find an antidote, they'd need to know the composition of the virus. And especially now, time was of the essence. If Ted did something stupid, the repercussions—contagion, death and panic—would be almost instantaneous.

And not only the human population would be at risk. No one knew how this virus would act on Shape-shifters.

"Follow me," Gus said, reaching into his pocket and withdrawing several keys. He took off for the barn/laboratory. Carmen and Rick followed.

When they reached the entry door, Gus unlocked it and turned to face them. Now that he was away from his men, he allowed his worry to show. "I'm really afraid," he said. "Everything I was planning was controlled. I asked for war to be declared in West Latvia. For this, I would be paid one billion dollars. After that, we'd planned to put the virus on the open market and let all the superpowers bid."

"Wait," Rick interrupted. "Someone paid you to have war declared? Earlier you said you were doing it for power."

Gus shrugged, his expression unconcerned. "Money is power, don't you know?"

But Carmen wasn't having it. "How much of what you told us is actually true?"

"None of your damn business. Unless you want me to put a bullet in you like Sheldon, you'd best shut your mouth and get to work."

Carmen allowed a slow smile to spread across her face. "Go ahead," she said. "Shoot me. I'm your best chance—no, your only chance—of figuring out a way to recreate this thing. But if you want to be left with nothing while Ted holds all the cards, then go ahead. Pull out your gun and shoot me, right this instant. Otherwise, don't ever threaten me again."

Apparently, Gus hadn't expected her reaction. His mouth dropped open and his already squinty eyes narrowed before he recovered. He looked at Rick and shook his head. "She's crazy, you know?"

Rick grinned. "Maybe, but I can tell you she meant every word that she said."

"Really?" Gus pulled out his pistol and pointed it at Carmen. "Not so brave now, are you?"

Carmen couldn't help but laugh. "Go ahead. If you're going to shoot, do it."

Instead, Gus jammed his weapon back into his holster. "I didn't even take the safety off," he said. "Here." He tossed her the keys, appearing surprised that she effortlessly caught them. "Get to work," he ordered, spinning on his heel and stomping off.

Carmen waited until he'd left before going inside. "Strange man," she commented to Rick as she felt along the wall for the light switch. While she could see just fine in the darkness, she knew Rick couldn't. Plus, she needed to see in every nook and cranny if she was going to find those notes.

When the fluorescent lights kicked on, she turned around and gasped. A quick glance at Rick revealed he shared her surprise.

"This is…" She had no words. She'd expected at least a semblance of sterility, so necessary in a biological lab. But no. Glancing around at the piles of manila folders and haphazard pieces of paper, she grimaced. This looked like something used by a mad scientist.

A rat scurried across the floor, veering away when it saw them. Carmen gasped. "What the…?"

Rick crossed the room, lifting a pile of what appeared to be rusted machine parts. "Maybe there's more. Another part, where Sheldon did actual work."

"I hope so." Privately, she had her doubts. In fact, she was beginning to wonder if this virus was actually real.

Chapter 9

The Pack Protector who'd been parked outside Jake's had made no attempt to follow Maddie home. Which meant he no doubt already knew where she lived. Great. Just great. Even more proof she was being watched. What she didn't understand was the logic behind it.

Maddie took pride in her reputation as someone who could be counted on to do what was right. *Reliable* and *loyal* could have been her middle names. Same for her family. Her father's reputation had been stellar, right up until the day he'd died. Having a brother who'd been promoted to a powerful position high up in the Pack Protector organization used to mean something. As in, someone like her would be considered above reproach.

Clearly, that was no longer the case. And she had no idea why. The simple fact of Jake hanging around the alley that led to Broken Chains didn't seem to be an adequate reason. There had to be more to all this. She needed to find out what.

Right now, she wasn't sure what to do, what course of action to take. The only thing she knew for certain was that she wanted to protect Jake as much as she could. Which meant she had to somehow dissuade him from the crazy idea he had about unmasking the truth about werewolves.

But how? He seemed so determined, so focused. So damn cute. Even his not-so-sly attempt to get her to take him into Broken Chains made her smile. She admired him for trying.

Her phone rang. Glancing at the screen, she groaned. Her brother. As if he'd known she'd been thinking about him. She could only hope he wasn't calling her in his official capacity as a Pack Protector.

"Hey, Colton." She put a lot of effort into sounding carefree. "How are you? It's been a long time."

Never one for pleasantries, he cut to the chase. "What have you gotten yourself into now, sis?"

She knew better than to bother trying to deflect. "It's nothing I can't handle," she said. "For the life of me, I don't understand why anyone would think this is a big deal."

"Maddie, if it's been elevated to enough of a threat that the Field Protectors are notifying me, then I'm not sure you can handle this. Now tell me what's going on."

With a sigh, she gave him the short version. "This human guy happened upon the alley leading to Broken Chains. He became obsessed with what was behind the door, especially since he saw a lot of people coming and going."

"And?"

The way he prodded told her he probably already knew the rest. But then again, if he did, the Protectors would have already rounded up Jake and taken him in.

No way was he finding out from her.

"One night two guys beat him up and I stumbled across him and helped him. He claims he's seen me go inside and has been trying to get me to take him with me. Of course, I can't."

"What did you tell him?"

She sighed. "That it was a private club for members only. He asked to go as my guest. So I told him that wasn't allowed. He keeps pushing. I keep refusing."

"Why?" Colton asked. "Why does he want to go inside so badly?"

"I think it's the lure of the unattainable. You know how you men are. Put something out there and tell a man he can't have it and he'll move heaven and earth. That trait must be built into the masculine DNA."

Colton laughed. "It sounds as if you like him."

"I do," she admitted. "He's human, but he's cute."

"He's also a journalist. A well-respected one. Did you know what?"

"Yes." Closing her eyes, she braced herself for her brother's reaction. "I think that's also the reason he wants to find out what's really behind the door. The journalist part of him believes it might be his next big exposé, like he'll uncover a terrorist cell or some huge, earth-shattering story." *Like the existence of Werewolves, Vampires and Merfolk.* Good thing Jake had no idea about the others.

"That's not good," Colton commented.

"No, but right now it's manageable. What I don't understand is why your field operatives are so worried about this. Don't they have better things to do?"

"That's their job." Colton's tone went sharp. "Worrying about the potential possibilities of situations like this."

A little taken aback, she swallowed. "Okay. I get it."

"Then I don't have to tell you to be careful, do I?"

"No, not really." Suspicious now, she waited. No way would Colton let her off this easily. But when he didn't speak again, she cleared her throat. "Can you call off the goon?"

Colton didn't even pretend not to understand who she meant. "He's there for your own safety."

"He threatened me. I didn't like that. If I didn't have you on my side, he would have scared the hell out of me."

"Threatened you how?" Colton's flat voice told her how little he liked her words.

"He felt it was his duty to warn me that the Protectors knew about Jake. And he advised me about the severity of my crime if I were to betray the Pack."

"That's standard protocol."

Disappointed in his dismissal, she sighed. "Intimidation tactics should never be the first line of offense. I'd think you'd know that better than anyone. What'd Dad always say?"

"To lead off with courtesy and respect." Colton could recite their father's creed as well as she could. "People are always more willing to help you if they like you."

She had him there, and he knew it. Still, she couldn't resist pounding the point home. "Exactly. Enough said. Maybe you should point that out to your goon."

"That's ridiculous," he protested. "Besides that, I don't even know which Field Protector has been assigned to your case."

"Oh, now I'm a *case*?" she asked. "And I know good and well that you can find out. That guy has been following me around, stalking Jake and bothering me at Broken Chains. I could understand if I was some known criminal. But no. I'm the sister of an upper-level Pack Protector. Surely that should buy me a little respect."

Colton laughed outright at that. "I'll see what I can

do," he said, his tone dry. "But be aware, someone will always have eyes on the journalist. I don't care how cute you think he is, I want you to promise me you'll always be aware what a threat he could be."

"I promise. And Colton, if I see any indication that he'll be taken seriously, I'll call you immediately."

"Good enough," he replied, and then he ended the call.

Shaking her head, she scrolled over to check social media. She'd barely started to read her news feed when the phone rang again.

"What'd you forget?" she asked, not bothering to check caller ID. "Because, Colton, believe me, I get it. I understand."

"Colton? Who's Colton? This is Jake."

Yikes. Glad she hadn't said this out loud, she apologized. "Sorry, I'd just finished another call. What's up, Jake?"

Now he hesitated. "I think maybe we should talk in person," he finally said. "If you want to give me your address, I can swing by and get you."

"I'd rather meet somewhere."

"Of course you would." His tone had gone glum. "Listen, maybe this isn't a good idea. I shouldn't have bothered you. Especially if you're in the middle of something."

Was he *jealous*?

"I'm not in the middle of anything. I was just on the phone earlier. Colton's my brother," she said. "In case you were wondering."

"Okay."

He didn't sound relieved. Or skeptical. Or anything, really. Maybe she'd misinterpreted. Yikes! Now she felt embarrassed. "I just thought you might want to know."

She spoke fast. "In case you thought he was my boyfriend or something. Because I don't have a boyfriend."

Awkward silence. Gripping her phone, she wished the floor would open up and swallow her.

Finally, Jake laughed. "I get it. I'm glad you don't have a boyfriend."

Warmth spread through her at his words.

"But what I don't understand is why you don't want me to know where you live," he continued. "At least, that's what I surmise is the reason you don't want me to pick you up at your house. Do you think I'm going to start stalking you or something?"

Now she had a reason for the earlier silence and the reserve in his tone.

"Of course not." And she had to admit, he had a point. "I guess I'm just a private person." But she'd been to his house. And logistically, there was no reason why he couldn't come to her apartment. "You're right," she finally said. "If we're going to have a relationship, I've got to be more open."

There. She'd put it out there.

"I agree," he replied, to her relief. "I'll head that way if you'll give me your address."

She did. Once she hung up, she rushed around her apartment, tidying up. Mostly, she kept her living space pretty neat, but she couldn't help wanting to make it look perfect for Jake.

As nervous as if she was going on a blind date, she paced, unable to resist continually checking the window for the sight of his vehicle. Finally, common sense prevailed and she opened a can of Diet Dr. Pepper and carried it onto the front porch to wait. From here, she could see not only the parking lot, but the turn-in from the street.

She took a seat in her favorite wooden rocking chair,

sipped her soft drink and willed herself to calm down. This behavior was not like her and she didn't like it. But just when she finally felt normal, she caught sight of his SUV pulling into the parking lot, and her heart rate kicked into overdrive.

Wiping her hands on the front of her jeans, she went inside and waited.

When he knocked, she opened the door. Jake smiled when he saw her, his appreciation sending warmth all the way to her toes. "Hey," he said.

"Hey yourself." She stepped aside. "Come on in."

As he moved past her, he looked around. "Nice place," he said. "Great location. You can almost see the ocean from here."

Since proximity to the beach had been one the reasons she'd chosen to lease this apartment, she grinned. "Thanks. I like the sound of the waves. It's soothing." Especially at night, when the traffic on Seawall Boulevard had died down.

"You look great."

The compliment made her blush, which was one of the curses of being a fair-skinned redhead. She couldn't help but let her gaze travel over him. Everything about this man called to her. From the light brown tone of his skin, to the angle of his masculine jaw. She liked his broad shoulders, narrow hips and the way he towered over her. He had a sensual mouth, the eyes of an old soul and a wicked grin. "So do you," she responded.

"Here." Oblivious to her decidedly carnal thoughts, he handed her a brown paper bag. "For you. Wine."

"Wine?"

"Yeah." He grimaced. "It's a nice chardonnay." Eyeing her, he appeared to realize something. "Do you even drink wine?"

"I have. Though I typically prefer beer." She checked

her watch. "Since it's a little too early to drink this, I'll put it in the fridge so it can chill."

He nodded, practically bouncing on the balls of his feet, vibrating with energy. "I have news," he said.

"Just one second." All she could think about was how badly she wanted to kiss him. Needing to give herself time to regain her equilibrium, she carried the bottle into the kitchen and placed it inside the refrigerator. Reminding herself to breathe, she straightened her spine and headed back to her living room.

His intense gaze tracked her every move.

"Okay. What's your news?"

In response to her question, he dragged his hand through his short hair and inhaled. "Maddie, you're probably not going to like this, but I thought it was fair to tell you first. I've made contact with someone who says he can get me inside that club."

At first, his words didn't register. When she realized he meant Broken Chains, she shook her head. "I don't know what this person is asking for in return, but you need to be supercautious. There's no possible way he can do this."

Judging by the stubborn set of his jaw, Jake didn't believe her. "You don't know that," he said. "In my line of work, there's always a source who can do what others say is impossible."

"Oh, but I do know." Arms crossed, she shook her head, biting down hard on her anger. Not at Jake, never at Jake, but at whoever was trying to dupe him. "What's he asking you to pay him for this privilege?"

"Not too much," he hedged. "A thousand dollars."

"Ha." She snorted. "You might as well set a match to your money. He's just trying to swindle you."

"Are you always so negative?" he countered. "If I

thought like you, I'd have missed out on numerous good stories."

"Negative?" Incredulous, she stared. "Try *realistic*. I can even guess how it all went down. You were doing your usual watching the alley. This person happened to run into you and struck up a conversation. He seemed nice, genuinely perplexed why you couldn't get in. Then, to prove he could, he left you and went inside."

Now Jake viewed her with open suspicion. "That's exactly what happened. How do you know this?" He narrowed his gaze. "Is he a friend of yours?"

"Nope. But I know a setup when I hear one. I grew up in a family of private investigators. I've honed my instincts." Plus, she knew, though she couldn't tell Jake, that if anyone were to take a human inside Broken Chains, they'd be set upon within minutes and killed. The Vampires would smell his blood and hear his heart, the Shifters would scent his humanness and notice his distinctly human aura, and the Merfolk would know by a look. Though this had never happened within Maddie's lifetime, she'd heard tales of a human once breaching the club's defenses. He'd been killed instantly.

The thought of such a thing happening to Jake made her shudder. And then she realized this could actually be the plan. Not only to relieve Jake of his money, but to get him inside. His death would neutralize the threat he posed. Would the Pack Protectors go that far?

Jake dropped onto her couch, his frustration showing in his face. "That makes no sense. In my world, when a journalist is looking for leads for a big story, sources sometimes show up with information and want to be paid. It's considered unethical, but sometimes the story is just too big. This guy did exactly that. What would be his reason for setting me up?"

Again, she stuck as close to the truth as possible.

"Because only certain people can go inside that door. There are many who will do anything to stop an outsider—such as yourself—from entering. Can you give me a description of the guy?" She needed to know if he was a Shifter, a Merman or a Vampire. Right now, she was betting on Shifter. Probably another of her brother's employees.

Jake leaned back. "Sure. He was a big guy, like a football player. My first thought was to wonder if he worked as a bouncer. Shaved head, wore dark sunglasses. He did ask me if I'd seen anything unusual outside in the alley."

Her heart skipped a beat. "What did you tell him?"

"Nothing, of course."

Relieved, she smiled. He wouldn't be here talking to her right now if he'd told a Pack Protector he'd seen someone shape-shift. They'd have already dragged him away for reprogramming.

He had no idea how much danger he'd placed himself in.

"Where and when are you supposed to meet this guy?" she asked.

"Sorry, I can't reveal my sources." One corner of his mouth quirked. Hounds help her, but her mouth went dry.

"Seriously?"

"Yep. Obviously, I can't have you trying to ruin it for me." He patted the couch next to him. "Come here. Sit. Tell me about your day."

His rapid switch of topics, no doubt meant to throw her off balance, amused her. Because she needed to buy some time to come up with a better way of explaining to him the impossibility of what he'd suggested, she sat. But she prudently kept a few feet of distance between them.

He chuckled. "Why are you way over there? I don't bite. Come here."

Staring at him, she swallowed. Her entire body tingled. She wondered if he realized the power of his sexy smile. Of course she slid over, inch by inch, until her hip bumped his. Even that small bit of contact sent a shiver of longing through her.

Talk about distraction techniques. He was good, she'd give him that. Except she had no idea if Jake even knew how he affected her.

But the warm glow in his dark eyes told her he did.

Determination set in. Two could play this game. Maybe this would be her only chance to convince him to abandon the idea of trying to get inside Broken Chains.

One ability Jake prided himself on was being able to read other people's reactions. And Maddie meant what she said. Not only did she worry about him being swindled, but she appeared truly worried, even afraid for him.

Why? Granted, she'd found him after he'd been jumped by the two thugs. He'd been caught by surprise that time. That wouldn't happen again—he wouldn't allow it. Not only did he now carry a knife, he'd looked into applying for his concealed handgun license and planned to purchase a pistol. Plus, he'd purchased—on the black market—a body camera similar to those used by police officers. It was on back order. He couldn't wait until it arrived. Once he had it, anything that happened to him would be sent to secure storage in his personal cloud, with a scheduled and timed release to all his social media accounts in exactly one day.

He'd taken, as the saying went, precautions. However, though he hadn't yet admitted it to Maddie, his always reliable gut instinct warned him to be wary of the entire thing. "Maybe you're right," he told her. "Something doesn't feel right."

Some of the tension drained out of her body. He could feel it, even though they were just hip to hip, shoulder to shoulder. "You were really worried about me," he mused, turning to face her. As usual, being this close to her sent his every sense into overdrive.

From the way her pupils dilated, she felt the same way.

"I was," she murmured, tilting her head. "I really wish you'd just let this obsession you have with Broken Chains go."

"Broken Chains?"

"Damn." Briefly, she closed her eyes. "I shouldn't have said that. I don't suppose you'd be willing to pretend I didn't?"

Since he suspected she already knew the answer to that one, he didn't immediately reply. Instead, jubilant, he leaned in and kissed her. What he'd meant to be a quick, celebratory kiss caught fire and turned into something more.

Arms wrapped around his neck, she kissed him as if she'd die without him. Her ardor fed his own, until he could scarcely breathe, never mind think. If she meant to distract him, he didn't care. Around her, rational thought ceased to exist. One touch and he craved more. One press of his lips to hers and he became so hard it was painful.

"Oh," she gasped, coming up for air. He barely let her inhale before claiming her mouth again.

Earlier, he'd given himself a stern talking-to. This constant craving for Maddie bordered on obsession. Definitely not healthy and, for a man in his position, and not safe, either. Being pretty sure she felt the same way, he'd resolved to talk to her about it.

Of course, every time he tried, they couldn't seem to keep their hands off each other.

Dimly he realized she was speaking. With his blood roaring in his ears, he'd missed the first part.

"Get it out of our systems," she concluded. "What do you think?"

"I…" He swallowed, trying to concentrate on anything other than how good her body felt pressed up against his and how badly he wished there weren't any clothes between them.

Clearly still unaware he had no idea what she'd said, she wiggled against him, possibly to underscore her point. He found himself even more aroused—something he wouldn't have believed possible.

"I want you," he managed, stating the obvious. "More than you can imagine."

"Um, no." She grinned, glancing at his spectacular bulge. "I can see that. And I want you. So, what do you say? Maybe if we go ahead and get it out of our systems, this attraction between us won't be so intense."

Relief mingled with desire as he finally realized she'd managed to put into words what he'd been trying to articulate.

As he reached for her in agreement, she eluded his grasp. Moving back, she lifted her T-shirt over her head, and then shimmied out of her denim shorts. Standing proudly before him in her black lace bra and matching panties, she was the most beautiful, sexiest woman he'd ever seen.

"Your turn," she said.

Glad she hadn't offered to help him undress—because he knew if she touched him right now, he'd lose his tenuous grip on self-control—he rapidly divested himself of his shirt. Removing his khaki shorts was a bit trickier, due to the sheer size of his arousal. Finally, he decided the hell with it, and stepped out of everything. He stood before her, naked, aroused and aching.

Her grin widened. Without taking her eyes from him, she made quick work of removing her bra and panties. The instant she was naked, he reached for her. She met him halfway and they fell to their knees together onto the couch. Skin to skin, finally, he let himself touch her in places he'd only dreamed of.

She guided his hand to her lady parts, warm and wet. "I need you inside me."

"Wait," he managed, with his fingers half buried inside her. "Not here. The bedroom." He wanted their first time to be in a proper bed.

Head back, eyes half-lidded, she moaned. "Only if you swear to keep touching me exactly the way you are right now."

"Oh, I can do better than that," he promised. "Let me show you."

They made it to the bedroom, limbs still intertwined. Separating from her, he went to the nightstand, found a condom and managed to pull it over him. She watched, her full chest rising and falling with her rapid breathing.

"Now I'm ready," he growled, reaching for her as she came around to the side of the bed. She pressed against him, so close he could feel the rapid beat of her heart.

He entered her as they fell back onto the comforter, already moving, moving inside of her. She enveloped him, he filled her, a perfect fit.

She moved with him, crying out in pleasure. When her climax came and her body pulsed against him, he gave himself over to his own release, knowing with absolute certainty that one time would never be enough.

Chapter 10

When Carmen started to speak again, Rick held up his finger. "Let me sweep for bugs," he mouthed, pulling some sort of device from his pocket and walking around the room with it.

She nodded.

After making a thorough sweep of the room, he went again. Nothing like being thorough. After all, if the gang had bugged their living quarters, it made sense they'd want to listen in on their biologist as he worked in his lab.

But no, he found nothing. "It's clear," he told Carmen, letting his confidence show in his voice. "Maybe it's just us that they want to keep ears on."

"Yeah, maybe." Frowning, she turned in a slow circle, surveying the room, her slender figure and graceful neck reminding him of her stunning beauty. "After seeing this, I have to wonder if the bugs in our room are even active."

"Come on," he said, managing to stop himself from reaching for her hand. "This is a big barn. Let's check out the rest of it."

"Fine." She strode past him, disgust evident on her beautiful face. "Look at this place. There's no way to avoid contamination. If anyone developed anything here, I'd be surprised. No, more than that. Shocked. I call BS."

While he didn't know anything about biology or laboratories, he tended to agree with her. Nothing about this place screamed *high-tech lab*.

They crossed the center of the barn, stepping around a rusted out old tractor, three or four semi tires, and a pile of junk. As they passed, a large rat scurried past them. Instead of screaming like a human woman would have, Carmen hissed and bared her fangs. For a split second, her eyes glowed red.

"Impressive," he said. "But be careful about who sees those."

Though she gave him a narrow glare, she nodded and continued moving, the stiff set of her classical features revealing her discomfort.

In the back section of the barn, they came to a locked door. Rick felt along the top of the sill, finding a key. "Lax security, too," he said, shaking his head. Once he'd inserted the key into the lock, he turned the knob. "After you."

At first, she didn't move. Noticing his quizzical glance, she forced a smile. "I'm bracing myself for more disappointment."

"Maybe we'll be surprised," he said, though he privately doubted it.

Carmen squared her shoulders and opened the door. She stopped so suddenly he nearly ran into her.

"Now this is what I expected," she breathed. "Take a look."

Moving around her, he stopped and stared. They stood in a small area that appeared to have been converted to a washroom. There was a sink, a soap dispenser, and a box of rubber gloves. Two white clean-room suits hung on the wall. Unlike the rest of the barn, this room was immaculate.

"There." She pointed. Separated by a clear glass wall, the next area over was even tinier, the size of a small elevator. Some sort of keypad blinked on the outside, and it appeared to be the only way to unlock the door. Someone had helpfully posted the code on a yellow sticky note taped up above the keypad.

"What the heck is that?" Rick asked.

"A decontamination area. The only way one can control contamination is to control the entire environment. I would be surprised if this isn't up to Federal Standard 209E."

Since he didn't want a long explanation, he didn't ask. "That's good, right?"

"Yes. Very good." But then her excited expression fell. "But look." She gestured. "They haven't been maintaining this. Once a clean-room has been built, it must be maintained, cleaned to very high standards. If it isn't, it's no longer considered clean."

He squinted, trying to see what she saw. "Where are you seeing contamination?"

"Everywhere. Look closely. Dust in that corner." She pointed. "And there, rat droppings. It's no longer up to par."

"I see." Pushing back his disappointment, he touched her shoulder. "How long ago do you think it became contaminated?" he asked. "Can it be brought back up to par quickly? Maybe it's just been since Sheldon was killed."

"No." She immediately shot that idea down. "From the looks in there, this has been going on a while. I wouldn't be surprised…" She stopped, pushing him back. "There's a possibility that the virus is growing inside that room, unassisted. Since we don't know how it would affect you, I'm going to have to ask you to step away."

"No." He didn't have to even think about his response. "If I put on one of those suits, I'm protected, right?"

Expression reluctant, she nodded. "Assuming they're intact. Given the state of the rest of this place, it's probable they have rips or tears. I can't let you risk it."

"You're not in charge of me," he began.

"But I am." Her eyes flashed. "You agreed to those terms if I consented to help you. So, if I say I don't want you in the lab, you will remain out here."

Frustrated, at a loss for words, he did the only thing he could think of to do. He hauled her up against him and kissed her until they both were breathless.

When he lifted his head, she gave him a slow smile, her sexy eyes glittering. "Now that you got that out of your system, I need you to wait out here while I ascertain the risk inside the lab. Can you do that?"

"Now that you asked nicely, yes," he drawled. "Though I can promise you that I'll hate every minute of it."

"Sorry." Without a backward look, she crossed the room to the sink and began scrubbing up. Once she'd finished, she dried off and reached for one of the clean suits, checking inside to make sure there were no unwanted residents.

"Why bother?" he asked, confused. "If the lab is already contaminated."

"The less the better," she replied, pulling the garment up over her clothing and zipping it closed. Next, she grabbed a headpiece and put it on, making her look as though she wore some kind of bizarre spacesuit. Finally she pulled on gloves, after shaking them out first in case anything might have crawled into them.

Fully dressed, she stepped awkwardly forward, removed her glove and punched the code into the keypad, then slid it back over her hand while she waited for the door to swing open.

Inside, she stood absolutely still while water sprayed her and then wind dried her off. Despite himself, Rick was impressed. This small terrorist group apparently had big funding behind them, which meant the FBI knew only part of the story.

Once the machine had finished cleaning her, the door to the inner chamber swung open. Carmen stepped inside and turned slowly, surveying every bit of the place, inch by inch. From Rick's vantage point, he could make out a gleaming stainless steel table, a refrigerator and several empty glass vials, similar to the ones Sheldon had been carrying when he'd been shot.

While Carmen did her thing, Rick prowled the outer room. Even though she'd claimed the place had been contaminated, as far as he could tell, that would be only this outer room. The inner room where she was now appeared to be inaccessible except through the purifying room. The glass went all the way from floor to ceiling. And it appeared the outer barn wall had also been sealed off with the same kind of glass or Plexiglas.

He checked for bugs or cameras twice and found nothing. Either Sheldon and his assistant Ted had cleared the area, or they had never been there at all.

* * *

Something was off. First thing, Carmen could see no evidence whatsoever that this lab had ever been used for work. Any kind of work whatsoever. Which meant this Sheldon person had either brought the virus in with him, or the entire thing was some sort of elaborate hoax.

She frowned, trying to think. Rick had said there'd been a victim. And that the CDC in Atlanta had been working on identifying the virus and developing a cure.

Which meant a new virus did exist. But the likelihood that this group, the Sons of Darkness, had anything to do with creating it seemed nonexistent.

Then why? What could possibly be the reason for creating such an elaborate setup? Building a clean room wasn't cheap, and the fact that they'd brought her in to assist their existing biologist made no sense if they were aware Sheldon hadn't created anything. Clearly, Gus and his ragtag crew had no idea that anything was amiss.

However, Sheldon and his sidekick, Ted—well, that was another story. Damn, she wished Sheldon was still alive. Evidently, he'd panicked when he'd learned Gus was bringing another biologist on board. He'd known she'd find out the truth. So he'd staged a protest, not figuring the men would actually harm him. And when Sheldon had been shot, Ted had grabbed the vials and fled. Why? Because they contained the virus? Or, more likely, because they'd contained nothing at all.

Anger warred with curiosity. She made another sweep of the room, again noting that everything, every single freaking tool and beaker, appeared to be brand-new. Some still had the plastic on them.

Opening the refrigerator proved her theory beyond a shadow of a doubt. The pristine inside of the fridge housed nothing. And she'd bet there'd never been any contents. This entire thing—the messy barn, the expert attempt at replicating the clean room—all was a sham.

They were being played. Whether or not these Sons of Darkness people were in on it or not, she had no idea, though she tended to think they had no idea whatsoever.

Furious, she strode through the door to the connecting spray, allowed it to do its thing and then exited. As soon as she was clear, she yanked off her headgear and gloves and made a face. "How certain are you that this place isn't bugged?" she asked, keeping her voice low.

Rick's brows rose at her tone, but he shrugged. "I'm sure. I did two sweeps while you were in there. I found nothing. It's clear."

Though she nodded, instead of blurting out the news, she went closer, putting her mouth against his ear so she could whisper. "This place is a setup. It's never been used as a working lab."

He froze. With her Vampiric hearing, she could detect the immediate increase in his heart rate. "You're positive?"

"Yes. I'm not sure if Gus and his crew know, but probably not. Otherwise why would they have brought me in?"

Turning slightly so that he faced her, he jerked his head in a nod. "That puts all of this in an entirely new light."

"It does," she agreed. "The question is, do we tell them?"

"Not yet." He checked his watch. "I think we've been in here long enough. We'd better go back. I want to see how this shakes out."

She nodded. They exited the clean area, moving slowly through the cluttered and filthy barn.

"At least now I understand why there aren't any

notes," she mused. "Imagine how Sheldon must have panicked when he found out they were bringing in another biologist."

His grim smile told her he'd already thought of that.

"For now, we'll just play along like we know nothing," he said. "If these guys don't actually have the virus, if they never had it to begin with, that is an entirely different ball game."

"But it still leaves the question of where the virus came from to begin with."

"Exactly," he agreed. "Let me ask you. Is it possible that a previously unknown virus strain could appear naturally?"

"Emerging disease is usually a yet-unrecognized infection, or a previous one that expanded with a significant change in pathogenicity," she said. "Many so-called new strains originate in the animal kingdom." Noting the way Rick's eyes had glazed over, she shrugged. "But the CDC is well versed in all this. If they have reason to believe this thing was artificially created, then I have to think they're right. It's what they do. They have the brainpower and the resources to make these kinds of calls."

"That makes sense."

"Which begs the question. What's these guys' angle?" she asked.

"Or who is actually behind them pulling the strings?" Rick added. "Either this goes deeper than we originally thought, or this group is being played."

"And I'm thinking that's an answer you're never going to find out," Landers said, stepping from behind a stack of moldy bales of hay. He had a pistol pointed directly at Rick.

"I should have known it was you," Rick responded,

his tone even, though his body had gone tense. "I'm guessing the others have no idea."

"Of course not." Motioning with the gun, Landers apparently wanted them to move forward. "They all think we're going to get rich. They have no idea."

Neither Carmen nor Rick moved. She exchanged a quick glance with Rick because she was thinking of simply using her Vampire ability to move and snatching the weapon out of the puny human man's hands.

But Rick gave a miniscule shake of his head, letting her know that for now, she should see what Landers intended.

"You're going to shoot us and pretend we were escaping, aren't you?" Rick asked. "Kind of like what happened to Sheldon."

"Smart guy," Landers sneered. "But I have bigger plans for you."

"Oh, really?" Carmen kept her voice cool. "What would those be?"

"I need you to create a virus," he said. "You've got the lab and the know-how. I can get you anything else you need."

Her mouth fell open before she quickly snapped it shut. "Do you have any idea what you're asking? That's insane."

"Is it?" Landers waved the pistol from her to Rick. "I'm going to give you one week. If you don't have something by then, your husband is going to die."

"One week?" Not bothering to contain her disdain, she had to keep her lips locked tight to hide her aching fangs. If this fool had any idea how badly she wanted to snatch him up, clamp her fangs to his neck and drain him of every drop of his blood, he'd throw down the gun and run away. Naturally, he didn't and he wouldn't, not until he died.

"Carmen." Rick's quiet warning brought her back to rationality. "Maybe you should at least try to do what he's asking."

"Try? Try?" She rounded on him. "What he wants is impossible."

"Not for you," he prodded, gently reminding her that they needed to stall. At least for now. "Can't you give it a shot?"

Landers snorted. "Listen to the man. He's begging for his life."

Except he wasn't. Unless Landers had a silver bullet in his gun, he couldn't kill Rick. And since she had already died a long time ago, nothing short of a stake through her heart would do her in now.

Landers knew none of this. And if Rick wanted her to play along, then that's what she'd do.

"I guess I can try," she said, pretending to be deeply in thought. "I'll need Rick to assist me. I'll make a list of what I need and get it to you. Most important, I'll need a working computer and access to the internet."

"No can do." Landers didn't even blink. "I can't take the chance of you alerting the authorities. You'll have to figure everything out on your own, without the internet."

Clenching her jaw, she nodded. Apparently, Landers had no clue that what he asked was simply impossible. She had no idea how to even begin to create a new virus. It would have to come from a genetic mutation of an already existing one. She'd need access to research papers among other things.

Again, the clueless human thought she could work miracles.

"Oh, sure." She flashed a humorless smile, hoping her eyes hadn't turned red. "No problem. I'll get right to work. And don't worry about supplies. I'll have no problem creating a completely new virus out of thin air."

Either her irony was lost on Landers, or he was playing along for his own reasons. She'd bet on the former.

Landers nodded. "Perfect. I heard you were the best."

"True, I am." She dipped her chin with false modesty. "Since you expect results so quickly, I guess Rick and I had better get to work immediately."

"One slight change in plans," Landers announced, his voice pleasant. "I'm afraid Rick will be staying with me until you have what I want. Insurance, you understand."

"No." Both she and Rick spoke at the same time.

"That's not going to happen," she said. "No Rick, no virus. That's nonnegotiable."

Landers waved his pistol. "Neither of you are in any position to negotiate," he said.

"That's it, I've had it." Carmen shot a quick glance at Rick, though at this point she didn't particularly care if he agreed or not. To her surprise, he gave a tiny nod, as if telling her to go for it.

Perfect. Grinning, she turned her attention toward Landers, who'd started to laugh at her frustration. When he saw her eyes, he choked.

"U-um," he stammered.

She moved. Before he could tighten his finger on the trigger, before he knew what hit him, she took him down. The weapon went flying—without discharging—and she left retrieval of that to Rick. She sunk her fangs in Landers's neck, drinking deeply.

At the first coppery taste of human blood, energy flowed into her. She hadn't realized, not until that very instant, how starved she'd become. Used to subsisting mostly on a diet of frozen blood, having her meal come fresh and warm was a gourmet treat.

As Landers went limp in her embrace, she looked up and saw Rick watching with a kind of revolted fascination.

"Is he dead?" he asked, his detached tone at odds with the look in his eyes.

"Not yet." She looked away, hurt stabbing her heart, oddly enough. She'd long ago come to terms with what kind of being she was and refused to make apologies. She imagined Rick would be ten times more savage if she were to watch him as wolf, taking down a kill.

"Maybe you should leave him alive," Rick suggested. "Won't he turn into a Vampire if you kill him?"

Considering, she swallowed. He was right. The last thing she wanted to do was to create another Vamp. Doing such a thing came with heavy repercussions. This was never to be undertaken lightly. Which made her wonder. Had she become so crazed by the taste of fresh blood that she hadn't thought things through?

"What will happen to him if you stop right now?" Rick pressed. "If you let him live, how much will he remember?"

"Nothing." She glanced down at the still-swooning man in her arms. A single drop of bright red blood glistened on one of the puncture holes in his neck. The sight made her fangs ache, but she ruthlessly shut down that craving.

"For humans," she continued, "this process is perceived as sexual. I'm not sure how he'll remember it, exactly—I've never stuck around long after drinking from a person. Most likely he'll believe it to have been a particularly sensual dream."

Though he merely nodded, her words sparked a glint of something in Rick's gaze. He hid it quickly, turning to survey the junky barn. "We need to come up with a quick plan," he said. "I'm not sure, but I'm gathering from what Landers said that none of the others were in on this scheme. But then again, we don't know for sure."

After gently easing Landers to the floor, she stood. "I know what I want to do. We need to get out of here and go after Ted. Once we catch up with him, we'll know if these Sons of Darkness ever even had a virus."

"I agree," Rick said immediately. "If not, we've got to find out who's using this group as a cover-up. And where the virus is."

"Exactly. I wonder how close the CDC is to figuring out an antidote."

He took her arm. "That's some more information I'll find out once we're clear of here. How do you propose we escape?"

Laughing felt good, so she did. "That's simple. You change into your wolf self and run. See if you can keep up with a Vampire at full speed."

After a moment, he laughed, too. "I doubt I can, but it'll be close. My wolf side will appreciate the opportunity to try."

"Perfect." The fresh blood had energized her, making her feel as if she could do anything. "If you change now, go ahead and strip first. I'll carry your clothes for you so you'll have something to put on when you change back."

He eyed her and then nodded. "Good thinking. At first I thought you just wanted to see me naked."

"That, too." She saw no point in lying. "Another time, I'd definitely take advantage of that. But we need to hurry. There's no telling how long it'll be before someone decides to come looking for us."

Without hesitation, he removed his shirt, then kicked

off his shoes. As he undid his belt and prepared to take off his jeans, she couldn't look away. Despite the circumstances, and maybe because of the fresh blood flowing in her veins, the simple act of him getting undressed aroused her.

The luck of bad timing. In a few seconds, he stood before her in all his magnificent male nakedness. He scooped up his clothes and shoes, bundled them together and handed them to her. She couldn't help but notice that his body was also aroused. And large. Very large.

"I've never seen a Shifter change form before," she said, her husky voice betraying her.

"Then you're about to." Dropping to all fours, he winked at her and then initiated the change.

Firefly lights surrounded him, twinkling as brightly as miniature stars. Fascinated, she watched as his bones began to lengthen and change shape. His human features blurred, elongating, and fur started to rapidly take over his previously smooth skin.

The multitude of lights swirled, hiding him momentarily. When they abruptly vanished, a massive and dangerous-looking wolf stood in Rick's place.

Nonplussed, she stared. Then, gathering her composure, she headed toward the door. "Are you ready?" she asked.

Wolf-Rick made a rumbling sound, a cross between a growl and a bark. For whatever reason, that lupine voice filled her with a fierce joy.

She opened the barn door and stepped out into the warm sunshine. After sidling past her, Rick took off, streaking away in the direction of the woods. She inhaled, glanced once at the house and took off at full Vampire speed.

Chapter 11

Held tightly in Jake's arms, Maddie felt a sense of contentment steal over her as she marveled at how powerful their lovemaking had been. She felt...changed. This had been more than just a simple slaking of physical need. It was like their souls had connected. They'd fit together as if their bodies had been made for each other. Even now, after all that, Jake didn't seem to be in any hurry to let her go.

He was unique, that's for sure. One of a kind. Hers.

Mate. Unbidden, the word flashed into her consciousness. She instantly rejected the thought. She'd never been prone to romantic fantasies or notions and she had no intention of starting now.

Sheesh. Give her a taste of some mind-blowing sex and she went all mushy. Luckily, Jake had no idea.

Turning her head to look at him, she caught him studying her, his brown gaze as warm as melted chocolate. "What?" she asked, curious.

"You're amazing, you know that?" His grin took her breath away and made her stomach flutter.

"So are you." She used a brisk tone to cover up how he made her feel. Too fast, too soon. Scooting out of his arms, she grabbed a T-shirt and pulled it on. "I don't know about you, but I'm starving. How about we get dressed and go grab something to eat?"

"Sure." He yawned, not sounding particularly enthused. "I guess I could eat."

She almost offered to go get them something and bring it back, but that felt wrong. Too…girlfriend-like. No, they needed to get moving so she could feel normal again.

"Great." Jumping up, she headed toward the bathroom. "Let me get cleaned up and then you can have a turn."

The hot shower brought back rationality and eased the tightness in her chest. After drying her hair, she applied a light touch of makeup, got dressed and opened the bathroom door.

Sauntering past her fully naked, Jake seemed completely aware of his effect on her. He grinned as she caught her breath. She could breathe again once she heard the shower turn on.

This. Had. To. Stop. She'd vowed never to let any man turn her into goop, and it wouldn't be starting now with him. Surely she could enjoy fabulous sex and a friendly relationship without becoming *that* girl. Right?

When he emerged, his short hair still damp and his shirt unbuttoned, the stab of longing she felt was so strong she had to look away. "Are you ready?" she asked, her tone too bright.

"Sure. We'll take my car."

While he drove, Jake kept glancing sideways at her, one corner of his mouth quirking in a half smile.

"What?" she asked again, battling the urge to smile back.

He shrugged. "Don't take this the wrong way, but I really like you."

Secretly pleased, she nodded. "Ditto."

"But," he continued, "just because we made our relationship physical doesn't mean I'm going to abandon the chance to get inside that club of yours."

"Seriously?" She groaned. "Well, I've said all I can say. Don't blame me if you end up getting fleeced."

They pulled into the parking lot of her favorite Mexican restaurant. After he parked, he turned in his seat to face her. "Wouldn't it just be a lot easier if you could take me inside yourself?"

She shook her head. Not wanting to ruin a perfectly good evening, she opened the car door and got out. Maybe in his line of work, he'd learned if he kept pressing, he'd get results. Not this time.

As she reached for the door to go inside, someone opened it for her. Not Jake, as he'd just now gotten out of the car. But another man, and one she recognized. The Pack Protector who'd been parking outside Jake's house. The same one who'd confronted her inside Broken Chains.

"You." She glared at him. "My brother said he was going to tell you to back off."

"Really?" His smug look infuriated her. "Well, he hasn't yet. I see you're still slumming around with the human."

Right about then, Jake noticed something was going on at the entrance and came hurrying up. He glanced blankly from Maddie to the other man, clearly not recognizing him.

"Is something wrong?" he asked, directing his question to Maddie.

"Nope. This man thought I was someone he knew. That turns out to be wrong." She gave a hard smile at the Protector. "Now if you'll excuse me," she said pointedly.

Immediately, he stepped out of the way, having no choice. She knew enough about how Pack Protectors operated to understand he wouldn't start something here, in a popular restaurant filled with tourists.

But why hadn't Colton called him off? Knowing her brother, he'd simply gotten busy and the thought had slipped his mind. She'd text him and remind him.

"Are you okay?" Jake eyed her. "Whatever you and that guy were discussing looked pretty heated."

"Did it?"

"Yes. You can tell me all about it once we're seated."

Of course mild deflection didn't work on him. She figured once his journalistic instincts were roused, he'd pursue it until he had his answer.

Part of her—the private investigative side—admired this. It was sexy, even. However, the Shape-shifter side found it not only annoying, but dangerous. No matter how much she liked Jake, she had to protect her people.

The hostess led them to a booth. As Maddie slid into the seat, she sighed, bracing herself for an onslaught of questions.

"Hey." Jake reached across the table and took her hand. "Are you sure that guy wasn't your ex?"

"My ex?" Reminding herself that she'd promised not to lie, she shook her head. "No. He's someone who knows my brother."

"I take it your brother is a bit overprotective?"

A server delivered a basket of chips and two small bowls of salsa. Right after that, the waitress appeared to take their drink order.

Maddie ordered a margarita. She figured she'd need a little help in order to relax.

After they placed their food order, Jake sat back and studied her. "You're a very private person, aren't you?"

"I guess." She shrugged. "But you also tend to forget to put your reporter side away."

"What does that mean?" His frown told her he truly didn't understand.

"You ask a lot of questions."

Was that hurt flashing across his handsome face? Telling herself she must have imagined it, Maddie reached for another chip and dipped it into the salsa.

He waited while she chewed. Then, leaning forward, he met her gaze. "How else am I supposed to get to know you? I know nothing about you, really. I know you have a brother. Whether he's older or younger, I have no clue. Where he lives, if you two are close, those are the sorts of things people in a relationship should know."

In a relationship. Stunned, she took a sip of her margarita. As usual, she knew honesty was always the best policy. "Is that what we are? In a relationship?"

Again he flashed that devastating grin. "Unless you want to be acquaintances with benefits, then yes." His casual shrug fooled no one. "Up to you."

Their food arrived just then, giving her a few seconds to decide how to respond. "You're right," she finally said. "We should try to get to know one another better. I guess we kind of went about this backward, but that's fine." Spearing a chunk of her enchilada, she smiled. "Tell me about yourself. Where you're from, if you have siblings, all of it."

Over the course of their meal, in between bites, she learned Jake had been an only child, born and raised in Terrell. After graduating from Texas A&M University in College Station, he'd moved to Houston to take a job as a special correspondent for KHOU. His parents were both still living out near Tyler, and he visited them a couple of times a year.

For her part, she told him she had one older brother, and that they'd grown up in Missouri City, where her father had run a private investigative agency he'd taken over from his father. "When he died, my stepmother sold the agency right out from under me," Maddie explained, taking care not to sound too bitter, though she was. "I'd hoped she'd at least give me a chance to buy it and continue my family's legacy."

"So instead you started your own." His eyes gleamed with interest. "That's admirable."

She felt a warm glow at his praise. They'd both cleaned their plates and he was debating whether or not to order sopaipillas when her cell phone rang. Normally, she would have ignored it, but caller ID said Carmen.

"Sorry, I have to take this," she told Jake. "Hello?"

"Hey," Carmen said. "Are you home? We're on our way over."

No explanation for her disappearance, though Maddie hadn't really expected one. "First, I'm not home. I'm in a restaurant, eating dinner. And second, you said *we're*. Who's with you? Shayla?"

"No. Shayla's still with her new husband. You know that." Carmen's typical impatience rang in her clipped words. "How soon can you get home? Rick and I need someplace to hide where no one will think to look. That means Broken Chains is out."

"Hide?" What had her Vampire friend gotten herself into this time? And did it have something to do with that new case she'd mentioned taking on?

"I'll explain later," Carmen said. "Can we come to your place or not?"

"We're just finishing up our meal," Maddie replied, keeping her voice calm. "Jake and I will be home shortly. You know where I keep the extra key. Just let yourself in." She ended the call before Carmen could protest.

Across the table, Jake waited, his expression curious.

"Well, you said you wanted to get to know me better," Maddie drawled. "That was one of my best friends. She and a guy friend of hers—someone I don't know—are on their way over to my apartment. How'd you like to meet them?"

Jake put down the dessert menu and grinned. "Sounds great. Let me take care of this check and we can get out of here."

By the time they pulled into her apartment building's parking lot, Maddie figured Carmen and Rick—whoever he was—were already inside. Since she'd been wanting to come up with a distraction to keep Jake away from his earlier disastrous plan, she figured this one would be as good as any.

Either way, her invitation to meet her friends appeared to make him happy. As they walked up the sidewalk and climbed the stairs to her apartment, he turned to her and planted a quick kiss on her mouth.

Surprised and pleased, she smiled up at him, her lips tingling. "What was that for?" she asked.

"Just because."

She decided *just because* felt wonderful.

As she unlocked her front door and stepped inside, she saw Carmen sitting on the couch, next to a dangerous-looking, handsome man whose aura proclaimed him a Shape-shifter. They both jumped up when Maddie and Jake entered. Introductions were performed all the way around. Maddie couldn't help but notice the protective way Rick Fallin eyed Carmen. As if she was his to protect. Even stranger, Carmen allowed it. In all the time Maddie had known the Vampire, she'd never seen her even come close to allowing a man, any man, to have the upper hand.

She also couldn't help but see the narrow-eyed glares Carmen directed at Jake.

"Maddie, do you have a minute?" Grabbing her arm, Carmen propelled her into the kitchen. "What's the deal with the guy, Jake? We have a lot of sensitive information to discuss. Why would you bring a human around and let him hear all this?"

"Because I need a distraction." Talking quickly, Maddie filled her friend in on everything that had been going on, except for the fact that she and Jake had made love. "If he keeps on pushing, he's going to end up either dead or with his memories erased. I thought if he had an actual story, he'd drop the other. I'm hoping you can help with the story. Highly edited, but still."

"I see." Expression thoughtful, Carmen finally nodded. "And you feel this is somehow your responsibility?"

"Yes. I like him, Carmen. A lot. He has…potential."

"Okay, okay." With her usual elegant grace, Carmen combed her fingers through her short platinum hair. "Rick's a bit freaked out, so let me talk to him."

"I'll do it," Maddie replied. "He's a Shifter, so I can make him understand."

"I'm not sure you can." Carmen seemed doubtful. "I know you don't know what's going on, but it involves a deadly virus, a terrorist cell and a dead junior senator."

"Wow. I'm intrigued and impressed," Maddie said. "That's way more interesting than what's been going on in my life. Jake will eat this up."

Carmen tilted her head, frowning. "I don't know. If

he's a reporter, maybe letting him hear about this isn't a good idea."

"Does this situation involve humans?" Maddie asked. "Because if it does, it wouldn't hurt to let him know. This could be the scoop of the century."

"And you think it would force him to abandon his other story about Broken Chains?"

"Yes. And about proving the existence of were-wolves." Maddie shuddered. "I don't have to tell you how awful that would be. Especially once the Protectors got a hold of him."

"No, you don't." The frown smoothed out and vanished. "Come on then. You talk to Rick. If he's okay with it, then we'll let Jake hear a slightly sanitized version of our case."

When they emerged from the kitchen, they found Jake and Rick deep in conversation about baseball. It appeared they were both Houston Astros fans, though Jake also liked the Texas Rangers.

Joining the two men, Maddie exchanged a glance with Carmen. She'd need Carmen to lead Jake away on some pretext so Maddie and Rick could have a quick talk.

Both Jake and Rick turned to stare as the two women emerged from the kitchen. They were both stunning, though in different ways. Carmen's platinum blond, pale-skinned look seemed edgy and sexual, while Maddie had a more wholesome sexiness that Jake much preferred.

For whatever reason, Jake could tell Carmen wasn't thrilled to have him there. He wasn't sure why, at least not yet. He had no doubt he'd find out before the end of the evening. Carmen seemed really...direct.

In fact, she made a beeline over to him. "Do you

have a moment to speak privately?" she asked, her husky voice full of confidence that he wouldn't turn her down.

Jake glanced at Rick, who shrugged. Maddie gave him an encouraging smile. "She doesn't bite," she said.

For whatever reason, both Carmen and Rick found this comment hilarious. "Inside joke," Rick finally said.

"Yes. Sorry." Carmen wiped at her eyes. "Will you talk to me?"

"Sure," Jake answered. "Lead the way."

She took him into the kitchen she and Maddie had just left. Though he could make out the quiet hum of Maddie's voice, he couldn't discern what she and Rick might be speaking about.

"How do you know Maddie?" Carmen demanded, folding her arms across her ample chest. Immediately he forced his gaze back to her face.

"Didn't she tell you when you two were in here a few minutes ago?" he shot back, wondering why she seemed so antagonistic.

"Maybe. But I want to hear it from you."

He decided instead to use a different tactic. "If you're worried about your friend, don't be. We both know what we're doing. We're adults. I won't hurt her."

Carmen didn't immediately respond. She just continued to eye him, her stare both bold and frank. "You're pretty," she pronounced. "I see why she likes you."

He grinned. "Pretty, huh? While I'm not sure if that's a compliment or an insult, I'll take it as a compliment. So, thanks."

When she didn't smile back, he shrugged. "Well. Nice talk. We'd better get back in there and rejoin the others." He turned and started to leave.

"Wait."

What now? Slowly, he swung back around to face her.

She took a deep breath. "In a few moments, you're going to hear some sensitive information. Information I don't feel you need to know. But Maddie believes you're a good reporter and will do well with this story. Understand that we're all trusting you. There are lives on the line here. Don't mishandle this."

Though he had no idea what she meant, he nodded. Her use of the word *story* had his journalistic instincts on full alert.

"Assuming," she continued, "that Rick's okay with filling you in."

"Interesting," he said. Because it was. "Are you ready to go and find out?"

"Sure." Now she seemed indifferent. He couldn't help but wonder if her mercurial mood changes were normal for her. Or if he just rubbed her the wrong way. He'd ask Maddie later.

When they emerged from the kitchen, Maddie and Rick appeared to be arguing, though they both kept their voices low. They immediately stopped when they saw him.

"We need a few more minutes," Maddie began.

"No." Rick dragged his hand through his hair. "We don't. I'm good. Just be careful."

"I will."

Now every journalistic instinct Rick possessed had flared to full alert. "Let me go out to my car and get a pad of paper and a pen," he said. "I also have a little voice recorder, if that's okay."

"No recordings," Rick pronounced. "You can write stuff down. This is very sensitive information. You'll need to give us your word that you'll handle it responsibly."

"Of course I will." Jake didn't even hesitate. "You don't become an award-winning, respected journalist by cutting corners. I'll report the facts without embellishment."

Rick and Carmen exchanged glances. "That might be a bit difficult. We don't actually know all the facts."

If anything, this intrigued him even more. "Let me grab my pad. Just a second." He dashed out the door and jogged to his car.

When he returned, the other three now seemed to be arguing among themselves. Again, everyone went silent the instant he stepped into the room.

"Guys, if you keep doing that, I'm going to get a complex," he joked.

Maddie was the only one who smiled. "Come on in, Jake. Sit down. They've decided Rick will tell you the story. Since I haven't heard it either, it'll be news to me, as well."

"Perfect." He made his way to the couch and sat, motioning to the spot next to him. Maddie didn't hesitate to take it, plopping down right next to him, close enough that their hips bumped.

He could get used to this. The fleeting thought made him smile at her, before he turned his attention back to Carmen and Rick. They both had chosen to remain standing.

Rick cleared his throat. "What we're going to tell you has to be off the record, at least for now. Agreed?"

"Agreed." Jake loved when people began with *off the record*. Things tended to get really interesting then. And although sometimes that meant he couldn't ever use what he'd been told, every now and then when *off the record* became *on the record*, the payoff was great.

"Perfect." Rick and Carmen exchanged a glance. "Where should I begin? There's a small cell of domestic terrorists who call themselves Sons of Darkness."

"A motorcycle gang?"

"Nope." For some reason Carmen appeared to find this funny. "Not even close."

Rick glared first at her and then at Jake. "Are you going to let me tell this story or not?" he asked her.

"Go ahead." She waved at him, covering her mouth with her other hand.

He shook his head and then continued.

Jake listened to the rest without interrupting, jotting down notes. When Rick finally finished, Jake nodded. "Interesting. I have a few questions." He looked pointedly at Rick. "Assuming I'm allowed to ask questions."

"Ask away."

"Considering that this group had a fake lab and, most likely, no virus, how do you know this virus even exists?"

Again Rick and Carmen exchanged looks, giving the sense that they weren't revealing everything. "The CDC is working on it. What we don't know is if this Ted person has an actual virus or not. If not, then the thing is currently completely contained inside the CDC lab in Atlanta."

For the first time since Rick began his explanation, Carmen spoke. "Most important, there's the matter of whoever really created the virus. I'm a biologist who specializes in diseases. I was excited when they contacted me and wanted me to join their operation, even if I'd be working undercover with the FBI. I welcomed the opportunity to learn from a scientist who, while he might have been evil, also appeared to be brilliant."

"Because he came up with a new virus?"

"Exactly. You have no idea how rare that is. And if I worked side by side with him, then I'd be more likely able to develop an antidote." Carmen's animated expression fell. "But that didn't happen. We thought it was this Sheldon out at the Sons of Darkness compound. He's dead, so we can't actually ask him. And while it's possible he might have stumbled across the perfect combination by accident, from the looks of the lab, that's highly unlikely." She grimaced. "In fact, I can state with 99.9 percent certainty that no virus was developed in that lab."

"So what are you going to do now?" Jake asked.

"That's where you and Maddie come in," Carmen said. "She's a private investigator and you're a reporter. You two should have enough skills between you to locate the missing guy—Ted—and find out what he does or doesn't have."

Jake turned to look at Maddie. Judging from her closed-off expression, she wasn't too keen on the idea.

"I'll have to think about it," he said, nudging Maddie with his knee to let her know they'd discuss it later. "But I have to ask, why are you telling me this, off the record?"

"Because once a solution is found, think of the story. It won't be off the record any longer. And you'll have an exclusive."

"Put that way," Jake replied, grinning. "It's an offer almost too good to be true."

"I'm in," Maddie said suddenly, startling him. "I personally enjoy a challenge."

She met his gaze, a challenging look on her face. "Well?" she demanded. "What do you say?"

Something still felt off. But he trusted his instincts and knew he'd figure it out eventually. "Working together, right?"

Maddie nodded.

"Then I'm in, too," he said.

Chapter 12

Rick almost felt sorry for the reporter. No one could help but notice the way Jake and Maddie looked at each other, or the way sparks seemed to crackle between them. But then again, Rick could actually relate. He felt that way about Carmen. Too quickly, too soon.

Especially now that she'd seen him shape-shift into wolf. That knowledge alone boggled his mind. Among the Pack, such a thing was forbidden with other species—unless they were mates.

Mates. He'd never really given the idea serious thought. In fact, he wasn't sure he even believed in the concept. If he ever mated with anything, he'd have to say he was mated to his job. Most definitely it wouldn't be a Vampire.

Yet Carmen was…different. The more time he spent with her, the less Vampire-like she seemed. The initial impression, of her blazing hot sexiness, had become enriched with her dry sense of humor and mocking wit. He liked her, he had to admit. And while he found himself craving her, he knew enough about couples and partnerships to realize that wasn't enough.

"What's your plan?" Jake asked, bringing Rick out of his reverie.

"We're going after Ted, of course," Carmen put in.

"Okay. But what about these Sons of Darkness people? It seems to me you went through a lot of trouble to develop undercover identities. I get that you fled their hideout, but wouldn't it make more sense to continue to work with them?"

Jake had a valid point. Rick glanced at Carmen, who shrugged.

"The thing about them," Rick said, "is that we got a real inkling that they are a front for something else, something worse. The entire plan about starting a war in West Latvia to anger the Russians didn't make sense to begin with. And this was even before we realized they didn't have the virus."

"And most likely never had the virus," Carmen continued.

"But don't you want to know what's behind them?" Jake pressed.

"You'd better believe we do." Rick didn't bother to keep the impatience from his voice. "And we will find out, eventually. What matters right now is the virus. It's out there somewhere. We've got to find it before it's released into the general population and starts an epidemic."

"Meh. I'm skeptical." Jake directed his words to Carmen. "One body with a virus doesn't prove the existence of more, am I right?"

"Well, it's highly unlikely to mutate on its own. Plus, we've already confirmed that someone fed the virus to the victim, most likely in a drink or meal he ate at a restaurant right before he became ill." Carmen sighed. "So unfortunately, while I like the way you think, we pretty much are guaranteed that someone, somewhere, developed this virus."

"And has more," Rick said.

"Exactly. And has the capability of making a large enough supply to cause a pandemic."

Pandemic. Even nonscientific types like Rick hated that word. Maybe he'd seen too many movies, but the thought made him shudder.

Especially since they didn't have an antidote.

"Rick," Carmen said, touching his arm. "I'm going to call the CDC again, just to make sure they don't need me."

"Okay." He didn't tell her that he'd already checked, before recruiting her. She might be one of the top biological disease specialists around, but there were others. And some of them had connections. The CDC considered their staff full. Who knew—perhaps something had changed.

"While you do that," he said, "I need to make a few calls and find out what my boss wants me to do now that we've left the group. I haven't given a full report yet anyway."

Already scrolling through her phone, Carmen waved at him as he stepped outside onto the apartment balcony to talk privately.

As Rick had suspected, his boss wasn't happy.

"You what?" Special Agent in Charge Olson Ferring roared. "Do you know how long it took to get you set up for this undercover assignment?"

Then, without giving Rick a chance to answer, he continued. "You get back in, make contact with them. Come up with some sort of plausible story for doing what you did."

"Just a minute," Rick interjected. "You haven't heard the full story." And he proceeded to tell him the lab hadn't truly been used, that the biologist named Sheldon had been murdered, and someone named Ted had run off with vials that supposedly contained the actual virus.

Olson went silent for a full five seconds. When he spoke again, he'd lowered his voice. "Do you believe that he might actually have it?"

"We're not sure," Rick responded. "It seems highly unlikely, but there's still a minute chance."

"In that case, I want you two back in the group. Back undercover immediately. You need to hunt down and find Ted and those vials. Being part of the Sons of Darkness will afford you better protections in that world than if you go on your own. Understand?"

Rick allowed that he did and ended the call. He turned to go back inside, but Carmen stepped out onto the balcony instead and closed the door behind her.

"You look glum," she commented. "I'm assuming your work wasn't happy with you?"

"Nope." He relayed the conversation.

"Seriously? That's not so bad." She shrugged. "Especially since we'd planned to do that all along."

"No, we just involved that reporter," he said, jerking his head toward inside the apartment. "That *human* reporter."

When she put her hand on his arm, his entire body tightened. "It's okay. Maddie will make sure he stays protected. Let them search, too. The more eyes out there looking the better."

"Maybe. Though we need to let them know it's dangerous. Since Maddie's a Shifter, I have no doubt she'll be all right. But that poor human. He's already been jumped on by two Protectors in the alley outside Broken Chains."

She grimaced. "I heard about that. But this case will get him away from all that, at least for a little while. And if Maddie is willing to work to keep him safe, why not? You know as well as I do that sometimes reporters have ways to access information outside regular channels."

She did have a point. "Fine," he said. "Let's go back in and inform them. Then you and I need to get on the road. I'm going to have to call Gus and grovel in hopes he'll take us back."

"Oh, he will." The confidence in her voice made him smile. "Especially when you tell him what we discovered in the lab and that we want to go after Ted. I can pretty much guarantee that."

Side by side, they headed back into the apartment.

Still seated next to each other on the couch, Maddie and Jake looked up when they entered.

"That looked like a serious discussion," Maddie observed. "Is everything all right?"

Rick explained, careful to keep from focusing too much on Jake. He didn't like working with humans and preferred to work with other Shifters as much as possible, especially on dangerous cases. Humans were too…fragile. They slowed him down and distracted him, especially if he had to worry about keeping them from getting killed. They could be headstrong and impulsive and unpredictable.

Maddie needed to understand this, as well. Rick would talk privately with her before he and Carmen left.

By the time Rick finished his explanation, Jake practically vibrated with excitement. Rick had to like the guy's enthusiasm.

"Sounds good." Jake rubbed his hands together. "My

favorite kind of investigative journalism. I've got to get busy and do some research. I assume you don't want me to directly contact the CDC?"

"No." Both Rick and Carmen answered at once.

"Okay. I have back channels."

Though they glanced at each other, Rick and Carmen let that one pass for now.

"Do you have a moment?" Rick asked Maddie.

Though she lifted one brow in surprise, she nodded. "Out on the patio?"

Once there, he reiterated what he and Carmen had discussed. "Not only will you have to keep an eye on him, but you'll have to keep the two of you safe. Do you think you can do that?"

She grinned. "I relish the challenge."

"Good luck." The words came out gruffer than he'd intended.

Instead of taking offense, she laughed and hugged him. "You're a decent guy, Rick Fallin. I like you."

Not sure how to react to that, he simply nodded and turned to go back inside.

But she wasn't finished. She grabbed his arm. "Carmen likes you, too, I can see."

Hounds help him, but he fell for the bait. Turning slowly, he eyed the female Shifter. "Sometimes I have to wonder if she does. Because with all that Vampire aloofness, sometimes I have my doubts."

Her grin widened, telling him his casual tone didn't fool her at all. "You make a great team. I think with you two as partners, you'll solve this case in no time."

Partners. Now he really felt foolish. Glad she didn't know he'd been thinking romantically while she meant in a working relationship, he nodded. "Good to know. I'm hoping we will in time."

She laughed again before pushing open the door and stepping inside, with him following right behind her.

Carmen and Jake were deep in conversation. As he approached, Carmen looked up and winked. "I was just telling Jake how the CDC works. I took a tour there and did quite a bit of research when I was thinking about seeing if they would hire me a few years ago."

Rick made a big show out of checking his watch. "Sorry, but we need to get on the road."

"Give us just five more minutes," Jake pleaded, finally looking up from his notes. Apparently, he'd been scribbling furiously into a spiral notebook the entire time Carmen had been talking. "This information is really going to be beneficial in writing the story."

Rick frowned.

"It's fine, Jake," Carmen said, her voice as cool as the icy glare she directed at Rick. "I don't have to ask his permission to do anything. You'll have your five minutes and more if I feel it's necessary." Her tone contained a warning.

Since Rick didn't want to start this leg of their assignment off on bad footing, he didn't even attempt to argue. "Let me know when you're ready," he told her, escaping again to the balcony, where he could breathe the fresh air. Her mercurial mood change confused him. He didn't know if it was because she was a Vampire or if it was some feminine thing. Either way, he had no clue. He just wanted to get on the road. Like ten minutes ago.

Though maybe some alone time would do him good. Hopefully, Maddie wouldn't feel a sudden urge for more conversation.

To his relief, she didn't follow him. A quick glance back showed she'd joined the discussion with Carmen and Jake. Good. Because right now, Rick needed to get his head back in the game and stop obsessing over the gorgeous and sexy Vampire when he needed to figure out a way to relate to her only as a teammate, a partner. Nothing more, nothing less. Now was definitely not the time to allow himself to get distracted.

The one thing Carmen would never permit was for a man—any man—to boss her around. This was why she'd set up the working dynamic with Rick in the beginning. Her nature would not allow him to be in charge. She wasn't sure when this strong belief had taken place, but because she'd spent nearly her entire human life under first her father's then her husband's heel, she'd spent nearly a century after being made a Vampire exploring her strength. She'd vowed to remain independent and strong and so far, she had.

Damned if she'd let a bit of sexual attraction cut the legs out from under her.

After Rick's directive, she stretched things out and kept talking to Jake for fifteen more minutes rather than five. From the corner of her eye, she could see Rick standing out on the balcony, his back to the room while he gazed out into the darkness. For whatever reason, this made her feel vaguely guilty.

Finally, she took pity on him and wrapped things up with Jake. "Good luck," she said, uncoiling herself and pushing up off the sofa. She squared her shoulders and lifted her chin as she made her way to the balcony.

Stepping outside, she waited for Rick to turn. When he didn't, she touched his arm. "I'm ready now."

He swung his head to look down at her, the tightness of his expression revealing his leashed emotions. "I don't like playing games," he told her.

"Games?" she drawled, her tone mocking, unable to help herself. "I wasn't playing a game back there.

I told you up front early on that you weren't going to be the one in charge. You can't come and interrupt my conversation—it was important, too." Surely he could see the validity of her point.

A muscle worked in his jaw. "We needed to get going."

"Did we? Please. A few more minutes wasn't going to hurt anything."

She had him there and he knew it. But that didn't mean he liked it. She'd lived long enough to understand how it was with men and their pride.

"Look." Placing her hand once again on his arm, she felt the way his muscles bunched and tensed. There was power there, leashed yet fierce, and she liked that. "Don't take this personally. It's more my thing than anything else. I find it difficult to let a man call the shots."

"Ever?"

Judging by his incredulous tone, he found this hard to believe. And she had to admit, it did sound kind of ridiculous.

She shrugged to cover her confusion.

"Carmen," he pressed. "Are you saying that you always have to be in charge? Every single time?"

His question made her frown. Put that way, it made her seem both egocentric and bossy. Not to mention far too controlling. "I don't know. Aren't you making too much of this?"

He sighed. "Maybe," he answered, much to her surprise. "And I think you are, as well. If we're going to be partners, there's got to be a give and take. I promise, there will be times when I'll know or see something you don't, and I'll bark out an order. I'd do the same whether my partner was male or female. It isn't sexist. It's survival. Teamwork."

"There's no *I* in *team*," she joked.

He didn't even crack a smile. "I'm serious. I know for a fact that I won't be able to work with you if you're going to do the exact opposite of anything I say, just because you have control issues."

Since she wasn't sure how to respond to that, she did the only thing she could think of to distract him. She pressed her body up against his and kissed him.

As usual, instant sparks combusted. Except after a few seconds, she realized they were all on her end. Rick didn't react at all. In fact, after the first initial shock, he closed his mouth and took a step back. "Not fair," he said quietly. "You no longer get to play that card."

For whatever reason, this made her want to cry. Which infuriated her. She'd gone centuries without shedding a tear over a man and she wasn't going to start now.

"You are absolutely correct." Her clipped tone revealed her emotions, though she figured he didn't know her well enough to realize how truly upset she was. "From now on, we're just partners."

Her declaration didn't appear to impress him.

"Just partners?" he repeated. "Only if you tell me you understand that we have to be equal. Sometimes you might have to do as I say. Other times, it will be reversed. Unless you can see that, I don't think we can work together at all."

Stunned, she took a moment to swallow her injured pride. Intellectually, she knew he had a point. "I agree," she finally managed, wincing as she spoke. Then, she tried to lighten her eat crow moment with a bit of humor. "What do you know? It seems you actually can teach an old Vampire new tricks."

He laughed at this, his eyes crinkling at the corners. "Come on, then. Let's hit the road. My SUV is parked nearby."

The rush of warmth she felt in her chest at his smile was like nothing she'd ever experienced. In fact, if she hadn't been a badass Vampire, she would have been frightened at the things this Shifter made her feel.

They rushed through their goodbyes, though Carmen hugged Maddie a bit tighter than usual. "Be careful," she whispered.

"I will," Maddie whispered back, her gaze sliding past Carmen to land on Jake. "And I'll do my best to keep him safe."

Carmen peered at her friend, wondering if the warm glow in Maggie's eyes meant she had strong feelings for the human man. She bit back the urge to utter a warning, still stinging from her earlier conversation with Rick.

Heading out, she caught herself shaking her head. Ever observant, Rick eyed her but didn't ask. He led the way to his vehicle and opened the passenger door for her. Once she'd climbed inside, he went around and got in, then started the engine. He backed out of the parking space and pulled out into the street.

"Now, what's the plan?" she asked. "How are we going to get back in with Gus and his guys?"

"I'm hoping a phone call will do it," he said. "But I need to buy a disposable phone. I can't take a chance on them tracing my number, especially if they decide we have to pay for running away."

"Why would they decide that?" Perplexed, she stretched. "They need us more than we need them."

"How so?"

"Think about it. How many biologists like me do they have access to? They need to recreate the virus, especially if they can't find Ted. Or worse, if they find Ted and learn they never had the virus after all."

"Which means they've been played."

"Or someone is pulling their strings still," she continued. "The question is who."

"Another possibility," he said, glancing at her sideways as he drove. "They could be aware that they're pawns or a shell for whoever is behind the big picture. Their little terrorist cell really hasn't done much other than funnel some guns to other terrorist groups. They're on the ATF's radar, but they've held back at the FBI's request. We've been hoping they could inadvertently lead us to whoever is pulling the strings."

Carmen nodded. "And all of this has something to do with West Latvia. Someone wanted a war with them, for whatever reason."

"Exactly. That is another bit of info we need to find out. Why?" He grabbed his cell, keeping one hand on the steering wheel. "I'm about to call Landers. Even though he pulled a gun on us and you bit him, he's the only one I have a number for."

"He won't remember much," Carmen promised.

"Good. I'll put it on speakerphone so I can drive. Feel free to chime in if you come up with anything you think will be helpful."

"I will."

But it turned out she didn't need to. As soon as Landers learned it was Rick calling, he put Gus on the phone.

"Where the hell are you?" Gus demanded. "Landers told me some bullshit story about you hightailing it out of here after seeing the lab."

"Was he acting on your orders when he confronted us at gunpoint?" Rick asked, his voice hard. "Or when he told Carmen to get to work while he intended to hold me hostage?"

Silence.

"So, yeah," Rick continued when it became apparent Gus wasn't going to answer. "And when we saw your lab had never been used, we figured it was in our best interests to go."

"I see." Gus had now become a man of few words.

"Were you aware?" Rick pressed. "About the lab, I mean? And if you were, then is it safe to assume Ted stole worthless vials?"

"I wouldn't assume that," Gus said. "It's entirely possible he and Sheldon had the virus, even if they weren't actually the ones to develop it."

Carmen perked up at this, though she didn't speak. Not yet.

"Explain," Rick prodded.

"Before I do, I need to know what side you're on. Are you still in?"

"Yep. We're definitely in," Rick hastened to reassure the other man. "But we need to know if we should even bother trying to hunt down Ted and see what's in the vials."

Again a moment passed before Gus spoke. "We didn't know they weren't working in the lab. One of Sheldon's strict criteria was that we stay out. Believing he needed space and time to develop large batches of the virus, we did as he asked."

"Where did you find him?" Rick asked.

"We didn't. He found us." Clearing his throat, Gus sounded uncomfortable. Unusual for him. "Actually, someone sent him to us."

"Who?"

"I'm not at liberty to say." On that, Gus sounded firm. "I need you to find Ted."

Carmen and Rick exchanged a glance. Since this

was exactly what they'd hoped he would say, she figured Rick would wrap up the call.

Instead, Rick asked a question. "Why? What are you hoping we will find?"

"The vials," Gus barked. "The damn vials. We don't need that stuff being released among the public. Not yet."

Not yet. Chilling.

"You've got to give me a bit more information," Rick pressed. "You believe Ted does have the genuine virus. I need a logical reason why."

"No. You don't. You follow my orders, not the other way around. Understand?"

Nudging Rick's arm, Carmen nodded. Clearly, Gus felt Rick had overstepped. She had to agree. Rick never would have acted like this when they were at the group's location.

"Yes." Voice surly, Rick shook his head and made a face at Carmen. Careful to hide her smile, she gestured that he should continue.

"I'm sorry," Rick muttered. "What Landers did pissed me off. And the one thing both Carmen and I despise is being lied to. When we saw the lab and realized it had never been used in any way, we thought we'd been duped."

The words he hadn't said echoed in Carmen's mind. They still were being played, though they weren't supposed to understand that. And truth be told, they didn't. At least as far as the reason why.

That's one of the things they'd have to find out. After they stopped the virus from taking out an entire country or more.

Chapter 13

Even before Carmen and Rick left, Maddie wanted to jump Jake's bones. Once they were gone, she could barely control herself. Unfortunately, he had no idea. He'd asked to borrow her laptop and had immediately become engrossed in research. He kept his spiral notebook open and used a pen to continue to make furious notes.

She'd never seen him like this. He was on fire. Determined, enthused and sexy as hell. With her body aching and throbbing, she couldn't take her eyes off him.

Oblivious, he continued to simultaneously type and jot stuff down. She watched him, burning.

How was this possible, that he made her so hot just being in the same room? And conversely, the fact that he hadn't even the slightest clue made her want him even more.

Should she attempt to distract him or simply wait

him out? As she mulled this over, considering all the delightful ways she could entice him, he looked up.

"Maddie? Are you okay?"

She blinked. "Um. I'm not sure."

"What's wrong?" Expression concerned, he immediately pushed up out of his chair and sat down next to her on the couch.

It took every ounce of any willpower she possessed to resist him. Instead, she slid sideways so her head rested on his shoulder.

To her immense relief, he put his arm around her. "I've got a distant cousin who works for the CDC in Atlanta," he said. "I've emailed him and let him know I'm working on a story—I didn't get more specific than that—and asked him if he'd mind answering a few questions."

"Great." If she turned her head slightly, she could nuzzle his neck. She loved the scent of him. Human male, spearmint and something else, something earthy and musky that called to her primal wolf self.

He glanced down, catching her about to go for it.

"You're beautiful," he mused. "And sexy and sweet and smart and…"

Unable to resist any longer, she pulled him down to her for a kiss. The instant their mouths connected, the fire that had been simmering low in her belly erupted into a blaze, consuming them both.

Out of control, they shed their clothes. Naked, skin to skin, she let her fingers explore every inch of him. His hands were all over her also, his touch driving her to madness. She tried to climb on top of him, but he was having none of that and pushed her onto her back instead.

"Slow down," he ordered. "I want to savor this."

Part of her thrilled at the way he took charge. And when he used his talented mouth to taste her breasts, her skin and, finally, the throbbing spot between her legs, she lost all capacity to think.

The first climax came quickly, rocking her world. And then, while her body still quivered, he rose up over her and pushed himself inside her, filling her completely. Then, to her surprise, he held himself perfectly still while her last spasms clenched and released him.

She caught her breath, a quick gasp of air before he covered her mouth with his, letting her taste her own nectar on his lips. Suddenly, she felt desperate to have him move. She squirmed and arched her back, rotating her hips as she urged him on.

He groaned. "Maddie…"

Grinning, she pushed harder, up and down, until he used his hands to still her hips. "Wait." He spoke through clenched teeth. "Give. Me. One. Second."

But as he ground out the last word, he apparently lost whatever grip on self-control he had. With a roar, he released her and drove himself into her, hard and deep and fast.

She met each thrust halfway, baring her teeth, feeling so savage it felt like her wolf self had taken over her human one.

As the tension built within her, Jake cried out and shuddered. This was enough to send her once again over the edge. Together, as one, building upon the other's pleasure, they reached new heights. Though even in her own mind it sounded corny, she felt as if they'd blazed a path directly to the stars.

He held her while their breathing slowed and their perspiration-slick bodies cooled. For once in her life, she allowed herself to snuggle close, something she usually avoided. But with Jake, cuddling felt right. Especially after…that.

"Amazing," he murmured, kissing her forehead. "You're absolutely—"

"Shhh." She cut him off with a lingering kiss. She'd wait to move until he fell asleep, which in her experience with men seemed to happen within twenty minutes after sex.

But not Jake. Instead, he gently disengaged himself and padded to the bathroom. She watched him, admiring his toned naked body, until he closed the door and she heard the sound of water running.

While he cleaned up, she got up and collected her own clothes.

A few minutes later, he emerged, still naked. He gathered his clothing, picking it up from the floor, and got dressed right there in front of her. She watched him with interest, amazed when she felt another twinge of desire.

"I hate to make love and run," he said, grinning. "But I've got tons of research to do on this story and I know I won't get much done with you to distract me."

Amused and bemused, she nodded.

"Bye." He pressed a quick kiss on her lips. "Lock up after me."

And he was gone. She turned the dead bolt and headed toward the bathroom. The pleasurable way her body ached made her smile.

After a hot shower, she fixed herself something to eat and tried to decide how to occupy herself for the rest of the evening. While Jake was all hot on the trail of this story, she knew Carmen and Rick planned to handle it on their own. Her job was to keep Jake out of harm's way. If they happened to learn any useful information along the way, even better.

She made scrambled eggs and toast and ate standing up.

Now with Jake long gone, the edgy restlessness that had simmered all day returned. She roamed her small apartment, a completely different type of ache filling her. Not sexual, as Jake had thoroughly taken care of that need. When she finally realized what it was, she actually laughed out loud, shaking her head at her own foolishness.

She needed to change. It had been far too long since she let her inner wolf come out and play. She'd take care of that now.

Decision made, she grabbed her car keys and headed out. Nothing like a good hunt to help improve one's perspective on life in general.

Because there were limited places on the island that would be deserted enough to shape-shift safely, she headed north toward the mainland. Since she had plenty of time, she drove all the way to Clear Lake City. The wildlife preserve. There was one of her favorite places to let her wolf run free.

Once she arrived, she parked. Since it was now dark, the lot was empty. All the tourists had gone on to other, more well-lit pursuits and the locals knew better than to roam around this place at night. The only others she was likely to encounter now would be actual wildlife or other shifters.

Grabbing her empty backpack from the passenger seat, she started up one of the hiking trails. She'd learned a long time ago that it was better to bring something she could store her clothing in. That kept out insects and damp and who knew what else.

A creature of habit, when she reached her favorite

spot, she set the backpack down on a fallen tree. Since the complete and utter darkness made it impossible to see anything farther than her own hand, she listened. Nothing but the normal sounds of nocturnal animals doing their usual thing.

Satisfied she was alone, she removed her clothing, once again marveling at her body's pleasant aches. After stowing everything in the backpack, she tucked it into a hollow in the side of the downed tree.

Then she dropped to all fours, relishing the feel of the damp earth beneath her, and initiated the change.

As her bones elongated and changed shape, sparkling lights surrounded her like a thousand fireflies. While sometimes shape-shifting could be painful, this time she felt only pleasure. When at long last her body was no longer human, she lifted her snout and sniffed the air.

Damp earth, wet leaves. A nearby rabbit or two. Even an owl lurked somewhere on a branch nearby. As wolf, she relied on her sense of smell the most.

Her wolf eyes immediately adjusted to the darkness and she could make out the ghostly shapes of trees and plants. She began to move, relishing the strength of her lupine body, loving the way her claws sank into the moist soil.

The hiking path stretched out ahead and she began to run, stretching herself out to her full length. The landscape blurred as she reached full speed, her paws thundering on the trail.

Only when she'd burned up her reserve of energy did she allow herself to slow. At the point where the path reached a small pond, she wandered near the water's edge and sat. Again she checked the scents drifting on the wind. Sifting through them—the usual rabbits and mice—she lifted her head when she located deer spoor.

It had been a long time since she hunted such a large animal. Deer were usually brought down only by packs, a group of Shifters who'd become wolves together for the express purpose of hunting.

Which meant she'd take a pass on deer meat tonight. She'd go for something small or maybe even skip hunting altogether.

It was enough to be wolf again. She'd forgotten how much changing centered her, made her feel whole again.

Returning to the clearing by the downed tree, she laid her belly on the damp earth and breathed deeply. Humans couldn't seem to understand the connection between the earth and her creatures. When she was in her human form, that knowledge felt abstract and distant. But as wolf, she could feel the energy linking her to all other creatures, and to their home.

Since dwelling on such philosophical matters wasn't what she usually did as wolf, she sighed and initiated the change back to human. Again, the sparkling lights, a few flashes of pain, and she finally lay naked on the forest floor.

Wincing, she got up, shaking herself as if by doing so she discarded any last, lingering remnants of wolf. She reached into the tree truck and pulled out her backpack, dressing quickly. It wasn't until she'd turned to head back to her car that she realized something was different. Every Shifter, upon returning to their human form, experienced an almost overwhelming sexual arousal. Mated pairs often took advantage of this, as did younger, unmatched, sexually adventurous singles. Those who were alone simply suffered through it until it passed, or pleasured themselves.

But tonight, Maddie felt...nothing. Correction—she felt sated. Apparently, making love with Jake earlier had satisfied even her deepest primal urge. Interesting.

While she knew she should probably try to figure out how this could be possible, she put the thought away for later.

Jake refused to allow himself to dwell on how amazing making love with Maddie had been. But try as he might, he couldn't stop thinking about her as he drove home.

This story! The endless possibilities—from saving the world, to being the first journalist to be able to share the inside details! More than exciting, the thought was intoxicating.

While he still hadn't forgotten his earlier obsession with the mysterious door at the end of the dead-end alley, he'd put that on the back burner for now. Something like that couldn't come close to this, which might be the story of a lifetime.

One of his favorite songs came on the radio, and he cranked it up, singing along. Up ahead, the light turned green as he approached the intersection, which felt magical. At least until he'd gotten halfway through and the speeding truck hit him broadside on the passenger door.

The force of the impact spun him around, his vehicle going up on two wheels. As he fought to control the steering wheel, he thought he might actually roll, and braced himself. Instead, miraculously, the car landed back on all four tires, spinning once more before crashing into the guardrail. The shriek of metal on metal made an inhuman wail as the vehicle screeched to a stop.

Stunned, Jake maintained enough coherent thought to kill the engine before unbuckling his seat belt and attempting to open his door. The door wouldn't budge.

And even when he turned the key in the ignition, the electric window refused to open.

One step at a time. The next rational move would be climbing over the console and trying the passenger door. He did and to his relief, it opened. He climbed out, suddenly dizzy, squinting and trying to locate the vehicle that had hit him.

There, engine still idling, a large box truck sat in the middle of the intersection, likely right at the same spot where it had hit him. Why hadn't it moved? Was the driver injured? Jake started to head that way and check, but a shiver of warning crawled up his spine and he paused. He knew enough to trust his instincts, even if they didn't seem rational at that exact moment.

He glanced north and then south, east and west. No other cars. The road seemed abnormally quiet for this early in the evening. Was it his imagination, or did the large truck appear menacing?

No matter what, he didn't have it within himself not to check on the driver. He couldn't leave a potentially hurt person alone without help, so he was going over. Before he did, he quickly dialed 911 and gave his location and a brief description of what had happened. Even though the dispatcher encouraged him to remain on the line, after informing her that he was going to check on the other driver, he ended the call.

When he reached the box truck, it didn't appear there was anyone in the driver's seat, though the window was open. He eyed the shoulder and the grassy embankment, wondering if the driver had been ejected. A quick search didn't reveal a body, so that meant the driver remained inside the cab.

His legs felt surprisingly wobbly. Shock, most likely. In fact, when he looked over his shoulder at his car, he seemed to be looking through a thick haze. Damn.

When the paramedics arrived, he'd be sure to have them check him out.

Again, he faced the box truck, stepping up on the running board and reaching for the door handle. He intended to use it to pull himself up and look inside. Instead, someone hit him over the back of the head and he crumpled to the ground.

When he came to, the violence of his headache made him groan. The metal floor beneath him bounced and jolted him. Disoriented, at first he couldn't figure out where he might be, or remember what exactly had happened. It all came flooding back to him—the accident, the truck and, last, being attacked. And now, judging from the sounds and motion, he was in the back of that same box truck with his hands and legs bound by what appeared to be duct tape, heading down the highway.

This made no sense. As he struggled to clear the cobwebs from his brain—as well as battle the knifing stabs of pain—he tried to find the logic. That was the first thing he always did when pondering the why behind a story. Some things were obvious, like a terrorist driving a rental truck into a crowd of pedestrians. Others were not quite so clear. Like this. Why would anyone target him?

He thought back to the night in the alleyway near Harborside Drive. The one that led to that mysterious door. He hadn't staked out the place in a while, and the accident tonight was nowhere near that area. Heck, this time he hadn't even been on the island. Yet it all seemed to be tied to that alley, that door. He'd been beaten, stalked and now abducted.

The truck hit a particularly large bump in the road, sending him bouncing. The swift spike of pain in his head made him wince. Though he couldn't reach up and feel the back of his head due to the ties, he'd bet he had a good-sized knot there.

Since he could tell it wasn't in his pocket, he guessed they'd taken his cell phone. At least he'd managed to call 911, so the police would be aware he was missing.

Maddie. His stomach lurched. No one would know to notify her. Would she think he'd simply taken off, intent on chasing their story on his own? He wasn't like that, not at all, but she didn't know him that well. Even worse, she'd believe he'd disappeared right after making love, which ranked up there as inconsiderate.

Once more, he tested his bonds. The duct tape had been wrapped around his wrists numerous times and it held tight. The same went for his feet, though he had a bit more wiggle room there. Didn't matter. He had to get his hands free.

Though he twisted and clawed, trying to reach an edge of the tape proved futile. Instead, he began looking around the darkened interior of the cargo box to see if there was anything—a sharp corner, an edge—that he could use to cut through the tape.

But there wasn't anything else at all. Except…on the back door. The handle that was used to raise the door. He wasn't sure how sharp the edge would prove to be, but it was better than nothing.

Gingerly, shuffling on his knees, he made his way over there. He sat with his back to the door and uttered a quick prayer. Then, pressing hard, he pushed his bound hands against the handle.

The tape caught and held. The metal wasn't sharp enough to cause a tear, even if he tried sawing back and forth. He attempted it anyway, desperate to get his hands free before the truck came to a stop.

After several minutes and numerous tries, all in different positions, Jake lowered his aching arms and admitted defeat. As he shuffled back to the front corner, he spied some sort of loop built into the side of the box. Clearly it had been designed to act as a tie-down. Since it was round, he knew it would be of no use to him. Just in case, he checked the one on the other side.

Jagged. Unable to believe his eyes, he scooted over. The bottom edge of the loop had broken off, just an inch or so of it, but enough to create a sharp shard. Like a homemade shiv, he thought, giddy and dizzy at the same time.

He backed up, caught the duct tape on the edge and yanked his hands down. Again and again he did this, until finally he felt the smallest tear.

Hope gave him energy and he worked furiously, putting every ounce of his flagging strength into getting free. The first tear grew, a bit at a time. Since there were several layers, as soon as he cut through one, he started on another.

Eventually, he had torn through enough to separate his hands. From there, it was a matter of simply removing the tape.

Except he decided to leave it on. Now that he had full use of his hands, it would give him a better advantage if his abductors still believed him to be tied. And he'd need every advantage he could get. Next, he removed the ties on his feet, though he made sure to leave the duct tape wrapped on each individual ankle. If he kept his legs close together, the initial impression would be that his bonds remained.

The truck made a sharp turn, nearly sending him flying. He scooted back to his corner, keeping his arms behind him as if he was still bound.

Judging from the sounds and feel, they'd left pavement and now traveled on a gravel road. Which had to mean they were getting closer to their destination. He couldn't help but wonder if they meant to kill him and bury his body out in the country, where no one would find it. He set his jaw grimly. He wasn't going down without a fight.

Finally, they slowed. Jake braced himself, wondering how many there were, and if he had a fighting chance.

As the vehicle shuddered to a stop, the driver killed the engine. Jake listened, waiting for conversation, something to tell him if there was a single assailant, or two or three. He heard nothing. Nothing but the sound of footsteps on gravel.

Someone raised the door with a squeal of metal. Jake blinked against the sudden brightness, momentarily confused. They hadn't driven long enough for the night to become day, had they? He supposed it depended on how long he'd been unconscious.

"Get up," a harsh voice ordered. Male, and somehow familiar.

As his sight adjusted to the light, Jake blinked. He recognized his assailant. "You," he said, struggling to his feet. "You're one of the guys that jumped me in that alley."

"Good for you," the man said. "Now less talk and more movement. Get up."

Though not an easy feat with his ankles supposedly bound, Jake managed to hobble toward the door on his knees. He knew he had to get up, but had to be careful not to reveal the fact that he'd managed to remove his bonds. He needed to keep his eyes open for an escape possibility. As soon as one presented itself, he'd take it.

With a muttered curse, his captor reached up and hauled Jake the rest of the way out of the truck. Because he let go before Jake's feet connected with the ground, Jake fell. Seizing the opportunity, Jake allowed himself to roll, putting a few more feet of distance between himself and the other man. Who, at least at this very moment, appeared to be alone.

Better odds, at least. Even if his captor outweighed him by at least forty pounds, Jake bet the other guy couldn't outrun him. Especially if he got a good head start. The only problem would be if he guy was armed.

With that sobering thought, he decided to adopt a wait-and-see attitude. If an opportunity presented it-self, he'd definitely respond, but he wouldn't take fool-ish risks.

Plus, he had to admit to being curious about what this guy wanted with him.

A second later, he was glad he hadn't tried running. Two more guys the size of pro football linebackers ap-peared, seemingly out of nowhere. Flanking him, they lifted him up and carried him into a long cinder block building. Down a dimly lit hallway, and into a better lit room that resembled a police interrogation setup.

"Sit," guy number one growled.

The two goons deposited Jake in a metal chair. Care-fully, he kept his ankles close together and, though his arms had begun to ache, his hands behind his back.

His captor stood on the other side of a battered wooden table and glowered at him, silent.

The door opened and another man strode in. Tall, with a thick head of dark hair, everything about him spoke of confident authority. He nodded at the first man, who immediately vacated the room.

As soon as they were alone, he faced Jake, his calm, gray-eyed expression unsmiling. "Explain yourself."

"I would if I knew what I'm supposed to be explain-ing. I have no idea what you want from me," Jake re-plied. "I haven't been back bothering your precious alley, if that's what this is about."

"That is where this began," the guy in charge said.

"Let me introduce myself. I'm Colton Kinslow. I'd like to know what you're up to behind my sister's back."

It took all of three seconds for the name and the statement to register. "You're Maddie's brother?"

"Yes. And we've picked up enough chatter to know you're involved in something big, something top secret. Something someone like you has no business being involved in."

Someone like you. The words made Jake bristle. All his life, there was always that one person who made assumptions about him due to the color of his skin. To blacks, he wasn't dark enough. To whites, he was too dark. With his mixed parentage, he personally thought his skin tone was the perfect compromise between the two. Clearly, not everyone felt that way.

Something of his thoughts must have shown on his face.

"I'm not talking about race," Colton explained.

Jake crossed his arms. "Then what did you mean?"

For the first time, Colton appeared uncomfortable. "I can't explain. Not at this time. Let me just say that we consider you quite a bit more vulnerable than Maddie, Carmen or Rick."

He knew their names. Fully alert now, Jake wondered if this guy, who claimed to be Maddie's brother, had something to do with the virus. If so, then Jake had just lucked into the middle of the action without even trying.

Now all he had to do was keep himself alive.

Chapter 14

They drove until Rick started seeing double. While he wasn't sure if Carmen wanted to drive, he knew he had to get some rest.

"I can drive," she said when he asked her. "But I'd prefer not to. At least not tonight. How about we find an inexpensive motel and catch a few hours of sleep? We can get back on the road at the crack of dawn tomorrow."

Relieved, he took the next exit, pulling up in front of an unassuming two-story motel that looked both inexpensive and clean. He went into the office, paid for a single room and emerged with a card key. Per his request, the room was on the ground floor near the back. Of necessity, he always had to consider if there might be an urgent need to escape.

The small room appeared neat, though the decorating looked like it had been last updated in 1982. Two full-sized beds with a nightstand in between them, a

small desk-like table with a chair, plus a faded blue re-
cliner were the extent of the furnishings.

"Not bad," Carmen said, gliding around to inspect
everything. She flicked on a light in the bathroom, and
smiled. "I'm going to take a shower."

"I'll go after you," he replied, even though images
immediately assailed him of them both naked in the
shower together, water running down their slick bodies. Shaking his head, he pushed these thoughts away,
turning on the television to help distract him.

Ten minutes later, her short blond hair still damp,
Carmen emerged. "Your turn," she called out. "Nothing like a nice hot shower to make you feel better."

Oh, he could think of a few other things that would
work, but he wisely kept them to himself.

However, the shower did reenergize him. Toweling
off, he emerged to find her engrossed in some talk show
on the TV. She held a little plastic bag with a straw in
one hand. Though it looked like a child's juice pouch,
upon closer inspection he realized it contained blood.
Of course. Since blood was how she got nourishment.

His stomach growled, reminding him it had been a
while since he'd eaten. He went to the curtain, peered
outside and spotted the huge illuminated sign of a fast
food restaurant next door. Hopefully, it would still be
open.

After telling Carmen he'd be right back, he walked
over and ordered a burger, fries and a chocolate shake.
He brought those back to the room and sat at the desk
and ate. Still watching her show, Carmen glanced over
her shoulder at him, gave him a thumbs-up sign and
continued sipping her own meal.

When his cell phone rang, Rick's first thought was
that Gus had thought of something else. But instead,
he found himself once again on the phone with Olson,

his Special Agent in Charge. He listened to what the other man had to say with mounting disbelief.

When he finally ended the call, he had to sit in silence for a moment and let what he'd heard sink in.

Carmen waited, impatience plain on her face. "Well?" she finally asked. "What's up? I'm guessing whatever it is, it isn't good. At least, judging by what I heard on your end."

"The CDC called my boss." Rick tried to keep the panic from his voice, not sure he succeeded. "They are about to release a public health warning."

Her head snapped up, instantly alert. Inhaling, Carmen nodded. "About the virus?"

"Yes. They're calling it a plague."

She froze. "Where is the outbreak? Please tell me not a large metropolitan area."

"Not yet. West Latvia."

"The very country in Europe where the terrorists behind this were wanting to start a war. What the hell?"

"Exactly." His stomach roiled. "Casualties are increasing by the hour. Apparently, there's a twenty-four-hour period from infection to death."

"What's the fatality rate?"

"My boss said 100 percent. This thing seems unstoppable."

She'd started shaking her head before he finished speaking. "Nope. We can't let that happen. How close is the CDC to an antidote?"

"No idea. All I know is that they don't have one."

"Yet." The fierceness in her voice matched the shine of determination in her beautiful eyes. "Do they want me to go there and help?"

"No. They want us to go back to the Sons of Darkness hideout and use the lab. They're sending us samples of the actual virus. Oh, and they found Ted. Looks like he really did have the virus."

"Is that where they're getting it, then?"

He hesitated. "Sort of. Ted must have had the real thing. I don't know what happened, but he got infected. He got really, really sick, and fast. He's as good as dead. They're having another Vampire transport him to you."

"Brilliant." She shot to her feet, her gaze glittering with excitement. "Working with a live subject will be much more intense. In fact, that should help me get quicker results than lab work. We need to keep him alive for as long as possible. When do we leave? I'd like to get on the road."

He stared at her, aware that he hadn't yet told her everything and not sure if he should. "Wow. That's not quite the reaction I expected."

"Why not?" She appeared the most animated he'd ever seen her. "I fail to see a downside. I mean, I feel bad for poor Ted, but he kind of brought this on himself. He was dead anyway. You know Gus and Landers would have taken him out if we'd brought him back."

"True. But at least it would have been quick. From what I understand, he's suffering greatly. All the victims suffer. And then they die."

"Well, this way, at least he will have done something good for his fellow humankind," Carmen pointed out, eyeing him curiously. "But how on earth are we going to explain this to Gus?"

"That's easy. Ted—in an airtight, sealed container— is going to be delivered to us. We're to take him back to Gus's lab."

"Perfect," she exclaimed.

He only grimaced.

"I'm sorry." Carmen squeezed his shoulder. "I take it you're not a fan of the idea. Can you explain why?"

"I'm not." Still he struggled with how to find the right words to say what his bosses wanted him to do. Finally, he decided to just say it. "And my reasoning is purely selfish. This virus is deadly, and I'd love for you to find an antidote. But…"

"But?" Arms crossed, she waited.

"But, so far all of the victims have been human, and no one knows how it interacts with Shifters." He took a deep breath. "Because we really need to find out, they're offering me up as a test case."

At his words, all the animation vanished from her face. "They?"

"The Pack Protectors. My real job."

Expression thunderous, she took a step toward him.

"Why would they do such a thing? You're a valuable agent."

"Because they don't have anyone else. I know about it. They're trying to slam the lid shut on any leaks until they know more. If word got out to the rest of the Pack Protectors…"

"There'd be a panic."

"Exactly." He scratched his head, wishing he could feel honored or relieved rather than horrified. "We can't have the ones who are sworn to protect all Shifters worried about this…plague."

"Then why release a public health warning at all? Seems contradictory to me."

"They have to, at least for the humans. A thing like this can't be kept hidden. The human press is starting to notice. People are dying. You know as well as I do that most Americans tend not to panic when an epidemic occurs on a faraway continent. But at least they'll be aware. And when it starts to spread to other countries, it won't come as a total shock." He looked her square in the eye, hoping he seemed calm and resolute. "That's why this is so important. You've got to develop an antidote."

Arms crossed, she began to pace. She finally came to a stop right in front of him. "No. I won't do it. I won't be able to do my best work if I'm worried about you."

His heart skipped a beat but he kept his face expressionless. "You have to. If the worst happens and I become infected, I'll be collateral damage. This is too big, too important, to let the life of one Shifter get in the way."

She didn't react. "Surely you don't believe that."

"I do. And you should, too." When she didn't respond, he shrugged. "And we don't know for certain that the virus can kill me. So far, only a silver bullet or fire can do that. Otherwise, I might get sick, I can get wounded, but I always heal. I'm hoping it will be the same with this virus."

"But you don't know," she cried out. "I'd rather you don't get involved."

For the first time since taking the call, he smiled. "Me, too. But I have my orders. And either way, we have no choice. We leave in the morning."

"What if I refuse to go?" she asked.

"Then I'm traveling without you." One of the worst bluffs he'd ever made. She had to know how badly they needed her and her scientific expertise. Without it, he was just a shape-shifting guinea pig.

Her eyes widened. "Seriously? Because you have to know there's no way in hell I'm letting you go in this without me to at least try to protect you. We're partners, remember?"

"Yep." He grinned. And then, because who knew what was going to happen to him once they reached the lab and took delivery of Ted, he pulled her into his arms and kissed her. Thoroughly and slowly, taking his time.

When he finally raised his head, they were both breathing hard.

"Yes," she said. "Not that you asked." And she kissed him again.

Hungrily, greedily, they clung together. Somehow, they shed their clothes, or at least enough of them to matter. Still standing, they were skin to slick skin. Carmen, so pale, so smooth, arching her back for him to taste her breasts. His body had become so hard it was painful, pulsing with need and desire. Almost frantic now, he pushed himself up and into her while they still stood, her back against the wall.

Inside, her body sheathed him like a glove. Wanting to prolong the moment, he gritted his teeth and tried to slow down, to contain the urgency. But Carmen, making sexy sounds low in her throat, became a wild woman. Shoving up against him, rotating her hips, she fought to make him go faster. "Hard and deep," she ordered, raking her nails down his back. "Now."

If control had been tenuous before, he now found himself clutching frantically to what tattered shreds remained. Four seconds in, he gave up, and abandoned himself to the mindless pleasure of making love with Carmen.

Fast and furious, they came crashing together, each meeting the other halfway, as if racing for an as yet unclimbed peak.

She cried out, a guttural sound, a cross between a moan and a scream. Determined not to be the first to lose control, he tried to focus on other things, anything but how amazing he felt inside her.

But when she climaxed, her body clenching around him, his self-control shattered. He let himself go, riding the waves of pleasure right alongside her.

They clutched each other close until their breathing

slowed. He would have bet a million bucks that Carmen wasn't the type to cuddle after sex. But when she burrowed into his side, snuggling up against him, he gladly held her. He'd never really thought about what a Vampire's body would feel like, but Carmen felt warm-blooded, just like a human or Shifter. Weird, but great.

"What am I going to do about you?" she mused, her lips against his chest. "I don't want to lose you. I really like you."

He couldn't help but laugh. "I like you, too. And we'll figure out something. What matters more than anything is you figuring out an antidote."

When she didn't respond, he looked down at her. She'd fallen asleep. Astounded, he studied her, memorizing her exquisite features with his gaze. He couldn't really afford to let himself go soft. Allowing that sort of weakness could get him into trouble.

Still holding Carmen, he let himself doze.

Somehow, morning arrived without either of them moving apart.

Now that she and Rick had allowed themselves to do what both had been circling around for days, the air should have been much clearer. When she woke to realize that she'd somehow managed to have fallen asleep in his arms, she nearly pushed him away and leaped out of the bed. But something about the serene look on his handsome face as he slept stopped her.

Usually, she wasn't a big fan of Shape-shifters. But Rick wasn't an ordinary Shifter. And there was no way in hell she was going to let him endanger himself by acting as a Shifter guinea pig for a deadly new virus.

She needed to have Rick ask his boss if he could send her the CDC's notes. It would be extremely helpful to know what they'd tried and failed. This would save her tons of time.

"Hey." Rick's voice, gravelly from sleep, drew her attention.

She shifted, twisting herself slightly toward him.

"Hey yourself." Immediately, she realized he was magnificently, spectacularly aroused.

And of course, they indulged themselves in a replay of last night's lovemaking. This time, they were much more leisurely about it, allowing each other the luxury of a slower, less urgent exploration.

After each taking another quick shower, they packed up and got back into Rick's vehicle. He ran through the drive-thru next door, ordering a breakfast sandwich and coffee after asking her if she wanted anything. She brandished another shelf-stable bag of imitation blood and declined.

When she asked him about getting records from the CDC, he liked the idea and sent off a quick text to his boss. He got an immediate response, confirming that his request would be met ASAP.

"Perfect." Carmen sat back, wrinkling her nose at the smell of grease and cheese. "I don't know how you can eat that," she said. "It smells terrible."

"To each their own." He nodded toward her blood. "Next up, I need to call Gus and tell him we're on our way back with Ted. The special team delivering it to us will meet us near Kemah."

"It's going to be interesting to see how they react once they learn Ted's been infected with the virus."

He glanced at her and grimaced. "I imagine they'll stay clear. Or they will if they have any sense at all."

Making the call while he drove, after the initial greeting, he didn't say much. Finally, when Gus apparently took a breath, Rick explained he'd be bringing back an infected Ted. "He's terminal," he said. "Just like everyone else who's contracted this virus. You need to take steps to make sure no one else gets infected. We'll be taking him back into the lab."

Rick listened a moment long before ending the call. He glanced at Carmen and shook his head. "They've brought in another biologist."

Her heart sank. "Did he say who?"

"No, he never mentioned the name or anything about credentials. Just that we'd have someone else helping us work with the virus."

"I don't like that," she murmured. "Not at all. But since we weren't given a choice, I hope at least they found someone with excellent qualifications."

The exchange in Kemah went off without a hitch. Rick pulled over down a winding country road. A few minutes later, a black Ford Expedition pulled up. Two men wearing full hazmat gear got out, went to the back and opened the hatch. Rick did the same with his vehicle.

They transferred what looked like a large plastic cocoon and had Rick sign off. Then they drove away.

"That was weirdly efficient," she commented.

"Yeah." Now Rick seemed fidgety, uncomfortable. He made no move to get back in the driver's seat and she couldn't say she blamed him.

"He's sealed up tight," she told him. "Besides, this virus isn't airborne. You'd have to touch him or have him cough on you to become infected. It's safe."

He nodded, eyeing Ted's body. "How can he breathe in there?"

Pointing at a loop of plastic tubing, she gave a short explanation of the air circulation system. "It's enough to keep him alive. Even though we're not sure how long he actually has to live."

When he winced, she apologized for sounding callous. "I've already shifted into my scientist mode."

Finally, he climbed into the vehicle. Once she'd done the same, they took off, heading for the Sons of Darkness compound.

They arrived in the early afternoon. Only Landers came out initially to greet them. Rifle at the ready, he circled around their vehicle as if he expected them to start throwing out vials of the deadly virus.

After he'd made two complete circles, he gestured for Carmen and Rick to get out. Slowly, keeping their hands where he could see them, they did.

Carmen stared at Landers, fantasizing about how easy it would be for her to snatch that rifle away from him. But of course she didn't.

A moment later, Gus and another man—one she didn't recognize—emerged from the house.

Gus grinned as he made the introductions. Landers stood off to the side, glowering at all of them.

The new biologist's name was Scott. He smelled of cigarette smoke, perspiration and rotgut whiskey.

While she wasn't entirely sure what to make of the human man, she kept her doubts hidden. She'd been able to sum him up in one look—or smell. His hands shook and his bloodshot eyes were far too bleary. Drugs or alcohol, probably both, and that answered her other question. Why he was here instead of at another, more reputable lab.

"Carmen here has a reputation as one of the top biologists in the country," Gus said. "The two of you working together should be able to replicate the virus."

"I worked for the CDC for twenty-seven years," Scott bragged. "It wasn't my fault they let me go."

Right. Wisely, she didn't voice this thought out loud. He'd been caught drinking or doing drugs on the job, had failed a random drug test or had made the kind of mistake that could have been disastrous while under the influence.

She glanced at Rick, who stared straight ahead, distaste plain on his handsome face. This nearly made her laugh, but she throttled that, instead resolving to speak to him later about perfecting a better poker face. Of course, since he was a seasoned undercover operative, the possibility existed that he wanted Scott to know how he felt about him.

"Considering that the virus has broken out in West Latvia," Carmen interjected, "is it possible someone obtained a blood sample or tissue sample? That would definitely help us get quicker identification."

Scott laughed, a bit maniacally, she thought. "I managed to snag a test vial from the CDC lab before I left. They have several, all locked in high-security areas. When I found out they intended to let me go, I took it while my clearance was still good."

Finally, the man had said something interesting. And judging from the rapt expression on both Gus's and Landers's faces, they were enthralled.

"That should help," Rick commented, his voice level. A quick glance at him revealed he'd managed to once again mask his feelings.

"Definitely," Carmen drawled. "As long as you're careful and don't allow yourself to get infected. That would be unfortunate. And deadly."

For a brief second, Scott appeared uncomfortable. "Yeah, that's true. But that's what he's for." And he pointed to Rick.

Carmen froze. "What do you mean by that?" she asked, her voice ice. What did he know? And how?

Scott grinned, malice shining in his small eyes. "They promised me a living test subject." He turned to face Gus and Landers. "Am I wrong in thinking it's him?"

Carmen turned. The glare she directed toward Gus left no doubt how she felt about that possibility.

"One of my men will do it," Gus finally answered. "For now, Rick is going to act as your assistant."

Careful to hide the relief that flooded through her, Carmen nodded. "That's what I thought." Though she now had a sneaking suspicion that Gus might be lying. She couldn't imagine any of his men willingly stepping in.

"I'll send someone along shortly," Gus continued. "Right now, why don't you all get to work. We've got to get this right before the CDC comes up with an antidote. Whoever does that first holds all the cards."

"They aren't even close," Scott said confidently.

"What about replicating the virus?" Carmen wanted to know. "What's their progress on that front?"

Scott shrugged. "They're still working on that, too. Pretty frantically, let me tell you. Once that thing crosses the ocean to other continents..."

The thought made her shudder. The human population would be swiftly decimated. And since no one yet knew if Shape-shifters and Merfolk were immune, the virus could possibly ravage the paranormal community, as well. This would leave Vampires. And the thought of a world full of only Vamps sounded like a grim place indeed.

"We've got to figure this out," she declared, allowing eagerness to leak into her tone. "Let's get started immediately. We need to move Ted from the vehicle to the lab."

Though Scott appeared appalled at the idea, Gus nodded enthusiastically. "My thoughts exactly. You two, get to work right now. And Rick, your job is to find them whatever they need."

Rick nodded. Only the way his jaw tightened gave away how much he hated being ordered around by Gus.

As for herself, Carmen had to carefully mask her excitement. Finally, the brand-new lab would be used. Add to that the fact that she would be able to get her hands on the actual virus and things couldn't have been better.

Scott grunted and began shuffling off toward the barn. Following, she wondered if he'd been working in the lab alone and unsupervised. Originally, she'd planned on trying to work around him. Now, though, she'd begun to reconsider. He might seem incompetent, but he had been working at the CDC and had access to the latest developments. She'd pick his brain for those. And who knew? Maybe they could actually work together and solve this puzzle.

However, if either of them succeeded in developing an antidote, there was no way she'd be turning that over to the Sons of Darkness. Not only would that make them the most powerful group on earth, but it would be a betrayal of all humanity.

Chapter 15

The next morning, Maddie puttered around her apartment while waiting for Jake to call. Knowing him, he'd stayed up late doing research on the internet and had slept in. If she didn't hear from him by nine, she planned to call and wake him up. She wanted company for a late breakfast.

On her third cup of coffee, and a bit jittery, she watched the clock. Out of necessity, she'd made herself a single piece of toast and slathered it with peanut butter since she'd needed something to settle her stomach.

At five until nine, she gave in and called him. His phone rang and rang and rang, finally going to voice mail. Which meant he was most likely still asleep.

Her conscience warred with her grumbling stomach. She could be nice and let him sleep, or she could continue to dial his number until his ringing phone finally woke him.

Having no choice, she went with choice number two.

Again just ringing and no answer. She hung up and immediately called again. This time, someone picked up on the third ring.

"Maddie?" a familiar voice asked. "As least that's what shows on caller ID."

Stunned, at first Maddie couldn't find the right words. Instead of Jake, her brother Colton had answered. "What are you doing with Jake's phone?" she asked, even as a horrible realization dawned on her. "Please tell me Jake's not in Protector custody."

"I can't tell you that, because he is," Colton replied. "Sort of. Actually, he's in my custody. Which is, as you know, much safer for him than if he'd been taken in to headquarters."

While he did have a point, this still worried her. She swallowed. "Why? What did he do?"

Her brother sighed. "As you know, we've been keeping an eye on him for a while."

"Right, but I thought you were backing off once I told you I was handling him."

"I always have a backup plan," he chided. "You know that. So we've been watching him. Turns out he was seen meeting with one of our other operatives, a guy who's been working deeply undercover."

"Rick Fallin?" she asked.

Either because he liked her to think he knew everything, or because he already knew the answer, he didn't ask her to elaborate. "He refuses to tell me what he's doing with him or, for that matter, you."

Poor Jake. She grimaced, keeping her thoughts to herself. Colton could be formidable when he wanted to be. She was impressed that Jake had resisted giving anything up.

"You aren't torturing him, are you?" She put a

threatening note in her question. "Because so help me, if you touch one hair on his head…"

Colton chuckled. "No torture. Come on, Maddie. I'm not a savage. This human hasn't broken any laws. Yet. He's just come onto our radar one too many times. We need to find out what he knows."

"I think you should ask Rick Fallin. He's one of your own, plus he's fully briefed on everything." It dawned on her that this entire situation might be a bit above her brother's pay grade. No doubt Jake had reached the same conclusion and that was why he'd gone silent.

"You know," Colton mused, "that's exactly what Jake said. How are you involved in this, little sister? You've been seen with him numerous times and you were spotted with him and Rick and another, unknown woman yesterday."

Now she went silent. And then, she tried to salvage everything the best way she could think of. "Jake is my…boyfriend," she said, wincing internally at the actual term. "He might even be my mate."

"He's human," her brother protested immediately. "Please tell me you aren't serious."

"Since when did you decide to be against Shifters mating with humans?" she asked, honestly perplexed since such a thing was very common. The children who resulted from such unions were termed Halflings. While not as invulnerable as full-blooded Shifters, Halflings were much more resilient than humans. They healed much faster, for one thing.

"I'm not, but this is *you*," Colton responded. "My baby sister. I've been hoping you'd meet another Pack Protector."

Disappointment warred with anger. "Let's cut to the chase. You need to let Jake go."

"Really?" His icy tone matched hers. "Let me remind you that I don't take orders from you."

"Maybe not. But this could be a matter of not just national security, but Pack security. I'd suggest you contact Rick Fallin or his superior and clear this through them. I have a feeling that you're going to have to put Jake back where you found him."

"That won't be so easy," he grumbled. "Since that was at the scene of an automobile accident."

Her stomach clenched. "Is he okay?"

"He's fine." Colton paused. "His vehicle isn't. I believe the police department towed it."

"Tell me where he is and I'll come pick him up." Though she felt frantic, she kept her voice calm and cool.

"Not yet. I'm not quite done talking to him. This new info you've given me has brought up totally different questions."

"Like what?" Though she still sounded collected, an edge had crept into her tone.

"I'm going to find out what his intentions are toward my baby sister." And Colton laughed, the exact same way he used to when they were just kids and he'd managed to pull one over on her.

"Don't you dare," she began, and then realized her brother had already ended the call.

Next, she did what she had to do. She dialed Rick.

Of course, he didn't pick up. Most likely since he was back undercover.

Then she tried Carmen, just in case. The call went straight to voice mail. Of course. But it had been worth a shot.

Her doorbell rang. She froze. These apartments enforced a strict no solicitation rule, so she doubted it was someone selling something.

She rushed over to the peephole and peered out. And silently groaned. It was that same Protector who'd been staking out Jake's house.

She decided not to open the door. Colton hadn't said anything about sending someone over. She had the uncomfortable feeling that this guy might be acting on his own. For whatever reason.

He rang the bell again, once, twice, and a third press in rapid succession. Judging by that, she thought he seemed agitated. Not a good thing.

Running for her phone, she punched Redial, praying Colton would pick up again. Instead, it rang and rang before going to voice mail.

She cursed. Her apartment was on the second floor, so the only other exit would be the balcony. While she could probably figure out a way to get herself down, she wasn't nuts about leaving her apartment available for that man to rummage through and trash.

And for what reason? The more she thought about it, the angrier she got. If the intruder had been human, she would have been confident in her ability to fight him off. But since he was also a Shifter, it would be tougher. Not impossible, just unlikely.

Crash. The front door shuddered. She swore. Damn fool was trying to break through her door.

"Stop!" she yelled. "What the hell do you want?"

"I need to talk to you," he hollered back. "It's urgent."

"I just got off the phone with my brother, Colton Kinslow. If there was anything I urgently needed to know, he would have told me."

"He doesn't know," the man replied. "Please. I'm begging you. Let me in. I promise I won't hurt you."

Right. Because she was so gullible that she'd believe

what a stranger who was actively trying to break into her apartment said.

"Go. Away. I'm dialing 911."

He groaned. "Don't. Please. I work with Rick Fallin's unit. Your brother isn't authorized to know about this. Rick is being set up."

Now he had her interest. "Set up how?"

"Let me in and I'll tell you."

Stalemate.

"I'm sorry," she finally said. "I don't trust you. Go away. Or call Rick yourself and warn him."

"I tried. He's undercover and not answering his phone."

Since that was correct, she again reevaluated. Then, finally deciding to take a chance, she opened the door. "I warn you," she told him. "You try anything stupid and you'll have an epic battle on your hands. I might be a smallish female in my human form, but my wolf is fierce."

Nodding, he stepped past her into her apartment.

"May I?" he asked, gesturing toward her couch.

"Sure." Standing near the door, she eyed him when he lowered his large frame onto her sofa.

"Sorry, it's been a long day. They'd kill me if they knew I was here."

"They?" she asked.

"My unit. Rick's being betrayed by the very people he trusts to have his back. I refuse to do that to him, so I'm here trying to warn him."

"He's not here. He only stopped by last night."

"I know." He rubbed his chin. "They're tracking him. This was the last place he visited before going back undercover."

"Which means—" she swallowed hard "—there's a very real possibility they know you're here right now."

He nodded.

Great. Now it seemed entirely probable that the crazy in her living room might be hunted by other deadly and determined Pack Protectors. It hadn't been too long ago when that organization had gone through a major purge, ousting the corrupt and cruel Protectors and reconfiguring with honest, decent agents.

Or so they'd said. Now, with this man telling her Rick was being set up, she had to wonder.

"They had Rick pick up a body that had been infected with the virus," he continued. "A guy that had escaped from the group Rick's pretending to be part of."

A chill snaked up her spine. "Go on."

"They're going to ask Rick to be their guinea pig, to see if the virus works on Shifters. The thing is, they already know. Apparently, this thing doesn't just kill humans. It's deadly to our kind, too."

She swallowed hard. "That's bad. If it is fatal to us, it's probably lethal to Merfolk, as well."

"Probably," he agreed. "But there's no reason for Rick to sacrifice himself when they already know the answer."

"Who's *they*?" she wanted to know.

"People in the higher echelon of government. Not just our country, but internationally. They are Shifters and Vampires, and who knows what else. The one thing they're not is human. They have…" Gesturing, he appeared briefly at a loss for words. "A master plan," he finally continued. One that originally involved the extinction of humankind."

At that, Maddie narrowed her eyes. She wasn't entirely sure she could take this guy at his word. "Are you saying that a Shifter created this virus?"

"Yes. The one thing he didn't expect was for it to be able to harm his own kind."

"But why?" This, as far as she was concerned, was the million-dollar question. "None of this make sense. Our people have gotten along with humans for eons. Why change?"

"Power," he answered. "Some say a Vampire is behind all this. It's sort of logical, since Vampires will be all that are left once the virus decimates humankind, Shifters and Merfolk."

While she still wasn't entirely convinced she believed him, clearly *he* believed he spoke the truth. "Who all knows about this?" she asked.

"My unit—Rick's unit. One of our guys accidentally intercepted a communication stream between two men who are on the high council. Now that we have access, we've continued to monitor the chatter."

She nodded. "And you're confident this information is accurate?"

"Yes. One hundred percent." A muscle worked in his jaw. "We've got to warn Rick. It's imperative that he play along without endangering himself. We don't want to alert the ones behind this before we can take them down."

"Take them down?" she repeated, wondering why it felt like she'd walked onto the set of a television drama.

"Yes." Mouth tight, he shook his head. "The less you know the better. Suffice it to say, this is bigger than just finding an antidote. It's about power. Whoever can control that virus can control the world."

And whoever came up with the antidote would have the most power of all.

Finally, she nodded. "I'll continue trying to reach Rick or Carmen." Still uneasy, she walked to the door and held it open. "And you go back to doing what you were before you came here."

The hint to leave couldn't have been any clearer. To

her relief, he nodded and took it. As he stepped outside, he turned and faced her. "May I have your phone number? That way we can stay in touch."

"I'm surprised you don't already have it," she said, only half kidding.

"I do." He smiled. "I'll text you so you have mine."

And he left.

Judging from what he could hear of Colton's side of the phone call, Maddie's brother wasn't pleased with what he was hearing from her. And while Jake wasn't sure what Rick would want Colton to know, it wasn't his place to reveal anything. One of the hard rules of successful journalism was to keep one's head down and avoid revealing anything too soon, especially information about the source. Which, in this case, would be Rick himself. If, as Colton claimed, the two men knew each other, then Colton could simply speak to Rick directly. That way, Rick could fill him in at his own discretion.

When Colton concluded his call and walked back into the room, Jake worked hard to keep his face expressionless.

"That was interesting," Colton said, grimacing. "Now I've got a whole other set of questions for you."

"I couldn't help but overhear. Are you seriously about to ask me my intentions toward your sister?"

To Jake's surprise, the other man grinned. "Maybe," he allowed. "Are you two dating?"

To his dismay, Jake felt his face heat. "That's none of your business."

Colton laughed. "I'm going to need to make another phone call," he said, thumbing through the contact list in Jake's phone. "What, no number for Rick Fallin?"

"I don't think he's in a place right now where he can

receive calls," Jake responded, even though he had no idea where Rick might be. "I suggest you call the Special Agent in Charge at whatever FBI office he works out of."

"FBI?" The notion appeared to surprise Colton. "Uh, yeah. Sure. I'll call them." He started to put down Jake's phone and then reconsidered. "Here," he said, walking it over and placing it on the ground next to Jake. "And you can take the rest of that duct tape off. I saw you'd managed to cut through it. Pretty enterprising. Kudos on that."

Jake nodded. "Thanks." Feeling slightly foolish now, he brought his arms around to his front, rubbing his aching wrists. As he began peeling off the remaining duct tape, Colton left the room to go make his call.

Once he had all the tape off—both hands and feet—Jake stood and began walking around, trying to get the blood flowing back in his arms and legs. He had to admit to feeling relieved knowing he wasn't in any real danger. Though he still didn't understand why Maddie's brother would have deliberately caused a car crash in order to grab him. Especially since he worked for the FBI. Surely they didn't allow such unorthodox methods.

He eyed his phone. Maybe Maddie could shed some light. Plus, he really needed to hear her voice.

She picked up on the third ring. "Oh, thank goodness. Colton, what on earth is going on?"

"Not Colton," Jake said. "He's in another room trying to reach Rick. You sound panicked. Are you all right?"

She exhaled. "I'm okay. I think. I just had another operative come to my apartment looking for Rick. He said he's trying to warn Rick that he's being set up."

Though his journalistic instincts were now screaming, Jake kept his voice level. "Popular guy. You know, no one ever told me exactly what covert operation your brother actually works for. I find it kind of odd that they'd concern themselves with a reporter like me. I'm not even famous."

She hesitated, just long enough for him to wonder if she'd tell him the truth.

"That's classified," she finally said. "I'm sorry, I can't tell you more than that."

"Kind of like what Rick does for the FBI?"

She hesitated a tad too long. "Um, yes. As for how you came to be on their radar, Colton received some intel on you and apparently the meeting with Rick and Carmen—and me—was the last straw."

"The last straw?" he repeated, incredulous. "Let's see. Colton broadsided me with a box truck and then tied me up and transported me in the back because he found it *annoying* that I met with you, Rick and Carmen? That's crazy."

"You're right, it is." She sounded genuinely upset. "I'm sorry. Tell me where you are and I'll swing by and pick you up."

"That's just it. I couldn't see where we went, so I have no idea where we are. You'll have to ask him."

The hiss of her sharp intake of breath showed her reaction to that. "Seriously?"

"Yes. Like I said, he transported me here in the back of a box truck. There were no windows. No matter what his reasons, this was really extreme," he continued. "I think my car might be totaled. I'm damn lucky I wasn't hurt." The anger he'd been keeping banked threatened to erupt. Directed at the wrong person. He swallowed hard, hoping he could maintain his equilibrium.

"I'm glad you weren't." The warmth of her tone took the edge off. "And if you don't have insurance on the car, I'll make sure Colton pays to have it repaired."

She'd make sure? "Are you saying you can tell your brother what to do?"

"No, not at all. I'm telling you I'll go to bat for you with my brother. What he did was wrong and he needs to make reparations."

For the first time ever, he finally understood the term *mental anguish and suffering*. This was more than the damage that had been done to his vehicle. He'd been run into—on purpose—and tied up and kidnapped. By her brother. For no good reason at all.

"That's it? The extent of your outrage?" Though he tried, he wasn't able to keep the bitterness from his voice.

"Jake, I'm as appalled as you are. And shocked. But whatever else I might be, I'm not my brother's keeper," she explained. "Like I said, he works for the same outfit Rick does. These guys are used to operating under the radar. Sometimes they go to extraordinary lengths to get what they want."

Something in her voice…

"What are you not telling me?" he demanded. "I can always sniff out when people are trying to hide the truth."

She laughed. "Don't go all reporter on me. It's me. I'm as upfront with you as I can be. But there are some things I can't say. Just like we can't pass on what Rick and Carmen told us. If they want Colton to know, I'm sure they'll fill him in."

"I didn't say anything," he said, relieved. "And I believe your brother is calling Rick now."

"Good. Then it's out of your hands. Look around and see if you can find any clues as to your location."

"Doubtful." He pinched his nose. "Considering that I'm in a windowless room in some kind of bunker."

"Are you talking to my sister?" Colton had come

back into the room. He leaned against the door frame, arms folded.

"Yes," Jake said. "Can you tell me where I am so she can come get me?"

One brow raised, Colton nodded. "Let me tell her myself. I need to ask her something anyway."

"Hold on," Jake told Maddie, and then handed over the phone.

"What's going on?" Colton asked his sister, his tone urgent. "As soon as I started trying to reach Rick Fallin, I was ordered to back off. Wait—don't answer me. Not on an unsecured line. We need to talk in person."

He listened for a moment. When Colton spoke again, a thread of urgency undercut his tone. "Rather than an address, I'm going to give you a clue. Remember when Dad used to take us camping when we were kids? Same place. And make sure you're not followed."

Evidently Maddie understood the reference. Colton punched the off button and handed the phone back to Jake. "She'll be here in a few hours," he said. "Might as well make yourself comfortable. There's a bathroom through there." He pointed. "And a kitchen with a fridge stocked with soft drinks. Or beer, if you'd prefer. I've even got a TV." He shrugged. "You don't have to stay out here in the garage."

"The garage?" Stunned, Jake looked around. "This is a garage?" There were no tools, no machinery, nothing to indicate the usage of this room. "I thought it was a bunker."

"Nope. You were wrong." Colton grinned. "This is my father's hunting cabin. He used to bring Maddie and me up here when we were kids. That's how she knows where to go."

"How far are we from Galveston?"

"A couple of hours. Come on." Motioning Jake to follow, Colton turned and went inside the house.

Curious, Jake followed him. The cozy, rustic retreat was so far opposite of what he'd been expecting that he couldn't help but laugh.

"What?" Colton asked, turning to eye Jake over his shoulder.

"Nice place," Jake said, shaking his head. "Though it's not the sort of place I would have expected an FBI agent to bring a captive."

"Oh, that." Colton tugged at his collar, grimacing. "I was actually acting on my own behalf, not the Bureau."

"Figures." Wandering around the room, Jake realized he could picture a younger Maddie here. Outside, he could see a lot of tall pine trees, as well as live oak and silver leaf maple. A bucolic scene, under ordinary circumstances. However, this situation was far from ordinary.

He didn't see a single other person. Or house. Nothing but forest and sky. Looking out the big picture window, Jake realized they were miles from civilization. East Texas, most likely. Still, none of this made sense.

Jake turned to face the other man. "Mind telling me why?" he asked quietly. "None of this fits. Why'd you go through such extremes to capture me? Wouldn't it have been a hell of a lot easier if you simply asked to have a word with me?"

"Easier, true. But not nearly as much fun." Colton chuckled. "I'm kidding. I did what I did for a reason. Other people are watching you, getting ready to pounce. I wanted to make them believe you'd been abducted so they'd back off."

"Other people are watching me?" Jake asked. "Again, why?"

"Because you represent a threat." Colton's ambiguous response didn't help at all. Obviously, he knew that. He clasped Jake's shoulder and squeezed. "Let's wait until Maddie gets here. Once I speak privately with her, it's entirely possible we can clear this entire thing up."

Head aching, Jake nodded.

Maddie. The one person he'd believed he could trust. Clearly, he'd been wrong.

Chapter 16

Rick caught up with Carmen and grabbed her arm. Her skin felt soft and smooth under his calloused fingers. Though she flashed a quick smile at him, she shot a clearly disgruntled look at Scott's back. The other man sure moved fast, especially considering he hadn't appeared all that eager to get started. His jerky movements reminded Rick of the crabs he sometimes picked up on the beach, trying to run away. This made Rick wonder if Scott might be on drugs.

Naturally, he couldn't ask. He couldn't even give the other man a rudimentary sobriety test. Since Gus and Landers brought up the rear and were only ten feet behind them, Rick didn't speak.

He might not know all of what was going on, but his sixth sense was working overtime. In an already weird situation, something else was definitely off. He hoped they'd find out what before all hell broke loose.

Once inside the barn, little had changed. Dust still

coated everything, though their footsteps from before remained. When he spotted the wolf paw prints, she wondered how they'd escaped notice, but no doubt everyone assumed some wild animal had entered and then left when no food had been found.

As soon as they reached the back corner, Scott stopped, swaying slightly on his feet. He eyed Carmen with bleary red eyes. "I've brought the vial here and it's in the cooler. We must use extreme care when handling it."

"Vial?" She stared at him. "Of what?"

"The virus." He stared back. "What else would I have a vial of?"

"Point taken, but I thought we'd work on the infected subject first, not a vial. With an actual body, we can skip several steps right away. It's important to see how this virus mutates in a live body."

His smug grin made him look drunk. Rick revised his thought about drugs to include alcohol. "We can do both. You work on the body and I'll take the vial." Scott puffed out his chest. "I'm sure you know, but I'll say it anyway. It's imperative that we take precautions so we aren't infected." His condescending tone had Rick gritting his teeth.

He wondered what it cost Carmen not to snap at this fool. Cool, calm and collected, she only nodded and stepped away from them both. "Full suits," she said, gesturing to a wall of closed lockers. "I checked them out before. They're old, but I did a cursory examination and found no tears or holes. There are enough for all three of us to have one."

"We'll check them again," Scott interjected. "Not that I don't think you're thorough, but I personally don't have any desire to die because these people skimped on proper precautions."

Now Rick had to curl his hands up into fists to keep from doing anything foolish. Judging by Carmen's narrowed gaze, she felt the same way.

"I second that," she finally said. "I don't want to die, either." Her first lie, at least to Scott, since the virus wouldn't affect her. She was already dead. Again, Rick admired her acting ability. There were many facets to Carmen and her beauty was the least of them. He thought he might really enjoy getting to know her, which surprised him.

"Landers here is going to stand guard," Gus announced. "He'll remain in position outside the lab until someone comes to relieve him."

Landers strutted around, glaring at them. He obviously considered himself a deadly menace. One look summed him up. A bully.

Still, of course it would have to be Landers. Judging from the menacing way he held his rifle, he hoped someone would give him a reason to use it, whether smashing someone with the butt of it or firing off a few shots. Rick entertained a brief fantasy of shifting into a wolf and ripping out the other man's throat.

"I don't think he needs a suit, though," Scott said slyly, pointing at Rick with a shaking finger. "Why waste one when we might need a backup? He's only your assistant. There's no reason for him to come inside the lab."

Inwardly tensing, Rick waited for Carmen's response instead of reacting and telling this fool what he thought of him.

"I want him there," she said smoothly. "That's reason enough."

Though Scott mumbled something under his breath, he didn't challenge Carmen any further.

Once they'd all suited up, Scott and Carmen went

through the purifying process to get into the sterile environment. Though wearing the claustrophobic and cumbersome suit, Rick remained outside the chamber, announcing he was ready to bring them whatever they needed.

Carmen nodded, her smile letting him know that this setup pleased her. Him, too, despite his orders. If something went wrong, neither of them wanted Rick to be the test subject for ascertaining whether or not Shape-shifters were immune to the virus.

Something about Scott's movements worried Rick. However, even if the other scientist planned to "accidentally" infect Carmen, the virus wouldn't hurt her. What Rick couldn't figure out was the other man's agenda. Clearly, he had a grudge against the CDC. Yet he seemed intelligent, so he had to realize the fact that he'd successfully stolen a vial of the virus made him a force to be reckoned with.

He could have had all the power to himself. Instead, he'd chosen to align himself with a fringe group of crazies.

Unless... Once again, Rick realized there had to be a lot more to this story than he realized. It was like peeling back layers on an onion.

Right then he decided to join Scott and Carmen inside the lab. In there, he could keep a closer eye on things.

When she'd first begun working with biological diseases, Carmen had found the suits cumbersome and awkward. These days, she actually liked them. They reminded her of the old days, when Vampires had believed it necessary to sleep in coffins.

"The vial is in here," Scott said, his voice muffled

due to his headgear. "I waited for your arrival before running any tests."

Something in his voice. She gave him a sharp look. "Are you absolutely certain of what you have?"

Before he could answer, Rick stepped into the cleansing room. A moment later, he joined them inside the lab.

"I'm so glad to have you here," Scott said, rubbing his gloved hands together. "You can be of much more assistance than if you'd stayed out there."

For herself, Carmen felt the opposite. For safety's sake, she'd much rather have had Rick stay where he'd been. Of course, she couldn't vocalize that. She didn't want any of the people to have the slightest inkling how important Rick was to her.

The knowledge slammed into her like a punch to the gut. Despite everything, she loved him. Even though she had no idea how he felt about her.

Scott said something and she shoved the newfound knowledge away. She'd examine it later.

"We need to bring the victim in," Scott said, carefully placing the vial back inside its Styrofoam nest. "After we do blood samples, I want to make sure he has the same virus."

Carmen shrugged. "Sounds good."

Barking out his request to have Ted brought in to Landers, Scott gestured to Rick. "You go and help him. See if there's an extra protective suit he can wear."

To her surprise, Landers instantly obeyed. Since one suit remained, he clumsily put it on while they all watched.

Once Landers finished, Rick went back through the disinfecting area and joined the other man. Together they left the barn.

She and Scott waited silently until they returned

with the still sealed carrier that contained the hapless Ted. Each man held one end, though due to the rigid shape of the container, she couldn't tell which was the head and which was the feet.

Poor Ted. She couldn't help but wonder if he'd even be alive once they opened the enclosure. Either way, it wasn't going to be a pretty sight. The virus wasn't just lethal, it was disfiguring, as well.

Landers and Rick stood in the decontamination chamber, holding Ted between them. When the light turned green, they entered the clean room.

"Over here," Scott directed, gesturing at a long stainless steel table. He stood watching, impatiently shifting his weight from one foot to the other. Once the container was settled, he ordered them to step aside.

Landers complied immediately, going so far as to leave the room. Carmen noticed he didn't remove his protective suit, though, even as he made sure to put as much space as possible between himself and the virus.

Just as Scott reached to unfasten the first of the three clips, shots rang out, coming from somewhere outside the barn. Landers attempted to spin, but the heavy protective gear made him clumsy, and he fell. Hard.

Rick grabbed Carmen, attempting to push her to the ground. She twisted away from him, or tried to. Moving in these suits was like trying to swim in quicksand.

"Take cover," he ordered, clearly forgetting momentarily that she was a Vampire and invulnerable to guns and bullets. Just as he was, unless the shooter happened to be savvy enough to have used silver bullets. Humans never did, since they had no idea Shape-shifters even existed.

Another volley of shots. Scott, who'd frozen in place, cursed loudly. "Those idiots," he said. "How can they not understand the importance of what we're doing in here? They swore they'd keep us safe."

"Yeah, well, I guess they failed," Carmen told him. "And if you want to stay alive, I suggest you drop to the floor and take cover."

"Drop? In this suit?" He shook his head. "Impossible. I notice both of you are still standing."

Carmen and Rick exchanged looks. "True," she admitted.

Through the clear glass, they all watched as Landers struggled to rise to his feet. It would almost have been comedic, if not for the sound of more gunfire, closer this time.

Rick shook his head. "What the hell are they up to?"

"I don't know," Scott answered, as if the question had been posed directly to him. "But we need to protect this virus. We can't let anyone else get their hands on it."

Great. The last thing Carmen would have suspected was some rival group attempting a raid. But then again, why not? This entire situation had been crazy.

A moment later, the barn door crashed open. Five fully armed men stood in the opening. Landers cursed again, fumbling to remove the suit so he could reach his own weapon.

"Freeze," one of the intruders yelled, training his rifle on Landers. Landers froze.

Carmen again glanced at Rick. Unbelievably, he wore a wide grin on his face.

"Friends of yours?" she asked.

"You might say that." Rick waved. "Hey Pete, over here."

What happened next seemed to go in slow motion. Rick unclipped his headgear, pulling it off his head in one easy motion.

Horrified, Carmen shouted at him to put it back on. For a second he only stared at her, clearly having forgotten the danger. Then, realizing, he slammed the headgear back into place, securing the clips with fumbling gloved fingers. "It should be okay," he said. "We haven't opened Ted's container or the vial. Since the virus isn't airborne, I should be all right."

Scott nodded in agreement. "He's correct."

Meanwhile, the team of armed men came closer. "Clean lab?" the one named Pete commented. "Fancy."

"Yeah." Rick grinned. "Give us a second and we'll be right out."

"Wait a moment." Scott stepped in between Rick and the exit. "Do you know these people?" Then, without waiting for an answer, he groaned. "It's an inside job. You two are working with them, aren't you?"

"I have no idea who these people are," Carmen protested. Though Rick clearly did. She wasn't sure how all this factored into his undercover role, or what the men were doing here, so she'd let Rick take the lead.

"Relax," Rick said, glaring at Scott. "They're not here about the virus. They're working with me on something else. Now if you'll excuse me…" Without a backward glance, he went out into the cleansing chamber and finally out into the other room where Landers still stood as still as a statue.

This time, when Rick yanked off his headgear, he took a deep breath and smiled. "Much better," he commented, before relieving Landers of his rifle. Shedding the rest of the bulky suit, he stepped outside with the other men and closed the barn door behind him.

"Do you trust him?" Scott asked, glancing sourly at the closed door. "Or are we about to be killed in the midst of some sort of coup?"

She told the truth. "Honestly, I have no idea what's going on."

"I thought he works for you."

"Rick?" She shrugged, as if she didn't care. "We're partners. But I don't know everything about him, and he doesn't know everything about me."

Scott's scowl told her what he thought of that. "I can assure you that there are powerful people behind this backward group, the Sons of Darkness. How else do you think they got funding to build this lab? There are forces at work here that you—and he—cannot possibly comprehend."

"Ah, but I do," she said quietly. "The future of the world is at stake. Power and powerful people will crumble before the death and destruction that this virus can bring. That's why it's imperative that an antidote be found quickly."

His jaw went slack, as if he found her statement not only shocking, but absurd. "If the combined forces of the best infectious disease biologists working for the CDC can't find an antidote, how can you possibly believe we can?"

"Because I'm just that good," she responded. "Now, while we don't have any idea what's going on outside this barn, how about we get to work? No one is going to be foolish enough to interrupt us while we're working with an infected body."

Considering for a moment, Scott finally agreed. "Who knows," he said, his tone bleak. "Maybe we can come up with an antidote before someone shoots us."

"Maybe we can," she agreed. "Let's get to work."

Seeing Pete not only was a major surprise, but Rick knew immediately that something had to have gone terribly wrong. Otherwise, his team never would have risked unmasking his cover.

But first, they all exchanged greetings, amid much back clapping and arm clasping. "Sorry, man," Pete said. "But we had to take out the others up in the house."

Gus and his crew. "How many were there?" Rick asked. "The number of people at this place seems to fluctuate quite a bit."

"We rounded up five." Pete grimaced. "We were just going to contain them, but one of them—the bald one—decided to try something stupid. As soon as he started shooting, the others went for various weapons. We had no choice."

Which meant Gus and his gang were all dead.

"What about the ones in the barn?" Pete asked. "I know you're working with Carmen, but who are the other two men?"

"One is part of the gang. The other is a former CDC scientist they've brought in. Or so he claims." Rick shook his head. "What the hell are you guys doing here?"

"We heard you were given orders to be the test case for the virus, to see if it affects Shifters." Pete's narrow-eyed gaze told Rick what his friend thought about that.

"True. I was. I don't like it, but I can't fault the logic. One person is acceptable collateral damage, especially if my sacrifice saves others."

"It's a trap." Pete crossed his arms, his expression grim. "They already know the virus kills us. They have documented proof. Several of the dead over in West Latvia were Pack."

Stunned, Rick wasn't sure how to respond. When he did, he could come up with only one question. "But why? Why would they ask me to die if they already know?"

"I don't know. Who have you pissed off lately?" Pete asked, clearly only half kidding. "Or did you find out something you weren't supposed to?"

"Not that I know of." Genuinely perplexed, Rick thought back. "Olson Ferring's been giving me my orders. Does he know you guys are here?"

"Hell no. As soon as we found out what was going on, we headed out to rescue you. No way we're letting one of our own go down without a fight."

Grateful, Rick nodded. "I appreciate that."

"Good. Let's go. We want to get you out of here before the powers that be find out what we've done."

While that idea held a lot of appeal, Rick wasn't running off and leaving Carmen. "I can't," he said. "This mission is too important."

Pete eyed him. "You're not making sense. I just told you that you're being set up."

"And I appreciate that. I can now take effective precautions. But if there's even the slightest chance that the two biologists in there can come up with an antidote, I've got to make sure it gets into the right hands."

Squinting at him, Pete finally slowly nodded. "It's your funeral."

"It's all of our funerals if we don't find a way to stop this virus," Rick said. "I honestly believe this may be our last hope."

"Seriously?"

"Yeah. Unfortunately. I appreciate you guys having my back, but I can't leave."

Slowly Pete nodded. "Then we're staying with you."

Touched and honored, Rick nodded. "You need to understand you all could die if this goes south."

Pete shrugged. "We will all die anyway if what you say is true and this virus starts running rampant through our population. Better to be on the right side and go down knowing you did whatever you could to prevent it."

Those words were, in a nutshell, the reason why Rick's unit was the best of them all.

"Go on back in there," Pete directed. "Me and the guys will stay outside here and guard the place."

Taking a deep breath, Rick turned to head back into the barn.

Working carefully, Carmen and Scott opened the container that held Ted's body. Once they got it fully opened, inside was another body bag that they had to unzip.

The instant they did that, a horrible odor hit them, so strong it sent Scott reeling away from the table. Even Carmen, who'd smelled many awful things over the centuries, fought to keep from gagging.

Then she caught sight of what had once been Ted. "Will you look at that?" she breathed. "It's not even recognizable as having been a human being."

Her statement brought Scott rushing over to see for himself. Eyes huge, he stared down at the writhing mess of goo inside the body bag. "What the hell is that?"

"What the virus does to its host, if allowed to incubate after death," she replied. "That's why they've been burning the bodies over in West Latvia."

Though he nodded, Scott didn't take his gaze from what Carmen now thought of as virus breeding ground central.

"We should be able to get some good samples from this," she said. "Can you please bring me three new test tubes?"

Moving like a man in a dream, he complied. When he handed the first one to her she saw his hands were shaking. For the first time, she wondered if he'd truly have the balls to handle this type of work.

"What department did you say you worked in at the CDC?" she asked, keeping her voice casual.

"I didn't."

Not a good answer. Since time was of the essence, she decided to cut to the chase. "Do you have any idea what you're doing?"

Instead of his usual bluster and bragging, Scott merely swallowed hard. "I wasn't on the front line in the lab. My job was more data focused."

In other words, he entered the data into a computer.

While that job, too, held some importance, the fact that he'd passed himself off as a top research scientist infuriated her. "Why?" she asked, knowing he'd understand the question.

"Because I wanted to do some good," he responded. "I am a degreed, trained biologist. I took a data entry job as a way to get into working at the CDC with the hopes I could eventually move into the research lab. When I saw my chance, I took it."

"Your chance? You stole a vial of a deadly virus and took it from a controlled environment out among mankind."

He at least had the grace to appear ashamed. "What else could I do? When the Sons of Darkness contacted me, telling me how they had a clean lab and offering me the opportunity to save humankind, how could I refuse? How could anyone refuse?"

She opened and closed her mouth, not sure how to answer.

"Anyway," he continued, apparently taking her silence for agreement, "what's *your* story? You act like you're some super hotshot scientist, but did you ever even work for the CDC?"

"Nope." And that was all she intended to say about that. "If you want to help me analyze these tissue samples, you'd better get busy."

To his credit, he once again stepped up. Looking as if he might vomit at any moment, he watched while she filled the first test tube halfway and placed it in the metal stand. When he handed her the second, his hands weren't shaking as noticeably, though the tremor was still there.

Once all three test tubes had been filled, they carefully zipped up the body bag and also reclosed the container. "We'll need to burn that," Scott commented.

"True," she agreed. "But not yet. Right now, I want to take advantage of all the active tissue samples."

The barn door opened, sending a beam of brilliant sunlight to light up the other part of the barn. Rick stood silhouetted in the door for a moment before he closed it. He hurried back to the lab area, entered the antechamber and quickly suited up. After rushing into the decontamination room, he once again entered the lab.

"Well?" Scott demanded. "Are you going to tell us what's going on?"

"No," he answered, his voice muffled behind the headgear. "That's on a need-to-know basis. And right now, you don't need to know."

Chapter 17

Though it had been years since Maddie had visited her father's old hunting cabin, she knew the way there as if she was still a regular visitor. Once upon a time, she had been. Before she and Colton had been born, their grandparents had gone in with their own siblings and purchased a hundred-acre parcel of land in Southeast Texas. Each family had constructed several small cabins, careful that none of them were in sight of the others. Young Shifters learned how to change here, and how to hunt. They'd had family reunions and group hunts, and celebrated birthdays and anniversaries there. Despite the pall of the occasional divorce and remarriage, the tradition continued strong.

But then Colton and Maddie's father had been killed. This horrific act, a brutal murder with a silver bullet, had forever changed their tight-knit clan. After his death, their stepmother had wanted nothing to do with the rest of the family. She'd sold what she could and moved away. Since the cabin remained deeded to the still-living grandparents, she'd been unable to get her greedy hands on that.

These days, with all the kids grown and their elders traveling, the cabins weren't used much. But they would be, as soon as the next generation of Shapeshifters was born.

Driving, Maddie's heart quickened at the thought. She'd been too busy establishing her career to even think of having children. And to be honest, she hadn't met anyone she'd even consider mating with. Until now. Until Jake.

Now that she'd had the thought, instead of shutting it down, she allowed herself the luxury of trying to imagine what their babies would look like. She'd hope they had Jake's beautiful skin tone rather than her freckled, pale one. In fact, she'd rather they'd totally resemble him, as he was the most handsome man she'd ever met.

Damn. Gripping the steering wheel, she shook her head. When had she become so far gone? Jake's capture, even if by her own brother, had forced her to face the truth.

She loved him. Truly, madly, deeply. Amazed, she turned up the radio, singing along as she drove. She drove fast in the passing lane, noted what vehicles were around her, and then switched to the far right lane and a much slower rate of speed.

None of the original group of cars stayed back with her. They all passed her.

She did this several times on the trip, with the same results. Then, just before she made the turnoff to take her east, she pulled in to a fast food restaurant. After sitting in her car for a few minutes and checking out all the other vehicles that pulled in after her, she got out and stretched her legs. Inside, after using the restroom, she bought a large coffee and a sandwich. When she returned to her car, she locked the doors and sat there until she'd finished eating.

Again she went through the parking lot, noting vehicles, before pulling out. She kept a close eye behind her, but saw nothing of interest, so she got back on the highway and took the necessary exit.

Once more, in an overabundance of caution, she performed her little test. Fast, then slow. Finally satisfied that no one was trailing her, she continued on to her destination.

Not a single other car in sight, she turned off the main road onto the familiar gravel one. As she drove through a set of open iron gates marked Private, her heart rate sped up. Odd how even with so many years since her last visit, this still felt like returning home.

Finally, the first cabin came into view. Set deep within a copse of trees, the weathered wood blended with the rich colors of earth and forest. A flood of memories rushed back, but Maddie continued on. Her family's cabin was much deeper, near the river.

After passing three other cabins, she finally rounded a curve in the road and got her first glimpse in years of the one belonging to her family. The faded gray color gave it a homey look. She felt a rush of nostalgia as she turned in the horseshoe-shaped drive.

Parking behind the white box truck, she got out of her car and headed toward the back door. Despite the sidewalk, no one ever used the front entrance to the cabin. The back side, with its large wooden deck, had been deliberately made more inviting. As she crossed the walkway and the overgrown flower beds, the back door opened and Colton came out.

"You made great time," he said, enveloping her in a quick hug.

"I did," she agreed, looking past him for Jake. "And I made sure no one followed me."

"Perfect." His gaze followed hers. "Looking for something?"

"Quit." Pulling away, she punched his arm. "Where is he? Please tell me you don't still have him locked in the garage."

"Where else would he be?"

She stared in disbelief. "Judging by your frown, you don't see how awful that is."

"What? He's fine. I didn't want to bring him into the house until you got here."

"Why not?" Turning to face him, hands on her hips, she glared. "Afraid of a human man?"

He actually appeared offended at her words. "That wasn't it. I needed to talk to you first and find out how much he knows. Is he aware that you're Pack?"

"No." She swallowed. "We haven't reached that stage in our relationship yet. It's all too new."

His gaze searched her face. "Yet you seem pretty certain about your feelings."

"I am. When you know, you just know. I can't explain it any more succinctly."

Though she could tell he had no idea what she meant, he slowly nodded. "I haven't had a chance to get to know him very well. Actually, he's really pissed at me. And I can't say I blame him." He shrugged. "Eventually, he'll understand what I did was for his own good."

"Was it?" she asked, crossing her arms.

"Yes. Some of the other Pack Protectors got wind of the fact that he is planning to write an exposé on Broken Chains. I have to tell you, that went over like a ton of bricks."

"Where did they get that info?" she asked. "As far as I know, he's only mentioned it to me."

"Apparently, he approached who he thought was some random guy and offered him money to help him get in."

She groaned. "Yes, he mentioned that. Let me guess. The guy is a Protector."

"Bingo. Orders came down from Headquarters yesterday that he was to be brought in and interrogated. If they learned he knew too much, he was to be…reprogrammed."

A shudder crept up her spine. "He doesn't know anything, I promise. All I've done is misdirect him."

"I believe you. But you know how it is. Once a report is made, it has to be investigated. That's why I staged such an elaborate abduction."

"Because you want them to believe…what, exactly?"

"That a Protector unit has grabbed him. There's still the occasional infighting in the group. Competition is fierce to see who can find the most threats and neutralize them."

"Are there truly that many?" she asked, still skeptical. "I mean, come on. Everyone knows about the consequences of revealing the truth to humans and no one wants to be picked up by the Protectors. I'd think that alone would act as a huge deterrent."

He shrugged. "What can I say? People can be stupid."

Since she had no answer for that, she glanced at the house. "Can we go get Jake now? I imagine this has all been stressful for him."

"Sure." Colton shook his head. "But if you ask me, that guy's plenty capable of dealing with stuff like this. He's a well-respected journalist who's written articles from all over the world, including dangerous war zones."

"You looked him up?" she asked, incredulous.

"Didn't you?"

Instead of responding, she punched him in the arm and pushed past him to get inside the house. As she hurried toward the garage, Colton stopped her. "I was kidding. He's not in the garage anymore. He wanted a shower, so I let him use the bathroom." He pointed at the closed door. "Unless you intend to go in after him, you might as well wait with me in the kitchen."

"Don't tempt me," she muttered.

Hearing that, her brother made a face. "Gross. Don't even think about it."

The bathroom door opened before she could reply. Maddie's thoughts scattered at the sight of Jake, his close-cropped dark hair damp, button-down shirt open to reveal his muscular chest. Unable to help herself, she let her gaze roam to where his jeans rode low on his hips. To top it all off, he was barefoot. He hadn't yet seen her because he appeared to be preoccupied rubbing at one of his wrists.

"Rein it in, Kinslow," Colton murmured, elbowing her hard. Raising his voice, he invited Jake to join them in the kitchen.

Jake looked up and his gaze locked on Maddie. Swiftly he crossed the room and went to her, took her in his arms and held her. Heart hammering, she snuggled close, relishing the warmth of his skin, the feel of his muscular body, his unique masculine scent. *Mine*, she thought, unbidden. *All mine.*

"Oh, for the love of…" Colton turned away. "Anyone want coffee?"

Raising his gaze, Jake's expression hardened. "Will it be laced with something to knock me out?"

"Ouch." Colton shook his head. "Look, as I told my sister, I had good reasons for doing what I did."

"And they are?"

Maddie swallowed. Now came the tricky part. She wanted to tell Jake the truth, just not all of it. "There's another group that's after you," she said. "Colton did what he did to make them believe you were abducted. That will buy you some additional time."

Judging by his closed off expression, Jake wasn't buying it. "After me? Why?"

Colton took over. "This group believes you might have stumbled on some classified information. They'll do anything to keep you from revealing it to anyone."

"Classified?" Now Jake frowned. "I haven't come across anything like that. Believe me, I'd know. I'm a reporter. We're good about quickly comprehending things like that."

Aware she couldn't glance at her brother, which might make Jake realize they weren't telling him the full story, Maddie kept her gaze trained on Jake. "You know that and we know that, but this group doesn't. They want to bring you in for questioning."

The ever-observant Jake picked up on her use of that particular phrase. "Are they law enforcement?" he asked.

"More like covert ops," Colton interjected. "That's why letting them nab you wouldn't have been safe. They operate outside the constraints of the law."

"Where's your evidence?"

Both Colton and Maddie froze at Jake's question.

"You'd better believe he wants evidence," Maddie said, finally looking directly at her brother. "He's a reporter."

"And as such, I need proof." Jake shook his head. "Facts, not speculation. What hard evidence do you have that this story you're telling me is true?"

"Because I'm one of them," Colton finally said,

anger flashing in his gaze. "And believe me when I tell you that you're a wanted man."

While Colton's story had holes in it large enough to drive a truck though, Jake could also see elements of truth. He understood they—and this included Maddie, which bothered him—were trying to manipulate him. For what reason? That had yet to be revealed.

"All right," Jake finally said. "Let's say I decide to believe you. I'm a wanted man. But I also know top secret government agencies don't go after someone on a hunch. They need proof. Hard data. So tell me, what do these people have on me?"

Neither Colton or Maddie responded. When Maddie reached over to take his hand, he moved away. Though hurt flashed across her mobile features, she didn't say anything. Of course not. What could she say, other than an outright lie?

"I trusted you," he told her. "The one thing I thought I could always count on was you being straight with me."

"I *am* being straight with you," she exclaimed. "There are just certain things I can't tell you."

"Sorry, that doesn't cut it. If you want me to believe any part of what you say, you've got to tell me everything."

When Maddie looked down, Jake felt like she'd just stabbed a knife into his heart.

"I can't," she whispered. "Believe me, if I could, I would. But this is the very information those others are worried you already know. If either Colton or I were to fill you in, it'd be like marking you for dead."

The pain in her voice only compounded his own. Hardening his heart, he looked from the woman he'd thought he might love, to her brother. "Are we finished here? If so, I'd like to go."

Instead of answering, Colton glowered at him. The ferocity of the stare reminded Jake a bit of a wild animal, attempting to prove dominance with only a look.

"Stop it, you two." Maddie's voice seemed to catch in her throat. With a strangled sob, she ran out of the room.

"Great," Colton groused. "Now look what you've done."

Dumbfounded at the comment, Jake strode over to the window, hoping if he stared long enough at the beautiful forest, some of his feelings of betrayal would fade. Of course, that would be wishful thinking. He wasn't sure he'd ever get over the knowledge that Maddie wasn't at all the person he'd believed her to be. That kind of hurt ran deep.

"Do you mind if I ask you a question?" Colton asked. "It's important, so I'd like you to really think about it before you answer."

Both impressed and appalled that Colton seriously believed Jake would do anything he asked, Jake didn't even acknowledge that he'd heard the other man.

However, that didn't seem to faze Colton. "What exactly is your relationship with my sister?"

Jake ignored him.

"Are you friends," Colton continued, "or more than that?" Colton came closer, even going so far as to dare to reach out and grip Jake by the shoulder.

Jake spun, knocking the other man's hand off. He felt like all of his regret, his bottled-up rage, blazed from his eyes. A warning. "None of your business," he said, his voice hard. "Whatever might have been between me and Maddie is dead now anyway."

"Aha! Now you're admitting there was something between the two of you."

"Enough." Jake wandered away from the window and sank back down on the couch. "You and your stupid games are exhausting. I just want to get out of this place and go home, back to my normal life. Back to reality."

"If you do that, I can guarantee those other guys will grab you." Colton sat down on the other end, as far away as the sofa would allow. "And what I'm asking you is important. It speaks to the things Maddie couldn't say. You see, among our kind, there are certain truths one can only admit to someone who is the one who will become our mate."

"Mate?" The change in subject only made Jake's head hurt worse. "As in soul mate?"

"That, too." Colton shrugged. "I think if you and Maddie took the time to talk about how you feel about each other—about your expectations—that might help her know what to do."

"You're not making sense." Jake dragged his hand through his hair. "None of this does."

"I get what you're saying, but I promise you, there's sound logic behind it." Leaning forward, Colton spoke earnestly. "If you care at all—even the slightest bit—for Maddie, go find her and talk to her. She's hurting right now."

Since Jake was hurting, too—though he'd be damned if he'd admit that to Colton—he pushed to his feet. "Any idea where she might have gone?"

"Yes. Out in back there's a trail that goes into the woods. Follow that to the pond. There's a small fishing dock there. When we were kids, it was always her favorite place to go when she needed to think."

Throat tight, Jake nodded. When he turned to go,

Colton called after him. "Don't you hurt my sister, understand?"

Ignoring him, Jake left the cabin, and started down the path. He had to admit, the beauty of the apparently remote area surprised him. The pine trees and tall live oaks meant they were in East Texas, a part of his state that he particularly loved.

He spotted her in the distance as soon as he rounded a curve in the path. Like her brother had said, she sat with her back to him at the end of a short wooden pier. Her legs dangled in the water and the breeze lifted strands of her long red hair. Just the sight of her had his chest feeling tight.

Everything about her…her inner and outer beauty, her kindness, her compassion. To him, she was perfect, she was everything that was good and right and true. Of course, this made her apparent betrayal that much more difficult to bear.

Though Colton had hinted there was more to the story. Of course. There always was. Jake could only hope Maddie cared enough about him to reveal her side.

"Hey," he said softly.

When she turned to face him, he saw that she'd been crying. "Hey," she replied, the despair in her voice matching the hopelessness in her eyes.

With every fiber of his being, he wished he could offer her comfort, that he could simply open his arms, pull her close, to tell her everything would be okay.

Instead, he jammed both hands into his pockets so he wouldn't touch her and walked out to the end of the pier. "Mind if I join you?"

"I'm not sure," she answered. "What do you want?"

Fresh hurt stabbed him. "Maddie, when did we become so adversarial?"

"When you started pushing for answers I couldn't

give," she cried out. "All I've done is try to protect you. And right now, I'm not even sure why. You've made it clear you value getting a story more than anything else. More than…me." She turned her back to him, her shaking shoulders evidence of her silently crying.

He stood, frozen, while an awful certainty filled him.

"Maddie, whatever you've gotten yourself mixed up in, let me help you. Not for a story, but because I genuinely care about you. I can't protect you if I have no idea what the danger is or where it's coming from."

"You want to *protect* me?" She made a sound, some sort of awful cross between a laugh and a sob. "The best way to protect me would be to let Colton help you stay safe."

Before he could respond, a sound behind him made him turn. Colton came jogging up. He stopped when he reached Jake and he motioned to Maddie to come closer.

To Jake's surprise and annoyance, she pushed to her feet and joined her brother.

"What's up?" she asked.

"I've got news," Colton answered, excitement ringing in his voice. "Rick's unit is already on the move. They're going in and attempting a rescue."

Maddie gaped at him. "But wouldn't that be going against the chain of command?"

"And their own orders?" Jake interjected. "What gives?"

"They stick together, the guy I spoke to said. No man left behind and all that. No way do they plan to let the Protectors make Rick some sort of sacrificial lamb."

"Protectors?" Jake asked. "What do you mean?"

Maddie and Colton exchanged a quick look.

"That's the name of their unit," Colton responded.

Jake wasn't sure how, but he knew the other man was lying.

Again.

"What about the virus?" Maddie rubbed her hands together as if she was cold. "Any news on any front on progress in developing an antidote or a preventative vaccine?"

"No. I can only assume they're still working on it."

Still stewing over the way both Maddie and her brother felt compelled to exclude him, Jake cleared his throat. "Hey, if they're Protectors, how about you ask them to protect me?"

Though the question made sense to him, clearly it didn't to the other two. Maddie appeared horrified, while Colton tried hard not to laugh.

"That's the thing," Maddie said. "Unfortunately, the Protectors are actually the ones who want to harm you."

Judging from the sharp look Colton sent her, she'd said too much. Maybe she had, but once again, Jake didn't understand the subtext.

He waited to see if she—or Colton—would elaborate, but of course neither did.

"Whatever," he said. "Since we seem to be at a bit of a stalemate, I'd like to be heading back to Galveston now. If one of you wouldn't mind dropping me off in town at the bus station, I'm sure I can get myself home."

"Bus station?" Colton spoke in a tone of utter disbelief. "There's no bus station within fifty miles of here."

"You can't go back now," Maddie added, her voice slow and measured. "There's no telling what they'll do to you if they bring you in now."

"I'll take my chances." He looked from one to the other. When neither of them spoke again, he sighed. "Fine. Then point me in the direction of civilization and I'll walk."

"I'm sorry, Jake." Colton stepped in front of him. "Maybe we weren't clear. You're not going anywhere."

"Step away from me," Jake ordered. "I'm not tied up, so if you plan to stop me, it's going to get physical." He moved to go around Colton, but the other man grabbed him.

Jake shoved. Hard. Clearly, Colton wasn't expecting this. Jake wrenched himself free and shouldered the other man, hitting him hard in the gut. Colton staggered backward, trying to regain his balance, but couldn't. Off the edge of the dock he went, hitting the murky water with a huge splash.

Though he wanted to laugh, Jake knew better. Instead, he dusted his hands off on the front of his jeans, and took off at a jog toward the gravel road.

Except he hadn't counted on Maddie. She moved so fast he barely had time to evade her. Launching herself at him, she tried vainly to knock him to the ground.

He spun and the second time, he caught her, pinning her arms to her sides. "Settle down," he ordered.

Eyes spitting green fire, she continued to struggle. Just long enough for Colton to come up behind him and clock him under the chin.

When he came to, his hands and feet were bound. They'd left him lying on the ground, with Maddie— the traitor—watching over him.

"He's awake," she called out, and Colton came into his view.

"Help me help him up," Colton ordered. When they had him standing, Colton informed him they were going to march him back to the house. "Don't try yelling," he said. "There's no one else up here now, so no one will hear you."

Ignoring the other man, Jake looked at Maddie. Despite the pain in his pounding head, his heart hurt more.

"Don't do this, Maddie," he implored. "I've done nothing to warrant being treated this way."

She swallowed. "I know it might not seem like it, but it's for your own good. This is the only way we can keep you safe."

Drawing himself up, he shook his head, which sent bolts of pain through his jaw and head, making him wince. "Let me make this clear. If you don't help me get free, I'm done. I want nothing further to do with you, ever. Understand?"

Eyes dark with emotion, she gave a slow nod. "If that's the price I have to pay to save your life, then yes."

Chapter 18

Though she might have wished for less masculine posturing between the two men, Carmen couldn't help but thrill at Rick's refusal to clue Scott in on whatever had just happened with the intruders. She wasn't sure she still trusted the other biologist, and apparently Rick felt the same way. The fact that Scott had lied about his qualifications still pissed her off. Though no doubt he had his own reasons, the seriousness of this task left no room for anyone to fall short.

Another time, she might have stewed about his ignorant delusions. Not now. She knew she couldn't let anything distract her. Not this time, not when she was so close to obtaining an analysis and identifying the exact biological makeup of the virus.

Excitement thrummed through her. Sure, no doubt the CDC had felt the exact same way, and those biologists were just as qualified as she was. But something—call it gut instinct or woman's intuition—told her she was right on the edge of a major breakthrough. If she could just keep Scott out of her way while she worked. Judging by the bumbling way he fumbled around the lab, it would only be a matter of time until he made a costly error.

No one could afford the luxury of cleaning up a catastrophic mistake. Due to the urgency of the task, they would be working fast, which carried another form of risk. While vaccine development was usually a long and complex process, the world didn't have the luxury of waiting ten to fifteen years.

Later, when all of this was over, she planned to have a long talk with Scott about the importance of being honest about one's credentials. Right now, since she didn't have time, she had to get right to work and see what she could discover. Anticipation raced through her body as she set her tools out and prepared to begin.

Even though she knew the CDC would have followed these same steps, she began her exploratory stage. She needed to go through the hopefully weakened virus particles. By having Ted's corpse, she had already been able to skip a step—the one in which she'd use cultures to identify the cellular response to the virus in humans.

She planned to develop numerous candidate vaccines, since she knew most of them wouldn't produce the needed immune response. Once again, in a noncrisis situation, this process usually took one to two years.

In this part of the experiment, she intended to act in as close to a nonscientific manner as she could. While still following protocol, she planned to develop all kinds of radical combinations and hope one of them worked. More like gambling than true science, but desperate times called for desperate measures. All she could do was work hard and hope the metaphorical lightning would strike. Not her usual painstaking and methodical way of working, but she knew she'd have to be bold if she wanted results.

At least she trusted Rick to keep them safe.

As if he'd read her thoughts, Rick stepped into the antechamber and once again went through the brief cleansing process. Though Carmen continued working, she remained überconscious of him, almost as if she was tracking his every movement.

Not good. No distractions. As he entered the actual lab, she looked up to tell him exactly that. Before she could, he crumpled to the floor in midstep, his bulky protective gear settling around him in a puff of inflatable padding.

"Rick?" Putting aside the sample she'd been working on, she rushed to him. She rolled him over so she could see him. Stunned, she gasped. What she saw horrified her.

Sores had begun blooming all over Rick's handsome face. Even under the headgear that was supposed to have kept him safe.

Which meant something had happened to his suit. Frantic now, she managed to unclip his headpiece and remove it. When she did, he managed to open his eyes.

"What happened?" he croaked. "I feel like I've been hit by a freight train."

While she tried to formulate an answer, a tear sneaked out of her eye and streamed down her cheek.

Seeing this, he cursed. "The virus?"

Slowly she nodded.

"How?" He licked his cracked lips. "I thought this outfit was supposed to protect against infection."

"It is," she answered, watching as more and more sores appeared on his skin, right before her eyes. Brushing away her pointless and useless tears, she leaned down close, putting her mouth near his ear. "I promise you, I won't let you die. I'm going to continue to work on figuring out an antidote and vaccine. But if I don't find it in time, I'll bite you and kill you that way." And hopefully, that first death would end the virus. When he reawakened as a Vampire, it wasn't illogical to assume that he'd be invulnerable, as well.

But right now, Rick's condition rapidly worsened. He was dying right before her eyes.

"No. Not even as a last resort," he managed, even as blood vessels burst and turned the whites of his eyes red. "I'd rather die than join the undead. Develop the antidote and save me. Save the world." The last word trailed off into a gurgle as he slumped over again, unconscious.

Muttering a string of curses in a language that had been long forgotten, she eased him into what she hoped was a comfortable position and climbed back to her feet.

When she looked over at Scott, she realized the other man had been watching them intently. "What?" she asked, confident he hadn't been able to hear what she'd said to Rick.

"He looks bad," Scott said, shrugging. "I'm thinking it won't be long until he's in as bad shape as the first guy." To her annoyance, he sounded surprisingly comfortable with the turn of events. Of course, why wouldn't he, since clearly his protective suit still did its job?

"I think he's going to die really quickly," Scott continued.

Carmen lurched toward him, as quickly as she could in the bulky suit. "So help me, if I find out you're the one who sliced his protective gear, I'll ram this virus down your throat. Was it you?"

Scott blanched, taking a step back. "Of course not,"

he protested, stumbling over the words. "I'd never do a thing like that. Are you certain it was cut?"

"I didn't take the time to look." She kept her voice cold. "We don't have that luxury. I'm going to get back to work immediately. I'll need you to stay out of my way. Understood?"

"Crystal clear," he replied, nodding. And then he, too went down, hitting the cement floor hard. Hopefully, his suit helped cushion the blow, though judging from the sharp crack she heard, his facemask most likely had been compromised.

Which clearly no longer mattered. Cursing the cumbersome gear, she rolled Scott over. Huge sores had also begun to erupt on his face, which meant someone had sabotaged his suit, too. A spidery web of lines showed she'd been right about the facemask.

If both men's suits had been compromised, most likely hers had been, too. However, she had one advantage here that the saboteur knew nothing about. The virus couldn't touch her. In fact, she saw no need to continue to wear the cumbersome protective suit.

"Screw this," she muttered, removing her own headgear and gloves. She quickly stepped out of the rest of her gear, aware that whoever had messed with them had no idea she would be invulnerable.

She didn't care. None of that was important. What mattered now was the need to save Rick's life. And Scott's, too, after Rick's.

Rick groaned, a tortured sound. Judging by the rapid progression of this virus, she had less than six hours to either come up with an antidote or she'd have to bite him and turn him into a Vampire to keep him from dying on her.

Despite Rick's request that she not do that, she wasn't about to lose him. She'd do whatever she had to in order to keep him alive, even bite and turn him. Hell, even that possible solution had an uncertain outcome. While Vampires were impervious to the effects of the virus, she wasn't sure that would still apply to someone who had been infected before becoming a Vamp. She hoped she wouldn't have to actually find out.

She had to come up with the antidote. While wanting to save the world was altruistic and noble, saving Rick hit much closer to home.

Working at near Vampiric speed, she examined slides, worked calculations, tested and did it all again. And again and again, refusing to let her rising frustration deter her.

While both Rick and Scott lay on the floor nearby, the virus continuing to destroy their bodies.

One hour passed, or maybe two. Hell, it might just as easily have been three or four, for all she knew. Time flowed in a continuous stream of awareness, and while she knew she was working against a ticking clock, she couldn't allow that knowledge to throw her off her game. Scientific fact had little room for improvisation, but she'd learned long ago to trust her gut and go with her instincts. Sometimes a move that might at first seem illogical turned out to be the exact detour that had needed to be taken.

Testing. Nope. Move on to the next. And again, not the response she'd been hoping for, or needed. Every now and then, she'd leave her work area to check on the two downed men. The virus continued to spread with alarming speed, but they were both still breathing.

Aware they wouldn't be for much longer if she continued to fail, she renewed her efforts, increasing her speed. Though Rick's supposed friends remained outside, ostensibly guarding the lab, she was glad they didn't look in on her. If they did, they'd only see a crazed woman working so fast she appeared as a blur.

Though supremely focused, fear of losing Rick guided her every movement. She couldn't lose him. Not now, not ever. If she could save him, she could save the entire world.

Growing more and more desperate as each test failed, she tried to take an objective step back in her mind. She was missing some common denominator, but what? Though she racked her brain, she couldn't hit it. Again, she tried. Again. And again.

While meanwhile the virus continued to devour the bodies of the two men on the floor. Time was running out.

"Hey!" One of the new men, Rick's friend, entered the antechamber and peered at her through the glass wall. "What's going on in there? Why is Rick on the floor? What did you do to him?"

"Stay back," she ordered. "Someone sabotaged their suits and they were infected with the virus. No one is to come anywhere near this lab. Understand?"

Instead of recoiling in horror, he didn't move. "Why are you not wearing your protective gear? Are you infected, too?"

"Whoever messed with the suits probably ruined all of them," she explained. "I work faster without it, so I went ahead and took it off."

His eyes widened. "That's a huge risk to take."

"Maybe." Letting her impatience show, she returned to her microscope, viewed the next slide and entered the data into a computer program. "I don't have time to chat."

When she looked up again, he'd gone.

After running through all her slides, she returned to poor Ted's decomposed body and extracted another round of samples. As time had passed, what had once been flesh and bone now resembled a soupy sea of organisms. It horrified her to realize if she didn't make some sort of breakthrough soon, Rick and Scott would look like this.

They were running out of time. Once more she ran her tests, hoping, just once, for a change in variables. But she found nothing. Learned nothing. This had become beyond frustrating. She wanted to throw the vial against the wall and watch it shatter.

Of course she didn't. Vexing, true. But she wouldn't consider a total failure. She couldn't. Not yet.

Another glance down at Rick. Neither he nor Scott had moved at all. She hurried over, horrified at how quickly the sores had spread. This thing was brutally quick.

Rick's eyes opened and he gasped for air. She forced herself to turn away and ran one more round of tests, fingers flying as she entered the data into the computer.

The tightness in her own chest made it difficult to breathe. She couldn't lose him. Not after waiting so many centuries to find someone like him. She'd waited so long to find…love.

Love. Of course. If all the poets and singers were correct, the magic of love would prevail. The antidote would be found, the vaccine developed, and the world would be saved.

Carmen, however, knew better. She'd lived through the Black Plague. Seen the death and destruction of religious purges, more disease, and murder and mayhem. There'd been love then, too, for others rather than her, and still they'd died by the thousands.

She would not let Rick die.

Decision made, she left the computer running the last batch of calculations and hurried over to Rick.

Dropping to her knees, she found a spot on his neck still untouched by sores. Pressing her mouth against his skin, she felt her fangs elongate. With a quick, savage motion, she pushed them into him, piercing the vein, and began drinking his blood. She hoped she hadn't waited too late.

He went rigid, then let out a slow sigh. As he relaxed into her deadly embrace and the metallic taste of his beloved blood filled her mouth, she nearly swooned.

This was the point where she normally would stop. Right before the heart stopped beating, so the human would wake in the morning slightly weak and confused, with no memory or idea what had happened.

For Rick, she'd take this all the way. Even though she hadn't made another Vampire in well over one hundred years, this wasn't the kind of thing one forgot. This was, however, the first time she'd made a Vampire because of love.

Dimly she heard the computer chime. A moment later, it chimed again. Carmen froze, slowly releasing Rick. That particular sound meant a successful combination had been reached. She'd entered the variables and let the program run the tests. Success? Setting Rick gently on the floor, she hurried over and peered at the screen.

There. Flashing bright red. A possible antidote, which meant a plausible prototype for a vaccine.

She could make a syringe of this in minutes. Did she even have minutes? Glancing at Rick, she let her fangs retract while she tried to decide what to do. Should she risk it, knowing the antidote might fail to save him? Or continue making him a Vampire, even though he'd expressly asked her not to?

Pleasure mingled with pain as he relaxed into a gentle yet fierce embrace. Was he dreaming? Whose arms held him? He tried to find a scent, but couldn't. Carmen? Or was there someone else, a doctor, a nurse? Was he still in the lab or had he been moved? He had no idea. Hell, he didn't even know what day it was.

Then he floated. Straight up off the floor and out of his body. He'd heard of such things happening, right in the hour of death. Was he dying, then? He'd been sick, he remembered. That hellish virus. The last thing he'd seen had been Carmen feverishly working to find a cure. Had she? If anyone could save the world, he'd be betting she could.

If she had, then why had he died? He couldn't see Carmen allowing that to happen. She was a warrior Vampire, that woman. No way would she let him die, not on her watch.

Maybe he wasn't dead. Experimenting, he inhaled. The instant he did, he was no longer floating and he slammed right back into his body. With that came horrible, pulsing hurt. Fever and the awful, horrible knowledge that the virus was busy eating away at his body.

Nope. Definitely not dead.

Then where... Listening, he heard nothing. No sound, not even the steady beat of his heart that he'd always taken for granted. If he didn't have a heartbeat, that would mean Carmen had turned him into a Vampire. Even though he'd expressly asked her not to.

Pain knifed through him. Did Vampires suffer as their human body died and they became undead? He'd never thought to question, hadn't cared enough to wonder. While he knew he should be furious, he couldn't seem to summon up enough strength for even anger.

Some kind of internal struggle seemed to be going on inside his body. Either the virus was dying or he was—and he couldn't be sure which.

"Rick." Carmen's voice. Pleading. "Rick, can you open your eyes?"

He tried, oh he tried, but the lids felt stuck together and he couldn't manage to fight his way through the murk.

"Can't," he managed to say, though most likely the word came out garbled. "What's happening to me?"

Silence. He figured she probably couldn't understand him. He didn't blame her. His tongue wasn't working right. "Help."

That word rang clear as a bell.

"Sit tight," Carmen replied. "I've figured out a potential antidote and made a small test batch. You're going to be my lab rat. I just injected you with it."

Which meant she hadn't made him a Vampire. Relieved, he tried to nod again, failed. Instead, he succeeded only in drifting back to sleep.

The next thing he knew, he snapped open his eyes, squinting at the bright light shining at him.

"There you are," Carmen said, almost chirping. "I've been monitoring your progress and I'm 99 percent sure the antidote worked. I've already put a call in to the CDC. However, no one there would even talk to me, so your friend who's helping guard the place is pulling a few strings. We need to get this stuff processed in huge batches, and for that we need their help."

Confused, he blinked, finally closing his eyes to protect them from the glare.

"Oh, sorry," Carmen said, and moved some sort of lamp she'd had shining at his face. "I used that so I could chart the progress of the sores as they receded."

He turned his head slightly and saw Scott lying prone nearby. Carmen followed the direction of his gaze and nodded. "Yes, I gave him a shot, too. After I was sure yours was working. He hasn't come awake yet. I think yours happened more quickly because I..." She looked down, before resolutely raising her chin and meeting his eyes. "I bit you."

"I thought you did," he managed, still struggling to push out the words. "For a moment there, I felt myself dying."

She grimaced, though she appeared unashamed. "I came really close to changing you so I could save your life. The computer pinging to let me know I'd finally found a successful calculation was the only thing that stopped me."

He tried to smile, but knew it probably appeared more like a grimace.

Apparently, she did, too, judging by the stricken look on her face. "I'm sorry, okay? I know you said not to, but I just couldn't let you die. I...care too much about you to do that."

A wave of warmth flooded him, giving him just enough strength to push up onto his elbows. He tried to search his muddled mind for just the right words, aware he needed to tell her how he felt, but instead exhaustion slipped back over him. He lay back, let his eyes drift closed and went off once again to oblivion.

Time passed. How much time exactly, he wasn't sure. When he next opened his eyes, the third reawakening, he felt as if he'd been reborn. Energy surged through him, enabling him to push to his feet. He turned slowly, stunned to realize he was still in the lab. Scott remained motionless on the floor near him. A quick glance revealed the other man hadn't survived the virus. Evidently, the antidote had been given too late to save him.

"Carmen?" Rick called, puzzling over the realization that she wasn't there. He tried again, louder. "Carmen? Where are you?"

Nothing but silence. Okay. Maybe she'd gone to the CDC with her antidote. That was the only reason she'd leave.

"Pete?" he hollered next, knowing his teammate had to be still standing guard. "Pete, I need some help in here."

Still nothing. It felt...eerie. Unsettling and worrisome. Something was wrong. He knew his team. None of those men would ever willingly abandon their post.

Then where were they?

He rushed to the door, amazed at how good he felt. Strong, alert, capable. As if he hadn't nearly died from a horrible virus. He exited the lab, quickly searching the barn. Other than shadows and dust, he saw nothing.

Outside, the compound appeared deserted. Moving carefully, wishing he had a weapon, he searched the house first, noting that Pete and the team had moved the bodies of the Sons of Darkness. Most likely, they'd been buried. Or burned, if burial wasn't an option.

But where the hell was everyone? When he realized all the vehicles were gone, he swore loudly. He cursed even more when he finally saw the warning signs that had been posted all around the property.

"Warning! Deadly Plague Contaminated area. Stay away. Entrance will result in death."

Who had done this? What had happened to Pete and the rest of the team? Rick knew his guys wouldn't have left willingly, even with the threat of a virus.

He thought back. The last he'd heard, Carmen had been trying desperately to reach the CDC. Had she succeeded and if so, had her phone call triggered some sort of crazy reaction? As in, a small army had been dispatched to bring everyone in?

Or had the situation been even worse? Had Carmen's call actually alerted the real terrorists, the ones who'd pushed so hard for a war in West Latvia, finally unleashing a deadly virus that nearly decimated the population?

Since Carmen had developed an antidote and a vaccine, that made her existence extremely problematic for anyone who didn't want the virus stopped. The fact that her findings were priceless would be their sole reason for keeping her alive. Of course, they had no way to know there were only one way to kill her—a stake through the heart. He knew Carmen would be careful not to turn over her findings to anyone but the CDC.

With no vehicle, he had no way to go looking for her. So he did what he had to do. He put in a call to the only other Protector besides his team that he trusted. Colton Kinslow, Maddie's brother.

When he learned Jake and Maddie were with Colton, Rick felt relieved. If anyone could successfully locate Carmen and the precious antibodies, those three could. Especially—and surprisingly—Jake. Rick had spent some time looking up the journalist and he'd come to realize the other man had great instincts. He couldn't have been as successful as he was without them.

Together, they all made a great team. And together, they'd find their missing fifth, plus Pete and the guys. Rick was betting on it.

Chapter 19

The hard fury in Jake's eyes as he gazed at her damn near broke Maddie's heart. "It's for the best," she whispered, almost under her breath. So low, she couldn't be sure Jake heard.

But her brother did. Colton grimaced and shook his head. "You're right. It is all for the best," he said. "You know that, even if he doesn't. Better to keep him alive, even if he hates you for it."

Though *hate* was a pretty strong word, she considered it an accurate depiction of Jake's feelings toward her right now. Ignoring her brother, she crouched down near the man she loved. "I'm sorry," she told him. "If there was any other way to keep you safe, I'd take it."

"You're full of it," he responded, glaring at her. "You and him. I don't know what you're up to, but now I'm positive it isn't good. And I'm willing to bet whatever it is ties in to the door in the alleyway back in Galveston. Whatever illegal activity you're involved in, you should be aware that it will eventually come to light. No matter if I'm the one to expose it or someone else."

"Illegal activity?" Colton interjected, incredulous. "What makes you think that?"

"Ha." Jake spat the word. "Think about what you just said, man. Really think about it."

"Jake," Maddie began.

"No." Now he wouldn't even look at her. "I have nothing left to speak to you about. You or your crazy brother, with your secrets and lies. Everything bad that's happened to me since I found that damn door that won't open, is tied to you. Don't bother to deny it." He lifted his chin. "I'm a great journalist and I trust my gut. Every instinct I possess is screaming that you're lying."

"Lying?" Colton snorted. "More like omitting what you don't need to know."

"Same thing." Jake's hard tone matched his unyielding expression. "Just cut the BS. I know I'm right. All of this is related somehow. And once I get away from you two, I'm warning you, I'm not giving up until I find out what it is."

Colton shot Maddie a meaningful look. She ignored him, focusing all her attention on Jake. When Jake met her gaze, he didn't look away, and she swore she could see the tiniest bit of softening in his eyes.

Or perhaps that was wishful thinking.

"Well, Maddie?" he demanded. "Tell me I'm wrong."

"You're not wrong," she replied, her voice soft. "It does all tie together. Everything."

At her words, he swallowed. His jaw hardened. "Is there really a deadly virus? Or was that a cover for more unlawful activity by Carmen and Rick?"

Before Maddie could even respond, Colton laughed. "Come on. You watched the news. You saw what's happening over in West Latvia. I know you think we're trying to pull the wool over your eyes—for whatever reason—but come on."

Still focused on Maddie, Jake ignored him.

She dragged her gaze away from him to look at her brother. "Colton, Jake and I need some privacy. Will you give it to us, please?"

Her brother started to protest, but she silenced him with a quick glance. Grumbling under his breath, Colton left the room, slamming the door behind him.

"It's time I tell you something," she said. "No, not just something. Everything. Beginning with this. I love you."

Though his gaze softened, Jake didn't reply in kind. She squashed her disappointment, reminding herself that she couldn't blame him right now. He didn't even know if he could trust her.

Nothing ventured, nothing gained. She had no choice but to go all or nothing. If he didn't feel the same way, she'd have to walk away.

Except she knew, deep down inside her, that Jake cared for her as much as she did him.

"Jake?" she prompted. "I know this is pushy, and I'm aware you're mad, but I need to know how you feel about me?"

"Why?" he shot back. "So you can use my feelings against me? No thanks."

"Do you really think I would do that?" She didn't bother to hide her hurt.

"I have no idea, Maddie. The way you've been acting since your brother ran into me and kidnapped me makes me wonder if I really know you at all. You tell me."

She pushed to her feet and paced, trying to find just the right words. When she turned to face him, she hoped she could somehow make him understand.

"I know there's been a lot of craziness going on," she said. "And that's an understatement. But we have laws. I can't tell you everything without knowing how you feel about me." Actually, Pack law forbade her revealing her true nature without being in a committed relationship—engaged or married—though she was willing to stretch the boundaries just a little. After all he'd been through, Jake deserved at least that.

"We?" His harsh voice matched his rigid profile. "Who is we, exactly?"

"My kind," she answered. "We're not like everyone else." Her heart began to race. She was too close to dangerous territory. *Forbidden* territory. Unless they were a committed couple, she could face serious consequences if she said any more.

As if he sensed this, Jake raised his face to hers. Their gazes locked. Maddie's heart skipped a beat as anticipation zinged in her veins.

"We've got a situation," Colton yelled, slamming back into the room. "I just talked to Rick. Carmen developed an antidote and a vaccine for the virus, but she's disappeared. Along with Rick's entire team of Protectors."

Maddie's nervous euphoria vanished. "Where is he?"

"At the compound of that fringe group that initially tried to barter the virus."

"Do we need to go pick him up?" she asked. "And does he have any idea where Carmen might be?"

"Yes and no." Colton grimaced. "He says all the vehicles are either missing or disabled. Short of hitchhiking, he has no method of transportation. We need to head that way now."

"Okay." Maddie jumped to her feet. "Let's get going."

"Take me with you," Jake ordered. "There's no way you're leaving me out of something like this."

Colton eyed him. Then he slowly nodded. "He's right," he told Maddie. "Did the two of you have time to have your little talk?"

"No." She didn't bother to hide her disappointment. "We didn't. But there's plenty of time on the drive south, if I can get you to put your earbuds in and listen to music. We'll use my car. I have satellite radio and Bluetooth."

Colton gave a slow nod, looking from her to Jake and back again. "I was going to congratulate you, but I think I'll just wish you good luck instead."

Since the closed-off expression had returned to Jake's handsome face, she understood exactly what he meant. "I'll take it," she said. "And thanks."

"Ahem." Jake cleared his throat as he held up his bound hands. "Are you going to untie me?"

"Not until we have your word you won't try to escape," Colton replied.

"My word?" Now Jake mocked him. "How do you know whether or not my word's worth anything?"

Colton's response came quickly, direct and to the point. "Because I know my sister. She wouldn't have fallen in love with a man who didn't have integrity."

Touched, Maddie patted her brother on the shoulder. "Thank, Colt."

He smiled down at her. "You're welcome, sis."

"If you two are done heaping praise on each other, I'd like to get going," Jake interjected. "And cut the crap about being in love with me," he told Maddie. "I know better."

His words made Colton's smile vanish. "Get in the car," he ordered. "Before I say something I might regret."

"Go ahead." Jake didn't back down. "The two of you are nuts. This all is beginning to feel like a very bad dream."

Despite everything, hurt stabbed Maddie. Deep. Somehow, she managed to lift her chin and meet Jake's eyes. "Are you going to give us your word or not?"

Though he swallowed, he finally nodded. "You have my word. I won't try to escape."

Immediately, Colton cut Jake's bonds. "Perfect. Let's get on the road."

Without another word, Jake marched to the car and got into the back seat. Maddie sighed. "This is going to be more difficult than I thought."

"Yeah, I'd say so." Grimacing, Colton shook his head. "Injured male pride is hard to work around. But I have faith in you, baby sister. If anyone can do it, you can."

"Thanks." After several deep, calming breaths, she walked over to the car and got in on the opposite side from where Jake sat. Colton climbed in the front seat and she handed him her keys. He started the engine, put in some earbuds and synced them with the radio, put the car in Drive, and they were off.

Next to her, Jake sat in stony silence. Mentally, she rehearsed and discarded several different ways to get him to open up. Finally, she realized she'd need to go with her gut instinct and speak from her heart.

"Jake," she began. "You know me."

He didn't respond at first. When he finally swung his head around to look at her, the mingled anger and pain in his chocolate eyes made her entire chest ache.

"Do I?" he asked. "I'm beginning to wonder about that. Ever since the day we first met, you've done nothing but hide the truth from me. The door in the alley, the secret club, the virus, this group of people you called the Protectors. I have no idea what's actually going on, though clearly you and your crazy brother do. You say you want to tell me, but then it's like you need a declaration of love from me first. Have I gotten this right?"

Slowly she nodded.

"That's what I thought. No way, Maddie. I refuse to allow you to use my feelings like that. I'm not bargaining with you, telling you that I love you, just to finally get the truth. That's wrong. All kinds of wrong."

Though she hated her desperation, she seized on his words. "What exactly are your feelings toward me, Jake? Can you at least tell me that?"

His jaw tightened. "Why does that even matter now, Maddie? Can you tell me that?"

When she didn't immediately answer, he nodded. "That's what I thought. I don't appreciate being used and treated like a prisoner. That's all you and your brother have done since he rammed me with his truck. It doesn't matter how I feel about you or you about me. Love can never flourish in an atmosphere of distrust and lies. Surely you can see that."

As his words sank in, she realized he was right. Had the situation been reversed, she would have felt exactly the same way he did. Quite possibly worse.

Now she owed him the truth. Even if it meant breaking Pack law, even if that meant she could face the ultimate punishment—reprogramming or...death.

Of course, if Colton knew, he'd try to stop her. She glanced his way. Earbuds in, he appeared to be intent on the road.

"Jake," she said quietly, leaning toward him. "Say something awful about my brother. I need to see if he responds, so I can make sure he's not secretly listening. I'm going to tell you the truth about everything."

Though Jake narrowed his eyes, clearly skeptical,

he finally lifted his chin and looked directly at Colton. "Your brother is a fool," he said. "A weak and ineffective liar. The only way he can accomplish anything is with tricks and unnecessary violence." His voice carried the ring of someone who believed he spoke the truth.

Colton didn't even turn around.

"Perfect," she murmured. "I'm going to start with what's behind that door at the end of the alleyway. It's a bar called Broken Chains, and the only ones allowed admittance are nonhumans."

"Nonhumans?" he repeated, frowning. "What are you going to tell me next, that you people are aliens or something?"

His comment made her smile, just the tiniest bit. "No. Actually, it's a bit more incredible than that. By Nonhumans, I mean beings like me and my brother. Broken Chains is a bar for Shape-shifters, Vampires and Merfolk."

Judging from the way he eyed her, he wasn't sure if she'd lost her mind or was seriously trying to pull his leg. Either way, she could tell he didn't believe her.

"Okay, I'll play along," he said, his tone sharp and cutting. "Which are you, then? Because you sure look like a human woman to me."

"I'm a Shape-shifter," she told him. "In the old days, people called us werewolves. I can change and become a wolf, and later change back to human. If we weren't in the car, I'd show you. Oh, and telling a human this without a promise of lifelong commitment is forbidden. In some cases, the punishment is death."

Though part of him privately considered the likely possibility Maddie had lost her mind, Jake also wanted to see how far she'd go with this. And—truth be told—

werewolves would explain the man he'd seen become a huge wolf that night outside the alley. Improbable, true. But technically not impossible.

"That's why those men attacked you," Maddie continued. "Humans aren't allowed anywhere near Broken Chains. It's our refuge, our recreational safe haven."

Not sure how to respond, he settled for simply nodding. One thing he'd learned in gathering information over the years was not to discount people with the most improbable tales. Sometimes the stories they told contained more than a nugget of truth.

But when Maddie proceeded to say Carmen was a Vampire while Rick was another Shape-shifter, he had to wonder if this time would be the exception to the rule.

Over the next several minutes, the things she said got even wilder. She spoke of a large governing body of Shape-shifters called the Pack. They were set up in councils, ranging from regional, to state, to country. And they were all over the world, in every country. Which would mean, if her statements were true, that there were a lot of freaking Shape-shifters in existence.

Though he had no choice but to take everything she said with a grain of salt, he continued to listen carefully. After all, until all this craziness had happened, he'd believed he loved her. Deep down, underneath the hurt and the incredulous realization that she truly believed every word she said, he still did.

More the fool, he. What he didn't understand was the *why*. People always had a reason for their actions, and while perhaps hers might be based on this fantastical world of hers she'd created, surely her brother didn't share in her delusions? That must have been why she didn't want him listening in to this conversation.

Except Colton had made a few comments earlier

that might be construed to indicate he knew exactly what Maddie was going to say. Jake filed that away to examine later. In the meantime, he continued to listen intently.

"Hey, you two," Colton said, removing one of his earbuds. "ETA is in about half an hour. The compound is a lot closer to the old cabin than I'd originally realized."

Wearing a distracted expression, Maddie nodded. "Okay. We're still not done back here."

Though he grimaced, Colton replaced his earbud and returned to listening to music.

Next, Maddie turned to face Jake. "You don't believe me, do you?"

While he hesitated to call her an outright liar, the fact that she even had to ask the question meant she understood on some level how bizarre her story sounded. "It's a lot to take in," he finally said. "But you haven't told me yet about these Protectors you and Colton are trying to keep me safe from."

"They're Pack Protectors, who carry the sacred duty of keeping the Pack safe. They were formed during the Dark Ages, when several of our people reached out to humans, hoping to form an alliance. Instead, they were hunted down like feral animals. The Pack had to do something to keep humans from eradicating our existence. Those first Pack Protectors were the ones who made sure humans believed anything they heard about people becoming wolves was a myth."

He nodded. "That makes sense." Assuming, of course, that he treated everything she said as if it was the truth. For now, he'd simply continue to try to keep an open mind.

"Over the years," she continued, "the Pack Protector organization evolved. Laws were created—and revealing ourselves to humans was forbidden. Telling the wrong person could endanger our entire species. Anything and anyone who was perceived as a threat was taken into custody. They are either eradicated or..." she shuddered "...reprogrammed."

Now he understood where she was going with this. "And they think I'm a threat."

"Exactly." She appeared relieved. "Colton knew I cared about you, so he stepped in and grabbed you before they could."

"I see." For such an illogical premise, it all made a weird kind of sense.

"And since he's a Protector, too," she continued, "he's put his own life at risk by helping us."

Us. A chill skittered up his spine. If what she said was true, she'd definitely broken her own laws, which she'd said were punishable by death.

"You shouldn't have told me any of this," he said. "I couldn't live with myself if anything happened to you because of me."

Her eyes widened. "Does that mean you believe me?"

Because he still couldn't bring himself to flat-out discredit her fantasy—and also because no matter what logic told him, part of it resonated with truth—he shrugged. "I'm still withholding judgment. But if it does turn out to be true, according to what you've said, you have put yourself in danger by telling me any of this."

She searched his face. "I know," she said simply. "That's why I asked you how you felt about me. Because there's that exception to the law. Those in a committed relationship are allowed to reveal the truth."

"But what happens if the human part of the equation changes his or her mind?" he asked, genuinely curious despite his skepticism. "I mean, say a man asks a woman to marry him and she accepts, but once she reveals that she's a werewolf, he backs out. What happens then?"

Maddie froze, her eyes wide. "Are you asking because that's what you want to do? Run away now that you know what I am?"

He could only give her the truth. She deserved that.

"Maddie, I care for you. But all of this—what's happened, what you're telling me—is making it difficult. Can you see that?"

Her eyes mirrored the moment when she realized what his gentle words meant. "You don't believe me," she said, her tone flat. Then, without waiting for an answer, she shook her head. "I guess I'll just have to show you. Not right this instant, but soon."

She didn't speak again for the rest of the drive.

Finally, they left the highway and turned down a paved two-lane road. After a series of turns, they ended up on a gravel road flanked by tall pine trees.

"We're almost there," Colton said, removing his ear buds and glancing curiously at them in the rearview mirror. "Did you two work everything out?"

"Not even close." The trace of bitterness in Maddie's soft voice surprised Jake.

"Bummer." Colton didn't sound too concerned.

"But we'll have it straightened out soon," Maddie continued, still refusing to look at Jake.

One more turn, this time onto a drive marked Private.

"There he is." Colton pointed. Rick stood on the porch of a long, narrow farmhouse, waving. Colton pulled the car up and Rick got in the front.

"Thanks for coming out here," he said, turning to eye Jake and Maddie in the back seat. "Judging from your expressions, you think someone died. What's going on?"

"Nothing," Colton said, at the exact same time as Maddie chimed in with, "I'm telling Jake the truth."

"Maddie," her brother hissed. "You know Rick's a Protector."

"So are you," she shot back. "So what?"

Colton groaned.

Rick looked from one to the other, his brow furrowed. "Jake, are you and Maddie in a committed relationship?"

Taking a deep breath, Jake ignored the stricken expression Maddie wore and the worry in Colton's eyes. He thought about all Maddie had told him, the risk she claimed to have taken, and how empty his life would be without her. Even if she had some sort of mental health issues, he knew he'd help her work through them. Because she was worth it.

"Yes," he said clearly. "We are."

Though tears brimmed in Maddie's beautiful eyes, she held herself together.

"Then I fail to see the problem," Rick concluded, glancing curiously at Colton. "Don't you agree?"

Slowly Colton nodded. He eyed Jake, his expression considering, before returning his attention to Rick.

"What now? Do you have any idea where they might have gone?"

"No. That's the problem," Rick began. Before he could finish, Maddie's cell phone rang.

"Caller ID says Unknown Caller," she reported before answering. "Hello?"

She listened for a moment, her mobile expression going from puzzlement to relief, then joy, and finally worry. "Got it," she said. "Watch for us."

Once she'd ended the call, she practically vibrated

with excitement. "That was Carmen. She stole some-one's phone and called me. Right now, she's playing along and pretending to be human. She says she wants to find out who is actually behind all this."

Again, Jake noticed that no one reacted at all to the strange part of Maddie's statement—about Carmen pretending to be human.

"Did she give you a location?" Rick asked.

"Yes. She's back in Galveston. In one of those aban-doned warehouses near Broken Chains."

Colton cursed. "That's an hour south of here."

"Only if you drive the speed limit," Rick interjected.

They made it in fifty minutes.

"Now what?" Jake asked. "Is there some sort of plan once we get to the warehouse?"

Both men stared at him as if he'd spoken a foreign language.

"No," Rick finally admitted. "We're playing it by ear."

As he pulled up to the curb and parked, shots rang out. Rick swore. "Get out. Everyone, out. Stay on this side of the vehicle."

Using the car as a shield, all four of them crouched behind it. Judging by the *rat-tat-tat* of the gunfire, they were either outnumbered or someone had a fully auto-matic weapon, or both. Colton cursed. Maddie winced each time a she heard a gunshot. And Rick, with his clenched jaw and a muscle working in his throat, ap-peared furious.

"You know what we have to do," Colton said. "That's the only way we can move fast enough to take the shooter down."

"I agree." Rick spoke without looking at anyone, all of his attention focused on the warehouse entrance. "And we need to go quickly. Not that Carmen is in any real danger, but we don't need that virus to be spread. Clearly, no one has thought about that or they wouldn't be shooting up the place." He swallowed. "I need to make sure you understand. This virus affects Shifters. If it's been released, you'll be putting your lives at risk."

There it was again. Jake kept silent, fascinated. The word *Shifters*, bandied about so casually. Either all three shared the same delusion, or Maddie had spoken the truth. But how was such a thing possible?

"True," Colton chimed in. "Except didn't you say Carmen developed an antidote?"

"I did." Rick still appeared grim.

"You're right. We have to go in." Slowly, Maddie nodded. "Sorry, Jake," she murmured. "I wanted to show you my true self, but not like this. The timing is bad, but this is necessary."

He tensed up. "What are you going to do? How can I help?"

Instead of answering, she cast one final long look at him before nodding at her brother and Rick. In unison, all three began shedding their clothes, right in front of each other and Jake, as if he wasn't even there. They didn't look at one another, either. Each appeared focused only on their own movements.

Jake had just come to the realization that their insanity had reached another level when shimmering pinpricks of light appeared, surrounding Maddie, Rick and Colton.

Jake froze. What the... Intrigued and alarmed, he watched as the light show swirled and danced, completely obscuring what had to be their by now naked forms.

When the lights finally winked out, three massive wolves stood where Maddie, Rick and Colton had been.

The largest of the three had to be Rick. His shaggy gray fur looked as if it had been dipped in black.

The next wolf, just a small bit shorter than the first, must be Colton.

And as for Maddie—her coat shimmered, a pearly sort of gray color that mirrored her human beauty.

Jake stared, struggling to process what he'd just seen. Then the three wolves took off, running directly toward the gunfire, crouched low to the ground.

They moved so fast they were a blur. Jake braced himself, wondering how to react if one of them were hit. But somehow, miraculously, they disappeared inside the warehouse, unharmed.

Despite the shock and tension of the moment, one thing stood out in his mind, like a blazing sign against a pitch-black sky.

Maddie had been telling the truth.

And if this—the existence of werewolves or Shape-shifters—was real, did that mean the rest of it was, as well? He didn't have more than a few seconds to ponder this, because a moment later, the gunfire abruptly stopped.

Maddie.

Heart in his throat, Jake didn't hesitate. Crouching low, he ran for the building, intent on reaching the woman he loved.

Chapter 20

If ever there'd existed a more disorganized bunch of criminals, Carmen hadn't met them. Infighting, power grabbing and a definite lack of respect for the power of the virus that so far remained inside the unbroken test tubes.

So far.

As far as she could tell, there appeared to be two separate factions. If they were connected in any way, she couldn't tell how. They were quite vocal, especially about what they wanted. Each group wanted different things.

But in the end, she figured they were the same. Money and power.

Though West Latvia had been mentioned a couple of times, she still didn't understand what the small European nation had done to deserve such a horrible fate.

The first group, a small, extremely loud trio of short, round men, wanted to destroy the antidote. Though

Carmen couldn't fathom how anyone could be so stupid, she carefully kept her face expressionless. She'd kill them before she'd allow them to do that.

The second faction was comprised of seven people—six men and one woman. They appeared more intellectual than the others, and in fact she'd heard snippets of their conversation that seemed to indicate they all had once worked at the CDC. They wanted to coldheartedly release the virus into six major US cities, in a timed and calculated manner. As people sickened and died, they wanted to hold an auction, for the purpose of selling off the antidote to the highest bidder. They then claimed they'd split the proceeds among all of them, including the other group. Carmen knew she didn't believe them.

When the men had come storming her lab, they easily captured the team of Rick's friends, led by a man called Pete. No one seemed to notice that the battle went too quickly, and that the rough and battle-scarred men gave up too easily. No one besides Carmen, that is. She figured they, like her, had allowed themselves to be captured in order to learn about what the terrorists wanted. And make no mistake, Carmen considered them to be terrorists. Anyone who harmed people and wanted to harm more, for the sake of ideology or wealth, should have been considered such.

When the right time came, she'd take them down. She'd even considered killing them all, but decided she wanted them to answer for their crimes.

However, right now she took care so that no one was the slightest bit aware of her power.

As time passed, the arguments became more strident, erupting into small bouts of violence. She, along with Pete and the rest of his team, watched silently, waiting for the fools to turn on each other.

Finally, one of the short, round humans pulled out a semiautomatic rifle and began shooting. He took out his entire group in the space of seconds before swiveling around to aim at the others, all of whom stood frozen in utter shock.

"Enough," Carmen roared. He laughed, bringing up his weapon to fire on her.

Except she was already on top of him. One of the advantages of Vampiric speed. She knocked him to the floor and snatched his gun away from him.

"Don't move," she ordered.

"How did you do that?" one of the former CDC group wanted to know. "One second you were there—" he pointed "—and the next..."

"Never mind that," Pete chimed in. "Carmen, when you have a minute, please cut us loose."

Just then, three large wolves streaked into the room. They'd obviously run straight into the sound of gunfire, probably aware that there were no silver bullets.

The humans, predictably, stared and gasped, nervously moving closer together. Since Pete and his crew were also Pack, they grinned.

"About time you got here," Pete said, eyeing the largest of the three beasts. "I don't know how much longer we could have kept up this charade."

"Gentlemen, let me remind you we still have a dangerous virus," Carmen pointed out. Keeping the rifle ready, she moved over to Pete and used one of her superstrong fingernails to sever his bonds. "You can free the others," she said.

Jake, the human reporter, appeared. Though wild-eyed, he took in the situation with a long look. "What do you need me to do?" he asked Carmen. She smiled to show him her appreciation. Then she directed him to tie up the remaining terrorists. When one of them began to complain loudly, she squeezed off a round of shots, deliberately missing him, but effectively silencing him. "Anyone else?" she demanded. "Next time, I promise you I won't miss."

No one spoke.

Staying close together, the wolves moved over to the group of captives. Baring their teeth, they gave growls of warning low in their throat. Wide-eyed, they struggled against their bonds, with no success.

"Jake," Carmen said loudly. "Why don't you take your wolf friends outside and bring back Maddie and Rick and their friend? I need to have a discussion with them." That way they could figure out what to do next.

"Okay." Jake turned to gesture to the wolves, but they'd already turned and begun to make their way toward the door.

As Maddie went past, she stopped and looked up at Carmen, grinning. Carmen reached out and tangled one hand in the soft fur. "Good to see you, girl," she said, before letting go.

At the door, Jake stopped. She noticed he didn't follow the wolves outside. She realized this might have been the moment he first realized Maddie's true nature. If she remembered correctly, the gift of that knowledge carried some heavy significance. She hoped Jake understood how difficult it must have been for Maddie to put herself in that position. And how much he meant to Maddie. That, too. Though Carmen had spent most of her long life staying out of other peoples' personal business, she felt sorely tempted to say something to Jake. Just this once.

"Hey," she called out. "Jake, come here for a second."

He glanced at the door before looking at her, as if torn. "I..."

"She'll be back in a minute," Carmen said. "I just have one quick question for you."

Expression wary, he crossed the distance between them. "Okay. What is it?"

"Do you love her?"

Clearly, whatever he'd been expecting, it hadn't been this. "It's complicated," he began.

"No. It's not. There's nothing complicated about it. Either you do or you don't."

He swallowed. Before he could answer, Maddie, Rick and another man rushed inside. With their heightened color and disheveled appearance, Carmen could tell they'd rushed through dressing immediately after shape-shifting back to human. From what she'd heard, they really would have had to hurry, as the act of changing brought often unwelcome consequences, unless one was with their significant other. Judging from the way none of the three made eye contact with the other, they were working on getting that under control.

"Carmen." Rick hurried over, wrapping his arms around her and pulling her close. She felt the force of his arousal and smiled.

"I'm glad you saved that for me," she purred.

"Always." He kissed her cheek. "Believe me, we're all so used to that happening when we change, we're able to control it easily. But when I saw you…"

His flattery made her laugh.

"Hello there." The strange man who'd accompanied Rick, Maddie and Jake walked over and stuck out his hand. "I'm Colton."

"Carmen." After they shook, she studied him. "You look familiar, but I can't say why. I'm usually pretty good at remembering faces, but I swear I haven't met you before today."

"I'm Maddie's brother."

That explained it. "Ah. And you two do resemble each other."

Maddie walked up, carefully avoiding glancing at Jake, though he tracked her with his gaze. "What's going on here, Carmen?" she asked.

"That's my Maddie. Straight to business." Carmen stepped away from Rick to hug her friend close. Again, she considered asking Maddie what was going on with her and Jake, but figured now was not the time. Maddie would tell her later, probably over a drink at Broken Chains.

"Jake," Carmen called, ignoring Maddie's almost imperceptible wince. "Come here. Everyone gather around and I'll tell you what I know. We've got to figure out what to do with these people."

When Jake joined their group, he stood as far from Maddie as possible. Not good, but she had other things to worry about beside the two lovebirds.

"There were two groups here," she said. "I'm not sure how they managed to work together long enough to capture me, but they did."

"What about my team?" Rick asked. "Pete and the guys were there to protect you."

"From what I could tell, Pete and his men allowed themselves to be defeated, so they could be captured."

"Right," Pete agreed. "Rick, sorry to leave you like that, but we knew you'd understand. Headquarters got intel that these people were about to make a huge move with the virus. We needed to stop them any way we could. Turns out, the infighting got so bad that one group took out the other."

"Saved you all some work," Rick said, his voice grim.

"Yes." Carmen felt that familiar tug of desire when Rick turned his blue eyes her way. "But the group that's dead was the one that wanted to destroy West Latvia. Now we may never know why."

"Oh, I'm sure there are more of them," Rick replied. "The head honcho always sends his flunkies to do the dirty work." He glanced at the now surly group, still tied up and clearly not happy about it. "What about those guys? Where do they come in?"

"From what I can tell, they used to work for the CDC in Atlanta," Carmen said. She'd been watching Jake from the corner of her eye, and that remark seemed to jolt him out of his shock. "They appear to be in it for the money."

"Of course we're in this for money," a tall, thin man with a hooked nose interjected. "The CDC didn't pay us enough, considering what we did. We came close to identifying the biological components of the virus, but then we heard some outsider had actually gotten much closer."

"How'd you hear that?" Carmen asked.

"Scott worked with us. We sent him in to talk to that fringe group of idiots. They were tied in with them." He jerked his head toward the dead guys. "We were understandably upset to learn he'd died after being infected with the virus." His cold gaze locked on Carmen. "Why didn't you give him the antidote like you did your boyfriend there? You let him die. That makes you guilty of murder."

Carmen laughed. She couldn't help it. And not the toned-down form of laughter she'd learned to adopt when around humans. No, this time she let loose with her real laugh, the Vampiric one, with all its glorious undertones of menace and fury. The one that had once sent people scurrying for churches and homes with doors they could lock, because that sound contained a warning that something awful was about to happen.

Immediately, the human man went silent, eyes wide. Head back, Carmen bared her teeth, allowing just the slightest portion of her fangs to show. As predicted, the entire group collectively recoiled. This filled her with a burst of savage joy.

Right then, Rick kissed her. A possessive crush of his mouth on hers, as if he, too experienced similar emotions. Surprised, she kissed him back, pouring all of her energy into the movement of her lips. Since she hadn't had time to retract her fangs, she accidentally drew blood on his bottom lip. The coppery taste only enhanced her enjoyment. In fact, she had to fight to keep from going wild.

When he finally drew back, they were both breathing hard. Grinning, Jake shook his head. "You two need to get a room."

"Maybe we will, once all of this is settled." Carmen turned, loving the way Rick kept his arm around her and his body close. "What I want to know is what we should do now. Has the virus been released anywhere else?"

"Not that we know of," Colton responded. "They've made threats. Do you have any idea who else has the virus besides these guys?"

Carmen shook her head. She glanced back over her shoulder at the man who'd spoken up before. "Answer the question."

"I...no." He swallowed nervously. "I can't do that. If I do I'll be a dead man."

"If you don't answer, your death will come a lot sooner." This time, she let her eyes turn red as she allowed a lot more fang to show. "Because I'll kill you. At least it will be a quick death."

She focused on the pulse beating rapid fire at the base of his throat. On the surface, he might not yet understand she was a Vampire, but somewhere deep in his psyche, he knew. And he understood exactly what her fangs would do to him.

"The CDC is the only other place that has the virus," he finally blurted. "Other than anyone who might have gathered their own samples in West Latvia."

She gave a slow nod. "Good."

"Not that it matters, since we now have an antidote," Rick interjected. "Thanks to you. Now all we have to do is contact the proper authorities and have large quantities manufactured."

Carmen closed her eyes, taking a moment to gather her composure. "Easier said than done. Finding facilities capable of that kind of mass production quickly will be a challenge, to say the least."

"Maybe so, but if they want to save the world, they'll have to figure out a way to do it." Rick sounded so certain, so confident that this would happen, she wanted to kiss him again.

Once, she had been like him. Before centuries of watching humans battle over all the wrong things. She'd witnessed plagues and battle and carnage, and seen firsthand the unspeakable things men did to each other in the name of love and religion. She could imagine the jockeying for power among those in charge, while people died. Seeing the hope shining in Rick's eyes, the honest conviction of his chiseled features, made her feel lighter than she had in ages.

"Have you contacted the CDC?" Jake asked, his own inquisitive expression mirroring the same hope as Rick's.

"Not yet." She looked at Maddie. "I wasn't sure who I can trust. Especially after learning those yahoos over there were all former CDC workers."

"You're right," Maddie said slowly. "We need to go higher up. Someone above the CDC."

At that, Rick and Colton exchanged a glance. "I think we know exactly the right person," Colton said. "Trent Paxton. He's head of the Protectors, but he also is in charge of the US Department of Health and Human Services."

Their confident hope felt infectious. "Perfect," Carmen said. "Does one of you want to make the call?"

"I'll do it," Colton said. "Trent and I used to golf sometimes, back when he worked here in Texas. He'll take my call."

While Colton walked away to take care of that, Carmen noticed Maddie appeared to be on the verge of tears. About to ask what was wrong, Carmen swallowed back the question when Jake took Maddie's arm.

"I was wrong," he told her, looking deep into her eyes. Though his words were meant only for her, he spoke loud enough so everyone could hear.

Since Carmen suspected he did this on purpose, she didn't move. Evidently, Rick had reached the same conclusion, as he stayed, too.

"I'm sorry," Jake continued. "Now everything makes sense. If I hadn't seen it with my own two eyes..." He looked down. "Thank you for trusting me enough to tell me the truth."

Though his words were kind, they clearly weren't what Maddie wanted to hear. She gave a stiff nod and crossed her arms.

Then Jake leaned in and kissed her. A rough kiss, possessive and decisive. The kiss of a man who knew what he wanted.

Seeing this, Carmen and Rick exchanged smiles.

"I love you," Jake declared, pulling Maddie close. Once he had her nestled into the crook of his arm, he turned to face Carmen. "I love this woman," he said. A second later, he told Rick the same thing. "When Colton gets back, I'll tell him the same thing."

Like the sun bursting out from behind heavy storm clouds, a brilliant smile appeared on Maddie's face.

But Jake wasn't finished. Before Maddie could speak, he kissed her again. "You're beautiful. Not just now, but *then*." He glanced over at their captives, clearly aware he couldn't say much.

Eyes huge, Maddie clearly hung on his every word.

"I'd like a committed relationship," Jake continued. "In every sense of the word. In fact, if you're willing, I think we should look for our own place. Once all of this settles down. For sure I'm going to need your help figuring out how to frame my story. There's so much and I'm not sure…"

Though he let his words trail off, his meaning rang clear. He wouldn't do anything to endanger Maddie and her people. The Pack Protectors would have no reason for concern with him.

With a glad cry, Maddie leaned in for yet another kiss. This one was the kind of kiss that should have been shared in private.

Marveling at all this, and overjoyed for her friend, Carmen turned away and took Rick's arm. About to suggest they leave the two lovebirds alone, she winced when one of the captors yelled out in a mocking voice, "You two should definitely get a room."

Maddie broke away from Jake, blushing. They touched foreheads and then, arm and arm, walked outside. Hopefully in the opposite direction from Colton, who still hadn't returned.

Careful to hide his annoyance at the interruption, Rick turned to Carmen. "Can't you do something about those fools?" he asked, gesturing toward their captives. "Like knock them out until someone from the government shows up to collect them?"

His question made Carmen laugh. "I wish. Unfortunately, I'm not a witch. There's not one stitch of magical ability in me."

"Lucky for them." Glowering, Rick took Carmen's elbow and led her as far from the others as they could get without leaving the warehouse. "What do you think about Maddie and Jake?" he asked.

Grinning up at him, she shrugged. "If Maddie's happy, I'm happy. He seems like a good guy. I don't think you Pack Protectors have any cause for concern, if that's what you're asking."

"It's not." He pushed away a sudden rush of nervousness, determined to say what he needed to say. "We make a great partnership, too, you know."

Carmen went very still. "I agree." She watched him, expressionless, as if bracing herself for whatever he might say next.

He refused to be nervous. "You know how I feel about you," he said.

One perfectly arched brow rose. "Do I?" Deadpan, until one corner of her sensual lips curled upward. "Maybe you need to show me again."

Though tempted, he shook his head. "I'm serious, Carmen. How do you feel about making our partnership a little more permanent?"

"You do realize I'm a Vampire, right?"

"Of course. Just like you know what I am. You've already seen my other self." They both kept their voices low.

"Is that what this is about? You're worried because I've seen your beast?"

He wasn't sure how to take that. "Of course not.

I've fallen in love with you." He waited for her to say something, anything, but she continued to stand still as a statue, looking down at the floor.

"Carmen, can you at least react? This has never happened to me before, so forgive me if I'm handling it the wrong way."

Finally, she raised her head. To his shock, her beautiful eyes were full of tears. "This has never happened to me before, either," she said, her voice husky with emotion. "Are you sure, Rick Fallin? Are you absolutely positive you want to be with someone like me?"

"Someone smart and beautiful and kind?" he countered. "Not to mention sexy as hell? Why wouldn't I?"

Though a smile tugged at one corner of her mouth, she shook her head. "You know what I mean."

Vampire. She meant Vampire.

He pretended to consider for a moment, before losing the battle and pulling her into his arms. She nestled in, the fit of her sleek body to his exactly right. "Without a doubt," he said. "What about you? Are you okay with having someone like me as your man?"

Instead of responding, she growled low in her throat, then spoiled it all by laughing. "Now that we've gotten that out of the way, I wonder what's taking Colton so long?"

As if her words summoned him, Colton appeared in the warehouse doorway. "We're all good," he said. "Not only did I notify Trent Paxton, but I let various other high-ranking people know. Just to cover our butts. The CDC is sending a team this way now, via private jet. They'll be here by nightfall. Trent's also going to work on getting some of the larger manufacturing companies geared up to start producing the vaccine and the antidote on a rush basis." He glanced back at their captives, who continued to watch with interest. "They're sending the FBI to get those guys, since they're being classified as terrorists."

Impressed, Rick nodded. "Perfect."

Jake walked over, making notes in a notebook he'd gotten from somewhere. "Thanks, Colton, for letting me talk to Trent Paxton. This will be the story of the year once I get it written up. I've already contacted people I know at all the major networks. I'm thrilled that I got an exclusive."

Colton grinned. "I owed you."

"Plus, we're only keeping our end of the bargain," Rick chimed in. Carmen bumped his hip with hers and he put his arm around her to keep her close.

The next several hours were a blur of activity. The FBI arrived first, taking the still bound group into custody.

Carmen stayed busy making copious notes in triplicate. She also took the precaution of taking pics of her findings with her cell phone and emailing them to herself. "One can't be too careful," she said. Rick agreed wholeheartedly.

When the CDC people finally arrived, looking frazzled despite their forced attitude of importance, Carmen handed them all her notes first, including the computer printouts she'd run. Next, she carefully gave them the padded case containing her tissue and blood samples. They took everything, thanked her for helping, turned on their heels and left. Carmen stared after them, her expression inscrutable.

Rick went to her and pulled her close. "Are you all right?"

"I expected more," she confessed. "Foolish, I know. But I single-handedly came up with a solution to save mankind. I thought at least I'd get a letter of commendation or a medal or something." She shrugged. "Shows even someone as old as I am can still be naive."

He hugged her and then nuzzled the top of her head. "Are you ready to go?"

"Yes." She didn't even hesitate. "Your place or mine?"

His breath caught. "I'd sure love to see where you live," he said. "My place is a pretty basic apartment."

"I live in a tomb," she replied. Then, as he stared at her, she laughed. "Just kidding. I own a condo overlooking the yacht basis. Lots of windows and natural light." She kissed him, a quick brush of her lips on his, and then once again, with the promise of more.

"Hey you two," Maddie called out. Hand in hand with Jake, she glowed with happiness. "Jake and I are heading to his house to finish working on the story. I'm planning to spend the weekend there. You've got my number if you need anything."

Carmen nodded. "I promise not to call unless it's urgent. Where's Colton?"

"He said he was meeting a friend for dinner, then planned on going over to Broken Chains for drinks."

"Broken Chains," Jake repeated. "Too bad I'll never get to see inside."

"It's just a bar," Rick and Carmen said at once. They exchanged quick glances, avoiding looking at Maddie lest they give away the truth. Broken Chains was much more than just a bar, more than just an anything. They'd gone there as singles, and as friends. None of that would change, even if they paired off into couples.

"Another successful case completed by The Shadow Agency," Maddie crowed, waving. "See you all later."

After she and Jake had gone, Rick took Carmen's hand and they walked outside. "We'll have to catch a cab," he said. "I rode here with Maddie, so I don't have a vehicle."

"Let's just walk." She smiled up at him, her white teeth gleaming. "We might even stop at Broken Chains for a quick celebratory drink."

And that's what they did.

* * * * *

We hope you enjoyed this story from

HARLEQUIN®

NOCTURNE™

Unleash your otherworldly desires.

Discover more stories from
Harlequin® series and continue
to venture where the normal and
paranormal collide.

Visit **Harlequin.com** for more Harlequin® series reads
and **www.Harlequin.com/ParanormalRomance**
for more paranormal reads!

From passionate, suspenseful
and dramatic love stories
to inspirational or historical...

With different lines to choose from
and new books in each one every month,
Harlequin satisfies the most voracious
romance readers.

SPECIAL EXCERPT FROM

H HARLEQUIN

I N T R I G U E

*Chief of police Jason Cash will do whatever it takes to
find the person who killed a woman in his town.
But could the criminal have harmed the wrong woman?
After all, Yvette LaSalle, a mysterious foreigner with the
same first name as the victim, recently relocated to the
remote area…*

Read on for a sneak preview of
Storm Warning
by Michele Hauf.

Jason Cash squeezed the throttle on the snowmobile he
handled like a professional racer. The five-hundred-pound
sled took to the air for six bliss-filled seconds. Snow sprays
kissed Jason's cheeks. Sun glinted in the airborne crystals.
The machine landed on the ground, skis gliding smoothly onto
the trail. With an irrepressible grin on his face, he raced down
an incline toward the outer limits of Frost Falls, the small
Minnesota town where he served as chief of police.

Thanks to his helmet's audio feed, a country tune twanged
in his ears. His morning ride through the pristine birch forest
that cupped the town on the north side had been interrupted
by a call from his secretary/dispatcher through that same feed.
He couldn't complain about the missed winter thrills when a
much-needed mystery waited ahead.

Maneuvering the snowmobile through a choppy field
with shifts of his weight, he steered toward a roadside ditch,
above which were parked the city patrol car and a white SUV
he recognized as a county vehicle. Sighting a thick, undisturbed
wedge of snow that had drifted from the gravel road to
form an inviting ridge, Jason aimed for the sparkling
payload, accelerated and pierced the ridge. An exhilarated
shout spilled free.

Gunning the engine, he traveled the last fifty feet, then braked and spun out the back of the machine in a spectacular snow cloud that swirled about him. He parked and turned off the machine.

After flipping up the visor and peeling off his helmet, he glanced to the woman and young man who stood twenty yards away staring at him. At least one jaw dropped in awe.

A cocky wink was necessary. Jason would never miss a chance to stir up the powder. And every day was a good day when it involved gripping it and ripping it.

Setting his helmet emblazoned with neon-green fire on the snowmobile seat, he tugged down the thermal face mask from his nose and mouth to hook under his chin. The thermostat read a nippy ten degrees. Already, ice crystals formed on the sweat that had collected near his eyebrows. He did love the brisk, clean air.

It wasn't so brutally cold today as it had been last week when temps had dipped below zero. But the warm-up forecast a blizzard within forty-eight hours. He looked forward to snowmobiling through the initial onset, but once the storm hit full force, he'd hole up and wait for the pristine powder that would blanket the perimeter of the Boundary Waters Canoe Area Wilderness, where he liked to blaze his own trails.

Clapping his gloved hands together, he strode over to his crack team of homicide investigators. Well, today they earned that title. It was rare Frost Falls got such interesting work. Rare? The correct term was *nonexistent*. Jason was pleased to have something more challenging on his docket than arresting Ole Svendson after a good drunk had compelled him to strip to his birthday suit and wander down Main Street. A man shouldn't have to see such things. And so frequently.

Don't miss
Storm Warning *by Michele Hauf,*
available March 2019 wherever
Harlequin® Intrigue books and ebooks are sold.

www.Harlequin.com

Need an adrenaline rush from nail-biting tales
(and irresistible males)?

Check out **Harlequin Intrigue**®
and **Harlequin**® **Romantic Suspense** books!

New books available every month!

***

CONNECT WITH US AT:

Facebook.com/groups/HarlequinConnection

 Facebook.com/HarlequinBooks

 Twitter.com/HarlequinBooks

 Instagram.com/HarlequinBooks

 Pinterest.com/HarlequinBooks

ReaderService.com

**ROMANCE WHEN
YOU NEED IT**

SGENRE2018

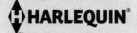

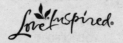

Love Harlequin romance?

DISCOVER.

Be the first to find out about promotions, news and exclusive content!

EXPLORE.

Sign up for the Harlequin e-newsletter and download a free book from any series at **TryHarlequin.com.**

CONNECT.

Join our Harlequin community to share your thoughts and connect with other romance readers!
Facebook.com/groups/HarlequinConnection

HARLEQUIN®

ROMANCE WHEN YOU NEED IT

HSOCIAL2018

Reward the book lover in you!

Earn points on your purchase of new Harlequin books from participating retailers.

Turn your points into **FREE BOOKS** of your choice!

Join for FREE today at
www.HarlequinMyRewards.com.

Harlequin My Rewards is a free program (no fees) without any commitments or obligations.

MYR18